THE TURNING
(FATE'S SEAL)

Part I

J C PEREIRA

DEDICATION

I dedicate this book to Sechat and Morrigan.

CONTENTS

ACKNOWLEDGMENTS

Thank you to Ornella who despite a busy and stressful job, remained close to me, reading my thoughts as I committed them to paper and providing me with welcomed feedback.

CHAPTER I

The sky was pissing down, oppressive and threatening. Black, thunderous clouds hung low, pressing gloom and foreboding onto the heads and shoulders of the frantically working deck-hands scampering about on the slippery, wooden-slatted, open deck of the small, fat and battered, cargo ship. This sudden squall was the harbinger of something worse. They could all feel it in their bones, and the very air, laden with brine and salt water, was laced with dancing electricity.

'Look lively, lads. Reef those bloody canvases before we lose them to this bitch of a wind!' barked the short, wiry Captain with a surprisingly loud and domineering voice.

The rough-clad sailors struggled to pull down the large, unruly, mainsail and the lesser one at aft, before the spiteful, gusting winds could tear them flapping from their vibrating masts. These men were tough and weathered. They knew little fear whilst their wooden island was secure beneath their feet, but out there -out there where the dark, fathomless waters were beginning to froth at the tips of ever-growing, erratic waves- they held a terror, like a man standing on the brink of a cliff; one step further, and oblivion. Their wide bellied, tub of a barge was beginning to wallow and roll, like the unfaithful sow of a fish-wife when her husband was called to sea, heaving and bucking for a new lover.

'Father Brine, I know she is a whore, but she is my whore. Please don't take her under,' prayed the Captain, covered beneath a muttered breath.

With a steady gaze, he tried to separate black sky from plunging, slate-grey sea and had to quickly avert his eyes from the disturbingly indistinguishable horizon as a fit of queasy dizziness sought to overcome him. His unsettled vision anchored onto the only figure on board not caught up in a desperate struggle to prepare for the oncoming, dreaded storm, and a deep frown creased his already lined face. A massive wave broke against the side of his ship making her shudder along every beam of timber in her stout frame and drenched his already sodden, wet body in cold, salt water. He dared not wipe his face free of the clinging and obscuring liquid for both hands were locked tightly to the quivering tiller as he tried to turn his whore into the waves so that she could take the pounding on her prow, but finding the right direction was near on impossible and this tub of pig's fat was very reluctant to respond to his demands.

He was the Captain of a Merchant ship, and this was his call in life. A man should concentrate on one thing and one thing only. He didn't take paying passengers. Now the god had turned his back on him for breaking his salt-code and being a greedy fool. The tall, lean man -wrapped from head to toe in a ragged, hooded cloak that hid his features despite the warm morning sun rising over the docks- had offered him a bloody diamond. He had been hypnotised, his imagination forming the illusory fleet he could buy with such a rare bauble. He was a stupid sod, and old Father Brine was hell-bent on revealing his stupidity so that all could plainly see. What's the use of a pretty stone when fishes were feasting on your eyeballs?

The man in question sat unmoving in the shadow of the bow, unperturbed by the growing maelstrom surrounding them.

'Landlubber bastard! Why wasn't he shitting his pants like everybody else?'

There was something unnaturally still and contained about this stranger. It had been quite clear that he wanted to be away from the Kingdom and to be unobserved while doing so. Whoever he was, he was a talisman of ill luck. Maybe it wasn't too late to throw his secretive carcass overboard as an appeasing sacrifice to the watery god. Still, a deal had been struck, payment given and accepted. A Captain who abandoned his cargo, animate or inanimate, was not worth his salt and would lose all future custom as bad word spread from port to port like a stinking pox. The distracted Captain threw himself to the decking as his mainsail went tearing by overhead, dragging with it a howling sailor who had managed to get himself entangled in the shredded bowline. He was a goner; doomed for an early, watery grave; the poor sod.

'Can't you do anything right!' he screamed at his surviving mates.

'Hold on tight, you bastards! We're in for it now!'

The storm was upon them. Where in hell's name had it come from? For all his years at sea, he had never been so taken by surprise. He had seen the cursed land-lubber staring into the distance, but he had uttered not a word of what he had seen, then 'boom' this roiling blackness had appeared. 'Dark magic, that's what it was!' He had brought a black-hearted magician on board. May the god protect and have mercy on his soul for a storm at sea was merciless.

The wind and waves now had him by his shrunken balls, and his little whore was running with them all. There was nothing they could do but lash themselves to the trembling vessel with corded ropes and pray. Racing dark water waves, mountain high, cresting with terror numbing white, churning edges of destruction, broke on the stern of the running sow, trying to pull her under and plough her to the seabed, but she fought them off gamely, trying to keep whatever virtue she still had.

'Good girl, run, you bitch, run!' yelled the Captain at the top of his lungs, his desperate words ripped and torn away by the roaring wind.

The black devil still sat in the lee of the spray battered prow, his body swaying and riding the waves as a peerless horseman would ride his galloping horse, smooth and one with the beast.

'Bastard!'

The storm tore through the night, taking them with it. Their tormented bodies were leached of all warmth, and their minds were soon frozen and numb. All thoughts of profit, even of survival, suspended in a veil that hovered at the boundaries of death.

Sometime towards dawn, the Captain lost hope and consciousness.

He came to with a fear clawing start and floundered into a world awash with sunshine, calmness and serenity. As he struggled to his feet on shaky sea-legs, he saw the cloak wrapped figure like the grim reaper himself, watching the sunrise filling the spaces with burning colour. He was still at his station at the stem. As the Captain looked around him in near panic, deep, even words, like rumbling thunder and smoked brandy, reached out and steadied him.

'Stand down Captain, you have steered your ship into a safe harbour.'

The still groggy Captain craned his neck around looking for his men on the swamped and broken ship.

'They did not make it. The sea has taken them as payment for your safety. May they sail the waves forever.'

These were the words of the sea initiates. How did the devil know them? Before he could get his salt-encrusted throat to work the black magician spoke again, still without turning.

'The current is now in your favour, Captain. In about an hour's time, it will drift you into the cove behind that jutting headland alee of your present position. The Fates have decided to let your thread continue, Captain. They have further plans for you, it seems.'

'Who in tarnation are you?' croaked the Captain.

The figure turned, smooth and oiled. The Captain caught a glimpse of a bearded face under the deep cowl, with eyes that shone with an unholy light, penetrating into his very soul and examining it. Gods, he wished he hadn't asked that question.

'I am somebody you have never seen, Captain. Remember this, and you may stay alive long enough to see time turn your hair grey. Thank you for an interesting sea passage.'

With that, the demon dove over the side making hardly a splash in the still waters and disappeared from view. The Captain stared for over five minutes, struck dumb and unmoving until a head emerged an impossible distance away in the shimmering sea and strong arms propelled the stranger away landward with hardly a ripple.

'Not bloody human,' muttered the bewildered and frightened Captain.

CHAPTER II

The boy sat wrapped in a dog-eared, sheep-skin cloak, tapping his staff idly on a moss-covered rock. Each tap punctuated his drifting thoughts as he dreamed the dream of becoming a warrior; his stick being a fearsome sword striking the armoured heads of his enemies. He had had a terrible night, huddled in a small cave whilst the frightening winds and terrifying rains tore into the headland where his small, coastal, fishing village lay snuggled. His father was the headman, and being the oldest son, it was his duty to guard the small herd of toughened sheep and goats. If it weren't for Crusher, his old, rangy and faithful wolf-hound, he wouldn't have been able to find them early this morning as the storm had scattered the live-stock in the same way that it had everything else during the dark hours of terror. However, everything was now back to how it should be. Crusher was noisily breaking open a mildewed and dirty sheep's bone, the sun was bathing the rugged and rocky landscape in a warm, golden blanket, and he had reclaimed his daydreams. Suddenly, a deep snarling rumble emanated from the huge chest of Crusher, startling the boy out of his fantasy world. His shaven head, balanced on a scrawny neck, popped up and craned around like a cockerel becoming aware of a fox outside the hen-house. He leapt to his feet, dropping his stick clattering to the rocks, as he saw looming above him a dripping apparition of doom, a sea bottom crawler for sure, with the sun rising dazzlingly behind its form, hooded and terrible. Crusher launched himself at the sea-creature of death, a deadly growl resonating from his savage throat. Just as he was confident that his alpha dog, fierce and indomitable, would rip this abomination spawned from the dark waves, from the face of the land of the living, Crusher inexplicably flopped to his stomach like a craven bitch and crawled whining towards the outstretched hand of the sea demon. The boy stared in horror as a sun-browned, long-fingered, elegant hand, scratched his betraying dog between its deceitful ears. It sat there panting happily and wagging its tail. 'Bastard mongrel of a dog!'

6

'Your friend is faithful and is the finest of animals,' reverberated a deep, sonorous voice from beneath the shadowed cowl.

'He is my dog!'

'Yes, of course, he is. Are you both from yonder village?'

'I won't let you hex my people! You'll get nothing from me, sea demon!'

'I see. You are a brave lad. I mean no harm to you or your people, son.'

'Then release my dog from your spell!'

'Your dog and I share a kinship, but that's another story for another time.'

The demon reached up with both hands and pulled his hood back. The boy tensed, ready to run for his life, but the face revealed stayed his intended action. It was the face of a king, majestic and proud, yet humble at the same time; the face of a father and a protector. Long hair streaked with the occasional grey, framed royally carved, high cheekbones above which were unfathomable brown eyes, steady and calm. Eyes that engendered trust and unfailing loyalty.

'You don't look much like a sea-demon!' said the boy with the direct words of a ten-year-old.

'Looks can be deceiving, son, but no, I'm not a sea-demon. I'm many things, but not that.'

'What do you want from my village then?'

'Nothing, son, nothing at all. I was just being polite. There is something you might help me with though.'

'Ah, here it comes now,' thought the boy. 'My Pa always says that the true colour of a man's under clothes always comes out after a bit of washing.'

Seemingly unaware of the boy's suspicions of him, the man continued.

'Who is the present lord of this region? Is it still Lord Bremford?'

'Are you daft, man? Lord Bremford died when my grandpa was still a youngling like me. So says my pa, anyway. His weak-kneed, raper of baby girls grandson, Lord Breakspear, now rules. He is a bastard, my pa says. Who are you anyway, Mister? You don't look that old.'

'I commend you for your varied and colourful vocabulary, son. You remind me of someone. Your pa has good cause to be proud of you. It has been my pleasure to have made your acquaintance, but I must be moving on. The best of regards to your father. Farewell, young shepherd.'

Before the boy could say anything more, the strange man moved away, his long strides flowing like a shadow over the uneven ground. It didn't take long before he disappeared from sight.

Shaking his head at the foolishness of outsiders the boy returned to his herd, his dog, and his daydreams.

The following morning, when his three nights stint as a herder of sheep and goats had come to an end, the hardy youngster returned to his village calling to his flock and his dog, keeping their movements tight and orderly. He had been doing this since his eight summer, and it was almost second nature to him. As he descended the narrow, rough path winding down from the headland, he paused to survey his home. Sandwiched between two craggy points over which white-water surf burst lustily, lay a part shingle, part sand covered, cove. Behind the sloping, rude beach was a sturdily built sea-wall forming a platform dividing unpredictable waves from the collection of low built, triangular, wooden-beam houses topped with turf which littered the spaces with their irregularity and dullness. A recently broken jetty pointed its way daringly into the now sheltered and calm sea, but its part destruction bore testimony to the battering it had received just two nights ago.

The village appeared deserted except for a brood of idly strolling chickens which pecked assiduously at everything and anything that seemed to be edible to their eyes, and two horses which stood patiently by a hitch-rail, occasionally switching their long tails at nonexistent flies.

'Another useless meeting, I suppose,' mumbled the young shepherd. 'Pa do love his meetings.'

Making his way between the silent houses the boy stopped at his father's and penned his flock into a covered, lean-to shed then trotted through the bare passages that served as streets to a large building facing the sea which was the village's communal hall. As he entered the cavernous, open-planned, smoky interior, lit by an open space in the high roof designed to let out the smoke from the roaring fire set in its central hearth, he saw sitting at the long table a wiry, haggard-looking man who was tearing into the carcass of a roasted fowl, ripping its flesh and crunching its bones in a breathless frenzy. The entire population of the village it seemed, was gathered around him in silence. Whether they were awed by his ability to devour food or by who he was the boy was not sure. After what appeared to be ages of wet, salivary munching and crunching the man said.

'He was a black wizard, I tell you. Didn't have a face, just burning eyes; like a cat's in the fire-light. Called up the poxy storm. For what dark purpose only Father Brine knows.'

'Didn't have a face?' enquired the boy's father, just to make sure that he had heard right.

'Well, not that I could see, anyway. Wore a hood like a shroud for the entire voyage.'

'And he called up the tempest you say? Did you see him do this?'
'Aye, that I did, Headman. Stood at the cutwater and chanted cursed words in a foul tongue.'

'Pa,' said the boy, pulling on his father's belt to get his attention.

'Not now, son!' whispered the Headman fiercely under his breath.

'The lord will have to be informed, Headman,' said a stout, white-bearded fisherman.

'Pa...'

'Not now, Severn! Yes, we will send word immediately. This strange wizard will have to be brought in for questioning. Can't have him wandering the countryside causing havoc and fear with the good-folk.'

'Pa...I saw him!'

All eyes turned on Severn.

'He hexed poor Crusher and asked questions about the village.'

'Did he hurt you boy or kill any of my sheep?'

'No, pa, but he thought that Lord Bremford still ruled.'

'What!' shouted the stocky fisherman. 'Old Bremford has been dead for donkeys of years!'

'That's what I said to im,' grumbled Severn.

After a period of uncomfortable silence, an old, crippled man who was noted in the village for his extensive travels and worldly knowledge quavered into the silence.

'Heard tell once that old Bremford had himself a pet magician. Got up one morning and disappeared into the sea during a storm. Dived right in he did. Not long after, old Bremford died mysteriously.'

'There you have it!' exclaimed the wiry man. 'A dark magician has reappeared in the midst of another tempest, dooming my ship and my men as his sacrifice. What do you make of that now, Headman? Still think I'm a fool of a sea captain? Disappeared in a storm, back in another.'

'It is a strange coincidence, I do admit,' was the troubled reply.

'We had better inform the lord,' said the stocky fisherman.

All heads nodded in unison.

CHAPTER III

'Hold her still, damn you! Gods what a hell-cat! Hold her still!'

'A word of caution, lord. This girl is the niece of Coulthain, Lord of the Stronghome Keep. She has been given into your care and protection. Think carefully before you do this thing, lord.'

The overweight and panting lord, sweating from his exertions, wiped a meaty hand over his fleshy, coarse-stubble face and looked over at his thin, ageing, gowned adviser and twisted his mouth in a grimace of disgust.

'What a sour, dried up prune of a man you've become, Tramford. Are they no juices left in those wasted ball-sacks of yours?'

'I only urge you to consider consequences, my Lord Breakspear; to weigh a moment's pleasure against possible sack and ruin.'

'Bastard! Alright, alright, you win. What a spoil sport you are. Take her away, Horace, and give her some sweat-meats to eat.'

The thin, prepubescent girl, about twelve summers old, pulled her ripped and torn clothing around her trembling form; her eyes desperate and haunted by shame and fear. She did not resist as the hulking, chain-mailed Horace led her away.

'The bastard is besieged in his fastness anyway. He will be lucky to get his muscle-bound brain out alive.'

'Then wait for this to be made certain, lord, before you indulge in what is his.'

'By then she might be too old for my liking,' grumbled the lord. 'Why have you come to my chamber anyway? I do not remember inviting you.'

'We have received an urgent petition from one of your coastal fiefs, lord. They claim that a dark magician has materialised out of the sea and is running loose in your kingdom.'

'Are you serious, Tramford!? And you saw it fit to bring this superstitious nonsense to me at this particular time? I'm not a fool, counsellor. I know that your true intent was to dampen my fire with your wet blanket. Bastard!'

'Be that as it may, my lord. We had best look into this affair. You know how excitable your subjects can be.'

'Stop pointing that sanctimonious, shrunken finger of yours at me, Tramford. There is only so much poking I will tolerate.'

'Yes, lord.'

'Yes, lord. Yes, lord,' sneered the lord. 'Go and handle this yourself, Tramford. Burn the bastard when you find him for all I care. We all must have our secret pleasures, eh?'

'As you command, my lord,' replied the pan-faced councillor, bowing low as he slid from the room, leaving the frustrated and fuming Lord Breakspear to his own restless thoughts and questionable devices.

In a way, Councillor Tramford suspected that the over self-indulgent lord was right. An aggressive Empire was seeking to dominate all the kingdoms, and if Stronghome Keep were to fall, they would be free to come flooding down on all of them. Time might well be running out for the old status quo. Maybe it was best to take ones pleasures now while it was still possible. Dark days lay ahead, and tomorrow might be too late.

As he moved along the stone corridor lost in morbid contemplation, he spied the large, brutish frame of Captain Horace, as he exited a side door, having completed his task of babysitting after his near escape in participating in the sordid task of despoiling an innocent. The Captain was a formidable fighter, a man designed for masculine confrontation, but the influence of his lord was leading him down an inglorious path to idleness.

'Captain, a word if I may. I have a task for you.'

The large man stopped and surveyed the councillor with shrewd, intelligent eyes hidden beneath over-prominent, brooding, brow ridges. He did not speak, being a man of few words, but waited patiently for the councillor to state his request.

'By orders of Lord Breakspear, take ten, competent men-of-arms and hunt down a stranger who may or may not be dangerous. Take no chances. You will be able to pick up his trail outside a small, fishing village on our northern peninsular. A young boy saw him first-hand. Question him.'

'Do you wish to speak with this man, this stranger?'

'In other words, can you kill him? Do as is necessary, captain, but it might be interesting to hear what he has to say for himself.'

'I will leave within the hour.'

'Very well. Oh, and captain. The rumour is that he is a magician.'

The big man simply eyed the councillor for a pause then turned away without comment.

'Interesting,' muttered Lord Tramford under his breath. 'Not weirded like most of the common folk then.'

True to his word, Captain Horace departed the lowland fortress keep within the hour, accompanied by ten of the roughest brutes he could find at short notice. Most of these men had honed their fighting skills as border reivers who had a reputation for boldness, mercilessness and cruelty when undertaking missions, sanctioned or otherwise. They were mounted on shaggy, sure-footed nags, noted for their agility and stamina. Like their riders, they had a disagreeable disposition and despised being fussed over.

A half-days ride over rocky terrain and through briny bogs brought the captain and his crew of killers to the small, seaside village where after a short discussion with the headman, they were led by the shepherd boy, Severn, to the place where the alleged magician had manifested from the sea.

'Can you see any signs, Luc?' asked the captain.

'I'm looking. I'm looking, big man, keep your trousers on,' grumbled a stocky, bow-legged, foul-smelling man whose eyes were blood-shot from last night's excessive drinking. 'Bloody sheep shit is everywhere!'

'Told you we should have brought the hounds, captain,' piped up a young, fresh-faced individual, with a puckered scar running down from his right eye into his cheek. 'Luc is in no position to find his way out of a latrine at the moment.'

'Shut it, Scar,' replied Captain Horace in a quiet, off-hand manner.

'Well, Luc?'

'Bastard is light on his feet. Seemed to have moved off in that direction,' replied Luc, holding his throbbing head with one hand and waving with the other.

'I could have told you as much if you had bothered to ask,' muttered the shepherd boy.

'Button it up, lad,' replied Luc. 'You're giving me a bloody headache.'

Scar sniggered and studiously ignored the glowering look that Luc gave him.

'Let's get on with this,' said Captain Horace. 'Lead out, Luc.'

Despite his self-inflicted affliction, Luc was good, in fact, he was the best tracker that Horace had ever seen. He followed signs that none of them could discern even though all of them were seasoned hunters steeped in wood-craft. So respected was he that not even Scar commented when he chose a direction based on evidence that to the rest of them was invisible.

'Any idea on what kind of man we're tracking, Luc?' asked Captain Horace when the trail reader paused to study something that only he could see.

In an absent and distracted voice, the man replied without turning to look at his commander.

'He's not very big, not heavy…but strong and floats over the ground like a ghost. He is also fast. Seems to be moving in the direction of the old castle.'

'Hmmm…I think you may be right with that. How do you know that he is strong?'

Luc glanced up at the commander as if he had just been asked a ridiculous question, the answer to which should have been self-evident.

'Do you recall a ways back when we had to go around a broken, steep-sided crag? No? Yes? Well, he didn't.'

'Are you saying he climbed it? It looked sheer to me; no hand-holds that I could make out.'

'Climbed or jumped; who knows.'

'Maybe it was magic,' chimed in Scar.

'Shut it,' responded the two men in unison, but the shadow of worry flitted across their eyes.

Luc and Horace knew one another from days of old; they were accustomed to watching each other's backs in the melee. Scar came later, but he had entered their circle and was one of them. The others were just killers to be used when a job was meant to be done. They had developed a deep understanding of when things weren't as they should be. Such a feeling was beginning to itch at the corners of their minds with each step that they were taking.

Towards evening they approached a large mound of plant growth growing atop the crumbling ruins of a once imposing fortress; nature reclaiming the futile ambitions of man. They fanned out and advanced, sitting alertly on the saddles of their steadily clopping, bog-trotters; leather creaking rhythmically into the silence between. Standing motionless on a chunk of fallen masonry, like a sentinel guarding the fractured remnants of what time had left behind, was a cloaked figure watching them as a hawk studies the movements of a sage hen, silent, patient and deadly.

'Shit!' muttered Scar.

'Oi you,' shouted Captain Horace at the unmoving figure. 'You have entered the domain of the Lord Breakspear without granted permission. You are hereby called before him to explain your presence forthwith.'

His words echoed around the broken dreams and crumbling memories of expired aspirations and touched them as much as they affected the statue still figure.

'I don't think the bastard is listening, Captain,' commented Scar.

'Let's get his attention, then,' muttered Luc grimly.

The Captain frowned but hesitated to give the command they were all waiting for and expected.

'Captain?' prompted Luc.

Jerking himself out of the place of his indecision, Horace opened his mouth to give the order to charge, but before he could utter a sound, the figure spoke in a deep, commanding voice which carried itself clearly to their ears.

'Stay your hand, Captain. Conflict is not necessary.'

'Well, it's going to happen if you don't get your mysterious arse down here in a hurry,' shouted back Captain Horace.

After a short pause, the figure replied in his steady, bass voice.

'Do as you must, men of war, but I will not be coming with you this day.'

'Is he for real?' asked Scar. 'There are eleven of us to his one.'

'Now that is magic!' mumbled Luc. 'You can count.'

'Up yours, Luc!' was the quick rejoinder.

'Stay focused,' interrupted Horace, his tone gruff. 'We'll go at him from all sides, fast and swift. Don't mess about, kill him quick and send him to hell. Let's go!'

The mounted killers kicked their bad-tempered, fleet-footed ponies into a sudden, neck-wrenching start and raced towards their prey, fanning out into a surrounding manoeuvre, yelling and howling like the blood-thirsty lunatics they were. The figure did not react but observed the avalanche coming towards him like a rock watches the sea, calm and unperturbed. They were almost on him, ready to tear him from his solitary perch, when everything happened at once, almost too fast for the human eye to follow. From stillness to offensive action in an explosive flash of lethal force and motion, the cloaked apparition was among them like a whirlwind. Horace and Luc were the first to go down. Moving with unnatural speed, the figure slipped under a powerful, sweeping slash from Horace's long-sword, and at the same time somehow avoided a gut-stabbing thrust from Luc's spear. He whipped between their two racing mounts and ripped them from their saddles and whilst still in mid-air hurled their shocked bodies into the oncoming rush of the men behind, sending both horses and three other henchmen crashing to the hard earth, breaking their limbs and necks. Landing with the agility of a panther, the cloaked demon spun, his arms swirling, sending two throwing knives spinning after with ferocious velocity, embedding themselves to the hilt in two more victims as they rushed by; they were dead before their bodies could hit the ground bouncing like broken dolls. The last four survivors pulled their horses around desperately, bewildered at what had just taken place in a matter of flown seconds. By some unknown instinct, Scar jerked his head aside as a spinning hand axe tore past his ear only to split the skull of the rider behind him with a loud, wet crack. He felt that his mind was caught in a slow-moving fog and he struggled to regain his bearings as a vision of death came hurtling towards him. In utter desperation he threw himself from his saddle as the devil in a flapping cloak tore through the space he had vacated and pounced on the two hapless would be killers behind him, bearing them to the hard, rocky ground and crushing their throats. Their limbs were still twitching when the creature rose in a fluid motion and turned to him. He fought the deep urge to wet his trousers.

'Mother,' he croaked.

As death glided towards him, he knew that his time was near and tried to prepare himself to meet his end bravely, but even so, could not stifle back the whimper that escaped his dry, parched throat.

'This was not necessary.'

'What...?' croaked Scar.

'This conflict...these deaths. Useless. I only wanted to revisit what once was.'

The deep voice had a removed quality to it, and Scar was not even certain that the creature was speaking to him or even, if it genuinely realised that he was there, lying helpless at his feet.

Then the demon lowered his head and regarded him with two luminous eyes sheltered beneath his dark cowl. He caught a glimpse of a bearded face but no more; the eyes were everything.

'Tell your lord that my destination is beyond Stronghome Keep and that I have no interest or business in his land. Tell him to leave me be.'

With these words, the creature turned and disappeared amongst the crumbling ruins of the almost forgotten castle.

It was some time before Scar allowed himself to move. He crawled over to the bodies of his two friends, Horace and Luc, and found them to his relief, still breathing but deeply unconscious. He could not find any external injuries and prayed to his father's god that they weren't busted up inside. He sat next to them and waited, not bothering to check on and not caring about the others whose bodies were strewn over the rough ground.

CHAPTER IV

Krarl knew that he was being watched. He had squeezed his large frame into the small, cargo hold during the middle of a moonless night, knowing that the ship would leave port at dawn with the rising of the tide. A guttural guffaw spat from his mouth as he recalled the strangled noises and looks of horror on the faces of the superstitious sailors as he emerged after a smooth and uneventful passage. Just to put on a show he had leapt up with one bound onto the towering jetty from the deck of the gently rocking ship, an impossible feat for any ordinary man. No one dared approach him, but they all gawked at his muscled, naked, hairy form as he strolled unhurriedly along the rough, planking of the jetty and across the busy, but now silent, fish market.

'Foolish monkeys,' thought Krarl. 'All noise and gabble, gabble, gabble; buying and exchanging worthless, shiny things dug from the earth.'

As he neared the vegetable and fruit stalls, two armoured and burly soldiers, plucked up the courage, drew their swords and moved towards him. Krarl did not hesitate. With a snarl, he sprinted from a standing start straight at them. Their jaws dropped open in surprise for this was not the normal reaction to their imposing menace. Uncertainty seized their limbs, and this was their downfall. They did not get a second chance. Vendors, customers, men, women and idle lay-a-bouts, screamed and scampered to get out of his way, and before the two befuddled soldiery could react, Krarl was on them like a cat on house mice. He grabbed the nearest one with both clawed hands and yanked him sideways with such force and velocity that his neck snapped, and hurled him into his fellow, throwing them both to the cobbled wharf where they skidded along and crashed into a stall, bringing it down with a clattering of wood and spilt fruit. Intimidation done, Krarl turned and roared at the top of his lungs at the fidgety gathering of pale-faced onlookers. All pandemonium broke loose as the pampered citizenry scattered, running pall-mall in all directions to escape from the beast that had appeared in their midst. Chortling to himself, he turned and trotted off into a narrow and twisting, side street, leaping over piles of rotting vegetables and fish guts.

'Mankind stinks,' he thought, 'foul of mind, foul in their deeds.'

His brother was out there somewhere to the east of where he was. He could feel him like a wavering spot at the back of his head, but his essence was off, unconnected. They had their differences, but they were one, and he had to get to him. Krarl no longer felt the overpowering rage he once felt. He occupied his time now in creating as much mischief as he could get away with without stirring up the proverbial hornets' nest behind him, just for the entertainment that it gave, but his brother, on the other hand, was growing darker. The constant disappointments over the long years were beginning to have a toll on him.

Looking back from the steep hill above the port town up which he was scampering, he saw a posse of about nine mounted soldiers whipping their horses in hot pursuit down the narrow streets.

'Shilly marn,' he muttered. 'They warnt to harv fun. I weel give them fun.'

He increased his rate of ascent with a burst of explosive speed, the muscle fibres and tendons in his legs standing out like steel cables from another time and place, now buried and almost forgotten. Instead of heading away from his pursuers, he veered towards the narrow road where he knew they would soon be pounding along. As always, Krarl was never anyone's prey; he remained always the hunter. It was his nature.

The nine men of horse galloped past on lathered mounts, bent on exacting revenge for the murder of their comrades. Krarl well knew the weaknesses of men, and the denting of martial pride, he was sure, was the real and prevailing emotion that instigated their vengeful actions. He laughed once more to himself as he slipped in behind their already straining horses. Caught up in their single-minded and he suspected, simple-minded attitude, he bounded alongside their nervous, wide-eyed mounts for a good space of time before he was noticed by their riders. A young tough with beetle brows and evil, pig-like eyes, caught a glimpse of him in his side vision and in startlement, yanked his reins sideways in a panicked reflex, causing his already skittish horse to shy across into the path of his fellow. The result was not pretty. The charging horse crashed its chest into the shoulder of the other and bowled it over, tripping itself in return and somersaulting in a screaming, tangle of thrashing legs, crushing their hapless riders in the process. Spurting past the calamity of horse and human flesh, Krarl leapt onto the back of the next animal in line and hurled its rider unceremoniously from his seat. Finally, the remaining six of the pack realised that something was truly amiss and were frantically trying to rein in and turn their now panicked mounts to face obvious danger from an unexpected quarter. This was a mistake, as they were like a ship that had turned side-on to the wind and was now dead in the water. He did not waste any time but was at them like the sprung, stone ball from a ballista. He kicked the terrified horse he was sitting astride of into a dead run aimed straight at his prey. Accustomed to dealing with unskilled opponents they sat there befuddled, frozen in place by the supreme warrior bearing down on them. One brave soul fumbled for his sword. Krarl grabbed his wrist in passing, twisted it and broke his arm. The others scrambled from their horses and fled into the nearby fields on foot, as their comrade's agonised screams echoed after them. He slid from the back of the now bucking horse, walked nonchalantly to the field's edge, placed his hands on his hips and guffawed loudly after the fleeing soldiers. Wasn't life fun? What made him think that and more importantly, when did he start thinking like that? That last hunt with his brother had sparked something in him; memories of someone beautiful, a companion of his soul, from a distant and misty past. Then came the hunting and killing of those who meant harm to his twin's two young friends; his rage had somehow been liberated by the very act of protecting two young lovers. Again those memories; surfacing from somewhere behind the pain. The curtain was gradually being torn by the passage of time.

Taking a deep, long breath, Krarl felt his body shudder from head to toe. He shook off the creeping feeling of melancholy and loped on along the scar in the earth that men called a road. Why did his brother waste so much time over them? They were hell-bent on turning whatever was natural into something ugly and unnatural.

After about five miles he left the road and struck out along the rugged coastline with its salt-ponds and jagged rocks. The terrain seemed to be gently sloping downwards until he found himself picking his way around sucking bogs swarming with mosquitoes, but this was the quickest way to get to his brother so onwards he went. To deter the biting, whining insects he rubbed his body in stink-weed and covered his skin liberally with oozing mud.

By mid-morning of the second day, he began climbing a rocky headland overlooking a pounding sea-surf and overlaid with coarse grass. The unshod hoof prints of eleven horses had trampled the place, but underneath were the tracks of a small boy and even fainter, his brother's. Already foolish men were after him; sheep hunting a wolf. Men were just plain idiots.

He wasn't in the least surprised when he eventually came upon the two days old, stiffened bodies of a group of armoured men and two horses, partly eaten by animals and scattered beneath a small hill of crumbling ruins as if in sacrificial worship. Grunting to himself in resignation he set about reading the story to their inevitable fate.

'Three survived,' he thought. 'My brother was always weak and overly sympathetic. More trouble is on its way.'

As if in answer to his thoughts he became aware of a large body of horsemen approaching in the far distance. With a great deal of irritation, he dampened the old fire of rage that was attempting to ignite deep within his chest. For some unknown reason, he decided to wait instead of seeking avoidance as was probably the better course. In the same manner, as his twin had done some days before, he stood and faced the oncoming confrontation; grim and unmoving.

CHAPTER V

Morgan could already make out the impressive walls of the ugly fortress that guarded the narrow pass to the lowland kingdoms nestled against the looming, ice-encrusted mountain face. It looked the same as it had ever done. Even before he had first come here over a century ago, it had been a prize. Every lord desired it and envied any who had it. It was a quick path to wealth, but unfortunately also a fast road to paranoia with a short life thrown into the bargain. Many driven by their near-sighted ambitions and greed tended to overlook this drawback or were willing to accept this real downside as a negotiable risk. Its position enabled any who commanded it to levy heavy taxes on any trade and even on travellers who had no alternative but to move through its gates in pursuit of their interests and concerns. Everything was different, yet everything was the same. Lords and their warrior bands fighting other lords and their followers, manipulation and politics – no changes there. Once occupied and thriving fortresses and towns, now lay abandoned and left to crumble in lonely, wind-swept places; replaced by new civic and military centres. In the past, he had tried to use his knowledge and power to influence promising men and women to rule within a universal law but they, in the end, fell in disappointment, swallowed by avarice and the inflation of their own self-importance. They each, in turn, had turned on him, trying to erase all trace of their vulnerability or sometimes, humble beginnings. Instead of fighting back, he had always slipped away and disappeared, leaving them to self-destruct, trying to find another patch of grass to restart from the beginning. Yes, he had once ruled a kingdom which had become successful, but it was in a land on the edges of everything, parochial and insular in its aims. As ever before, he had slipped away like a thief in the night, afraid that others would see that he was very different from them. At heart he had always wanted to fit in; to become a part of something great and outstanding. He could almost hear his brother laughing.

'Yuuu, brodar, are a wolf, thart warnt to be a sheep.'

Maybe he was right, but he did not want to be a wolf either. He had met and destroyed too many of them in his long life; or at least, men who wanted to be wolves.

He continued up the steep, stony path, moving in a slow, unhurried fashion. Even from this distance, he knew that something wasn't quite right. There was a discordant note at the edge of his extra keen hearing which heralded the jarring music of all too familiar martial conflict. Yes, some things did not change; the rhythm of war was ever ubiquitous. He felt a heavy reluctance to enter into its zone. Once, not so long ago, he would have marched right in, confident in his ability to alter dangerous situations and influence the heated minds of men. Here was a personal change he had not foreseen. It was not that time had allowed him to collect the baggage of useless fear. That was not his consideration. What bothered him was the impatient desire to just rip through the bothersome, little men who seemed to enjoy play fighting. What did they know? Trying to get them to listen and learn from their mistakes was a wasted enterprise. They were just foolish children tussling on the village common land. He repressed the snarl trying to form on his lips and took a deep breath to calm the fire in his chest, taking great care to concentrate on the movement of his entire body, slowing it down and controlling it with conscious thought.

Two hours later as he continued his measured progress up the last section of the snaking track to the mighty redoubt spread before the fortress, a group of belligerent, long-haired ruffians, clad in ill-sorted armour, pushed their small, shaggy ponies clattering and sliding down the precarious incline to confront him. Behind them a frantic siege was in place, filled with noise, dust, dirt and activity.

'What's your business here?' demanded a large, gap-toothed man with lank, dirty hair streaming untidily from his dented pot helm, and an equally dirty beard framing his thick, lipped mouth.

Morgan did not bother to answer, but continued on his steady climb, altering his course slightly to move around the mounted challengers.

Uttering a string of foul expletives, the unwashed leader followed by his aggressive entourage, kicked his mount around to intercept and block Morgan's silent advance.

'Answer me, you bastard, before I tear out your guts and send your corpse back down this hill. Last chance! What are you doing here?'

Morgan stopped and drew his cloak around him, like a hawk landing and folding in its wings. This small action managing to convey a heavily laden and explicit threat.

'Back off whilst you are still able to,' he said in a calm, even voice.

The rag-tag collection of pungent smelling horsemen stared at him incredulously, unable to believe what they had just heard but, at the same time, a bit unnerved by the complacent attitude of the lone, hooded man.

'Are you daft in the head, idiot!?' shouted the leader. 'Look, don't bother. Let's send this bastard rolling, boys!'

The wings of the hawk unfolded with a sudden flap of violence.

Morgan was in lethal movement before the last words had left the leader's mouth in a stink of hot breath.

Although positioned on the lower section of the slope, a point strategically inferior to the horsemen, Morgan attacked before any other could react.

In a blur of motion he leapt to the side onto an out-jutting rock and propelled himself the opposite way into the air, soaring clean over the startled pony of the leader, hauling the shocked man from his saddle as he passed, flinging him down the hillside even before his feet struck the other side, landing with perfect balance. The remainder of the horsemen seemed unable to comprehend what had just happened and sat their mounts staring after the bouncing, cart-wheeling body of their chief; their attention suspended in the frigid, dry air. Morgan did not wait. He leapt into their midst, silent and vicious, tearing men from their saddles and breaking them on the hard ground. The rest turned their mounts in panic and drove them back up the incline. Morgan raced after them and through the siege camp. Men stopped what they were doing and peered after this unusual spectacle with puzzlement. Some laughed in amusement at the sight of one man on foot chasing five mounted across a war camp. However, Morgan was not interested in any of them or their endeavours. As the fleeing riders peeled away to escape their demon predator, Morgan sprinted across the no-man's land separating defenders from attackers and flung himself at the thirty-foot curtain wall where it formed a sharp angle. Ten feet off the ground he struck the wall with force with both hands and feet. Whereupon like a coiled spring, he uncoiled upwards once again, spinning in mid-air, catching the edge of an arrow slot with clawed hands, and using this hand-hold, hurled himself skywards one last time, clearing the top of the bulwark and disappearing over it.

'Can anyone, in the name of the lord god, tell me what bloody well just happened here!?' shouted the big-bellied Protectorate general who lusted to be the next fortress master in the name of his empire, to his aids.

No one had an answer as they stared in wonderment at the top of the distant parapet.

Morgan landed like a cat on the other side of the battlements. He was greeted by surprised men of arms, bristling with weaponry, but who drew away from his sudden appearance with unsettled caution nevertheless.

'Can anyone tell me if Lord Abram Coulthain is still master of this stronghold?' asked Morgan in an even, conversational tone.

The soldiers glanced at each other nervously until a young, cock-sure captain stepped forward.

'Lord Cromwell Coulthain is now master here. His great uncle has been dead in his family tomb long before I was born. Who the blazes are you?'

'If it is permitted I would like to speak with him.'

'Nothing more will happen until you give up your name, sir,' responded the captain.

Morgan studied him and the men around him who held their weapons with tightened, sweating grips. Reaching up he pulled back his cowl and said.

'My name is Morgan Ap Heston.'

There was an audible in draw of breath amongst the listening soldiers, and the captain's face was drained of blood.

'Wait here,' he commanded and turned and hurried away.

Morgan stood quietly waiting, unmoving amongst the curious but nervously shifting warriors tasked with guarding the pass to the lower kingdoms. After a short interval, a worried looking and slightly distracted captain returned, pushing his way between his comrades in arms.

'Follow me, please,' he said curtly. 'The lord will see you.'

Morgan flowed after him without a word in response, like a shadow crossing the sun.

They descended the stairs from the battlements and crossed the circular courtyard within. Unnervingly, the young captain realised that this mysterious visitor seemed very familiar with where he was, and remained very self-contained, not bothering to gawk about as most strangers to the fortress usually did.

After a relatively short walk down thick, stone corridors, they entered a cavernous long-hall. A group of chain-mailed warriors sat huddled at a battered table discussing something; battle tactics no doubt. A tall, broad-shouldered man in his middle years, looked up and frowned at them. His head was completely shaven, and his nose was broken and overly long and pointed. Morgan almost smiled.

Some family genes had an annoying way of reappearing a few generations later, and this lord looked very similar to the lord he once knew so many years ago.

'Is this the man who jumped thirty feet up onto my battlements? Doesn't look like much to me. You call yourself by an old and dangerous name, sir. Are you for real or just a foolish charlatan? My bet is on the later.'

'I am what I am,' responded Morgan in a level voice.

'You will give proper address to my Lord Coulthain under his own roof!' exclaimed a hulking warrior with forearms like tree trunks.

Morgan did not even bother to glance at him.

'Easy Graham. Let's not provoke the fellow just in case he is who he says he is,' interjected Lord Coulthain. By the underlying humour in his voice, it was clear what he believed to be true. 'What do you want from us, Morgan Ap Heston? My great uncle once served with such a man, a man by-the-way, who by his actions and influence disrupted the politics of this region and beyond, and so by this reasoning, you should be now in your grave seven feet under in the bosom of mother earth. Explain yourself.'

'I am not sure why I came here, Lord of Stronghome Keep, but it certainly wasn't for anything that you might give me. Instinct led me to pay my respects to something that once was; to an old friend who once was.'

'Enough of this arrogant fool's nonsense, lord. Let me pound some humility into him then throw him out on his ear.'

After a thoughtful pause, the Lord Coulthain answered.

'Why not, Graham. Let's see what he is made of, eh?'

The young captain swiftly stepped away from Morgan as the giant Graham came steaming across the space, moving extraordinarily fast for such a big man.

Morgan did not move nor react in any visible way.

Graham was a man who wielded a war hammer in battle. Only the biggest and strongest are able to do this. As his ham-sized fist exploded around in a thunderous round-house swing, all present winced as they imagined the end result. Morgan, however, was unperturbed. At the moment just before fatal impact, the smaller man rolled sinuously under the terrible blow, slipped side on and lightly blocked and guided the force of the attacking arm away and downwards with a double knife-hand. Then with his left hand grounding the giant's bulging triceps, his right hand captured the wrist and twisted it, forming a lever of the straightened arm against the joints. As the big man bent forward with the surprising and painful manoeuvre, Morgan slid his hand from his opponent's triceps, reached up and cupped his chin, and with a casual reverse wrench, catapulted Graham backwards over his hip. As the colossal warrior crashed to the ground, Morgan stepped away smoothly.

Red of face with humiliation Graham surged to his feet and with a bellow, charged at the still form of his humiliator. Just as the juggernaut's arms were about to wrap around Morgan and rip him off his feet using his greater size and weight, the smaller man's left hand flew out catching his attacker between enormous skull and bull neck, depressing it and at the same time, as his body pivoted sideways, guided the momentum onwards. Instantaneously, the right hand slipped under the muscled shoulder of the giant and grabbing him by the under-arm, twisted from the hip and hurled the huge body effortlessly through the air where it spun full circle and smashed into the wall beyond. There it then lay unmoving. No one else moved. No one else spoke. The room was deathly silent.

'Maybe you are who you say you are. Whatever the truth of the matter, it does not reflect well upon you. You are not welcome here at my house. I respectfully request that you should leave without further delay,' said Lord Coulthain to a once again still and unmoving Morgan.

Morgan studied the lord for a heavy pause noticing the sheen of sweat gleaming from his shaven skull. The room was filled with withheld breaths and thick with tension.

'As you wish, lord. May you hold your roof against the storm coming against you.'

With these words, Morgan bowed and turned away, sensing that only the young captain dared to fall into step with him.

'Are you truly him? How is that possible?' was the expected questions from the young and bold.

Morgan nearly smiled, recalling another such young man who was as dear to him as any, other than his brother, could get.

'I am who I am, and there is only one other like me,' was his cryptic reply. 'May I ask your name in turn, son?'

'Guy…Guy Bastonet, Captain, first class,' replied the young man automatically, then grinned broadly, his face open and honest.

Morgan nodded but did not venture any further comment.

'I'll take you to the kitchens for some bread and cheese. If you keep low maybe no one would mind, then I'll show you to a hidden sallyport at nightfall. With luck, you'll be able to slip away without the bastards noticing.'

Whether he was referring to his own side or the besiegers, Morgan wasn't sure, but once again he nodded his thanks.

As hoped for, Morgan was left in peace at his corner table in the busy, sweltering kitchen. As dark drew in Captain Bastonet reappeared and guided him through side corridors out of the fortress main. For once things were quiet in the courtyard outside the redoubt, and the young Captain beckoned Morgan to follow him. However, the older man held up a hand to forestall him and walked over to a moss-covered statue standing above a small pond. Stepping up into the marble basin of water Morgan reached around the stone figure and fiddled with something at its back. Then to the astonishment of the Captain, the statue swung open revealing the dark mouth of a narrow tunnel. It was Morgan's turn to gesture to the wide-eyed Guy Bastonet, who being young, was ever ready to embark into the unknown. Without a word, he followed Morgan into the hitherto undiscovered tunnel.

'How in the name of the goddess did you know this was here?' whispered Guy in the darkness.

Morgan did not bother to voice the obvious answer.

After a while, the young soldier whispered again at Morgan's back.

'Why don't you stay and help us? Your reputation and deeds are well known and recorded. We still study and follow your written military strategies. Goddess, what am I saying!?'

'You seemed to have somehow accepted the unacceptable, son,' commented Morgan.

'Aye. Shit!'

'Ah, here we are,' muttered Morgan, pushing on a cumbersome stone portal that grated and rumbled on rusted sockets.

As they stepped out into the thin, cold air, the face of the ice-covered mountain loomed over them, dominating the moonlit night.

'This is a dead end,' observed Guy. 'You will never get out this way.'

'There is an old track that runs along its side. I will be fine. It is time for you to return to your people with the burden of a secret on your shoulders. It is for you to do with it as you wish. My thanks for your help and trust.'

'Stay. We need you.'

'In answer to your earlier question. Your lord well knows that although it is almost impossible to believe, I am telling the truth. He has to weigh up the advantages of using my help or asking me to leave. If I stay, men will say that the victory is mine. He cannot tolerate that as lord of this keep. He would not be able to tolerate my presence as a result. Therefore, win or fall he must do it on his terms only. This is the way of ambitious men.'

'Would you have stayed if he had asked?'

'No.'

'You no longer trust us. I can see it in your eyes.'

The lad was very perceptive and given the right circumstances and luck would grow into a great leader one day.

'Farewell, son. May fortune walk with you.'

Morgan turned and disappeared into the shadow of the mountain.

CHAPTER VI

'Lord Tramford, you had better come and see this!' said the big, raw-boned woman, dressed in the mail armour of a man.

'Sharleen, for the love of the goddess, can't you see that I've just sat down to meal?'

'Eat later,' replied the woman in a dead-pan voice. 'This you can't miss.'

'Alright, alright, I'm coming. It had better be good, Sharleen.'

'You can judge that for yourself. If I'm right, you owe me a night between your sheets.'

The counsellor quickly looked into the woman's eyes to see if she was serious. It was hard to tell for her expression never seemed to change. Not that he had ever seen, anyway.

'Sharleen, you know well that women do not appeal to me.'

'I'm no ordinary woman, and many say I'm like a man.'

The old councillor vented an exasperated sigh and muttered under his breath.

'I'm much too old for this malarkey. Please, Sharleen, lead the way if you will.'

Pressing a hand into the small of his back to help straighten his painful spine Councillor Tramford followed the warrior, his head coming only up to her broad shoulder. The many she referred to were quite correct in their assessment; she was definitely more man than a woman, yet the full curves of her buttocks were undoubtedly that of a woman.

'Stop ogling my arse. It's yours that I'm after.'

The councillor rolled his eyes and straightened his back with a groan, fixing his eyes higher.

Emerging into the muddy courtyard from the heavy timbered housing structures attached to the main, round, stone Keep where the lord lived, the counsellor pulled up short. Sitting on a pile of building stones was Captain Horace with his head wrapped in a make-shift bandage and looking much the worse for wear. Standing next to him were his two constant lieutenants, Luc and Scar. Luc was swaying on his feet and looked about ready to drop whereas Scar had a faraway gaze in his eyes that stunk of battlefield shock.

'Mother goddess!' muttered the old man, hurrying over to his once thought of indomitable team.

'What happened, Horace?' he enquired, failing to keep the anxiety from his voice.

'A bloody demon happened,' whispered Scar.

'Shut it, Scar,' said Horace weekly.

'A demon?' asked the councillor in a distracted and confused voice.

'Well, sir, to put it bluntly. One man defeated us all in less time than it would take you to spit on a stray dog.

'Or for Luc to have to have a fuck,' interjected Scar helpfully.

'Shut it, Scar,' said the old man grumpily. 'One man defeated the three of you? But you are our best!'

'Well, let's just say he wasn't impressed with our reputation. Killed all the others, we were just lucky.'

'But what you're telling me is not possible. Luc? Do you have anything to say?'

The burly, squat man just stared back blankly.

'We think that he received a nasty blow to his head. Hasn't said a word since he regained consciousness.'

'It certainly has improved his conversation though,' commented Scar.

'Shut it, Scar,' replied both men in unison, but they could see that even Scar was worried for his friend.

'Do we know who this man is? Where he is from and what it is that he wants?'

'Demon, not man,' corrected Scar, 'and he wants to be left alone. Said to tell our lord this.'

'Well we can't bloody do that, can we? Not after this humiliation! He will not be allowed to get away with it!' shouted Lord Breakspear as he stomped down the steps from the Keep and splashed his way through the mud towards them.'

'Oh, goddess!' whispered Councilor Tramford. 'Not now, please!'

'This is an affront to our dignity and demands an immediate and forceful response,' continued Lord Breakspear, the odour of alcohol strong on his breath.

'Lord...,' began Captain Horace, struggling to his feet.

'Gather a strong force together, man, and get back out there on your horse. That's what we hire you for, isn't it?' said the lord nastily.

'My lord, maybe we should consider things a bit...,' tried the councillor.

'You've had your say, old man! Now is the time for men of metal to take the reins, words are no longer useful here,' said the lord loudly, cutting off his adviser in mid-sentence.

'Will you lead us on this foray, lord?' asked Scar innocently.

'Are you mad, fool!?' replied the lord. 'Do you see me taking an axe to cut down my own trees? No, you don't! I hire foresters for that. You, sir, are supposed to be my foresters who harvest my enemies. Go and cut them down!'

With that, he spun away, gathering the soiled edges of his green, velvet cloak out of the mud and stalked back into the keep.

'Were you the one who alerted our lord to our predicament, Sharleen?' asked Councillor Tramford with an accusing glare.

'The bunch of you holding court outside his window was enough to get his attention, I think,' was the deadpan response.

'We'd best get on with it,' said Captain Horace in a fatalistic tone.

'None of you is in any shape to go out again,' reasoned Tramford. 'Let me try and talk some sense into him.'

'The lord has given a command. Come on you two, let's get together a fighting party of men who will make a difference,' responded Horace, walking away with his two weary companions in tow.

'Sharleen, you've just been appointed my personal representative. Go keep an eye on them and try to keep them safe. I'll have a note of command drawn up for you to present to Horace if he fails to take a reasonable course.'

The warrior woman nodded and moved off to collect her arms and horse.

Despite Horace's stubborn decision to carry out his duty to his lord immediately, finding a competent levy was not easy, and it wasn't until dawn before they finally set out to exact Lord Breakspear's imagined justice. Everyone was happy that the warrior woman, Sharleen, had joined their company for she was easily the best sword among them and her competencies in the field were well known and highly respected. No one objected when she chose to ride in the lead with Captain Horace, Scar and the still silent, but more alert looking Luc.

They drove their ponies hard, but they were bred for stamina and hardship and were up to the mark. Cutting across country, they made up time, for Horace, Luc and Scar knew precisely where they had to go to pick up the trail of their nemesis.

As they topped a rise in the land, they spotted a tall, black figure standing in the same spot where the demon had stood. In sheer startlement they drew back over forcefully on their horses' reins, bringing them to a dancing, fretful halt.

'Mother goddess!' exclaimed Scar. 'He is still here!'

'Is this your demon?' asked Sharleen in her usual unemotional voice.

'He looks somewhat different,' replied Horace with a puzzled tone.

'He is now butt naked, for a start,' commented Scar, his eyes appearing a bit too wide for his narrow face.

'Yes, I noticed. Puts you boys to shame,' observed Sharleen.

Despite their trepidation, the three men gave her a nervous glance.

'He's changed his colour as well,' ventured Scar.

'He's covered himself with mud, you fool,' said Luc.

They all jumped in their saddles. It was the first words they had heard from him since the incident.

'Magic!' whispered Scar. 'Let's ride away whilst we still can, Captain.'

'Stop your flapping, boys,' said Sharleen. 'What's your call, Horace?'

'This man is not the same as the one we encountered,' responded the Captain and twisting in his saddle he shouted in a commanding voice.

'The rest of you stay here unless I signal for you. Is that clear? Sharleen, Luc, Scar, you're with me.'

Without waiting for any acknowledgement or consent he spurred his mount forward into a gentle trot, approaching the motionless figure.

As the small group got to within ten yards of the figure they brought their ponies to a stop. Captain Horace raised his hand gently, palm outwards to show his non-aggressive intent.

Up close they could now see the figure clearly. He was tall, taller than most men, his shoulders powerfully built and his limbs unusually extended. His chest was huge and deep and his muscles were elongated and clearly sculpted under his skin. The hair on his head, although marred with mud, was long, curly and chestnut coloured along with his free growing beard. But most unsettling were his eyes, which were black, bottomless pools, which bore through them and into their minds. An inexplicable aura of power pulsed through the air.

An involuntary whimper escaped Scar's lips.

'We do not wish harm to you,' rasped Captain Horace. Then clearing his throat loudly, continued. 'We are looking for a man who stood exactly where you are standing about two days past.'

The strange man did not give any outward reaction or any sign that he had even understood what the captain had said but continued to regard them in an unsettling manner.

'We would like to speak with him as our first meeting did not go well.'

A small, mad, strangled giggle emanated from Scar.

Ignoring his companion with a force of will, Horace pressed on.

'May we ask who you are, sir, and why are you here on our lord's land?'

'Earth canort be owned just ars sky canort be owned.'

'Be that as it may, this region is claimed by our Lord Breakspear!'

'Don't annoy him, Horace,' whispered Sharleen evenly. 'You are doing well as a diplomat.'

The mud covered creature chuckled gutturally in amusement.

Pulling a rush of air through his nostrils and out again to settle his rising emotions, Horace tried once more.

'We do not wish conflict. We...I am trying to find a way to satisfy my lord's commands without sacrificing lives uselessly.'

'Arrh, my little brudar hars taught you humility, marnthing. He eez short on partience in theez days.'

'Your brother!?'

'My brudar. The one dart hars left heez mark on you. You shood nort harv challenged him.'

'Yes, we know that now, but we have to satisfy our lord's command. We must speak with him.'

'How carn a marn surrendar heez weel to another? Stupid. Do you wish to speak to or trick my brudar, little marn?'

'To speak merely...I need to find a middle way. He may be able to help me in this. Can you take us to him?'

'Be careful where you are going with this, Horace,' cautioned Sharleen in a hushed, uninflected voice.

'Listen to the womarn. Her words are wize. Your life weel be taken eef you cross my brudar. Eef you cross me. He eez growing dark. The day of turning is coming.'

Sharleen frowned slightly. It should not have been possible for the creature to have heard her.

As if in answer to her thoughts she felt the creature studying her. Its eyes sucking on the essences of her very soul. Despite herself, she shivered. No man had ever made her do that since she was ten years old. The day she had killed her father.

'Please, if you are able, guide us to him.'

'You arsk a dangerous thing. Dangerous for you, little marn. Come then, but only you four.'

Almost at once the creature turned and loped away, gliding like a wolf over the uneven ground.

'Quick Scar, tell the others to go home then follow after us as fast as you can,' commanded Horace, as he spurred his pony in pursuit of the strange demon. Scar was right. Two demons in so many days. The world was changing, and it was taking him with it. He truly feared that he would never find his way back.

CHAPTER VII

It was as if he were travelling down memory lane. Reviewing and examining his life, his decisions, by journeying back along the physical trail of his past existence from over a century ago. Every step taken was a tread deeper into his earlier life, the years falling away, the people he once knew, some of them friends, lovers, now dead. The land though had a different feel to it. It was more quiet, true, but it was also possessed by a skulking atmosphere. Danger lay hidden in every group of armed men trying to move around the countryside without being observed, but in addition, remaining on the look-out for any opportunity to take what was not theirs to have. Fear and uncertainty lay in the air. Villagers, farmers and peasants alike withdrew to a safe distance whenever he came into sight; housewives called to their children and closed themselves with their brood behind locked and shuttered doors. Suspicion was everywhere. The hand of the Protectorate was closing its grip, and the old order was unwilling to be squeezed by it.

Morgan was beginning to realise just how much of his life he had spent running. Running from himself, running from a destiny that he did not want; that others had wanted to thrust onto his shoulders. For all the advantages his engineered genes had given him he had never found the peace he had desired, the place to belong to that he had longed for. He was homeless and empty. His brother had had it right from the beginning; make your own path. People were only interested in what you had to say as long as it allowed them to profit and gain from your words and deeds. Once they had what they wanted, they stopped listening. Well, he had stopped talking, had stopped giving. Let the Protectorate conquer the world; he was certainly no longer in the game of trying to stop them. If they left him alone, he would leave them to their ambitions. Maybe enslaving mankind to their will wasn't such a bad thing. Men were like children anyway. A dictatorial father forcing them to follow - do as I say not as I do - may well be what was needed. It certainly had had the effect of reducing internal, never-ending conflict and strife in many of the subdued countries now under the yoke of the Empire. Wasn't that what 'the One' was supposed to have accomplished? There, the Protectorate was doing his job for him; he was free.

So far there had not been any attempts to molest or challenge him. Maybe that had something to do with the unpredictable surges of energy that crackled around him. As his iron self-control waned and his will darkened, the power in him -contained and condensed into a hard ball deep within him for nearly all of his life- began to leak, letting escape what he had always wanted to keep hidden. Morgan was never comfortable in releasing it, even in small measures, even when in great personal danger; once again for the fear or better still, for the self-acknowledgement, that he was somehow different. The mark of Cain -as he had once read from that ancient book of infinite trouble and contention- was engraved on his horsehead. He no longer cared.

Morgan had become so embroiled with the changes going on within him that for the first time that he could remember, his awareness of the world around him failed to warn him. Even his extraordinary senses had been nullified by the disturbing inwardness of his concentration.

'Well, what have we here?' the arrogant and sarcastic question brought his attention back to a sharp point.

'Looks to me as if we've caught ourselves a wandering, heathen monk.'

'Only one way to find out. We'll just have to expose him to cleansing fire so that god may find out what lies in his heart.'

The dismissive conversation sounded regretful, but Morgan knew it was the spiteful, bully tactics of the small-minded. Sitting their horses on a shallow rise leading into a small forest was a ten man Protectorate hunter pack. They were not soldiers but hired dregs of society who had found profitable employment in hunting their own people. When the law of the land was broken, the scum always managed to float to the top. Morgan felt a bitterness rising from within him. These people would never change, all that was left was for him to execute justice as he saw fit. The air around him thrummed, and the small stones at his feet jumped. Before Morgan was aware of what he was doing, he reached out for the sick minds of the thugs in Protectorate pay; reached out and held them tight. The horses were the first to sense that something was not right as nature had designed it. They tossed their heads and fought the bit in an attempt to get away, but their ignorant riders held them captive under their control. They should have taken heed of their mounts and let them run, but now it was too late.

The first realisation that something was not as it should be was the sharp, painful coldness clamping their foreheads. A thing that numbed their brains with icy trauma, like the odd and sudden sensation felt when drinking from an ice-melt stream on a hot day. From there icy tendrils crept throughout their skulls and down their faces, eating them with agony. They gasped like fishes thrown onto a river's bank, hands clasped around their heads, unable to breathe, unable to think, unable to talk. All crumpled from their now panicked horses and died where they fell, never knowing what had befallen them. Morgan walked on past their contorted bodies without giving them a glance. In fact, he had already forgotten that they were there. His mind was becoming an alien thing; removed from the concerns and restrictions of normal men. He was not one of them. Why should he continue to try? Had he been in a conscious state to look at himself objectively he would have been very consternated indeed by what he was looking at.

He walked steadily onwards for the rest of the day and throughout the night. He did not stop to eat, to rest, or even to sleep. He did not have a fixed destination or for that matter, an objective; he just needed to keep moving. He did not feel the rage that had been birthed in his brother so many generations ago, but he felt a vast emptiness, a void into which his hitherto locked away and controlled gift flowed, free at last of Morgan's self-imposed stop gates. Twinned with this unpredictable and ever-increasing power, his sense of responsibility was being eroded with each step along the road to his origins. Morgan was probably, even taking his brother into account, the most dangerous man alive on the earth. Every wild creature along his route detected this and swerved hurriedly away from his path. All except foolish men, who had so separated themselves from their mother, Earth, that they could smell, see and hear only themselves and the things of their own making.

Morgan stopped, as the sun rose over a swathe of green waving grass stretching out to the horizon like a vast inland sea, he felt the soft earth beneath his feet vibrating, rising to a dull throbbing, travelling up through his body. His sharp eyes picked out a fast-moving dot in the very far distance tearing along towards him under the big sky on a diagonal which would closely intersect his. Sweeping across the grass like a malignant blot of mal-intent were several other dots hell-bent on bringing their prey to ground. The dot grew into a horse, a fantastic animal, broad of chest and wild of eye, then the horse became horse and rider, which soon revealed itself to be a woman. Morgan could smell her fear, and taste the blood on her as it dripped into the air. He swayed slightly on his feet. His senses were becoming overwhelming. Despite her heightened emotional state and her injuries, there was something unusual about this woman. As he watched, she turned smoothly in her saddle and released an arrow from her short, composite, recurved bow, a powerful weapon, hard for even a strong man to draw. Just a split second before her fingers caressed the arrow free, Morgan caught something on the air, as if an invisible line had linked her iron point to its target. The arrow buzzed in flight, and a burst of blood mushroomed in the throat of one of the pack of killers on her heels. Morgan blinked. She had a gift beyond the gift of a master archer. He launched into action, racing faster than a galloping horse towards her.

The woman did not see him coming until almost at the last moment and although he picked up a spike of alarm from her, hormones ejected through her pores into the air, she delicately and expertly guided her horse away to either avoid or defend against this unexpected assailant.

Morgan leapt past her at great speed noticing that she already had a fresh arrow to bow as he swept by. Her pursuers were not so blessed.

The lead horseman flung his eyes and mouth wide in shocked surprise when an apparition from nowhere suddenly bounded up higher than the head of his flat-out racing stallion. Morgan pushed the great head of the animal to one side with his hand and kicked it solidly in the shoulder with his left leg. The thunderous blow threw the beast sideways, at which point, it tripped over its front legs and crashed down, catapulting over the grassy plain, crushing its bewildered rider and bringing to earth three more of its fast following brethren. Morgan using the rebound, brought both his feet together, still in mid-air, and smashed a hammer's blow into the shoulder of a companion horse running alongside, knocking it flying from its feet, only to be trampled over by its speeding fellows, the first two managing to half leap over but the third was brought down by its wildly thrashing legs. The hapless riders were thrown heavily onto the turf and did not get up after. As if from a spring-board Morgan was launched into the air and came down on a cringing and now terrified Protectorate cavalry trooper, ripping him from his saddle and flinging him bodily across onto his comrade, bowling them both under the clobbering hooves of the pounding animals. In the time it would have taken for a man to take a deep breath, ten men were down and not moving. The remaining five who had escaped his assault were in shock, craning their necks around, eyes wide and staring, to try and get a look at the demon that had sundered them and at the same time, trying to remain on the backs of their careening mounts. Their ordeal was not over. The hunted had become the hunter, and was now circling. Taking advantage of the reprieve granted to her, she rode like an implacable avenger, sending barb after barb, three flying before the first had found its mark, piercing and rupturing living flesh with their iron points. She did not stop her deadly dance till all lay dying and bleeding in the green grass.

The heavily blowing, sideways prancing stallion, kept under a tight and masterly control by its rider, was guided cautiously towards the now still and motionless Morgan. Only his eyes, with golden flecks swirling inhumanly in them, tracked her movements. As she tightened the reins and brought her superb mount to a stamping halt, he assessed her for the first time, just as she was doing to him. She was about his height, with a firm, taut, athletic build and wore high boots of stiffened leather with soft leather trousers tucked into them.

A thigh-length green tunic covered her upper body, and this was encased within a boiled leather back and breast-plate with a neck-guard rising at the rear where a second quiver of arrows was hung to match the near-empty one fastened to the pommel of her saddle. Her long raven hair was tied back into a warrior's pony-tail revealing a high, cheek-boned, proud and elegant face from which two unnerving, emerald-green irises pierced the world from its setting of oddly slanted eyes. Her movements were sinuously lazy and controlled. She reminded Morgan of a beautiful but highly dangerous cat.

'You have been a hard man to find,' she said in a clear, firm voice.

Morgan did not reply but kept regarding her steadily. She continued.

'You are one of the brothers. Which one, I am not entirely certain. By your mode of fighting I would say Lord Krarl, but by your look, I would venture Lord Morgan.'

Still, Morgan did not respond.

'By your lack of normal courtesy, my choice wanders back to Lord Krarl.'

'My brother would not be happy with such a statement and if I were he you would now be dead.'

The warrior quickly dismounted and bowed low.

'Lord Morgan, please forgive my rudeness. My brothers and sisters have endured many hardships in order to find you.'

To Morgan's ears, her words sounded almost like an accusation.

'You have a gift. Who are you and what do you want?' he responded abruptly, with his voice taking on a low, deadly tone.

'I was tutored very well in the use of the bow and...'

'You know very well that that is not the point of my statement. The words you use next will determine my actions.'

'I am one of the children of the Sacred Founder.'

'Sacred Founder?'

'Yes, he formed a refuge for children of certain abilities where they could develop their gifts free from persecution.'

'Where is this place?'

'It's in a region called the Blue Mountains, it's a...'

'You don't mean old Limp-foot, do you? The old codger was far from sacred.'

The woman bristled slightly, and her reply was tight with defence.

'We do not use such a derogatory and dismissive reference for our founder and I would advise you to refer to him respectfully as Master Brother Dragonet.'

Morgan regarded the woman quietly for a short time then shook his head thoughtfully.

'Old Limp-foot would turn in his grave if he knew that he had created a bunch of fawning sycophants to his name or even worse, fanatics.'

Morgan could taste the release of chemicals stimulating cold emotion within the warrior as she summoned her gift.

'Stay your hand, girl, unless you are tired of living,' he warned in a low voice that rumbled with power.

The warrior froze, struggling to regain her inner composure.

'When last I was at the Sanctum of Light the acolytes were much more disciplined with their emotions,' continued Morgan in a more conversational tone.

'You were there!? When…?'

'Your haloed Sacred Limp-foot wanted my help with the training of his stray dog initiates; never have I witnessed such incompetence.'

By now the warrior realised that for some reason she was being bated.

'You knew the Sacred Founder…?'

'Girl, your questions lack depth. Tell me about your gift.'

'I cannot explain it fully, but for some reason, I can call a target to me. Now after years of training I never miss, no matter the thrown weapon. My reflexes are also faster than most.'

'And these brothers and sisters that you mentioned; are they like you?'

'Yes and no. We all have different abilities at varying levels, but those of us chosen for the quest are the best of the children.'

'Quest…now what is it that you want?'

'Our mountain home has been invaded by the Protectorate Empire. Our Inheritor sent us out to find either you or your brother. He said the time was now or never.'

'Time for what, girl? Time is meaningless. I won't say this again, now that you've found me, what do you want from me?'

'Our Master said that you would lead us into the new beginning.'

'Limp-foot if you can hear me, I know that you are laughing, you old bastard,' muttered Morgan.

'What..?' asked the warrior woman hesitantly, becoming more confident with every passing minute that her long sought for mark was indeed a bit mad.

'I haven't got the patience for this, girl, or with you for that matter, and certainly not for the misconceived beliefs of your master.'

With these ending words, Morgan turned abruptly and walked away. The warrior, however, had come too far to give up so easily. She had no intention of allowing him to dismiss her in such a perfunctory manner.

'You cannot walk away from your destiny, Lord Morgan. You have been called for something greater than you are. It is your duty to answer the call.'

'Stop pestering me. Go find your brothers and sisters and follow your own destiny. Stop trying to piggy-back on someone else's,' replied Morgan, lengthening his stride.

Finding herself having to trot to keep up, the woman stopped, stuck two fingers in the corners of her mouth and blew a short, sharp, piercing whistle. Immediately, her spirited stallion cantered up to her, and she leapt smoothly into the saddle without bothering to bring her mount to a halt. Morgan ignored this display of showmanship and kept moving without even a sideways glance at them.

'So you admit you have a higher destiny to fulfil,' persisted the warrior. 'Don't you even want to know my name?'

Again Morgan did not bother to answer.

'How rude!' she muttered under her breath but did not bother to try to engage the silent man with any further conversation. She did, however, continue to dog his footsteps.

As evening encroached on the fading afternoon, Morgan diverted to make camp in the lea of a low, grass-covered mound. He appeared to be oblivious to the still present woman and went about his business as if she weren't there. She, in the same vein, was like his shadow, moving around him quietly and unobtrusively.

As they sat down to eat from their own stored supplies, Morgan suddenly spoke, causing the warrior to jump slightly.

'You should see to that wound.'

'It's nothing,' she replied in an off-hand way, rolling her shoulder.

Morgan observed the oozing of watery blood coming from the livid and open injury.

'Out here even small cuts tend to give way to the rot of flesh. That wound is high up. Death is long and hard in coming no matter how strongly you may wish for it.'

'You have a morbid way of looking at things, Lord Morgan if you don't mind me saying so. Please don't concern yourself, I heal fast.'

Morgan gave a non-committal grunt and finished his small meal of smoked venison in silence. He watched the warrior openly, his face expressionless, as she removed her breastplate and attempted to sew her torn skin together with a very thin and finely crafted bone needle and cotton thread. He did not offer to help nor did she ask. When this awkward task was completed to her satisfaction, she laid back on her blankets and closed her eyes, shutting him out of her world. Morgan could feel her building safeguards around her mind, but he was not interested in probing her, and his awareness of her efforts was only periphery. A lot missing from her training. The Inheritors, it seems, were not up to Limp-foot's rigorously laid down and passed on standards. The gifted were swiftly fading from the world. Once this would have evoked sadness in him; now he felt nothing.

Smoking in a deep breath through his nostrils he folded his legs under him and prepared to enter deep meditation, a ritual he had followed as long as he had memory. For the first time ever a sensation of fruitlessness and uselessness seeped into his mind, distracting him and taking away his centre. With another grunt, this time with disgust, he cancelled the exhalation necessary to cleanse his psyche, pulled his cloak around him and curled into the warmth of mother earth. He did not find the peace he needed wrapped to her bosom; sleep would not be summoned.

During the night a strong, hot wind blew in from nowhere carrying with it spiteful sand from a desert land, a forsaken place that lies only the goddess knows where. Morgan was glad for the interruption to his aimlessness. A challenge is a challenge, no matter its source. A thing to raise the blood like a hungry tide and to focus a waning mind. He was built to confront adversity and no matter his state of being he would never shrink from it. He stood up and walked into the scouring maelstrom of shrieking wind and stinging sand as it whipped the long grass into chaos and madness. When the warrior woke blearily in the dull, orange glow of an unearthly morning covered in shifting silt and dirt, he was gone.

CHAPTER VIII

The four riders were exhausted, their sturdy ponies sweat streaked and blowing loudly. The pungent smell of horse was thick around them, permeating the very air with its wet stink. The creature leading them snorted and increased its speed, surging further ahead.

'Goddess, bless us and keep us safe, for he is not of this earth, and we follow him blindly,' prayed Scar.

Luc glared at the muttering Scar, but then leaned in close to Horace and keeping his voice low, said:

'Scar has some truth to it. He does not tire, and our horses are being run into the ground. This is not natural, Captain.'

'We have to see this through. Turn back if you want to,' was the terse reply.

Scar angled his horse and brought it alongside Sharleen's.

'What do you think, Sharl? Shall we turn back?'

'I like looking at his buttocks,' was the serious reply. 'And don't call me Sharl.'

Scar eyed her but didn't say anything further.

At the foothills that would take them on the long undulating and the sometimes treacherous path to Strongholm Keep, Krarl suddenly stopped.

'We wrest here. One night, one day. No more.'

Then in a blink of an eye, he was gone, slipping like a ghost into the rugged terrain.

'Mother goddess! Do you think he has run off on us?' enquired Scar hopefully.

'You're a superstitious idiot, Scar,' responded Sharleen flatly.

Luc grinned broadly, and Scar put on a false outraged expression. This lightened the heavy, foreboding mood somewhat and they all dismounted to make camp and unsaddle their bone-weary mounts.

Twenty minutes later as they sat around a small fire sipping hot coffee, Krarl suddenly appeared in their midst with a small deer draped over one muscled shoulder. No one had heard or seen him approach. They all expressed startlement to varying degrees except Sharleen, who casually studied Scar who had spat coffee on his trousers and was frantically trying to wipe it off. As she looked up, she met the unsettling eyes of their strange companion and thought for a fleeting moment that she had glimpsed some sort of approval in their hypnotic depths. 'Shit, he was testing them with every yard that they covered.' Testing them for what, she wondered.

'Eat,' he said simply and dropped the butchered carcass wrapped in its own skin on the ground in front of them. Luc immediately bent to the task of quartering it. One of his unexpected talents was the great joy he took in cooking. A strange past-time for such a rough, uncultured man. Both Sharleen and Horace realised that this other-worldly creature had easily taken over the command of their small group and even Luc was obeying his wishes without question.

As the mouth-watering odour of roasting meat wafted around the camp, Horace cleared his throat and addressed the naked and silent creature.

'May we know by what name you are called?'

'Krarl.'

They were all surprised that he had bothered to answer, but after a pause, the captain continued.

'My name is Horace, he is Luc, the young fellow with the scar on his face, well, he is called Scar by all who know him well, and the woman is Sharleen. She is the most formidable fighter of us all and is known for her solid judgement on most things.'

Sharleen glanced at Horace but did not comment. His words were high praise indeed. The creature, however, did not look impressed and by his neutral expression, it was not quite plain whether he had even listened to Horace's introductions.

Horace, it seemed, was not fazed by this apparent inattention in the least.

'Lord Krarl, I cannot help but notice that you do not have any armour. From all accounts, we will be entering into the arena of a siege. I have some spare leggings, a tunic and a chain-mail shirt in my saddlebag. You would do me great honour if you accepted them as a gift.'

Sharleen eyed Horace with narrowed eyes whereas Scars' were wide open and he seemed to be struggling to keep something clamped into his mouth. The big fool was trying to get the stranger to cover up. She suspected that she was the reason behind Horace's suddenly loquacious persona; some misplaced sense of manly protection for her delicate womanhood. Her lips tightened slightly. She wasn't altogether pleased with his efforts or his attitude. She did not need protecting. Besides she liked what she was looking at.

The tall, rangy man, if a man he was, turned his gaze on Horace and all due to him, the fool did not flinch but returned the look with admirable steadiness.

'Showr me this gift.'

Moving a bit too quickly, a sure sign of his disguised uneasiness, Horace got up and picked up his gear where he had left them. Slowly opening the leather straps, he pulled out his offerings and handed them to the seated Krarl. To everyone's eyes, it looked uncomfortably like a supplicant addressing his king; his rock becomes a throne. Horace seemed totally unaware of the image he was portraying.

'Damn!' thought Sharleen. 'We're becoming his bloody entourage!'

'Good gift,' growled the man-like creature. 'I like.'

With one gnarled hand, he took the clothes and mailed shirt. As he got up and turned away, he glanced at her, and she saw deep amusement reflected in his black eyes.

'Shit!' she thought. 'He knows exactly what fool Horace was attempting and has twisted it to serve his own designs. He is no brute, unthinking animal, this one, no matter what we think he looks like.'

The companions sat in uneasy, reflective silence after their leader, and leader he was, had disappeared. They all felt deep inside that this was a turning point in their lives; there would be no going back.

Experiencing a sudden fit of aggravation, Sharleen got up abruptly and stalked after Krarl. She did not like being manipulated; she was no man's plaything, no matter how hairy he was or well-formed his butt.

She found the conniving fellow waist deep in a tepid, rain-filled, rock pool, scrubbing himself vigorously with a soap bush. He did not seem in the least surprised to see her. Hands on hips and face expressionless she watched his antics with far from embarrassed eyes.

Snatching a knife from her belt, she strode aggressively towards him.

He stopped his cleansing and carefully observed her approach.

'You are in need of a bloody shave and a haircut,' she muttered in a flat, no-nonsense tone.

He offered no resistance as she grabbed a handful of his hair, yanked his head back and began assiduously cutting and scraping. She was not gentle, but not once did she slice his skin with her razor sharp knife. When she had finished her task to her satisfaction, she gave his now shoulder length hair a final yank and whispered hoarsely.

'There, much more human.'

Then she stalked off, her boots squelching from their soaking in the water. At her back, she could hear a low, bass chortling and a pleased look flitted over her face which was quickly smoothed away.

When she strolled back into the encampment, three pairs of eyes flicked up at her, but no one dared to speak a word, not even Scar.

Soon after, Krarl arrived dressed in tunic and leggings with the chain-mail shirt draped casually over one shoulder and a faint, herbal smell drifting from him. They all stared at his face, even Sharleen, which was handsome enough if in a square-jawed irregular, long-faced fashion. He, in turn, ignored them all and picked up a piece of cooked meat to eat. At this point the illusion vanished as his overlong canine teeth broke into the clear light, shining with saliva. They all recoiled and quickly looked elsewhere, all except Sharleen once again, who caught the gleam of amusement in Krarl's eyes as he bit savagely into the deer's flesh. The man couldn't help himself from toying with them and their superstitions.

Late that night with the moon high and full in the cloudless sky, Krarl woke them roughly from their slumbers. He now wore his shirt of gleaming metal, and he seemed to glow the luminous light of the night goddess. He did not appear to respect normal travelling times, but the four companions were seasoned hunters and packed up their few belongings smoothly and quickly without a grumble. In under ten minutes, they had broken camp and were on their way up the steep trail. This time their unusual leader picked a steady pace which they all followed easily, strung out in single file.

As they climbed higher, the air became thinner and shivery cold. The companions drew their cloaks around them and huddled low over their sure-footed ponies unable to control the involuntary tremors flickering throughout their bodies. They envied the tall man floating sinuously up the rough trail ahead of them for he seemed immune to the biting cold they were suffering from.

About an hour before dawn they emerged onto an exposed, wind-swept ridge and paused to take in the formidable view of the legendary fortress, pulsing white across the separating valley. In all its history it had never been successfully taken and had a place of pride in all the lowland kingdoms. Politics and time, however, had overseen the turn-over of many of its caretakers, although certain dominant families held prominence.

Krarl stood on the very lip of a dizzying drop and appeared as if he had entered a trance, his hair whipping around his face from the icy fierceness of the wind. The others held their horses well back and tried to control the rising anxiety growing in the pits of their stomachs.

'He aez noo longer in the big rock shelter,' Krarl shouted to them over the buffeting wind. 'We go through farst and hard. Corm let's gowr.'

Two hard hours later as the slate-grey, cold light seeped into the glowering, pre-dawn sky, the four companions found themselves driving their tough, border ponies uncompromisingly up the steep, scree scattered slope, their unshod hooves slipping on the hoar frost covered rocks. Krarl had ranged ahead and was nowhere in sight, but they had already passed the broken bodies of three outlying lookout guards. This was enough of a physical sign of his deadly presence.

Breasting the lip of the climb without challenge, the four gave their horses full head and tore through the sleep-drugged, siege camp. The body count built up as they galloped recklessly, cornering and zigzagging their ponies around ice-covered tents. Any unfortunate enough to have wandered out of their military shelter at this forsaken hour of the morning had found a quick death from the unmerciful hands of Krarl. Behind their thundering hooves, they could hear a growing hue and cry as men floundered out of their bedding, bleary-eyed and confused, from the sudden and alarming hubbub. No one it seemed had the presence of mind to sound an alarm.

Leaping their racing mounts over the remnants of the curtain wall that once controlled the pass, they remained unchallenged as confused soldiers stared after them uncertain as to whether they were part of their besieging army or not. Their unorthodox leader was right, speed and boldness would win through where stealth and subterfuge would fail.

An hour later, still in the high mountains just above the tree line, they pulled up their lathered horses under the lea of an ice-crusted crag.

'I can't believe that we actually got through!' exclaimed a breathless Scar.

'Me neither,' commented a red-faced Luc. 'Where in heaven's name is the architect of our mad dash though?'

'He is waiting for us beneath the trees,' replied Sharleen in her usual calm and unemotional voice.

'Where?' asked Horace. 'I can't see a thing.'

'Look for the unmoving shadow that seems not right,' was the matter-of-fact reply.

'Would you stop talking like that, Sharl!' said Scar in a high, irritated voice. 'You're spooking me really bad!'

'I shan't warn you a third time, Scar. That's not my name.'

'Come,' said Horace quickly before things got more out of hand. 'Lead us to him, Sharleen.'

Krarl watched them coming, picking their way gingerly between the scattered and jagged rocks on their path to him. As an experiment, he had reached out to the woman. She was the strongest of them. He had been surprised at how receptive she had been to his call. He had found her mind open to him and although she had not realised it, had responded to his summons positively. It would have been impossible otherwise, for her to have detected the stillness of his camouflaged position.

As the companions slid into the tree line a shadow detached itself as if birthed from the trunk of a statuesque fir.

'Yuure did well,' said Krarl in a deep, guttural voice.

Even the horses shied away in surprise at his almost mythical and sudden appearance.

'Shit!' exclaimed Scar, struggling to control his pony as it fought hard against the bit.

They felt a bit embarrassed at the sudden flush of pleasure that went through them at his compliment.

Sharleen regarded Krarl who was examining their discomfort with his large head slightly cocked to one side; her face was unreadable.

'What now?' she asked in her usual deadpan manner.

'Argh…we find my brodar, the faster the bettar. Bettar for us all.'

CHAPTER IX

She was a member of the inner circle. No, she was much more than that. She was one of the nine. The first woman to join this august sphere and her star was on the rise. Under her exquisite beauty and soft, rounded curves she was as hard as granite and as ruthless as a scorpion. Many had listened to her delicate, sultry words and had felt dominant, until her poisonous sting had brought their posturing down, melting like wax before the flame, leaving them bereft of their pride, position and possessions. Now she was doing what none of the nine had done since the very beginning, from the time of the founders. She had taken to the field. In fact, she had made her way to the cutting edge, the waxing and waning frontier of the Empire. A place that was the sole domain of ambitious and experienced generals, men who risked their careers, their lives even, on a throw of the dice; win all, lose all. She did not ride in with a war stallion between her smooth, flawless thighs, but in a traveller's wagon, cushioned and decorated inside with sumptuous silks and velvets; no comfort denied. She came slowly with courtiers, sycophants and scribes, like an Empress with her travelling court.

'What do you mean a Cardinal is here!' demanded the fat, sweating general, his eyes wide with bewildered panic. 'What I don't need is you making absurd, unsubstantiated claims at this time. Things are bad enough as they are.'

Three braziers were pouring out heat around the large command tent, but it wasn't these that was making him sweat. He abhorred the cold, but winning through on this godforsaken mountain peak was the only ladder available for him to climb to a comfortable political life. Family connections were not enough, he had plenty of those. What he needed was a military victory to take home and a lucrative one to keep in the field. This bloody, barren place joined up all the dots. What he didn't need was one of the nine, supreme rulers looking over his shoulders and breathing hot breath down his bloody neck.

'The Conclave guards announced the presence of a Cardinal in Seat at the outer cordon and demanded immediate entrance and passage, Sir.'

'For the love of god, do we know which one it is who is gracing us with his presence?'

'No, sir,' responded the adjutant. 'He is travelling in a covered wagon without any crest on display and the guards although bearing Conclave colours remained tightlipped and wear no identifying coat of arms on their clothing or armour.'

'I find this all unexpected and unsettling,' grumbled the general, passing a pudgy hand through his thinning hair. 'The Conclave never does anything without some hidden agenda. Why now? We're in the middle of a bloody siege. This is not the time to play at politics! Cordon off and prepare a safe zone for our visitors. I'll go out and do the welcoming.'

'Yes, sir. It's already underway, sir.'

Stuffing a handful of cinnamon flavoured sweetmeats into his mouth, General Clarence Montford nodded approval and waddled fretfully in the wake of his adjutant, pausing to wrap a thick, bearskin cloak over his round shoulders before pulling open the tent flaps and stepping into the glacial air outside.

He knew that he did not strike the expected martial image, but he was the fourth son of a respected military family, all of whom had done active service in the name of the Empire and two of whom were still servicing generals. He was brought up on tactics and logistics and had virtually lived all of his life in one military camp or another. He knew his business despite his addiction to sweet foods and a tendency to worry overmuch.

His field staff were already waiting with his favourite warhorse saddled. As soon as he was assisted into the saddle, he became one with his horse, a superb rider despite his bulk. With a small jerk of his head, he led his small military entourage at a slow canter towards the dreaded encounter. Given a choice he would have much preferred charging single handed and naked at those confounded and stubbornly defended fortress walls. Two months of siege and still yet nothing to show for it but cold discomfort, frostbite and steadily mounting fatalities. He had conscripted a small army of the heathen locals and had them expanding and flattening the small plateau in front of the fortress to bring his heavy siege machines into play and assemble the full force of his command. At the same time, his engineers were trying to widen and improve the treacherous path that once served inadequately as an access road.

By the time he and his field staff arrived at the safe zone, the place was already in perfect order; tents laid out in regimented lines, latrines were dug, shelters erected for the horses, and even a defensive ditch perimeter excavated. 'Busy bastards,' he muttered.

To his annoyance, he was kept waiting in the freezing air for no discernable reason that he could see, and in his own war camp at that. He fought down the urge to fidget and tried to sit his horse with an attitude of nonchalance and unconcern, but with each passing minute, he felt himself growing more and more irritable. Just when he thought that he had had enough of this nonsense and was about to turn his horse about and return to the war he had started, the door to a large, imposing, white-washed caravan opened. Immediately, two rows of immaculately attired guards snapped forward in unison forming an escort phalanx for the most beautiful woman he had ever set eyes on. His mind went completely numb, and his heart skipped a couple of beats in trepidation. For all his sins in the world, why her? The almighty was already issuing his punishment. Why couldn't he have waited until he was at least on his deathbed? He knew who this woman was and her presence could harbour nothing but an ill fortune for him. Once again, sweat broke out on his forehead and trickled icily down into his fat jowls and neck. Hastily he dismounted and clumsily went down on one knee before her and bowed his head in an effort to buy some space and time to think.

Despite the bone-chilling cold, the woman drifted towards him in a low cut, gleaming white gown, cinched at the waist with a purple band of pure silk which accentuated her already curvy and sensuous form. Over her shoulders was draped a long, purple, ermine cloak, the folds of its hood pulled down and caressing her elegant, faultless neck; her skin glowing, naturally tanned and healthy. Her face was sultry and exquisite, her lips full and gently pouting. Her eyes with a slightly amused look that seemed only for the one she was focusing on, disguising a slicing intelligence behind the teasing gaze. General Montford shivered in dread at her approach.

'It's so lovely to finally meet you in person, General. I've heard so much about you,' her soft, husky words dripping with honey.

Fighting off the feeling of a fly caught in the sticky dew of a carnivorous plant, the general answered without raising his head.

'Your Eminence. Welcome to the frontier.'

'And a fine show you are putting on for us here, General. Although I was hoping that you would have been able to host us before a roaring fire in yonder keep. Ah well, no doubt we will all soon reach our goal.'

'All will be attained, your Eminence. It is only a matter of time, good planning and patience. Had I known of your personal interest, I would have sent you first-hand reports on our progress.'

'What a kind gesture, General, but no need. As you can see I'm here now. I look forward to hearing about your wonderful adventure. Your reputation is well known in the City of God.'

'What the hell does she mean by that!' wondered the suspicious general, but he simply answered, 'As you command Eminence. Thank you,' then struggled to his feet.

She noted his physical effort with a small smile, and he knew straight away to which reputation she had referred.

'She thinks I'm a lard-ass with no backbone to speak of or any get-up and go whatsoever. Well, damn her opinion, I've hard work to do. I shan't let her politicking get in my way,' thought the Honey General, for this was what men called him behind his back, and he did not care.

'The pleasure is mine, Lord Montford. It would be an honour to have you join me after the action of the day is complete. I will have my personal guard escort you to my command tent at let's say, one hour after nightfall? Until then, General, fare you well.'

With that, she turned her shapely back and glided away.

'Bitch!' fumed the General inwardly. 'Command tent, my arse! Escort me, my arse! This is my command, and she shall not have it!'

'Did you say something, General?' enquired his scribe; a little man with a myopic look about him, but faithful. Been with him since he was a young lieutenant.

'No, my dear Turpin. I'm just contemplating how blessed and lucky I am in life.' Then his voice took on a commanding ring which immediately transformed his appearance. 'Gather up the battle fodder and assemble the stormtroopers; ladders and battering-rams to the fore. We can only work with what is already at hand. We will renew our assault by noon. Make sure the trebuchets are firing within the hour. Am I clear?'

'Clear, General,' was the unified response from his following field-staff.

Things did not go well that day. Despite the heavy, incessant bombardment and repeated forays at the battlements, nothing changed significantly, except more casualties. As evening slipped her cold, grey veil around the fortress and her besiegers, the Cardinal's immaculately attired, personal body-guard located the General fretting well within reach of the enemy's return shot. He did not seem aware of the potential danger he was in, and as he saw them coming, he eyed their drilled and perfected advance and muttered:

'Ah, here comes my summons to high court. No doubt their axes are razor sharp.'

'Her Eminence, Cardinal Sybil Wuzetian, awaits your pleasure, Lord General,' said the commander bowing low.

'Of course, dear fellow. Do you mind accompanying me first to my camp quarters? I wish to wash the dirt of a hard day's work from this corporeal body of mine.'

'As you wish, General, but please let's not tarry overlong. Her Eminence is quite anxious to hear of your exploits and would be disappointed to have only a short measure of your time.'

'Well put, commander. You are wasted in the military. Come, let's to it then.'

In spite of his promise to hurry, Lord Montford arrived late at the Cardinal's tent. She, however, greeted him with flawless courtesy and resting an elegantly manicured hand on his arm, personally guided him into her sumptuous accommodations. A mouth-watering meal was served, prepared by her private chef, washed down with a deep, rich and very costly wine. Despite his caution, the general could not help himself and surrendered quite happily to his weaknesses.

Basking with a full stomach in the warm, queenly surroundings, bolstered by the soporific effects of alcohol, the soft-natured General did not realise that his defences had been infiltrated.

'General, I must bow to your military expertise in this, but tell me. To my untutored eyes, there is nothing to stop you from bypassing this incalcitrant rock and seizing the riches of the lower kingdoms. Why tarry here when you have all this lying at your feet, ready for the taking? Yes, we can't get in, but in the same measure, they are penned in like goats. Why not seize the moment?'

The General was and is a man who enjoys sharing – be it affection, food, wine, or knowledge – this night was no exception.

'You are correct in many ways, Eminence, but this is the reality of our position. Behind us, the land is still not truly pacified. Given the right circumstances and a gifted leader yet not identified, thank god, the heretics could unite and come at us like a storm of pests. Seeing this the lower kingdoms would grab fortune and attack us; classic hammer and anvil. Even worse, what a fine opportunity for our so-called penned goats to unleash hell on our heads. We wouldn't stand a chance.'

'Oh, yes, very insightful, General,' purred the Cardinal. 'But please, if you don't mind me asking. Why didn't you secure your rear before disturbing these wasps perched on this pinnacle of frost and ice?'

The General was beginning to sober quickly, but he already knew that he had been ensnared in the spider's silken trap.

'I…ah…it was necessary,' was his only response, lame and deficient even to his inebriated ears.

Her laugh was soft and playful.

'Oh, come on, my lord. Ambition is not a sin. We all keep our lips peeled for a bite of that juicy cherry.

She puckered her red painted lips as if for a kiss. Her white teeth peeping through.

'The trick though,' she continued, 'is not to put the enterprise of our Empire in jeopardy because of it. Our business is to spread the word of the true god to every nation; our enterprise is expansion, my lord.'

'I…I don't see where this is leading…'

'Let us consider leadership then, my lord. By failing to secure the lands that so many of our brave men have died to conquer, you have betrayed their memory, my lord, and exposed the Empire to appear weak in the eyes of our enemies; you have failed to take account of the bigger picture, my lord, in your unseemly rush to enrich yourself.'

The General could not find the words to respond. He understood war, but warring with words was never his strong point. She attacked ruthlessly.

'It hurts me to tell you this, General, but you are relieved of high command. However, we hold you and your family in high esteem so will allow you to remain with us in an advisory capacity. The Empire values your experience and knowledge. For this, you will be well rewarded. Goodnight, General. We look forward to working with you in your new capacity with the dawning of the morrow. A new day for all of us, my lord. I wish you a good night.'

She settled back down on her couch and for the first time he realised, placed her cup of wine to her lips and sipped. She behaved as if he was never there. His dismissal was a thing plain to see.

In a numbed fog he wandered from the tent into the frigid night, where he was immediately surrounded by her guards and escorted back to his quarters. He had no course for appeal; no champions within the circle of nine. His fate was sealed. In such a short time nothing had changed yet everything had changed.

CHAPTER X

She felt dizzy. Her body was burning hot to the touch yet she shivered with cold. Her faithful stallion carried her onwards, but she had no idea where they were or where they were going to. All she could do was cling to the saddle and his long mane and trust to his instinct. She had hunted in vain on the first day after waking to find the promised one gone. Now she thought that it was now the fourth day, but wasn't quite sure. The sea of grass had been covered by a thick layer of dirty sand, and any tracks that might have been had long since disappeared on that night of chaos. She tried to swallow, but the effort made her gag instead. Her throat was dry, raw and painful. Her canteen hanging on a strap over her shoulder was a third full or by the way she was feeling, two-thirds empty. It was all she had, and it would have to serve both her and her mount. It was up to him to find a water source; she didn't have a clue. In the shimmering heat haze on the horizon, she thought that she could make out movement. To her delirious eyes it seemed like a small herd of horses, but then again it could also be a mind trick, a mirage. She had seen plenty of those lately. However, this time she detected tension in the muscular frame of her stallion or was that too her imagination? She flexed her shoulder in preparation to withdrawing her bow from its protective casing on her horse's shoulder, but her left arm refused to obey; it was like a dead thing. The wound in her shoulder was throbbing dully, and despite her best efforts it was putrefying; her flesh eating away, poisoning her body. She had no idea when it happened but became aware of herself lying flat on her back staring up at the cloudless, azure sky with the warm breath of her horse on her face and it's velvet muzzle nuzzling her.

'Mother goddess,' she whispered and lost consciousness.

Her eyes fluttered open to reveal the hazy outlines of five familiar faces. Was it time already, to start training sessions? She had hardly slept. 'Go away,' she muttered weakly, and felt her head lull backwards on an unresisting neck, trying to shut out the annoying persistent voices clamouring above her.

'Is she injured?'

That voice, so easily swayed by anxiety, always disturbed her balance. She frowned in irritation and tried to go back to sleep, but they kept shaking and calling. 'Useless children, naive to the real world outside.'

'Yes, and it's gone bad. Wake up, big sister. Wake up! It has to be treated.'

'We can't let her go to sleep!'

'What do you think I'm trying to do? We've got to treat it.'

'How? We haven't got any herbs left!'

'We clean it. Re-open the wound to drain it and scrape away the dead flesh.'

Then a voice, deep, filled with quiet authority cut into the useless chatter, striking them dumb, even reaching down to her and arresting her steady fall into the beckoning bosom of tranquil oblivion.

'She will be dead in an hour.'

Guilty to be caught so unawares; embarrassed to be so shocked into silence and fear, the children scrambled to compensate. Swift hands snatched at sharp weapons, and youthful limbs leapt into aggressive defence.

Urgency flooded into her dying body and dragged her clawing back to the surface.

'No, stop,' she croaked. She knew to whom that voice belonged and if the children attacked they would all be dead.

'Rest, big sister, leave this to us.'

Kirk was always overconfident.

'Fool,' she muttered weakly and fell back into the grass. Then the low, bass voice laced with accustomed and natural authority gripped them once again.

'Stay your hand, son. There is no time for your nonsense. You have two choices. Let me through so that I may cleanse her or I leave you behind to bury her.'

'Who are you, bastard, to lay down ultimatums!?'

'Kirk! Let him through!' she groaned.

She felt the children drawing back cautiously and sensed rather than saw the confident, unconcerned approach of the man she had been trying to follow.

'Stand back,' he commanded quietly. 'What I'm about to do will cause her great pain. Do not interfere.'

There was a threat somewhere in the soft, deep voice.

'Who the devil is he, Kirk?' someone whispered.

'How the hell should I know,' was the irritated and hushed reply. 'We do what big sister tells us to do. Watch the bastard!'

The children watched the vexing stranger sit next to big sister's head on crossed legs with enviable and fluid grace. He placed the long, tapered fingers of his left hand gently on the pulse of her throat and with his right gripped her arm just below her nasty looking wound.

For a time nothing happened, and they looked uncertainly at each other as the faint, rasping breathing of their sister grated into the silence. Impatience was beginning to creep into Kirk's young features when suddenly his big sister stiffened, and a gasp escaped her lips.

Her body began to tremble and the stranger, his eyes closed and face immobile, tightened his grip on her arm. The children leant forward, concern and curiosity riveting them. Partly in fascination -partly in disgust and horror- they stared as their now thrashing warrior sister's wound burst open like an overripe mango and thick, gelatinous pus flowed out in gut-churning spurts. Heat like that of an oven in a small kitchen radiated from the sweating, moaning woman and a scream of anguish tore through her dry and blistered lips. In response, the impetuous Kirk stepped forward and had to be restrained by his companions. They had all learnt from their masters the process of gifted healing but somehow had never thought it to be possible on such a scale. Eventually, the livid flesh around the injury began to return to a pinkish colour, and a clear watery liquid oozed out instead of the foul infection. Without warning the stranger stood and walked through the children who hastily parted for him.

'Wash the wound and bind it with a clean cloth. Make sure she drinks and encourage her to sleep,' was all he said as he strode away into the distance, the rolling landscape swiftly swallowing him away from their sight.

No one moved.

A soft moan brought their attention back to their big sister.

'What happened,' she whispered.

The youngest of the five, a dark-skinned, long-limbed girl with tight, curly black hair took her head tenderly in her arms and replied with an amazed tone:

'A strange man with gold in his eyes and an aura of power around him marched up to us and healed you. I never thought it possible to do what he did…never.'

'He didn't march…he just appeared out of nowhere,' said the second girl who had short cut blond hair and laughing blue eyes. She was short and compactly muscled with a balance about her that denoted incredible agility.

'He came back for me in the end. All is not lost,' then she fell into fathomless sleep.

'I was thinking,' said a serious looking, thin lad who moved in a disjointed, loose-limbed manner. 'He brought her back from the brink of death; her system brimming with poison. Our teachers have always told us that healing is one of the most exhausting of the gifts, yet, he got up from this task as fresh as a spring daisy.'

'Yes, I did notice, Jacob,' replied Kirk, for once looking a bit reflective. 'You are our healer, Reginald. What's your take on this?'

'This kind of healing is not part of my gift. Herbs and potions are my expertise,' answered a stout young man who looked more like a blacksmith than a herbalist. 'Jacob has the right of it though.'

'Will the three of you stop your idle chatter and get a camp going!' interrupted the black-haired girl. 'Elder sister needs her wound cleaned, and for that, we need hot water.'

'Sorry, Vivi. You are right. We'll get on with it,' replied Kirk.

It was apparent that the five had a shared history and were comfortable in each other's company.

With the fire started and the water boiled, the three young men sat morosely around the fire-pit sipping the last of their coffee stores from tin cups while the two young women fussed over elder sister making her as comfortable as possible. They were all hungry but had little left to eat, and none of them had the inclination or the will to hunt, although Kirk had half-heartedly set a few snares around the camp perimeters. After an hour of this, each reluctant to voice their own thoughts, they all surrendered to their blankets, all except the blond girl Stephania, who had drawn the short straw for the first watch. She didn't mind, enjoying the time for herself in solitude under a star-lit night.

The sky was beautiful. An expansive awning of cold, glittering display, but the sea of grass spreading before her was dark and indistinct, where only glimpses of waving movement could be caught from the corners of her vision, leaving a great space for her imagination to fill. She was lost in this half-in, half-out world of her own creation when something unbelievably fast, powerful and elemental bounded from the cover of grass and darkness in one huge leap and landed directly in front of her. Her breath caught in her throat, blocked by the jump of terror from her heart. She scrabbled in the dirt to scuttle backwards, but the thing snatched her from her feet as if she were just a doll and suspended her easily in mid-air. Then it brought her face in close, studying her with an unemotional, unearthly gaze as if she were an interesting insect on a rock. All she was aware of were two pools of deep blackness that drew her consciousness and will inwards, sucking in her ability to think, to act, to speak. She wanted to give warning to the others as was her duty, as was the trust they had given to her, but everything that was her was held captive to this phantom who kept her hovering between the veil of the living and the dead.

The sudden sound of unshod, horses hooves and the jingle of harnesses burst through the silence, thundering from somewhere behind her head. She could not turn. They were under attack, and because of her they would all perish; her brethren, her friends. She could hear the flurry of motion as her brothers and sisters rolled from their beddings, but somehow she knew that it was too late for all of them. The calm, unhurriedness of the night creature that held her fast was enough to confirm this.

'Put my sister down,' the simple words were uttered with a coldness that matched the sky.

The glamour that had held her will helpless suddenly lifted and she kicked with all her strength at the sorcerous thing that held her aloft by her throat and jaw. She might as well have kicked a rock. A thick, rumbling sound emanated from its chest and she realised that it was chuckling.

'Sistar? Your sistar aes a dreamar. Not make good guard.'

'I'll not repeat it. Put her down.'

'I put her down. You put down little bow. No need for death. Warnt only brodar.'

Sweat dribbled down her back despite the coolness of the night, and her arms trembled under the strain of the bow. She could not remember ever feeling so weak. It took all of her will to keep from collapsing, but she had to keep her arrow pointing at the shadowed creature's heart. They had been surprised and flanked. Her only hope of saving them was nullifying their leader yet she had this nagging feeling that he was merely toying with her and knew of her weakened condition. He was playing for time, merely to test her. Drawing on all of her remaining reserves she responded in a flat tone.

'We know nothing of this brother of yours yet what is plain is that you threaten my sister without due cause.'

'Argh,' growled the creature throwing Stephania aside with nonchalant ease. 'No threart. You know my brodar. He has cleaned your blood. You owe him life, no?'

As she paused with the shock of the sudden realisation of whom this night creature was, a wave of fear struck her, and against her will, her arrow flew from her bow. In horror she watched it flashing like silver through the dark, flying to pierce the heart of one of those she had been commanded to find. She need not have worried. Like the flow of a changing breeze, the second object of her quest slipped his chest sideways at the very last moment and her arrow missed its mark and flew harmlessly by; a double shock for she had never missed a target since a little girl in training. From her kneeling position she bowed her head into the sand and cried:

'Lord Krarl, forgive me. I did not know who you were.'

She felt somehow that she had surprised him; not an easy thing to do. In fact, everyone present was surprised in one form or another and, for a short space of time, all were frozen into silence and inactivity.

'Who are youu, garl, to name mee in surch a way?'

'The name given to me by the master who found and trained me is Ahmya Yumi, Lord Krarl.'

'The bow that brings black rain.'

She stared speechless at the still form of the man from legend. How did he know the translation? Her master had been a man from a distant land with an almost unknown and forgotten language. Quickly taking a deep breath, she plunged on.

'These five here are brothers and sisters of my monastery. We were tasked to find you and your brother.'

Lord Krarl switched from immobility to action in one fluid movement and flowed towards her. She had always been amazed by the way Brother Jacob moved, but before this man, he paled into insignificance.

'Monastery? What monastery?' his voice held a lower tone, a definite hint of danger and violence.

'In the Blue Mountains, Lord Krarl. A place created by the Founder to help those persecuted because they were born with elements of the Gift.'

'Storp Lord rubbish. My name Krarl, that's all. Who aes founder?'

'The Reverent Brother Dragonet, Lo…Krarl. Your brother referred to him as Limp-foot.'

He sensed embarrassment as she said this, but he ignored that.

'Limp-foot! Pain in the arse foot! My brodar knows no end to folly and mischief!'

He sensed again growing anger coming from the woman in front of him but also from her companions.

'Storp that!' he commanded in an off-hand manner.

'Whart were youu to do when you found us?' he enquired.

'To tell you that the time was here and now.'

Krarl broke into a snuffling, growling sound which startled everyone until they realized that he was laughing. However, this did not reassure them. In fact, they were more than a bit disconcerted.

'Are youu strong enough to ride, garl?'

'Yes, Lord Krarl.'

'Then corm with urs,' he said, gesturing to the silent and immobile horsemen watching from the embankment above them. He did not bother to make introductions nor did she bother to ask where he intended to lead them.

She staggered to her feet and immediately commenced to saddling her horse. Her brethren followed her actions without question; she was Elder Sister, and they had sworn an oath to follow her onto death.

CHAPTER XI

Morgan knew that the girl would have followed him even though she had had little evidence of his trail or where it led. She had trusted what she had thought was intuition. It was much more than that, and despite his disillusioned state of mind, he was intrigued. She had a potential that was untapped, and she had no awareness of its existence. She would have also had died if he had not turned around to go to her aid. In the older days, he would not have hesitated in taking her as his student. Something told him that she would have proved the strongest of all of them. Now he just didn't want to care. Everything he had touched was futile. His brother had been right all along. As usual, his bothersome sibling was following him, and he was surprisingly close, but he couldn't be stirred to check on him, although he had detected a difference to his purpose this time. He wanted something from Morgan, but he had no intention of giving it; whatever it was.

In the short space of time since he had cured the girl of her poisoned blood, he had destroyed two more hunter packs and scattered a small, belligerent, war-party of locals who were hell-bent on attacking anything or anyone they did not recognise. He had no intention of skulking and hiding on his passage through the countryside. If they wanted trouble, they were free to try their hand. He was more than willing to take them on. He realised that such a strategy would draw attention to him like flies to fresh cow-dung, but in a dangerous and primaeval way, he relished the prospect, aimless as it was.

After a time he began to understand that his present path would eventually take him to the foothills of the Blue Mountains; a remote setting in an even more distant memory. Did the girl's mention of this location from his past affect him psychologically on a very profound and unconscious level? Was this the place he saw as home?

Was he running back there like a beaten dog with its tail between its legs? Or did he see himself as the prodigal son returning? Not likely, since he had had nothing but the clothes on his back when he had headed out into the world at large, and he had left nothing behind that he could have called family. His twin had never seen this place and probably never knew of it, and of course, Limp-foot had already passed over the bridge of light.

He stood at the edge of a ploughed field squeezed onto the top of a little plateau of baked and shallow soil and watched a troupe of ragged peasants scampering across open ground towards the illusionary protection of a small wood. In the far distance, he could see the curling brown and dirty mushroomed cloud of smoke billowing into the air. It didn't take much to guess that these few were the lucky survivors of yet another sacked village, or maybe not so fortunate, as many perils still lay ahead for them. As this thought ran through his head, a band of Protectorate mounted soldiers burst into view and riding in a double, outer circle, cut the terrified tillers of the land off from their safety goal, herding them like wayward cattle. Mothers pulled their grubby and wailing children in tight to their stained aprons and burly, rough looking men, wearing nothing but sack cloths for tunics and nowhere left to run, faced this threat to hope with pitchforks and grim, fatalistic expressions. What kind of man would rob and harass those with nothing left but fear in their hearts? Morgan felt a wave of sorrow flood through his system. Men were the worst of all mother earth's creations, but among this garbage of mankind, he had met a few pure and sparkling gems. It was for these and for the hope in adversity and the hopelessness of the doomed innocence below that he moved. A people who looked unflinchingly into defeat and obliteration and focused on faith were worth fighting for. Morgan was born, like his brother, to deal with violent conflict. He was an adversary that these cowards had not counted on ever confronting. He was the incarnation of the bringer of death.

He charged down the steep drop as a small boy would race down the garden path of his family's cottage; without hesitation, body and mind in focused harmony. He tore down on the yelling, bullying soldiers as they raced their horses in circles around the huddled peasantry, feeding off of their terror like a leech feeds off of blood. They did not see him until he was on top of them. Moving at an unnatural and frightening velocity he crashed his shoulder into a darting horse, bowling it ruthlessly over. At the same time, he reached up and snatched its rider violently from his saddle and pounded him into the hard ground. The sound of his breaking bones was audible to all, stalling the mad dash of the soldiers, and creating a shocked silence. Morgan was not waiting. Without pausing, his attack fluid, fast and unnerving, both hands whipped forward faster than the eye could follow as he straightened, sending a knife, then an axe, tearing through the air. Such was the force of these penetrating missiles that two more soldiers were literarily hurled backwards out of their saddles as if an invisible spirit had smitten them. He came flying after his fast flung weapons like a whirling dervish, straight for the throats of the now immobile and shocked horsemen. It appeared as if they could not accept what their eyes were telling them and even glanced at each other for confirmation. Morgan ripped into them mercilessly and with a savagery that stripped them of all courage and fortitude. The survivors fled in all directions kicking with panic-driven heels into the ribs of their terrified mounts who needed no such encouragement to flee.

The clustered men and women of the soil stared at their saviour with unbelieving eyes, still unsure of what was going to happen next. A short man with thickly, muscled arms and an incongruously large, rounded stomach, uncertainly stepped forward, eyes brimming with tears of relief at his deliverance from the evil that was scourging the land of his birth and that of his father's father as long back as any could remember.

'Thank you, Lord,' he said in a broad, thick accent, stumbling over his words. 'We have long heard of your deeds and have wondered why you have not come to our aid till now.'

Morgan frowned at him.

'I am no man's lord. If I were you, I would stop wasting time and continue into yon trees. More of those bastards will return before long.'

'Yes, Lord. We will do as you say. When you do call, we will come, Lord, to defend our land and that of our fathers.'

Morgan watched them go, bowing and waving timidly as they passed him, an even deeper frown furrowing his brows.

'What utter nonsense,' he muttered. 'Who has been filling these people's heads with such a thing? If I find the devil responsible, I'll skin him alive.'

Despite his annoyance, things got progressively worse.

As he moved deeper into this part of the land which was once ruled by a drunkard, but a just and well-meaning drunkard who was loved by his subjects, people seemed to recognise him at sight and would bow to him, some even prostrating themselves in the dirt and calling out to him. He did not like it one bit and took to skulking and stealth, unnerved by the whole affair.

At that time of day when the sinking sun turned the world it shined on and fed into an after-glow of golden warmth, transforming the land, Morgan arrived at a clear, green, mountain-sourced stream. A large group of men, women and children were gathered on its banks and were so riveted by something occurring in its cold depths that they did not see or acknowledge his approach.

Curious to see, Morgan manoeuvred himself as surreptitiously as he could around the edges of the silent crowd. There standing waist high in the fast-flowing water was a tall woman with long, wild, grey-streaked hair and a face burnt brown from constant exposure to the elements. She had a man gripped by the scruff of his neck and with her bared arm, corded with hard muscle she repeatedly plunged his head under, shouting words in a high, commanding voice. To Morgan, she seemed a bit mad and uncomfortably, a bit familiar.

'Wash yourself clean. Free yourself of the filth from these parasites that are invading our kingdoms. He is coming! Be ready! He will call for you! Be ready!'

'Be ready,' repeated the crowd. 'He is coming. Be ready.'

Morgan realised that he had wandered into the lion's den. A coldness came over him, but to withdraw now would attract eyes on him.

'He will stand at the head, tearing down what the parasites have built. We must be ready to follow in his wake and crush them underfoot. Be ready, he will come! Be ready, he will call!'

'Be ready, he will come. Be ready, he will call,' the crowd chanted back.

Morgan had had enough and pulled back from the stream thinking it best to leave this place quickly. As he moved a pair of shining, demented eyes fixed on him. He saw them flare in recognition.

'He is here! He is here among us! The time has come to be ready. Are you ready!'

Morgan felt fear for the first time in his life.

The crowd looked about them in confusion. As space was cleared from around him, they all stared at him in awe. Then in one mass hysterical move, they all fell to their knees before him shouting and chanting.

'We are ready, oh One. Call us. We are ready!'

Morgan turned his back on them and walked away, back into the wilderness. There he hid his face from all men for three days and three nights, hoping that the mad, crazy world would regain its senses.

In the early morning of the fourth day, before the dimmest of grey could touch the sky, he went hunting. From the banks of the madly gushing stream, he followed the fading traces on the ground, using his inner sight more than relying on what his eyes could see. Finally, he came to a small, ramshackle dwelling, nestled at the far end of the frontier settlement and tucked up against a sandstone embankment. He swung himself smoothly and silently onto its sagging roof and slid into one of its high windows. He could hear the faint, but deep breathing of his prey and knew that it was not genuine. He had been detected despite making no sound whatsoever. This prey was well deserving of its reputation.

'You are a long way from home,' he said in a soft, conversational voice.

'Aye,' was the husky response. 'Fate has a way of guiding our steps, but the first step was not of my making.'

 Morgan could make out the outline of the figure as it lay on a small bed covered by a thin blanket. The chemical scent drifting from it had an urgency in its flavour despite its owners controlled voice, but not one of fear; it was the smell of pure elation, adoration even. Morgan felt uneasy and began to regret his action in coming here.

'How so?' he found himself asking.

'I was sent into exile,' was the quick reply, with just a touch of bitterness.

'I see. By your king or by your abbot?'

'By my abbot for failing to kill a king.'

'A risky venture with little chance of a positive outcome.'

'This was my advice to those involved, Lord Morgan. It was not heeded.'

'So your path has led you here, but what has made you pick up this staff of madness? This prophesy that you advertise is sheer folly. You are misleading these simple folk with something that cannot be.'

'Ah, but here you are, Lord Morgan. Why is that, do you think? Did you come willingly? Were you called? If so, by whom? Do you have these answers at hand, Lord Morgan?'

Morgan could feel the heat of her madness like a physical thing, radiating like smouldering coal from deep within her. When she had been under his tutorship, she had always been cold and detached. Something had twisted her; turned her insane. Was it rejection? Was he suffering from the same fate? It only took a small thing, but that small thing which the unaffected would label insignificant could be the trigger to a man's, or in this case, a woman's, outlook on the things that matter in life. She had needed something or someone that had been constant in her past to hold on to; it was now blatantly obvious that she had chosen him as her anchor.

'Elisha, hear me. You are on the road to perdition, and if you continue to steer on this course, you will drag me down with you.'

'Your spirit needs to be awakened, Lord Morgan. The people need to see your star shining in the heavens. I will be your pathfinder, Lord. I shall walk before you and prepare the flock for your coming. I will bring them; let them see you with fire and sword as you cut down these parasites that cover their lands! I will wash them clean so that they may see the truth that you signify!'

Morgan was lost for words. No amount of reasoning could cut through the fog of Elisha's insanity. Limp-foot had been bad enough with his constant lectures on destiny and responsibility, but this was something else entirely. Unless he ended her life on this cold morning she would force him down a path he had no wish to travel; his destiny she had seized in her own hands. Mother earth, he just wanted to run, but he knew that there was nowhere left to run. She had started a spark and under her charismatic proselytizing the people, with their hope shackled, would fan this spark into an uncontrollable conflagration, whether he chose to lead them or not; it would be done in his name.

With an inward sigh he gave up the attempt and with a fluid movement joined the shadows and flowed back the way he had come, his mind numb and his spirit confused. Behind him mad words of fire and brimstone screamed out into the darkness, shattering the quiet of men's slumbers.

'Together we shall burn them to ashes, Lord Morgan. We shall smite them from this land on which they do not belong. We shall chase them back behind their walls of Sodom and Gomorrah!'

'That persistent book should never have been rediscovered or at best, never been written,' thought Morgan. 'Its words are pernicious and reaches the ears of the uninformed even though its pages have long since crumbled to dust.'

CHAPTER XII

The Honey General was dog tired. Once an army followed him, now just two trailed in his wake. His loyal scribe who would follow him to the ends of the world if need be, and his adjutant, who young as he was, had a misplaced, romantic sense of honour that insisted that when something was decided, the ultimate decision must be a just one. Once he was on the cusp of building a fortune and an unbreakable reputation, now he was disenfranchised, an embarrassment to his accomplished family and potentially disowned. He was not expecting a warm and welcoming homecoming.

Resignation had become his only option. He had become invisible. His once junior officers speaking of his work and plans as if they were theirs. His decisions questioned in his presence, but no one bothering to ask him for clarification. His very chair sat upon, and his brandy sipped. He exercised the only control left to him. As was his right as a first-class officer, he tendered his resignation in the field. He had seen the calculation behind her eyes. She knew next to nothing of military affairs. Could she afford to lose him? In a way he had trapped her in her ambitions for had she refused he would have gained political leverage back home where no doubt, she had plenty of enemies. So now, here he was, on a one-way journey to obscurity. In the end, pride matters.

They had not spoken to each other for the past two hours for it was dawning on them that they were riding in very hostile country. None could bring themselves to remove their uniforms, a thing that they saw as part of them, even though their badges of rank had been ripped free. This made them very visible targets; for the enemy, from their own side, and from those who had taken advantage of the lawlessness of the land to prey on those weaker than themselves. The danger they were in weighed heavier on their minds with each step back that they took; for going home was a journey backwards for all of them.

They had kept to the forest paths as much as they could without getting entirely lost; taking clues from the movement of the sun and the north star when they could see it through the constant canopy. In this drab green and brown world, they wandered, not really over-concerned with time, although their stomachs rumbled, unused as they were with this meagre, daily fare.

'I think we have lost our way, General,' whispered his worried-looking ex-adjutant.

'If you mean that figuratively, young Jason, I would have to agree. Other than that we are generally heading in the right direction, so let's not worry overmuch.'

Surprisingly, he felt much more sure of himself than he had for a very long time, despite his unenviable predicament.

They all smiled wryly at his answer, gaining reassurance from it.

However, as a demonstration of how ill-prepared they were to deal with the environment they were in, they all grabbed hastily at their saddles as a plump, teenage girl burst out of the underbrush, running full tilt, eyes wide in alarm, along the fern covered, narrow track they were following. Behind her was a tall, green-clad, solidly built man, with long, brown, lank hair. He was concentrating on something behind him and did not see them, but in a quick motion, he sent an arrow from his drawn, long-bow, flying backwards with a thrum of a bow-string. The girl, however, drew to a skidding halt at the sight of them and the man crashed into her back sending them both tumbling into the thicket of bushes. In a flash he was on his feet with a wicked, long knife, bared steel gleaming dully in his hand and a snarl on his face.

'Hold sir!' shouted the general in a commanding voice. 'We are not your enemy!'

'Well, you had better run then, for those bastards behind me are certainly mine!' was the fast rejoinder.

On impulse, the general shouted once again.

'Get up behind us then, man. We can move faster a horse-back!'

Neither the girl nor the man hesitated. With a bound they sprang onto the hind-quarters of the general's and adjutant's horses, which were turned on a coin and sent galloping back the way they had come with their double loads; the scribe following close behind.

'Left, turn left here!' the forester, for that was certainly what he was by his garb, shouted into the general's ear.

Without question, he followed the instructions although his eyes were telling him that he was about to smash headlong into a foliage covered, rock-face. Instead, his racing horse plunged through a narrow crack and thundered along a dark, twisting tunnel.

After a short time, the man yelled tightly once again.

'Here, here, turn left again, off the track! Stop, stop!'

The general pulled sharply back on his reins bringing his horse to a skidding halt. Immediately, the forester leapt nimbly to the ground, grabbed the horses halter and pulled it deeper into the shadows, covering his hand over its muzzle and whispering to it. It was obvious he knew how to handle horses. The adjutant and the scribe quickly dismounted and followed suit.

In the time it took them to take two breaths, the thundering and crashing sound of horses galloping full out in a dangerous fashion tore by their hiding place. As soon as they went by the forester snatched up his bow and raced off, fitting an arrow to string as he did so. The girl followed and so the three men, after a quick glance at each other, did the same, pulling their mounts behind them. As they turned the next corner in the tunnel, the mad din of torrential water and the terrified whinnying of crazed horses surrounded them, echoing off of the damp rocks and penetrating their ears, deafening them. They knew immediately what it was; an underground river. The shadow of the forester could be seen clearly outlined, sending arrow after arrow into the backs of men clinging to rearing and bucking horses. Even then the chaos of struggling, frightened, and panicked animals were causing others, fighting desperately to get back from the brink of the raging torrent, to slip and plunge over the steep edge into the maelstrom of water below, where they were dragged away and under as if by a mighty hand.

'Goddess!' whispered the adjutant. His heresy went unnoticed.

The forester suddenly threw himself to one side as wide-eyed, riderless horses came tearing back along the trail, seeking to escape certain death by the only route that they knew of. The three shocked men hastily pulled their now restless mounts tight against the wall of the tunnel to let them pass and held fast onto them so they did not follow their herding instinct.

As the forester sauntered back to them, the general looked at him in approval.

'That was quick thinking, sir, and a merciless trap you led them into.'

The forester nodded and said.

'I'm not sure why you're wearing the colours of these unwanted invaders to our lands, but I thank you for your aid. Without it both me and my daughter would have perished for sure.'

'It's the least we could have done under the circumstances. As far as your question is concerned, well, that's a long tale, but suffice it to say we no longer serve who we once did.'

'Deserters, eh? I tend not to keep company with disloyal men.'

'No, we are not deserters.'

The forester waited as if to hear more, but seeing nothing else was forthcoming, said.

'You can come with us a while as a payment for your help. I would guess that you fellows are lost. The Green Mistress does not like strangers under her branches, and she is angry. There has been an infestation of unsavoury folk of late, and I wouldn't like it if she included you in her revenge for their sacrilegious acts.'

Once again the three military companions glanced at each other but didn't comment. They hurriedly followed after the already departing forester and his silent daughter.

After about an hour's trekking through a green scenery which appeared to be all the same at every turn, the three realised that if they thought that they might have been lost before they now did not stand a chance in hell of getting out of this forest. They were completely at the mercy of their host, whatever his intentions might be. Eventually, they came upon a large log cabin tucked into the landscape up tight against a rock-face and didn't even see it until they were almost on top of it.

'This is our home,' said the forester, his first words since leaving the deadly tunnel. 'I'll see to your horses. Jenny will pour you a cup of coffee.'

They were not sure if they had just been taken prisoner or offered a safe haven. Neither Jenny nor her father seemed to notice their hesitation and headed off in their separate directions. The general gave his two companions a slight nod, and they followed the girl into the cabin. Inside the floor was on a raised platform and they noticed cunningly carved arrow slits at various points around the open and roomy interior. A ladder led to an upper floor and cured hides separated parts of the very, sturdy building. It was like a mini fortress.

The girl made her way to an iron, coal-stove and busily began to get it stoked up. Feeling a bit out-of-place, the companions sat at a roughly built table in front of a large, stone-built chimney-place and waited.

'Is your father the only family you have?' asked the general in a kindly tone.

The girl nodded but did not speak. The heavy, cabin door was suddenly pushed open, and the forester lightly ascended the two stairs to the raised flooring.

'Don't mind Jenny. She was born without a voice, but she can speak aplenty. Hope you're hungry,' the man continued, slicing off pieces from a slab of cured pork hanging from the ceiling and throwing them into a pan.

The father and daughter were a practised team, preparing different elements of a meal in fascinating harmony. The smell wafting from the stove made their guests mouths water with anticipation.

When the food was finally served up, they all attacked it with the gusto of the famished, not wasting any time on polite conversation. At the end, the forester leaned back in his chair and lit a pipe, the smell of his fragrant tobacco driving back the lingering, but now stale odour, of their finished meal.

'Now's a good time to hear the rest of your tale,' he said evenly looking at them through narrowed and sleepy eyes.

The general was not fooled. This man was alert and deadly.

'My name is Clarence Montford, once a General of The Protectorate Empire, still a Lord, I think, of that self-same Empire.'

The forester's expression did not change, but his daughter stiffened, and her glance flitted to a cleaver hanging on the wall.

'I not long ago offered my resignation to my position and fortune due to irreconcilable differences with my superior and the untenable position she placed me under. This white-haired gentleman is my scribe, Turpin Greyhound, who has been in my service for as long as I can remember. That young fellow with the purest heart that you can ever find, once served as my adjutant. His name is Jason Rhineheart.'

'That's an interesting tale, General. Many of my countrymen would love the opportunity to see your head on a pike.'

'If they are patient they may well see my own people do that for them.'

The forester studied him closely through the drifting smoke of his pipe.

'I like you, General,' he said quietly.

'Thank you, sir. At the moment that means a world to me. The three of us are at this instance in time, friendless. May we know your name in turn?'

'Of course. Please excuse my rudeness. I am known as Trevor Long-Ranger. My birth name I no longer use. You already know my daughter's name.'

'Well met, Trevor Long-Ranger. May I ask what you have decided to do with us?'

'Good question, General. I suspect that you know my initial intention was to kill you, despite your kindness, as I do with all invaders. It is my duty to kill them on sight, you see.'

'But?'

'But now I've decided not to. The information you have in your head is far too precious for you to lose it.'

'Ah, yes. I see your point. So are we your prisoners?'

'No, not at all. You may leave at any time you wish. However, I cannot vouch for the Green Mistress. She guards her paths jealously.'

'Ah,' responded the general. 'We are at your disposal then.'

After a short pause, he continued.

'Your words seem to hint that you do not stand alone in your fight, Trevor Long-Ranger.'

'Is that a question, General? Well, the answer to that is no. We foresters are not as many as we once were, but our sworn duty is to defend and protect the Green Mistress.'

'Is the Green Mistress the goddess of this land?' asked the General in a respectful tone.

'The Green Kingdoms are a union of many lands with the forests running thickly through all of them, binding them. But men forget when peace gives them time to pursue their own self-interests. They forgot their pledges and abused the benevolence of our beloved Mistress, cutting her many fingers down one by one. Their own greed left them exposed as they forgot the lessons that were taught to them; lessons learned the hard way. Our first forester, the Green Warden, knew that your Empire would come eventually. He taught us to work in harmony with the Mistress as we would need her when your armies descended upon us. The peoples of the great grasslands behind us, lost in their wanderings, would depend on us to shelter them, but we forgot.'

'It is natural for men to turn to farming when a population increases. It's the only way, sad for these beautiful forests as that may be,' replied the General in a sympathetic tone.

The forester did not respond and remained silent. The General cleared his throat and tried again.

'Is this Warden part of your old legends? He sounds a wise and informed man.'

'Yes and no, General. As you well know, the history of your voracious Empire is not so long in the measure of time, and he knew of your intentions. But yes, not only did he have foresight he had prodigious skills. He set up the first foresters and trained them rigorously. With us as his spearhead, he forced reason into the hearts of men and stopped the kingdoms from carrying on with their eternal bickering and warmongering. Peace brought prosperity and prosperity gave birth to forgetfulness.'

'So you keep reminding us, Ranger,' said the General with amusement in his voice. 'So, what happened to this legendary Warden of yours?'

'My great-grandfather used to tell my father that his father as a boy once saw a man at the head of an immense shield wall. Giant rangers stood guard at each side of him, and although he was a head and a half shorter than them, he seemed to tower over them, and when he went into battle, fully armoured men fled before him. He was called Morgan Green Ranger, Warden of the Mistress.'

'Morgan?' muttered the scribe Turpin. 'I've heard that name before.'

'Aye, wild rumour claims he is back among us; born again, re-incarnated, call it what you will. They say he is here to lead us against the parasites.'

'Parasites? Charming,' grumbled the General.

'Aye. We had best turn in. Tomorrow will be a long day. I can feel it in my bones.'

The forester's words turned out to be prophetic.

As first light filtered mistily through the cracks in the thick, log timbers of the cabin, teasing the General and his companions dreamily out of their deep slumber, the door crashed open and the forester barged in throwing his weight back against the heavy timbers and dropping an iron bar into thick brackets, barring it tight shut.

'Up, up!' he whispered harshly and fiercely through bared teeth. 'I've underestimated the bastards! They're on us!'

His daughter was the first to move; grabbing a bow and darting up the ladder to the upper level.

'Can you shoot the bow?' enquired their host with urgency in his voice. They all nodded assent.

'Then arm yourself and may the goddess have mercy on our souls. You,' he said to the young adjutant, Jason. 'Climb up with her.'

Grabbing a long-bow in turn, the young man leapt to obey. The General and his scribe quickly followed suit, each snatching up a bow.

A sharp, piercing yelp followed closely by an agonising scream, cut through the morning air.

'Bastards have found my traps,' muttered the ranger with a touch of satisfaction in his voice. 'Brought themselves some hounds by the sound of it.'

The twang of a bowstring then another scream from somewhere outside brought a wry smile to the forester's thin lips.

'Good on you, Jenny. Stick the bastards!'

The two military men settled at separate arrow-slits and peered out into the surrounding greenery, watching for any movement or out of place shadow. Despite the obvious fact that they seemed trapped, Trevor Long-Ranger seemed to be enjoying himself.

A darting shadow flitted briefly across an open space, but before either the General or the old scribe could react an arrow sprouted into it and a figure clad in mottled, brown clothing and leathers sprawled full length without a sound.

'Got you,' muttered the forester.

The man was indeed a master bow-man and his daughter it seemed, was also very well accomplished. They had killed two men before the others could even get a look at them.

However, before either of the defenders could send another arrow out, a barrage of missiles thudded into the timbers, all clustered around the arrow-slits, a few even whizzed through causing everyone to pull their heads back to safety in just the nick of time. The General put his hand to his cheek and felt the wet trickle of blood on his face.

He had been just a tad too slow.

'Watch yourselves now,' shouted the forester so that everyone in the cabin could hear him clearly. 'Some of these bastards know how to shoot.'

'What are their numbers?' asked the General.

'Too much for us to keep at bay for long, General, but what concerns me most is that these bastards are trained in wood-craft. Some may even be foresters.'

'Your own people?!' exclaimed Turpin the scribe.

'The promise of coins can seduce even the best of us, Scribe friend,' replied the forester in a low and bitter voice.

'Aye,' joined in the General. 'There's an old saying, "all that glitters is not gold."'

 Bluish, white wisps of smoke were soon seen drifting in tendrils from within the bushes.

'Ah, bugger!' said Long-Ranger. 'Was wondering how long it would take them to do that.'

'Do what?' asked the scribe.

'The enemy intends to smoke us out, sir,' came a warning shout from the adjutant above.

'Don't let the bastards get on the roof, whatever you do!' shouted back the forester.

Fire arrows were now being steadily shot into the timbers, and smoke began to infiltrate the cabin.

'By the smell, I'll say that they're using a mixture of pig fat and resin,' observed the General.

'Yeah, nice to know,' dryly commented the forester who was sending carefully aimed arrows through his hole. Whether or not he was finding his targets, no one knew for sure, but he seemed pleased with his efforts. Up high, on the upper platform, the occasional twang of an arrow string could be heard. Both the General and the scribe had yet to release a single arrow between them.

'Conserving your ammunition, eh, General? That's good to see, but here they come! Give them all you've got!'

The bushes seemed to burst outwards, and a dark mass of men came pounding across the open, killing ground, shields held affront.

'Aim for their legs,' commanded General Montford, pulling his staff back for the first time and letting loose.

His suggested strategy was successful for as arrows flew at the rapidly advancing shield-wall, many of its shield bearers fell screaming, clutching their pierced legs. As their brethren dropped their shields lower to compensate, the defenders switched their aim, catching a few in their necks and eyes. The noise of the wounded was unbearable, but also satisfying. Still, their numbers were too much for the five archers to deal with, especially with their vision limited by the narrow slots they were shooting through and hampered by the wafting smoke. This last got much worse as the yelling assailants flung their hoarded clay pots of resin and pigs fat at the wooden walls. The greedy flames from the burning arrows latched onto this new source of fuel and began to burn voraciously, sending roiling smoke in and around the building. The defenders all began to cough, and their eyes began to sting and water. The cabin shivered as full grown men began to clamber onto the roof. To the three military companions, it appeared as if all would soon be lost. However, the canny forester had other things on his mind.

'Down, get down! It's time to go!'

'I'm all for that, Long-Ranger, but go where?' asked the General through a hoarse and rasping throat.

The fellow did not answer but dashed at the fire-place just as a burning thicket of half-dried bushes mixed with fat came crashing down the chimney, filling the room with dark, evil-smelling smoke. At the same time, something heavy thundered against the front door rocking the abused cabin and making everybody except the forester, glance nervously back at it.

Without hesitation, he grabbed a spear from its bracket on the wall and began to pull out the fiercely burning nest of smoking nastiness onto the hard, cabin floor. The General stared at him as if he were mad. 'Was he trying to hurry them to a flaming end?'

The forester, however, seemed to know what he was about for he reached into the almost invisible, smoke-filled fire-place and began to tug firmly on an iron ring affixed to its stone-clad, back wall. With a grating sound, the wall came inwards revealing a hidden tunnel.

'Amazing!' muttered the General. 'Thank god for fore-planning and bolt holes.'

'Get in, get in!' hurried the forester, pulling and pushing his daughter first into the dark space. Then not waiting on ceremony or guests rights he ducked in after her. The ageing scribe followed by the rotund General went next. By now the floor of the cabin had caught alight, and dancing flames were creeping away in every direction. As the adjutant was about to bring up the rear, the front door gave way to the battering that was being brought against it and crashed inward with a cacophony of sound. Two terrible things then happened at the same time. An experienced besieger immediately send an arrow flying into the space before the door could hit the floor, catching the retreating adjutant square in the back, but also as fresh air reached the burning room the flames burst upwards into a destructive, explosive conflagration driving the attackers back and throwing the wounded adjutant into the arms of his General. Staggering under the weight the shocked man pulled his loyal subordinate into the tunnel and laying him on the dirt floor struggled to close the door to their escape before the heat melted the flesh from their bones. By now the forester had returned and was helping the scribe to drag the severely injured adjutant down the tunnel. Bent low and breathing heavily, the General followed as best he could, fighting back the urge to vomit his guts up. Ten minutes later they emerged on the other side of a cliff face, wheezing and blinking.

The General fixed the forester with a steady stare and said in a low, authoritative voice:

'There is more to you than just a simple forester, sir. I have just witnessed two over-kills in a short space of time. Someone wants you badly. Bad enough to send a top-notch team of highly capable hunters after you. And this tunnel! It would have taken a team to dig their way through this rock. All for a lone forester? I think not.'

The forester's face took on a blank, implacable look. The expression of a man on the cusp of killing, but a groan broke through the tension. Immediately, the girl Jenny ran to the adjutant's side. Blood was dribbling down from the corners of his mouth, and his eyes were beginning to take on a glassy look.

The General took his young, smooth hand into his pudgy ones and spoke gently into his ear.

'I'm here with you, son, me and old Turpin. I'm proud of you, boy. You are the son I have never had. We're proud of you. We will always walk by your side. Wait for us on the silver bridge, Jason. We won't be long.'

His tears dripped on the young man's face which seemed to bring him back from the start of his final journey. For a moment his eyes cleared and he smiled at the General, then he drifted peacefully through the veil.

No one moved or made a sound for many moments. Then the forester cleared his throat and said quietly.

'We have to go.'

The General nodded and folded the arms of his beloved companion over his chest and closed his sightless eyes. The girl and the scribe helped him to his feet, and they set out after the already departing forester.

After a long while the General said:

'Turpin, my old friend, life is a tenuous and precious thing.'

'Yes, General.'

'We cling to it desperately yet we never really give it meaning.'

'Yes, General.'

'That dear boy has taught me the greatest of lessons.'

'Yes, General.

'Turpin, in the time we have left for us we must find a meaning for our lives.'

'Yes, General.'

CHAPTER XIII

Her strength had almost returned to its normal level. They seemed to be moving in a great half-circle, turning back gradually on themselves. Their pace was steady and continuous, but not particularly fast or hard pressed. At camp every night and first thing every morning, she was given a brew of herbs and roots by Lord Krarl. He had not revealed from which plants they belonged, and the only one she could detect by taste was dandelion. Not even Reginald could tell her more. However, whatever the content, she was grateful, for her body felt cleansed and energetic, her mind clear and sharp. The two groups did not mix readily, and they watched one another cautiously. She felt disdain mostly from the two hard-looking, burly men. They were built to confront violence and did not seem to understand anything else. The slender one with the scar on his face regarded them with amusement, but even he had a deadliness about him. The worst, however, was the tall, muscular woman. Her face never revealed any emotion, but there seemed to be some undefined link between her and Lord Krarl. She felt disapproval from her whenever he brought her brewed tea; or was it something else? As for Lord Krarl he was oblivious to it all and did not seem to care one bit what anyone thought.

The grasslands were now giving way to a more diverse and mixed topography as the land climbed upwards. After two days of this, they came across what could only be called a frontier town that had never really lived up to promised riches. So far they had not been challenged, but she believed that this was due to Lord Krarl's intricate and well-chosen route. He seemed to be able to detect hostile intent and avoid it. For this too, she was grateful as she had had a bellyful of armed squabbling. The personalities of the Chosen Brothers were not what she had expected. Krarl seemed more like Morgan, and Morgan more like Krarl. They were undoubtedly an intriguing puzzle. At times she had caught Lord Krarl observing her in an absent, but introspective manner. He seemed interested in something about her, but what that could be, she had no idea. It certainly wasn't the usual interest a male would have for a female; it was something else. Right now he was gazing at the deserted looking town, his head cocked to one side. For a fleeting moment she felt something tugging at her consciousness and feeling a bit dizzy and disorientated, she quickly blocked out the sensation. Lord Krarl immediately turned and looked at her quizzically.

'Sharleen, yuuu take gurl and go into marn's lital nest,' he said indicating her. 'Look around. No cause trouble. Corm back.'

The tall, muscular woman walked directly to her horse and mounted smoothly without even a glance at her and clicked the stocky, little animal into motion.

Ahmya sprang forward in a short sprint and leapt onto her stallion's back without touching the stirrups. Before her weight could settle lightly into the saddle, it was already cantering off, taking the lead as they followed their instructions. Sharleen took no notice whatsoever, of this manoeuvre. She could hear Lord Krarl's deep chuckle reverberating behind them and felt a touch of embarrassment at her impulsive antics to demonstrate dominance.

Eventually, they rode in silence, their horses plodding along side by side, her large stallion towering over Sharleen's rugged pony who seemed to be taking every opportunity to torment her mount, nipping at it on every occasion that it drifted into reach. Sharleen ignored it all, her face deadpan and emotionless. Ahmya struggled to suppress her annoyance with the intimidating looking woman. She had always been looked up to and noticed for her abilities and competence, her attractiveness even, but never before had she felt in the company of others that she did not even exist, and with a fellow warrior woman at that. 'Respect is a thing that must be earned,' her teacher had always warned her. Now she truly understood what he had meant. It would take a lot for this hard woman to notice her. Not that she cared about that, anyway.

With nodding heads and the occasional nicker, their mounts ambled along the dusty main street, the thud of their hooves echoing dully between the silent, empty, almost ghostly buildings. A lone figure sat on the stairs of what was once a hardware store, now forlorn and abandoned, under its faded sign, swinging and squeaking in the dry wind. The two warriors nudged their indifferent horses towards it.

'Whatever you seek, you will not find it here,' came the hoarse voice of the figure, wrapped head to thigh in a brightly coloured, dirty blanket.

'I don't remember asking your opinion on anything, sister,' replied Sharleen rudely, although as always, her tone was void of any inflexion. 'But since you're volunteering information, where is everyone?'

'You are no sister of mine!' was the sharp reply. 'But since you asked nicely, the good citizens of this town have gone in search of their salvation.'

'Salvation? I'm not sure I understand you.'

'That is because you are still among the unwashed. Follow me to the river and I shall wash the mud from your eyes so that you may clearly see.'

'Thanks for the offer, but no thanks,' replied Sharleen, as if she were engaged in a normal conversation.

'Those who refuse to join The One will perish under his sword!'

'What did you say!?' interrupted a startled Ahmya, lancing her stallion a few dancing steps towards the seated, mad sounding woman. Her horse snorted through flared nostrils and tossed its head in aggression.

The woman on the stairs did not move. Instead, a deathly stillness seemed to settle over her.

'Back away slowly, child,' warned Sharleen in a low, even voice.

'I asked her a question,' persisted Ahmya, dismounting with fluid grace and stalking towards the still seated, blanket-wrapped woman.

The blanket exploded outwards in a burst of sudden, violent motion and the seated figure flew at the girl in a blink of an eye, a short, wicked, slashing sword appearing in her hands as if from nowhere. With incredible reflexes Ahmya drew her sheathed sword and parried the slicing attack with a matched speed and ferocity, slipping her body sideways to get behind the swift forward momentum of her attacker. However, once again she was surprised and almost overwhelmed by the sheer speed and balance of her opponent. Long black, wild hair blowing in the wind, the lithe woman spun, slashing a backhand stroke low, which was barely deflected, then spinning, brought around a vicious and powerful downward swing, which clanged shockingly on Ahmya's blocking sword, numbing her arm and sending her staggering backwards.

'Hold!' came a hard, commanding voice.

Sharleen had already dismounted and was slowly striding forward, her long sword held loosely in her hand and her eyes taking on the look of flint; unflinching, penetrating.

'You have potential, child, but this she-devil is mine. Leave her to me.'

From the short interaction, Ahmya knew that she was out-matched and out-classed. She backed away, leaving the space free for her tall, imposing companion. She sensed the battle-void descending around the two warriors as they prepared to face each other and felt awed in their presence.

The she-devil as Sharleen had named the odd, deadly woman, made the first move if move it could be called. From absolute stillness she launched into a blistering attack, her sword flying through the air with terrifying velocity and strength, each stroke a killing blow, no half measures, no feints. Sharleen her face calm, almost placid, seemed to move slowly in comparison, but that was just an illusion of styles. Each potentially crippling attack unleashed by the darting she-devil was deflected and parried with what appeared to be consummate ease, but that too was an illusion. After what was only a few moments sweat popped out on the big woman's brow and her opponent's breath was whistling through her nose and mouth. Ahmya had never seen such a display, not even from her masters. It did not take her long to realise that the two warriors were evenly matched and the killing strike would come from the one who made the first mistake. Disengaging from each other in a metallic unsnarling of heated swords, the two circled each other warily; grudging respect for each other evident in the cautious, loose-jointed way they moved. As Ahmya's eye involuntarily twitched from the tension, Sharleen stopped dead her prowling circle and lanced straight at her opponent with a speed that nearly seemed to match that of the Lord Morgan in his attack on the bastards on the plains. As was her signature, the she-devil did not bother with defence but sent her sword stabbing forwards with a sheer, reckless velocity intended to simply beat that of her opponent to the killing blow. Ahmya felt a sinking feeling of horror burgeon in the pit of her stomach. She saw everything in slow motion, and her gift blossomed, clearly pinpointing the mortal zones where unerringly guided weapons would rip both flesh and life away simultaneously; the outcome was inevitable mutual death.

A strong gust of wind whipped dust and grit into her eyes as something moving at an incomprehensible speed flew by, tearing itself between the two combatants and flinging them apart as if they were straw dolls. Then as the confusing commotion settled, they all looked uncomprehendingly at Lord Krarl, standing there as motionless as a dead man's shadow, holding in each of his hands a sword stripped from those of the two warriors who should now have been on their way across the veil.

'Good fight,' he said simply.

Blinking as if to clear fog from her mind, the she-devil crawled to her feet, her eyes fixed on Krarl as if she were looking at the creator himself.
'Who are you!?'

Ahmya snapped forward and bowed.

'You are looking at the Lord Krarl, twin brother to the Lord Morgan. Together their destiny is to become the One and reshape our world.'

Krarl snapped his jaws together in annoyance and growled low as Sharleen, making the situation even worse, climbed to her feet and face expressionless, bowed to Krarl as well.

The she-devil stared at each of them in turn, utterly non-pulsed as the truth she once held to be dear and irrefutable turned upside down.

'Foolish weemen,' muttered Krarl. 'Storp with this nonsense. Corm, time to find brodar.'

They all turned and followed him as he walked out of the ghost town.

CHAPTER XIV

He felt hunted and trapped. Foes that he could fight and evade were the challenges he was well prepared for, but this! This was beyond his capabilities. Strangers prostrating themselves before him and demanding that he deliver them from vile invaders; to carry them to salvation. What nonsense! Elisha should be better than that, but sadly her mind had been damaged by those she had trusted. It was far better for them to look to themselves. He had done this people champion thing before. He would not take back up that onerous burden again; a heavy stick to beat himself with. He needed a place where he could find solitude to once again master his emotions and control his gift which was threatening to erupt and overflow his once iron imposed, mental containment. Travelling still on memory's road, he entered the Great Forest in search of refuge; a refuge from the world of men and their delusional pestering. Even under the shaded, enveloping embrace of the Green Mistress, he could not access the void; that meditative state of complete emptiness. The spaces in his mind kept filling with the noise of past failures; failures attained in the service of the Mistress herself. Was she still displeased with him for abandoning her?

Nevertheless, despite his gloomy forebodings and the haunting by his past, Morgan spent a healing week without the interference from all things to do with man, communing with the Green Mistress. Her huge lungs breathed refreshing air through his mind and spirit, rejuvenating him and centering the increasingly unruly energy within him. Her capacity for forgiveness was huge and reassuring. He was floating deep within this timeless, vast world of the living trees -both anchored securely in their deep roots and at the same moment, light and carefree as their myriad leaves, rustling gently in the breeze- when he sensed them coming, like a banging on the front door in the middle of a peaceful night.

Morgan came back to himself wearing a deep frown of annoyance and pushed back down the surge of anger in his chest. Then reopening his centre, he allowed that heated ball of negative emotion to sink into his stomach and moving his diaphragm, strong and deep with slow breaths, purged it from his body. Then and only then did he open his eyes and rise to his feet, like smoke uncurling into the air. He drifted through the foliage without sound, without disturbing a fallen leaf, seeking that which should not be.

Ten men in drab greens and browns moved stealthily over the forest floor. Their sure-footed footsteps instinctively avoiding the half rotted, fallen branches hidden under the thick growth of ferns and bracken. In their midst were two men, who by comparison stumbled and staggered along with great awkwardness. To make it worse their hands were fastened behind their hunched over backs by bonds of corded rope. No one paused to help them when they encountered difficulty except for a young girl who by her sole efforts kept them going. The two captives' faces were grey with pain and exhaustion, but their eyes were filled with a determination that revealed their true characters; men who did not give in despite the adversity presented to them. The men herding them along did not spare them a glance, their eyes focused ahead were cold and pitiless, especially that of the leader, whose gaze shone with the light of a man called to something higher than that of human kindness. He held up a closed fist, and they all froze, the prisoners pushed roughly down into the damp undergrowth. After a moment of listening carefully to his surroundings, the leader, a tall man with lank, brown hair said:

'Here is a good a place as any. Hank, Clinton, take watch. Bring the stubborn bastards to me.'

The man, hard as he was, avoided looking at the young girl as he said this. Judgement day would be a damning one for him when it came, and he saw that day heralded in her eyes.

'Now, I'm going to ask you for the last time, General. How can I get to this Cardinal of yours?'

'Forester Long-Ranger, I can't tell you what I do not know. I have already freely given you all that I can,' replied the General, his voice sounding tired beyond belief.

'I would love to believe you, General, but you must understand, I cannot take that altruistic liberty. I'll have to see this through to the end, you understand.'

The General, no longer recognisable as the plump, Honey General, his body now haggard and thin, closed his eyes wearily and did not bother to respond.

'Bring him,' commanded the forester in an implacable voice.

Immediately, the girl, her eyes flat with hatred stepped in front of the helpless general to offer shelter against the misguided will of her father.

'Hold her, and bring me the scribe.'

The General's eyes flew open, and he made to surge to his feet, but a solid blow drove him back down. Rough hands grabbed the old scribe Turpin, who seemed to be clinging onto the vestiges of his life with the last of his strength, and dragged him uncaringly to the feet of the forester.

'You are a brave and determined man, General. As I said, I like you, but you have a weakness. You care for others. Will you stay silent and watch your friend here be separated from his old, wrinkled hide slice by slice? My bet is no. But let's see, shall we?'

So saying he slowly unsheathed his razor-sharp knife and said:

'Hold the old bastard down, I don't want him to get himself stabbed until I'm good and ready.'

As he bent over to start his wicked work, a deep, unemotional voice cut into the glade, freezing everyone in place.

'Torture is not permitted under the green shade. The Mistress will not allow it.'

No one had heard him come; no one knew how he had bypassed the sentinels. Not a whisper had betrayed his entrance.

They all stared in shocked silence, mouth agape, at the shrouded figure, so still that he was barely discernable, even though he was standing in plain view; the very shadows seemed to be bending around his form.

The Forester was the first to recover.

'Who are you, bastard, to speak in the Green Mistress's name!'

Behind him, the whisper of hard iron being drawn from oiled sheaths echoed as one.

The untroubled voice of the stranger spoke again making them all pause in their intent.

'You will all die if you move against me.'

The gathered foresters glanced around them nervously. Did this mysterious man bring more of his ilk with him? Were barbed arrow-heads this minute being aimed at their hearts from the shelter of the trees? They all were the best of the best in bush-craft yet this ominous stranger had appeared in their midst without a shred of warning. If he had done this maybe others yet unseen had also done so.

'You are a bold, bastard, I grant you that, but we will kill you in this glade nevertheless,' threatened Trevor Long-Ranger.

The man, if a man he was, did not bother to answer, but to the disconcerted watching foresters, his eyes appeared to take on a strange golden glow.

'Who the fuck are you anyway, bastard. I would love to have your name before we nail you to a bloody tree as sacrifice to the Mistress,' continued the forester in a rough, uncouth manner.

'My name is Morgan Ap Heston, known to your people in days of old as Morgan Green Ranger, First Warden of the Green Mistress, and your sentence is to be cast out of her embrace as a blasphemer.'

'Wha…what! Are you a bloody madman!' blurted out the forester, his scornful laughter rebounding through the watching trees.

Looking back on that fateful day, no one could recollect seeing the sinister figure move, but suddenly he was in front of the forester and had him dangling by his throat, his legs kicking uselessly in the air and his knife hanging forgotten in his hand for fear of having his neck crushed.

'From this day on, by decree of the Green Mistress, if you are caught within her domain, you will be killed on sight. Foresters, inheritors of the Green Rangers, heed these words and obey them on the oath you have sworn on the Union Stone,' came the dread words of the inhuman stranger, sealing the fate of the forester whose zeal to protect his land had over-shadowed his humanity and good judgement.

The foresters present were all stone sworn, a secret known only to the initiate. They knew an authentic voice when they heard it, and they all bowed their heads solemnly in confirmation. Trevor Long-Ranger realised that his end had come and much sooner than expected. He glanced at his daughter only to be met by hard, unforgiving eyes. He went slack in the iron grip of his fate, resistance fleeing his body as acceptance flooded into him.

Morgan put the outcast back down on his feet and simply said:

'Go.'

His shame was heavy and palpable as he hurriedly slinked off between the disapproving trees, his once companions gazing after his retreating back with uncertain and uneasy eyes.

Morgan addressed them.

'The Green Mistress demands that you remember your oath. If you cannot follow her path, then go now and follow in the footsteps of your fallen comrade. Choose and choose now.'

None of their company moved.

Morgan studied their faces for a slow count of three, then with a nod, strode over to the two exhausted, ex-Protectorate, military servants, now lying prone and weak on the damp carpet of ferns. Crouching down into a squat he looked searchingly into their eyes. He saw both pain and firmness of spirit in their returned gaze.

'I am truly sorry for the mistreatment you have suffered under the Green Shade. The Green Mistress offers you welcome and safe passage to wherever you wish to go within her domain.'

Both men nodded slightly, and the General tried to respond but discovered that he had not the strength to even talk.

Morgan reached out and rested a gentle hand on their heads. They eyes widened in alarm as they felt the cooling trickle of healing energy revitalising their depleted and abused systems. They stared at him with amazed eyes until dreamless sleep took them away to recover.

'Lord Morgan of the Green forest, what is it that you wish us to do?'

Morgan could feel the foresters all gathered reverently behind him. He could not help but betray his annoyance in the tone of his reply.

'I wish nothing of you. You are free men to act in good faith and in accordance with your given oath.'

'We know this, Lord, but now that you have returned we ask that you take up the wand and lead us as in days of old.'

'If you remember your history well, in days of old your forefathers abandoned me in the name of their ambition. Why should I be foolish enough to reenact such a tragic play?'

Morgan read a lot in the uncomfortable silence at his back. He had still not stood or turned to face them.

'We understand, Lord, but we cannot be judged or held responsible for our father's actions. We are unequipped to carry this fight due to the misguided actions of those who went before us. Our inheritance is incomplete. Our forests are under a dire threat. If we fall, nothing of the old bonds will be left to protect the Green Mistress. We need the man who forged these bonds to show us the way forward.'

'You are quite a speaker; a born politician. I have grown to become wary of men who are polished in politics; they tend to blur the lines of truth.'

'Lord Morgan, I…'

'Enough,' said Morgan curtly, rising to his feet in one smooth, sinuous movement. 'You've made your point; don't overdo it. Are you now the leader of these men?'

'No one has been elected as such, lord,' said a wiry, grizzled, grey-beard, stepping forward to stand in front of the tall, blond speaker. 'This one just has a smooth tongue and a quick mind; his true heart has yet to be weighed on the scale of life.'

Morgan surveyed them all, his face impassive.

'This charge may be levied against all of you here. You followed blindly a man who had clearly lost his way. You all lack good judgement. I have always been reluctant to lead such men for they have always proved wanting in the end.'

'We offer no defence against your judgement, Lord,' replied the man evenly. 'We make no demands, but merely ask and hope. Whether you choose to stand by us or not, we will all fight in the end and to the end. These invaders do not see us as men, merely a means to satisfy their avarice for dominance and conquest.'
Morgan stood for a long moment, his eyes closed. They waited.

'Summon a gathering. We will all meet in the old place a week from this day, but mind you, I make no promises as to my intent.'

'Yes, Lord. Thank you, Lord.'

Turning, the foresters vanished into the green surroundings.

'Yes, child. I can feel your thoughts.'

The girl jumped.

'Your voice is strong, but no one, it seems, has been prepared to listen. Not even your father, who sadly could only hear himself.'

The girl Jenny's eyes were burning with an inner fire of trapped need as they bore into Morgan's gentle calmness.

'Yes, child. I can hear you. In you, the gift has a form that is strong. There are others following in my footsteps who will also be able to hear you. You are no longer alone.'

A wave of tension flowed from Jenny in a warm wave and washed through his mind. She sat down next to the two sleeping men and gave him a small, shy smile.

The General and his scribe slept the sleep of dead men for the rest of that day and through the following night. When they finally woke the smell of coffee infiltrated their fogged but refreshed minds. Their bodies, on the other hand, were unbelievably stiff and aching. They looked at each other to find reassurance and shore up strength, then got shakily to their feet and made their way to the two silent figures seated around the small campfire. The girl, a familiar and welcome sight, briefly glanced up and smiled then returned to stirring the brown, fragrant liquid swirling in a small, tin pot. The other, a dark, bearded man, who seemed as firmly rooted as the surrounding trees, sat serenely with crossed legs and closed eyes. Strange energy appeared to be pulsing around him, making the two old friends a bit uncomfortable. They tried to make it not seem too obvious that they were avoiding getting close to him and sat down next to Janice. She pretended not to notice their nervousness.

'Thank you, Jenny,' said the scribe in a low voice, 'for standing next to us when no one else would. Do you know who our mysterious rescuer is?'

The girl nodded, gently placed a tip of a finger against her lips, and continued stirring. Both men settled back watching this soothing, domestic task and kept their uncertain thoughts to themselves.

'Going home will be a long journey,' the bass-deep, brandy voice startled them from their mesmeric time-out.

'We are not sure that a home still awaits us,' replied the General, after a collective pause.

'Have you decided on a course to follow?' asked Morgan, his brown, calm eyes instilling confidence into the two men.

'We would love the opportunity to witness this gathering that you mentioned.'

'Are you contemplating the bartering of information to buy back what was lost?' was Morgan's next enquiry, which was greeted with surprise, by the General, despite the question being an obvious response to his request.

Morgan sensed that his reaction was genuine, and felt an innocence surrounding the man despite his once high standing within a mercilessly ambitious nation. He was a man who understated his own abilities, an unassuming man who others may tend to overlook to their detriment.

'That is a possible scenario. One I must admit, I did not entertain. You have me there, sir, and I guess you have no reason or pedigree to base trust on my future behaviour; you do not know me, and I do not know you.'
'Maybe we should take steps to remedy that. My name is Morgan Ap

Heston.'

'I know of that name, General,' said the scribe with a worried look. 'I've had to translate certain secret, coded missives in the past for the High Enclave. This name has been mentioned more than once.'

'I see, Turpin, but why look so worried.'

'The thing is, General. I first saw this name when I was but a young scribe. I had a certain expertise in code, a hobby of mine at the time.'

'Ah, I see the problem,' replied the General, glancing nervously at the quietly observing Morgan. 'Sir, I fortunately or maybe unfortunately, overheard some of the conversations between yourself and my former captors. The implications were that you are someone revered from out of their history, although they called you by another name. May I ask just how old you are, sir?'

'I'm nearly three-hundred years old, General, give or take a few years.'

The two men stared at him dumbfounded with incredulous shock.

Jenny giggled.

The General recovered quickly.

'I can only assume you are not partaking in levity at our expense, sir, but what you say is difficult to accept.'

'Believe what you must, General. You asked a question, I answered. There is nothing more to it.'

'You misunderstand me, sir. The fault does not lie in the truth of your words, but in my acceptance beyond the world which I hold to be normal.'

'Do you still wish to tag along with me, General?'
'Most certainly, sir?'

'Then prepare yourselves for more of the abnormal. Jenny tells me that a Cardinal Sybil Wuzetian usurped your command charged with besieging Stronghome Keep.'

It was the second time in the space of a few moments that the two men were left speechless with shock. They both darted a look at Jenny and back at Morgan.

'But Jenny cannot…' stammered Turpin the Scribe.

'And so it begins, eh gentlemen? Your world continues to change before your very eyes.'

Jenny giggled.

CHAPTER XV

He was not a man to give up easily. This was his land, his forest, his fight. They were many who thought like him, and he wasn't about to let some outsider, fraud or the real thing, rob him of his chance to free the people of the Green Kingdoms. Whatever it took he was prepared to do it. As he moved through the shadowed trails, he made several stops, gathering to him those who wanted to fight and were fed-up and tired of waiting. Within a couple of days, he had a small, loyal army of two-hundred, hard-bitten foresters with him. He intended to use them before false messengers with false messages clouded their judgement. First, he would deal with the sympathisers; those who co-operated with the enemy. It was a dangerous precedent and the only way to stop it was to demonstrate in strong terms that it doesn't work.

'We are getting close, First Forester.'

The man's voice disturbed his thoughts, but he stifled his annoyance and replied in a flat measured tone.

'Give the word to spread out. We will hit them on all sides at once. No prisoners. Understand! We cannot allow ourselves to be slowed down. Half go in, half stay out.'

He saw the man's frown, but he knew he would follow orders.

'What of the settlement, First Forester?'

'We burn it to the ground. As I said, no prisoners.'

His second in command, a tough, short man with plaited blond hair and beard, frowned even more deeply, but without questioning his brutal, uncompromising instructions, slipped back along the lines to organize the attack. Good. These were the type of men he needed.

They may not like what they had to do, but they did it all the same. Not like this self-proclaimed Earl Flanders. He was once a respected and leading forester, but long before the parasites had come he begun to enrich himself, claiming that the old ways were dead and belonged to the romantic past. He had started cutting down the limbs of the Mistress, using her dead fingers to build his so-called fortifications. As usual the greedy and the sacrilegious gathered around him, building their hovels in the garbage strewn, muddy fields, tainting the pristine wonder that was the Green Shade. Now the time of reckoning was upon them.

When the large band of green-garbed men suddenly appeared out of the forest, no one was particularly alarmed. Trade between the ones who followed the old paths and those who preferred the new way of doing things had blossomed, forming an uneasy partnership which had been going on for many years now; both were gaining something from the alliance. Many eyes followed the newcomers as they padded along the muddy roads through the settlement and wound their way to the open gates of the log palisade protecting the Earl's place of residence. This was not an unusual occurrence, and as many of the green men stopped to examine the pottery wares at several of the stalls, the settlers soon returned to whatever chores they were doing before their arrival. The dirty children took this as leave to run forward and begin pestering the visitors for whatever hand-out they could get.

'Trevor Long-Ranger, what a surprise to see you here!' came a booming voice from a large chested man high up on a wooden balcony facing the open gate. 'Has the first of the foresters decided to come in person to trade with us? All reports claim you prefer enjoying our little benefits from your hidey-hole in that green swamp you call home.'

'A man uses whatever advantages he can, Earl Flanders. It is the bigger picture that always matters.'

'You are a man after my own heart, forester. We are not as different as you think.'
'Maybe not, but I'm not the one who sold out to the enemy.'

'Enemy? I'm not quite sure who that is, green man.'

'Well, maybe we can discuss that whilst my men trade for what you gave your soul to bargain for.'

'I don't understand a word of what you're saying, green man, but come on up anyway and join me in a wee draft of whiskey.'

Nodding to his men who dispersed throughout the rudimentary keep in an innocent and nonchalant manner, Long-Ranger entered the open, dimly-lit and cavernous interior of the Earl's house and climbed the rickety stairs to the second floor where the Earl awaited.

'Welcome,' said the Earl expansively, towering over the forester. 'Pull yourself up a chair and try this for size,' he thundered, pouring a dark brown liquid tinged with gold into two tin cups.

The forester sat down and sipped the fiery liquid, closing his eyes and breathing out heavily through his nose.

'That feels good,' he said.

'Compliments of the enemy,' replied the Earl with mischief in his booming voice.

The forester twisted his mouth to show his distaste and slowly put down his cup. The Earl laughed and looked out at the yard displayed below him.

'So what's your true reason for visiting my humble home and with armed men at that?'

'I'm glad you asked, Flanders,' replied the forester discourteously. 'I am here about trade, more specifically the selling of information.'

'Oh? Please. Go on.'

'Not long ago, a group of specialist turned up at my hidey-hole, as you so nicely put it. Not many people outside of the sworn foresters knew where that was, strangely enough. You wouldn't happen to know how these foreigners came by that knowledge, would you?'

'Can't help you with that one, I'm afraid, green man. But at least they didn't mean you any harm for here you are all in one piece. What was it that they wanted from you anyway?'

'My life.'

'Ah.'

'I'd best be going before my men nab all the good stuff. Thank you for your time, Earl,' said the forester offering the Earl a warrior's grip.

Suspicion flared in the big man's eyes, but he got to his feet and following the ancient guest code, turned to accept the offered forearm. As he did so, an arrow flew from the yard below and thudded sickeningly, square between his shoulder blades, tearing through his lung. His eyes widened in shock, and he staggered forward into the arms of Long-Ranger. Quick as a snake the man grabbed his host and stabbed him viciously up under his ribs, three times, stab, stab, stab. The Earl was a powerful man and with his dying strength gripped the cobra he had invited into his house and hurled him back into the wall behind with a force that shuddered the structure and caused the forester to bang his head and bite down into his own lip and tongue. With blood spitting from his mouth he snarled.

'Death to collaborators!'

The Earl tried to turn to shout a warning to his men, but his legs gave way, and he collapsed onto his back.

'You are a dog...,' he gasped, 'a bastard dog, green man!' then his eyes rolled up into his head and he died, his legs drumming on the floor with a death spasm.

The Earl's men reacted quickly, if too late, and as the treacherous forester spun away, two arrows thudded into the post where his head had just been.

What followed next was sheer mayhem and butchery as the foresters turned on people who were essentially their own. The Earl's men surprised as they were, were quickly overwhelmed and taken out. Outside in the settlement, the children became the first victims of the savagery of the foresters, who reluctant to fulfil their unsavoury role, were even more violent and merciless than regular warriors of war. Innocent bairns who were going about their normal business of tormented men, whom their parents had seemed to have vouched for, with persistent pestering and pleading were sent scattering, screaming in terror as the targets of their begging suddenly unsheathed sharp knives and plunged, slashed and stabbed at them. The survivors of this horrible onslaught fled panic-stricken in all directions, seeking whatever safety they could find. It was not to be. Shocked parents rushed forward only to be brought down by sword and arrow, bleeding into the ground. When it became apparent that their own foresters were killing indiscriminately, they tried to seek haven within the arms of the Green Mistress; she whom they had so blithely abandoned. The violators of all that was held to be decent and honourable became men possessed, dispossessed of their souls as they unleashed hell, burning hard grafted belongings and homes, killing any and everything that moved. With an inferno of shame blazing behind them they hurried out of the havoc they had wreaked and stumbled grimly over the uneven, tilled fields that had been carefully tended to feed men's hope for better things in their future. As they climbed the gentle slope which would take them into the green fronds where they sought to hide from their damning deeds, a tall, long-haired man wearing a gleaming, chain-mail shirt emerged into the sunlight. A single line of horsemen walked their horses, an odd mixture of ugly, bad-tempered ponies and elegant, high-stepping steeds, out behind him, keeping a respectable distance. With a simultaneous, flowing movement the foresters all brought their strung bows to bear. The eleven horsemen and their leader returned their fixed gazes calmly, quiet and unmoving except for an occasional stamp of a horse's hoof, as patient as if they were waiting for a wagon to roll by and clear the way for them to proceed along their path.

'You boys, whoever you are, just happen to be in the wrong place at the wrong time, there is nothing I can do to change that. Your fate is sealed!' shouted the First Forester, stepping forward, his bowstring like those of the men behind him, pulled hard against his ear.

The tall man in the chain-mail laughed, or they suspected that is what he was doing from the rough, guttural noises he was making.

'Did I say something funny, dog face!?'

'Dorg faach? Did baby-killar mean me?,' asked the tall man, turning his questioning gaze back at a broad-shouldered woman sitting on a small, sturdy pony, on either side of which were two other women, both warriors, one exotically beautiful and the other, hard-faced and mad of eye. The broad-shouldered warrior shrugged non-committedly, but the beautiful, young one pushed her specially bred horse forward and yelled in a strikingly, musical voice.

'You are addressing the Lord Krarl, be careful of what you say!'

'Lord who? Never heard of him, little girl. Kill…'

He never got to finish his sentence.

With unnatural speed, one that seemed to defy all known physical possibilities, the commanding figure referred to as Lord Krarl, warped across the intervening gap like dark smoke blown by a sudden, powerful gust of wind. Before the Forester could blink in comprehension, he was heaved off of his feet and his neck broken in a dull, wet, cracking of bones. His men stared in shock and disbelief at his limp, hanging corpse, still held aloft by the iron-banded arm of the strange, otherworldly man. In a contemptuous gesture, the tall creature tossed the lifeless body aside. Galvanised by a desire to live and by horned battle-reflexes, the green-garbed foresters pulled back on their bowstrings with a unified snatch of desperate breaths. A wave of fear crashed out from the tall, iron-shirted man, staggering them back onto their heels. At the same time, the line of horsemen on the low embankment behind the terrible creature, launched forward as one, a scream of utter defiance tearing from them as they leapt at the throats of overwhelming odds. Outnumbered they might have been, but speed, audaciousness and an unmatched elemental were on their side. The two-hundred combat seasoned foresters didn't have a chance; a tornado had descended in their midst. Split and scattered, they were cut down in a merciless swirl of aggression. Those who did not fall, fled, pride forgotten, into the frowning shadows of the Green Mistress.

'Run, you bastards, run! But you can't hide! We will find you, bastards! We are not women and children! We will find you!' shouted a pumped up Luc, his eyes wide, pupils dilated by the sudden flood of adrenalin surging through his veins and arteries.

'Come on, Luc,' said Horace, in a calming tone. 'Come, we're off again.'

Luc looked around him, his spiralling emotions coming back to earth, finding that only Horace and Scar sat their horses awaiting him. The others were already trailing after a loping Krarl, whose disappearing back was leading them to the goddess only knew where. Sharleen had attached herself to the two strange women and had become inseparable from them for reasons that she alone could tell, but in keeping with her nature, she wasn't bothering to do so.

As the miss-matched group cantered along the muddy, cart-track that once served as a road from the now devastated settlement, Kirk urged his horse alongside that of a thoughtful looking Ahmya.

'Why are we following this man, big sister?' he whispered fiercely, his voice seething with pent-up emotion.

'What do you mean? It was the task given to us.'

'He is not as we were led to expect. We were taught to follow a just cause. To be led by the One. To forge something better than what has gone before. He kills with impunity and follows no cause but his own. He is dangerous and answers to no one but himself.'

'Calm yourself. We will discuss this later. He leads us to Lord Morgan.'

Ahmya could tell that her two sword sisters were listening intently to their conversation, although they were pretending hard not to appear to be doing so.

'But…'

'Later Kirk, later,' she cut him off, spurring her stallion away from him.

After a time, Luc steered his mount closer to Horace and said in a low, troubled voice.

'The boy may well be right, Captain.'

It was not Sharleen and Elisha alone who had been eavesdropping.

'I've not felt such an uncontrolled emotion in combat since a boy with fresh snot in my nose. It was as if all reason had left me and I just wanted to kill. Where did that come from? I have my thoughts on the matter.'

Horace clenched his jaw grimly and did not respond. Neither did Scar, who unlike him, had a haunted almost frightened, expression swimming behind his eyes. Luc admitting that he felt like a child in the company of their not quite normal leader was not reassuring. His words echoed all of their hidden thoughts.

CHAPTER XVI

'I don't like excuses. What you are telling me sounds so much like an excuse, my darling man. Maybe you should try explaining all this to me again,' said the Cardinal, her sultry voice, husky and intimate.

'This time, please leave out the excuses.'

The man standing rigidly in front of her was sweating despite the hard cold outside the sumptuous tent.

'Eminence, I…'

'From the beginning, my dear General. From the beginning, and please, don't leave anything out. I love details. Tell me why we are still out here in the cold whilst a fine fire burns warmly behind those grey walls.'

'Eminence, it's not so simple…'

'Your predecessor alluded to the same thing. Simple? I'm interested in results, General. Are you the man to bring me this sweet thing, dear man? Are you equal to the great office I have bestowed upon you?'

'Everything is in our favour. We have time, resources. They are trapped with no-where to go. No one is organised enough to help them, or have the will even. They are a nut under our hammer, Excellency. Their mighty walls a weakened and fractured shell. Time, Eminence, just time. We must be patient and keep to the pattern.'

'Eloquently said, my lovely man. Thank you so much for your words of wisdom but what I really want is a general, not, unfortunately, a philosopher. On your way out, please surrender your stripes to my attendant. You are hereby relieved of the burden that you carry.'

'But your Eminence. I…'

'Your service to the Empire has been noted, dear man. Please, see yourself out.'

His mind, a fog thicker than the frigid mists outside, the short-lived General, risen up on the fallen back of his once upon a time superior, passed numbly his junior officer coming in as he made his way out into the cold. Lifting the heavy flap to make his exit into the unknown, he could hear that seductive voice, like silk, sticky with honey, fortune's trap, warming the ear of yet another ambitious man.

'Welcome, my darling man. I need something. Are you the person to get it for me?'

***

'Here they come!'

He could hardly see clearly, his eyes blood-shot and sore. A good night's sleep seemed a distant memory. The sticky, grimy feel of his skin under his hot, stifling armour, reminded him that a bath too was a distant memory. But they just kept coming.

'How long can we keep this up, Captain? I can hardly keep my feet I'm so bloody tired!'

The young, blond captain, although he felt somewhere around seventy, looked down at the impassive face of his sergeant. The man, flat nosed and stalwart though he was, had an unnerving tinge of panic at the very edge of his voice.

'It's them who should worry, sergeant. The bastards are dying in waves against our walls. How long can they keep it up? That my friend, should be your question.'

Slapping his sergeant on the back in a comradely gesture, he moved off along the line of defenders their eyes a mixture of fatalism and desperation. To them, he looked his old confident and cocky self. Inside, he was as desperate as they were, but he was in command of this section of the wall, and he swore that if he were to die, they would see the confidence of victory shining in his gaze to the very end.

'Steady men,' he said in an easy voice. 'When the nosy bastards peep over our wall, look them in the eye and send them to hell.'

Some men nodded, some smiled, and some laughed nervously, but they all tightened their grips on their weapons and firmed their stances. They were ready.

'How are you and your men faring, Captain Bastonet. If you would have me, I would like to fight by your side for a while.'

Guy turned his head to watch the heavy-footed approach of the hulking Lord Graham Stonerider, one of the twelve chosen Housecarls, a larger than life legend. The same man who Morgan Ap Heston had defeated as easily as a grown man would crush a child.

'There will always be a place for you, Lord Stonerider. You have given us honour on this challenging day.'

'We'll throw these whoresons off our wall as fast as they climb, eh son?'

Guy felt a flush of guilt as he experienced an unfair flashback of the boastful lord being flung nonchalantly against a wall into unmoving unconsciousness. To cover himself, he gave the Housecarl a shallow but respectful bow. Where was Ap Heston now? If he were to choose a man to stand by his side on this day, it would be him. A man who could change destiny itself.

A storm of noise, a wave of savage sound, fear, aggression, hate, anger, mixing together in one frothing turmoil, crashed into the wall on which they stood, sending tremors shivering through its stout structure and pulling Guy Bastonet's wandering mind back to the point of his present reality, survive or die. He swirled about and brought his shield up to guard position just as the reverberating blows of sling-shot missiles slammed into it in rapid succession, numbing his arm and sharpening his concentration. Three men, positioned behind him were slow to react and fell bonelessly to the hard, stone walkway with broken skulls. The resounding thud of ladders followed soon after and with a roar to dispel that cold worm in their guts, Captain Bastonet led his men at the persistent enemy yet one more time. The ladders were innumerable and appeared faster than their shaking limbs could push or kick them off. Soon the stench of alcohol and stale sweat flooded over the parapet heralding the ravening mob of uncouth, foul-mouthed Protectorate flunkeys, driven by the goddess knew what demons to claw their way over the blood-stained parapet no matter what the cost to their very lives. He did not care. He would kill them till his strength left his arms or death itself found him.

The loud, hoarse voice of the Housecarl bellowed out curses he had never heard before as he stood, legs apart and braced, swinging a huge, two-handed battle-axe in deadly and frightening figures of eight, cutting men down like rotten corn and hurling their fractured bodies catapulting back over the lip of the battlement. Despite the hard-pressed nature of his position, Guy grinned. No wonder the man was thought of as a legend. In battle, he became something terrible to behold.

He no longer comprehended the passage of time. Whether he had been fighting for five minutes or five hours, he could not tell. His arms were weighed down by something unbelievable and each stroke he deflected or blocked he was sure would be his last. His breath sawed loudly through his parched throat, his mouth as dry as an old crone's bits. He shook his head at the crude thought and that action saved him as the tip of a sharpened spearhead lanced through, nicking and slicing his scalp in a spray of blood. Where was his bloody helmet! He could not remember losing it. His tough sergeant was by his side, forever protecting his sword flank. May the goddess bless him. Blinking sweat from his eyes, he saw the Housecarl being overwhelmed by a horde of screaming men who threw themselves at him like ravening dogs on a wolf, bearing him to the ground and knocking his axe from his hands. His bellow of defiant rage was swallowed beneath their swamping and bludgeoning weight.

'To me!' shouted the captain. 'To me! A wedge! Form a wedge!'

Without waiting to see if anyone had heard his command, he gripped tightly onto his battered and broken shield, hunkered down, and shouldered forward. His sergeant was with him and another he did recognise on his left. The shouted march of voices behind him told him they were not alone. Step by step, they pushed and battered their way towards the fallen lord, the suffocating heat of their bodies incongruously giving them a shared feeling of brotherhood and purpose.

Grunting gutturally and digging deep, the Captain and his men laid into the enemy under which was the buried body of the giant Housecarl. They no longer had voice to shout or curse, every ounce of energy was needed to force their sword arms to rise and fall, rise and fall, again and again. The enemy scattered under their fierce, savage and almost silent onslaught.

'Shield wall! Shield wall!' commanded the iron-voiced captain. 'Pull him clear and let's go!'

Under the temporary shelter of the hastily assembled fence of shields, Guy watched as the dead weight of Graham Stonerider was dragged away, his head and face covered with bright blood, his eyes closed and mouth sagging.

'Abandon the wall,' shouted Guy. 'Sergeant, sound the retreat on my order!'

The sergeant did not hesitate. It was clear to all that their position was untenable.

Battle-weary warriors, behind the steadily retreating cover of shield walls, slipped through the narrow gates of the dividing towers that guarded the stairwells and slammed and bolted the wrought-iron doors, buying themselves a brief respite. Many did not make it through; many died, cut to pieces so that some of their comrades could get away.

***

'Well done! What a lovely man you are. Isn't he lovely, ladies and gentlemen? A true darling.'

Her voice was soft, husky and sultry with a little breathlessness of excitement running through it. An elegant, manicured, long-nailed finger ran a caressing path down the man's jawline as he stared adoringly up into her beautiful, captivating, large brown eyes. Newly elevated to General he had accomplished in one afternoon what his two predecessors had failed to do in months; he had seized the outer-wall. His glorious sponsor leant forward and as her perfume enveloped him his eyes feasted on a private viewing meant only for him. He was sure that he was drooling slightly from the corner of his mouth, but he was incapable of doing anything about it. Her breath, flavoured with the fresh smell of mint flowed over him as she whispered, drowning his senses with pleasure.

'Sweet man, you have brought me a slice of delicate fruit. Bring me the whole cake, and you shall taste a wonder that you have never dreamt of.'

Then she drew back from him with a high, girlish laugh, leaving him enthralled and a slave.

***

'Who gave the bloody order to abandon the wall? Who has sentenced us to be penned in like fattened goats for the slaughter?' shouted the Lord of Stronghome Keep.

As his voice echoed around the stone room, no one moved, all remained silent. Then a quiet, even voice filled with weariness, broke the pensive silence.

'It was my decision, Lord. I gave the order.'

'Ah, yes, Captain Bastonet. And weren't your orders simply to hold.

Was that too much to ask! Two other walls held. Why couldn't yours?'

'The boy did the right thing, lord,' answered a gravelly voice wracked with pain.

'I didn't ask for your opinion, Graham.'

'No, lord, you didn't, but if it weren't for this lad, I would be dead. We were overrun. His actions saved a lot of us from meeting our makers prematurely.'

'Heroes are supposed to die in battle. Didn't anyone tell you that, Graham? But here you are, eh? So much for legends.'

The big warrior watched his lord with steady, flat eyes but did not respond.

'Bah! We're in trouble, I can't deny it. Deep in pig shit. Defending this rock will be bloody near impossible. They will use our own walls against us. We've handed them the elevation they needed. Bloody hell! I would welcome some bright ideas if you have any,' said Lord Coulthain to his grim gathered commanders.

Everyone remained silent, including the brooding Housecarls.

'Well?' prompted Lord Coulthain.

'We are sworn to fight to the end, lord. We twelve Housecarls are all that is left of the pact signed by the Lower Kingdoms in days of old. We will hold to that pack till the day we die.'

'Yes, yes, Graham. I know this, but we still need tactics to make the bastards bleed as much as possible before that time comes.'

'We collapse the walls down on their heads, lord.'

Heads swivelled and all eyes turned to Captain Guy Bastonet. Lord Coulthain studied the young captain for a drawn-out moment then said:

'That may well be a fine suggestion Captain Bastonet, but even though every man in this keep was a sapper we would not have the time and…'

'There are tunnels, lord.'

His flat statement brought a shocked intake of breath from the gathered commanders.

'Tunnels? I am lord of this rock and have no knowledge of such,' responded Lord Coulthain in an ominous voice. 'From what fantasy have you obtained this information Bastonet? I would be very interested in learning more. What or who is your mysterious source? Such information if true threatens our very security and I am not even sure if you should be the one in possession of it. Were it not for our now blighted situation, caused by you in part by your independent actions, I might add, I would have you locked securely in a cell and have you put to painful questioning. Out with it Captain, I am waiting.'

'Maybe it would be best if we give the boy space to answer then, lord,' interjected Graham with his deep, gravelly voice. This earned him a rather violent stare from the Lord of Stronghome.

'Morgan Ap Heston gifted me this information, lord.'

'Fuck!' muttered an anonymous voice amongst the once again, shocked audience.

The lord of Stronghome Keep seemed to have forgotten how to control his mouth and left it gaping for all to gaze uncertainly into.

'He…What!…That charlatan! And you believed him! Incredible. Do you have any evidence to the truth of his words, man?'

'Yes, lord.'

'What!...'

'Show us, young Bastonet,' rescued Graham.

With a small army of bemused lords and high ranking soldiery trailing after him, Guy led them to the small, secluded fountain where Morgan had divulged a secret to him on that night not so many nights ago. How fortune changes quickly, he thought. Leaping up into the overflowing basin he spent some minutes fiddling behind the goddess until some of the more doubting began to frown up at him. Thanking the deity for small mercies, he was rewarded with an audible click, and the moss-covered statue swung open. Stepping to the side Guy gestured to Lord Coulthain.

'Lord,' he said.

'No, Bastonet, by all means, you lead the way. I prefer to have you in my sight at all times.'

Guy heard an annoyed grunt from Graham but turned anyway and disappeared into the mouth of the goddess.

Thank the heavens someone had had the presence of mind to bring along a torch. Under its unruly light Guy followed the memory trail first laid down by Morgan. At a point, he stopped where he had noticed a shadow darker than others. As he had suspected, it proved to be a divergent tunnel. As it turned out, only Lord Coulthain, Graham and five other Housecarls had followed him. Graham who had the torch stuck it into the opening of the second tunnel and examined it.

'This one runs along and under the curtain walls, I expect,' explained Guy.

'How did that charlatan know of this?' muttered Coulthain.

'Maybe that's just it. He is who he says he is,' replied Graham.

'You weren't thinking that when he was dropping you on your arse,

I'd bet.'

'That's precisely why I am thinking it now.'

'Maybe we should act on this boy's advice, eh lads? Instead of snapping useless words at each other,' rumbled an old, grey-beard who was known for not speaking very often but when he did it usually made good sense.

Surprisingly to Guy, both of the men rebuked, did not seem to have taken offence and nodded simultaneous assent.

'Go get our sappers, John. Organise every able-bodied man and women too. We'll work in shifts. Timing will be essential. Let's get a move on, eh!'

CHAPTER XVII

The Gathering was a much smaller affair than Morgan remembered. It was a rare and infrequent thing which traditionally took place on a rocky knoll situated within the shelter of a low range of hills deep within the Green Forest. Only under the most dire of circumstances or when great change was required was a Gathering called. In a natural amphitheatre cut into hard rock by countless years of exposure and erosion were representatives from all the various Green Kingdoms, those conquered, those still resisting and those whose names have long since been forgotten. Morgan sat under the shade of a small tree at the edge of it all, surrounded by his small entourage. He studiously ignored the curious stares and surreptitious whispers of the doubtful but hopeful. Hope he wanted to tell them, was a useless thing if poured into infertile soil but a man, he guessed, must hold on to something in order to make his life worth living.

'This is unbelievable! We didn't have a clue. And right under our very noses! Incredible!' said Turpin the scribe, drawing furiously on an old, vellum scroll.

'Ehr...Turpin, my old friend. Please be careful. We would not like your enthusiasm to be misinterpreted as espionage by our hosts.'

'What?', enquired the scribe, blinking in confusion. 'But I'm not a spy! I have no one to spy for.'

'Yes, but they do not know that, do they?'

'Rest easy, General. You would need more than a random sketch for anyone to find this place,' placated Morgan.

Jenny giggled.

Stationed at sentinel points around the trio stood green-garbed, hard-eyed foresters who made sure that no one approached closer than was necessary.

'Do they view us as their prisoners, Lord Morgan,' whispered the General.

Morgan made a small, irritable sigh.

'No, General. They see themselves as our protectors.'

'Or maybe they want to attach themselves to you so that you may protect them,' muttered Scribe Turpin.

Jenny giggled.

With hooded eyes, Morgan watched the grizzled, grey-beard climb the stepped slope towards him. From the corner of his vision, he could see the Swearing Stone of Loyalty in its prime position at the centre of the bowl. It had no power of its own. It was just a rock, but men for generations had endowed it with something sacred. And so, in the end, it had power over these men. A power he once used to forge his purpose – and now here he was again.

'They all have a desire to hear your words, Green Warden.'

'No. I'm not a politician here to grease their ears with a slick tongue that slides any which way.'

'But you must win their hearts…'

'No. They know who I am. This gathering is for them to talk amongst themselves and choose. Their decision made here will give direction to my next actions. Remind them not to talk for too long.'

'As you wish, Green Warden,' replied the man respectfully but with a deep frown clouding his already creased forehead.

'He was hoping for more from you, I think.'

'They always want more, General,' replied Morgan in a quiet voice.

'My old friend, Turpin here, has been bringing to light certain things. He has made me realise, now that we know who you are, that your battle tactics are studied in our military academy. You are known to us by another name, the Defiler. No offence. I remember thinking back then that you could have forged an empire, defeated ours even but you always fought small scale, always defensive, as if you were afraid of something. Sorry to say this, but to us, your vision seemed limited.'

At first, the General and the keenly listening scribe thought that Morgan was not going to respond. He appeared as if he had not even heard. Then in a deep, calm voice, Morgan said.

'When the demon is unleashed, beware, for nothing you can do will contain him again. You will become what you are not, and everything will be changed forever.'

The two friends looked uneasily at each other and, Jenny studied Morgan with concern in her eyes, her senses picking up a deeper emotion to Morgan's words than the other two could detect.

More foresters were arriving with every passing minute, and although the half-bowl had the capacity for many more, a sizable number had already gathered.

'They still look a bit expectant, Warden,' observed the General. 'I would say by the way they are glancing at you like shy girls at a party, they still want you to dance with them.'

'Bah,' said Morgan rising to his feet and centering the power spitting around him deep behind his navel, controlling it and balling it into a thunderous fist of force. 'I haven't got the patience for this.'

His companions sensed the unexplained surge of energy and their faces registered alarm to something felt that was not understood and could not be seen. For a moment, balanced on the knife-edge of time, Morgan struggled to master himself and come to a decision. He opened his mouth, and the very stones of the amphitheatre rumbled with resonant sound.

'Listen, Children of the Forest Green, do not look to me to cut your path. Your destination must be yours only to select. We can share the journey together, but its success must lay on your own shoulders. Do not load your hopes on my back to free yourselves of responsibility. Fear of failure is an unnerving thing, but you cannot escape the possibility of failure by piling your fears on me. I will no longer shoulder your blame. Your disparate avenues to your future are all here in this place of oath-making. Tomorrow is no longer an option. Today is the day of decisions and your hour of deciding is now. Tell me when you have come to one and do not bother me until then.'

The gathering of hardened fighters was stunned into incredulous silence and immobility, staring up at the apparition of power within the sacred heart of their domain. They were not released from their stasis until Morgan, pulling his cloak around him with a snap, sat back down and shut himself away from them.

They took more than an hour. In fact, they took the whole morning, deliberating, making speeches, breaking up into small groups, sending runners from group to group, on and on. Through it all, Morgan sat unmoving, like a stone statue. Not so much his companions, who napped, explored, eavesdropped till they were bored, then napped again, stretching out on the cool stone under the shade of the surrounding trees. They were very careful not to question Morgan, no matter how curious they were.

'How long do they need to say "I will follow" or "I will not follow"? whispered the old scribe.

'I guess you have the truth of it. Those are, in the end, the choices open to them. Almost like our former home, eh Turpin?' answered the General.

'No wonder they were so easy to defeat. They dither more than I do and I am only a scribe.'

'Well, I'm not sure defeat is the right word. We never followed them into these forests of theirs. If we had, we would still be here dying.'

'Do you think they have the numbers to challenge the might of the Empire?'

'It's not just numbers that matter,' said the grizzled, grey-beard, appearing from nowhere, and sitting down next to the lounging pair.

'If he leads us your Empire will pay dearly, and yes, there are many of us lying low beneath her fronds. They would flock to his call.'

'Why aren't they here now then,' gently challenged the General, his eyes closed as he enjoyed a refreshing breeze.

'Like most men they are waiting to see which way the wind blows before revealing their hands and committing their lives.'

'Do you think Morgan will take up your war banner?' asked Turpin. 'He seems very reluctant.'

'I believe he will aid us in some way but how I am not certain. We will have to wait and see.'

'And hope,' said the General.

'And hope,' confirmed the grey-beard.

Finally, a decision appeared to have been made as a small detachment made their way up the naturally carved steps towards the inhumanly patient Morgan. They stopped just below where he was sitting and when he did not acknowledge them a tall, lean, exaggeratedly erect individual with long, curly hair cleared his throat loudly. He seemed like a man who was not accustomed to being ignored and exuded great authority.

'We call on you to serve the Green Mistress once again Morgan Ap Heston. We…'

His voice trailed off as Morgan's eyes, now fastened onto him like a terrier onto a rat, swirled with a fierce and terrifying golden glow, fixing the self-important speaker and his entourage to the spot, leaching their will away and instilling within them a bowel-loosening fear.

'You do not have the authority to summon me. Do you understand? This is not what I asked you to do,' said Morgan, his bass-deep voice hissing with menace.

'Oh, shit!,' whispered the scribe, drawing away and pulling on his General who was transfixed with fascination and curiosity.

The lean, pompous man was as pale as a faded bed-sheet, and his limbs shook like a leaf in a gale. Still, beneath it all, he was a forester and foresters were bred tough. He strained through his short-comings and stammered.

'You..yo..uu, t-told us, t-to d-d-decide.'

'You heard but did not listen. Are you still the fools your forefathers became?'

'The grizzled, grey-beard stepped forward and gave Morgan a half-bow.'

'Please hear them out, Lord. Tobias Stumpcutter has always seen himself as royalty and is given to exaggerated pomp and ceremony. Maybe you should allow another to speak.'

This last he directed at the sweating, forlorn-looking representatives.

Morgan closed his eyes and the group in front of him to a man, sagged visibly, some struggling to keep their feet but all fighting the urge to sit on the hard rock.

'Speak,' he said.

A frightened looking man who had been hovering behind Tobias

Stumpcutter, turned to the grey-beard and said.

'Greybeaver, you know what we have decided. Would you speak to the Lord Morgan on our behalf, please? I do not think I have the strength.'

Morgan spoke before Greybeaver could respond.

'It is time to stop hiding in the shadow of others. Speak for yourself.'

Stumpcutter drew himself up to his full height and opened his mouth to address Morgan.

'Not you, Stumpcutter,' cut in Morgan, holding up his hand to forestall the jumped-up ass.

With Morgan's calm, brown eyes now resting on him, a short-legged, hairy fellow with a red face and bulbous nose, shuffled hesitantly around a flustered, frowning Stumpcutter.

'Erh, Lord, if it pleases you, I…'

'May I have your name, Forester?' asked Morgan.

'Clearwater, Lord. Francis Clearwater.'

'Very well, Francis Clearwater. Tell me what has been decided.'

'We would like you to stand at our side whilst we take back what is ours, Green Warden.'

'Waal saad littal marn, yuuu harv pleased my brodar.'

The sound of hard iron grating and slithering from oiled leather filled the air as startled men snatched their weapons into calloused hands and spun towards the unexpected interruption.

'You took your time in getting here, brother. What mischief did you bring with you this time?'

Morgan's calm response to the sudden, undetected and inexplicable appearance of the strange looking man in their midst steadied the nerves of the secretive Foresters and made them pause before launching themselves at the intruder who was stretched out nonchalantly on a tree branch above their heads.

'Do you know this creature, Lord Morgan?' asked a grim, hard-faced Greybeaver, his hands locked around the handle of his long-sword and his eyes fixed on the man in the tree.

'This creature, as you call him, is my brother. Try not to annoy him if you wish to hold on to your life,' was the level reply.

A woofing sound could be heard coming from the shaded branch of the tree that might have been laughter.

General Montford edged himself closer to Morgan and peered up into the branches.

'You have a brother, Lord Morgan? Fascinating! Is he like you?'

'Maybe we should ask him. Are you like me, Karl?'

'We are one,' was the strong reply. 'The time arrs corm for us to act as orn, brodar.'

'What does he mean, Warden?'

'I arv a gift for you, brodar,' interrupted Krarl, swinging smoothly to the ground.

The tense Foresters bunched together and crouched aggressively, extending the points of their weapons towards him..

Krarl ignored them all and walked towards his brother.

'You have brought a gift here for me?'

'Not here, Bark in trees. Too many littal green men skulking about.'

'What are you up to, brother?'

'I arv stopped running, littal brodar. Useless! Going nowhere. We must storp together. Turn, face world, face destiny. Become one in purpose.'

Morgan scrutinised his brother's face, waiting for the tell-tale signs of his usual mockery but nothing was revealed in his unusually open and earnest expression.

'This creature has not been invited here. He must be expelled immediately. He...'

'Stumpcutter if you don't shut it, I will do it for you,' growled Greybeaver.

Both Morgan and Krarl continued looking at each other and showed no indication that they had heard Stumpcutter and the rebuke he had received in turn.

'That's a fine speech, brother,' said Morgan, 'and does your gift have anything to do with your unexpected words? You have exposed your band of followers to some danger in bringing them here.'

'Not mine; yours. Many arv our curse flowing in them. It is the beginning. The time of turning.'

Morgan glanced around him. He and his brother were in the centre of a hushed army of the entire Gathering; all listening intently to them.

'So you've said, brother. So you've said. And what do you propose we do when we make this turn? Conquer the world?'

'We carn start with Empire. Drive tharm bark to the Gates orf their proselytising city and squeeze fat Cornclave a littal; mark tharm squeak.'

'What do you think of my brother's suggestion, General?'

'It would be a mountainous task. Akin to holding back the very tides of the great seas. The Empire has huge resources; an unstoppable army and remember, not all the conquered peoples resent their presence. All the Empire asks of them is to worship one god, pay their taxes and keep the peace.'

'They have stripped away choice and free will. These things are non-negotiable for those who value what their forefathers have fought for,' commented Francis Clearwater.

'You see, brother. The rights and wrongs of what you are asking are not so clear.'

'That may be so, First Warden, but the majority of us in the Green Kingdoms do not want these invaders and their meddling priests, even those who have opted for the path of collaboration,' said Greybeaver, emotion and conviction brimming in his voice.

'There arr also sorm from the Lower Kingdorms you may warnt to talk to, brodar. Then maybe you carn decide where we should make a start.'

'Come then, brother. Show me this gift of yours.'

'I weel bring them if littal green men not try to keel.'

All the Foresters within earshot nodded.

'I will come with you to guarantee safe passage,' said Greybeaver.

Greybeaver's mother gave birth to him under the never-ending trees of the Green Mistress, and he grew up under her protection, learning everything that she chose to teach him. He had never left her shade, and he had never entertained the desire to do so. He was one of the best of the Foresters but keeping up with this elemental made him feel like a flat-footed oaf. The not quite human he had sworn to protect from the fool-hardy amongst his one kind, moved through the forest like a wraith, always flowing along the path of least resistance, sometimes even taking to the trees without a moment's thought, never making a sound and hardly ever disturbing a single leaf. He was sweating and panting by the time they finally arrived at where his guide had left his band of followers.

An exotically beautiful, young woman was the first to detect their arrival, and as an arrow seemed to leap onto the bow that had mysteriously materialised in her hand, the metallic music of swords being drawn sang into the silent space. Two iron limbed women melted to her side, one large and imposing, the other lithe and supremely athletic, their swords held expertly in a guard position. The creature leading him grunted in approval. From the corner of his eye, he saw three men who had the mark of hard killers on them and behind the women five youngsters came hurrying up.

'Time to go to a party,' said the one called Krarl. 'Let's go.'

Without asking questions, the band sheathed their weapons, gathered up their few belongings and mounted their horses. They were efficient, and Greybeaver was impressed.

It took them double the time to return to the Swearing Stone as the thick forest was not designed for the swift movement of horses.

At the foot of the range of hills flanking the Gathering place, they left their mounts in the charge of a pair of young Foresters whose duty was to ensure that none of the uninvited was allowed to progress any further. Today they would remember as the day they failed in that task. Luckily for them, it wasn't any ordinary individual who had outwitted their vigilance otherwise their punishment would have been severe.

Nothing much had changed in the amphitheatre during their short absence except that the gathering was now more dispersed and Morgan was conversing with Francis Clearwater and a couple of other senior Foresters along with the ex-Protectorate General, his scribe and the ever silent girl who had made up their party. The three hard looking killers paused to take in the scene but the three women, led by the exotic beauty, immediately headed for Morgan the Green Warden, trailed closely by the five youngsters. Greybeaver thought the dynamics of the group to be very interesting. In fact, it wasn't one group but three. The knot that held them together was their undisputed leader, Krarl and he, interestingly enough, seemed to be deferring to his brother, Morgan. The conclusion of this Gathering would be, by all signs, a game changer.

The three women dropped to one knee, bowed their heads, thumped a balled fist below their left breasts and in unison said.

'Lord Morgan.'

Morgan watched them with an expressionless and unreadable face.

'Please, this is not necessary. I am not a king. Stand or sit but do not kneel.'

'Shilly wemen,' muttered his brother, shaking his shaggy head.

Morgan's gaze came to rest on the exotic beauty and after studying her for a short moment said.

'I'm glad you have recovered. May I ask your name?'

'Thanks to you, Lord Morgan. My name is Ahmya Yumi, Lord.'

Morgan glanced quickly up at Krarl, who nodded and shrugged his shoulders.

'An interesting name. I see that fate gave you my very brother to lead you to me in the end.'

'It was meant to be, Lord.'

Morgan frowned but didn't comment. Instead, he turned his attention to the lithe, hard-faced woman next to Ahmya.

'Elisha, I can't say that I'm overjoyed to see you again. I hope you've left that rubbish you were spouting behind you. It has caused me no end of trouble.'

'A man cannot run from his destiny, Lord,' she emphatically replied.

Krarl chortled loudly.

'Yuu see, brodar? I arm not the only warn bringing sound advice.'

'You have brought me a crick in my neck, brother,' replied Morgan, his eyes flicking to Sharleen then to the three hard-eyed men standing behind her.

'I know you four. You seem familiar.'

'They tried to kill yuu sorm time bark,' said his brother unhelpfully.

Morgan picked up a whiff of uneasy emotion straying from them. All, except the strapping, tall woman, who was as steady as a rock.

'You guard your mind well, warrior. Impressive.'

'She harz a way about har, brodar. I sense something hidden.'

Sharleen looked directly at Krarl, her eyes flat but penetrating.

'Haar, did yuu feel thart, brodar!' chuckled Krarl.

'Yes, I did. Intriguing,' replied Morgan, his attention focusing on the three men. 'What of these? They have the look of killers about them.'

'Haar. Theeze are men of the Lower Kingdoms, along with Sharleen here. It is to them thart I wish you to speak. Hear them, brodar.'

'I will,' said Morgan, turning his calm gaze on the five young followers of Limp-foot's mischief. They shifted slightly from foot to foot, unsure of how they should respond. Before they could come to a decision, Morgan turned back to the four Lower Kingdom citizens.

'The Foresters of the Green Kingdoms have decided to go to war. Where do the Lower Kingdoms stand in this? Do they wish to stop the Protectorate Order from descending on their necks? Will they fight in alliance with the Green Kingdoms?'

A tall, powerfully built man with heavy, protruding brow ridges stepped slightly forward. He was undoubtedly a man built for conflict, his hands thick from the constant use of weapons, his face scarred, but his eyes shone with intelligence.

'Our leaders have become self-indulgent and lazy, but above all, our people value their independence. They would not lie low for foreigners to stamp on their bollocks.'

The young one with the scar running down his cheek tried to smother a snigger, and the stout, broad-shouldered, pungent one frowned at his antics in annoyance.

'Fast friends, then,' Morgan thought, 'despite their odd differences, and dangerous.' The woman his brother named Sharleen remained silent, expressionless and self-contained.

'Would your leaders answer my call on your say so?'

'I do not know the answer to that, Lord.'

'Our Lord Breakspear would not stir from his cesspit until something crawled up his leg and bit his arse,' added Sharleen unexpectedly in a level, unemotional voice.

Once again the scar-faced individual sniggered and said.

'He only raises his lance for the spearing of little girls. Councillor Tramford does his thinking and Captain Horace here his fighting.'

'The fool says the truth of it, Lord,' concluded Sharleen, which earned her a glare from the scar-face.

'How well is your Councillor Tramford regarded by the other Lords?' pressed Morgan.

'He is mostly held in high esteem, for his skill as a deal maker and arbitrator have kept internecine warfare to a minimum over the years and allowed the lords to profit,' replied Horace.

Morgan nodded in approval, immediately reassessing the Captain's capabilities.

'Would you agree to return to your kingdom as my representative? Your mission would be to convince Councillor Tramford to set up a meeting between myself and the other Lords. Tell them to look to the mists above their heads. We intend to break the siege at Stronghome Keep.'

'But Lord, shouldn't we regain control of the Green Kingdoms first? We should not surrender the strong hand we hold. Our Foresters fight their best and their fiercest under the umbrella of the Green Mistress,' said Francis Clearwater with some concern in his voice.

'Not while a Cardinal of the Protectorate Order sits above us all with a hammer held over our heads. Stronghome Keep will be our place of turning. The Kingdoms, Lower and Green, must work together as one in this.'

'Aye,' said an impassioned Elisha. 'And when we win through, it will send a clear message to the god slayers that the One is coming!'

Morgan looked at her and frowned but did not pursue the matter. Krarl chuckled gutturally with mischievous humour.

'What a gift I've brought you today, eh Bruudar?'

CHAPTER XVIII

'My, my, messages from my esteemed colleagues. I am honoured, and all this way too, to the very frontier. How brave you are, Emissaries. Please, you must tell me, what urgent news have you risked life and limb to bring me?'

The three men in front of her bearing the colours of special agents to the Holy Conclave appeared uncertain but determined. She, on the other hand, dressed in immaculate, white robes, exuded confidence and tranquillity.

'The sitting Conclave urges you to return to the fold where you may be protected from the uncertainties of chance, Eminence.'

'Oh dear, have you travelled so far to tell me that the First Citizen is worried about my wellbeing? I already know the dear man's concerns, darlings. Surely, your presence must have a deeper meaning? If not I'll be disappointed.'

The three men glanced uneasily at each other. They were hungry, they were thirsty, they were tired and dirty. They had not been offered refreshments of any type. They knew their august host by reputation, and they were not reassured.

'The Conclave feels that you are putting ambition before country and state. They feel that your presence here gives the wrong image to the inhabitants of our Holy City. An image that puts self-interest before service.'

'My, my, but you lovely boys are blunt. No foreplay at all, straight down to business. Sometimes I like that; sometimes I don't. Today I'm ambivalent. Please, tell me more.'

The three Emissaries knew very well that they were treading a very delicate and dangerous path, but they had no choice but to plough on.

'It is forbidden for members of the Conclave to have armies of their own in the field. This is the domain of our generals.'

'Forbidden? Forbidden by whom, my darlings? I am extremely knowledgeable on the contents of our written laws, but I have no recollection of reading such a legal missive, and my memory is very, very good, you know.'

'It is a legal tradition handed down from the original Conclave established by First Citizen Crispin himself.'

'Come on, boys, get your facts straight. Is it law or tradition? I'm afraid you are getting me a tad bored, and I hope you do know that the primary Conclave was not the work of Cardinal Crispin.'

'We were not sent to argue points with you, lady. Our mission is to inform you that the sitting Conclave orders your immediate recall to your chair.'

'Lady, is it?'

Although she did not move or raise her voice, there was now a cutting, icy edge to her honeyed tone.'

'You will address me always by my proper title, or you will forfeit your tongues on the very spot where you are standing. Am I clear in this, darlings?'

The three men were stunned and dumbstruck by the direct threat. Emissaries of the sitting Conclave were always treated with the utmost courtesy with a pinch of dread. They were the voice of the Conclave and especially the First Citizen in the field.

'Eminence, we are mere messengers.'

'Then act so in accordance. Return immediately to your masters and reassure them that I am acting to secure our frontier and the best interest of our Holy City. This cold rock stands on a place of untapped riches if handled with a wise head. All trade must move through here, and this trade will fill the coffers of our Empire. It is best that one of us, one of the Conclave, be here to oversee its establishment. Since I am already in place, then the task is best suited for my hands. Now go. Fresh horses are already waiting for you.'

Bowing low the men hastily departed not even glancing at the harried-looking soldier who passed them on their way out.

'Your Eminence,' said the new arrival. 'General Cloner has sent me here with the news that the wall has collapsed.'

'This is either good news or bad. By your disposition, I would guess to the latter. Please clarify for me the meaning of this fallen wall.'

'The wall gave us the needed platform to eyeball our enemy. We were just finished carting our armaments onto it when it fell from under us killing most of the storming party and breaking our siege machines. We have lost quick advantage, Eminence.'

'Don't get excited, darling. Tell me, without a wall what do they have to hide behind? Nothing. Get more of these siege toys and blast an opening into their hidey rock. This is only a small delay. Tell my General to get on with it and stop being a cry baby. I like men not little boys.'

'At once, Eminence.'

Cardinal Sybil Wuzetian relaxed back into the embrace of her soft, leather chair, gently stroking the silk cushions with her tapered fingertips. 'On this throne of silk and leather I will one day rule the world,' she thought. 'If only I were not surrounded by imbeciles that time would come much sooner.' Her smooth, beautiful face did not betray any of her ambitious thoughts or the tension that was hidden in her body. She had spent a lifetime schooling those tell-tale signs that others might use in an attempt to manipulate her; now she was a true master. Her family were immigrants. Four generations ago they had come penniless to the Holy City, a once royal family running from a revolution that had overthrown their exalted status, turning them into something no better than dirty peasants. The enigma of their mixed presentation of poverty contrasting with poorly disguised education and intelligence fascinated a wealthy merchant who offered them patronage in return for the hidden gems of knowledge and ability that they had. By the time she was born, her family were the owners of a powerful and influential trading house, and she lacked for nothing. Still, this was not enough. She was born to be a queen and a queen she would become.

***

'They just keep coming, the whoresons!' panted the hulking Housecarl, flinging aside yet another madly charging soldier with a blow from the back end of his war axe, breaking his boiled exoskeleton with a resounding crack.

'We will hold the bastards here as long as it takes,' muttered Captain Guy Bastonet as he ducked under the massive arms of the gasping Graham Stonerider, taking his place in the small breach where the massive masonry had broken open and ignoring the blood from a scalp wound that was running freely down his face with bright blood.

'Hurry up with that blasted wall, will you!' he could hear the Housecarl shouting. 'I can't bloody well stand here all day swinging, I need a bloody tankard to drink. These bastards made me miss breakfast!'

No one answered him.

'Fall back, Guy! The sluggards are ready!'

Slipping backwards through the crack in the wall, Guy caught a glimpse of the oversized boots of Stonerider as he was hoisted upwards and over the newly constructed inner defensive construction. With a yell, he leapt for the dangling end of the second rope and was pulled swiftly up after the Housecarl. Before he was even over the lip, a barrage of whizzing arrows flew by his head, drilling into the enemy soldiers below who were pushing through and finding themselves trapped in a killing ground.

'This won't delay them long. Just gives us enough time to send a couple of prayers to the goddess,' yelled the big man in his ear, almost deafening him. 'Let's leave these boys to it and get back to the main party.'

Guy nodded grimly and followed the irrepressible Housecarl. Over the past few days, they had become constant battle companions and fast friends. They were everywhere, wherever the conflict was hottest, and their presence seemed to enliven the beleaguered defenders into greater efforts.

As their trotting footsteps echoed hollowly in a stone-lined corridor, Stonerider shouted a surprising and unexpected thing.

'I wish we had that Morgan fellow by our side at this moment.'

Guy burst out laughing as if it were the funniest thing he had ever heard in all the world.

'You had better be careful of what you wish for, big man.'

The heavy drumming of solid stone being bombarded by boulders of equal strength led them to a large open hall. The cavernous room trembled and rocked as if a mighty god was shaking the very earth to spite mankind and demonstrate his power. Five ranks of armoured, dust-covered, warriors stood silently waiting for the inevitable, their shields held before them to stave off the deadly pieces of flying rock shrapnel. In the second row stood the Lord of Stronghome Keep with a shroud of purpose hanging around his shoulders. The two comrades pushed their way through the waiting group and took their place in the front rank.

It wasn't long before the frightening sound of splitting stone rendered the air around the hunkered warriors. Lord Coulthain's voice spat between the loud, ominous cracks.

'Today we die as brothers in defence of our own. Let no man say we did not do our duty.'

The mighty wall that had protected the rock fortress since its conception and had never been breached, began to bulge with each new assault. Men felt their mouths so dry they could not even swallow, yet sweat flowed copiously down from their helmeted heads and dribbled under their body armour turning their tense and uneasy bodies into heated swamps. With palms wet from frayed nerves they gripped tightly onto the leather wrapped handles of their swords smelling the stink coming from them and drawing comfort from this familiarity.

The hall reverberated with a thunderous noise, overpowering the senses of the stalwart warriors, making them feel insignificant as if standing before the gods, overawed and anxiety-ridden. Then when they felt the climax of events building in the space in which they were waiting for their final battle, everything stopped, suddenly, unexpectedly. As one they all leaned forward into the dusty, deathly silence, ready to meet the onrush of the enemy. Nothing, nothing happened – only light playing on the settling dust - their ears ringing with emptiness; expectation left hanging.

CHAPTER XIX

Krarl, for reasons of his own, had decided to go with them. The occupying army was so elated and focused on their success that slipping through their large camp in the dark of night was an easy enough task. In fact, Krarl just led them along at a slow walk, using his uncanny senses to avoid the sentries but still appearing casual. Those who saw them suspected nothing out of the ordinary.

'The lord of shivery peak will soon lose his seat, by the look of things,' commented Scar.

'Their wall has been captured. Only a matter of time now,' added Luc. 'Wouldn't like to be in their shoes.'

'Nowhere to run, nowhere to hide,' finished Scar.

'Maybe it's best if the two of you keep the running commentary till a bit later,' cautioned Horace.

'Sorry, Captain,' responded Scar.

Sharleen glanced back at them but continued walking in her chosen place by Krarl's side. She had taken the position at his left side since they had departed the site of the Swearing Stone; a self-appointed guardian. Krarl had not seemed to have noticed.

'As if that bugger needs guarding,' thought Scar. 'And since when did Sharleen become so attached to others? First, those two scary women, now this ultra-scary man. Says a lot about what goes on in that hard boned skull of hers.'

'Scar would you stop that inane humming in my ear! You're giving me a headache and frightening the horses.'

'Eh? Oh, sorry Captain.'

After that, no one spoke but followed Krarl on the return journey as they had followed him out, only this time they had a different purpose, a broader purpose. They all sensed a point of turning, seducing them onwards, filling them with vigour but also trepidation. None of them could read Krarl's thoughts, and no one was prepared to risk asking him. All, of course, except Sharleen.

'So, will you lead us into war by your brother's side or behind him?' she asked, her voice flat and unemotional as ever.

Krarl stopped suddenly. They could feel the raw violence rising in him, like the rising of a black tide, even though his back was to them. Luc and Scar took a hesitant step backwards, and Horace set his feet, preparing to face death. They regretted having to leave their horses behind, for now they felt naked and vulnerable. On horseback, they might have been able to escape the devil-me-care attitude of Sharleen. Why provoke the man now? Krarl's words whispered out into the dry wind.

'You see murch but you knowr northing.'

Then he started walking again as if nothing had happened.

'Tell us then of the things we do not know.'

'Sharleen, for the goddess' sake, will you leave it out!' beseeched Scar with a panicky voice.

She ignored him as she always tended to do.

Five minutes passed, and he had not acknowledged her, and the three men started to breathe easily again thinking that maybe they had bypassed another of Sharleen's impulsive foolishness. She was always one to stir the pond to see what might float to the surface.

'When I luuk into the pool orf life my bruudar luuks bark out art me. For heem the same. One carnot be without the orther. We are two but one. None ees first, none ees second.'

Without a backward glance, he broke into a ground-eating trot.

'Oh no. Not again,' moaned Scar.

Three days of hard running brought them finally to the river that ran in a half-circle around the fortified compound of Lord Breakspear. As they crossed the log bridge, Krarl gestured for Horace to take the lead. Sharleen stuck by his side followed closely by a stiff-legged Luc with a panting and wobbling Scar bringing up the rear. A group of unkempt looking warriors stared at them in disbelief, and one called out:

'Captain, where the bloody hell have you been? You look like shit!'

'Long story, Pollock. Do you know where I can find the lord?'

A look of disgust flitted across the warrior's face.

'Tupping some poor peasant's daughter, would be my guess, Captain. Lord Tramford is over by the new mill, however.'

'Much appreciated, Pollock. Get the men together in the meantime, would you? Prepare for a hard ride, prepare for battle.'

The man's face lit up. Boredom did not sit well with these born raiders.

'Yes, Captain,' he replied and scampered away.

They found the aged Councillor side by side with the miller and the blacksmith wrestling with the stuck cogs of the mill, the sleeves of his gown rolled up to the elbows of his skinny arms as he grunted and heaved with the two other men.

'Lord Tramford, a moment of your time if you will,' said Horace as if he was well accustomed to finding the lord's councillor in odd situations.

'Yes, yes, just a tic...,' answered the Councillor, then realising who it was, turned with a genuine, warm look of surprise on his face.

'Captain Horace, Sharleen, when did you get back?'

'Just this minute, Lord. There is someone I would like you to meet.'

The old man's eyes rested on the still, imposing figure of Krarl, who was studying him as if he were deciding whether he was edible or not.

'Is...is this he?'

'Not exactly, Lord. It is his brother.'

A confused frown creased the Councillor's brow.

'His brother...?'

'It's a long story, Lord. May we find a place where we can talk in private and without fear of rude interruption?' interrupted Sharleen.

'Yes, yes, of course. Follow me. Carry on lads, we've almost got it back in place.'

Hiking up the hem of his gown exposing similarly skinny shanks he led them at a quick step across the dirt road, casting a furtive glance towards Lord Breakspear's quarters, and hurried through the oak door that led to his rooms.

'Here we are, now what's this...'

'My bruudar warnts you to arrange council weeth odar lords,' said Krarl without preamble.

'What…?'

'What he means, Lord, if I may,' said Sharleen quickly. 'Stronghome Keep is hanging over the abyss and will fall into it any moment now. When this happens, all hell will descend on our cosy little nests, the Lower Kingdoms. Lord Krarl here and his twin, Lord Morgan, are warlords without match. They intend to stop the plague that is the Protectorate Order in their tracks and liberate the Green Kingdoms. It is in our interest to be part of Lord Morgan's plans.'

'Slow down, Sharleen, I'm not young anymore.'

Scar sniggered.

'I, we haven't got the luxury to mull things, Lord. We have to move now.'

'Sharleen is right, Lord. Speed is essential,' interjected Horace. 'We must give men to Lord Krarl to join with his brother.'

'That name tickles at my memory. Morgan…Morgan Ap Heston, but that is impossible. Surely not the same man. He would be three times my age.'

'It is the same man, Lord,' said Sharleen.

'Carn yuuu do it?' asked Krarl.

'Yes, the lords will mobilize if they knew that Stronghome was breaking. We all thought it unthinkable.'

'It is happening now, Lord,' said Horace. 'When we passed through the defensive wall was taken.'

'Very well. Send out the runners, Horace. I will give you my mark for the convening of an immediate council of war. Tell the Lords to gather here as soon as possible and to send their forces to the foothills of Stronghome Keep and there to await our coming. Tell them that those who do not answer the call will be left behind and when we return there will be a reckoning.'

'Lord Krarl, welcome. I invite you to be my guest whilst we await the awakening of the lords. Sharleen would you stay with us. I would love to get to know our esteemed guest better. Wine, Lord Krarl?'

By the time Horace returned to report some forty minutes later, Krarl was on his tenth cup of wine but remained unchanged. He smacked his lips as he placed his cup carefully onto the table, edging it towards the old Councillor to have it refilled.

'Lord Krarl, would you have me believe that you are over three hundred years old! I may be aged, but I am not gullible.'

'He is telling the truth, Lord. I tend to like my men to be older.'

Both Krarl and the Councillor stared at Sharleen, trying to look past her impassive face to discern whether or not she was joking. Before any of them could respond, Horace cleared his throat politely.

'I estimate that the Kingdom Lords will be here in less than two days, lord.'

'Marn weak arnd slow,' commented Krarl.

'That's why we need horses, Lord Krarl,' answered the Councillor. 'Now tell me more of this brother of yours.'

True to Captain Horace's prediction, the Lords and their bodyguards began arriving before the two days were up.

'Can somebody tell me what the bloody hell is going on here!' screamed Lord Breakspear at his Councillor, as he struggled into his formal robes, which appeared to have slipped a size or two. 'Who invited these bastards under my roof? You will foot the cost of this from your private funds, Tramford! Do you hear me? Mark my words. Wine and food aren't cheap, Tramford, and these bastards know how to feast from another man's table. Pigs the lot of them!'

'The latest reports tell of Stronghome Keep being in a position dire, Lord. The Lower Kingdom Lords have called a council of war to discuss the next course of action. Since your lands lie closest to the Keep, here it was decided, was the best place to meet.'

'Decided by whom, Tramford. I feel your hand somewhere in this mess. Okay, let's get to it, shall we? The sooner I listen to these hogs, the sooner I can send them packing.'

Lord Breakspear closely trailed by his Councillor, were the last to enter the lively, noisy and crowded common hall where the council had been convened.

'Took your time coming, Breakspear,' shouted a stout, bearded, flaxen-haired lord.

'My lands, my hall, my prerogative, Kraxton,' shouted back Lord Breakspear as he headed for the pinnacle seat at the table. 'Now, who can tell me what the hell is going on!?'

'Why don't you ask your own Councillor, Breakspear? He is the one who orchestrated this little get together.'

'I knew it! Tramford, explain yourself and be very quick about it!' yelled the infuriated lord.

'Lords, Stronghome Keep is about to fall to the Protectorate Order. As we speak, it may have already fallen. At their head is one of their nine ascendant leaders, a high Cardinal. She wants the Keep, she wants our lands. She will be coming for us next. Our lordly heads will roll, and our kingdoms will fall into the dust of history.'

'Very poetic, Lord Tramford,' shouted Lord Kraxton, 'but may I ask how you came by all this knowledge and how do we know it is even true?'

'That's a fair question, Lord Kraxton. A quartet of our very best was sent to investigate the status of the siege of Stronghome and to venture beyond into the Green Kingdoms themselves. They have recently returned to us with this grave report. You are all familiar with the reputation of our Captain Horace here. He and his companions can give bold, first-hand testimony to my assertions.'

'We know you well Captain Horace, and Sharleen your exploits with the sword in battle has been a painful reminder to many of us over the years as to your skill and resourcefulness. Are things as serious as old fire-brand Tramford claims?' asked another thin, hawk-faced lord sitting next to Kraxton.

'I'm afraid they are, Lord Byron. The Keep is certain to fall, even I think, with our intervention. Time does not allow us to get to them before their end,' replied Horace in a grave and serious tone.

A sombre silence descended throughout the hall.

'This is all reactive nonsense. I for one will not leave these halls on a threat imagined. To take such a renowned fortress as Stronghome will have drained the Protectorate of men and resources. It will take them years to regain their strength before launching on another costly enterprise. I say we sit tight and watch their movements and intent,' said Lord Breakspear dismissively, gulping down a cup of red wine which dribbled brightly down his chin; the superstitious among the gathering seeing the foretelling of blood and death.

'Wait! Wait foar wart, littal fat lord? Foar your death? My brudar needs you now! Weel you heed his call or die?'

Krarl's deep voice, laced with pent-up power, reverberated through the hall, trembling the very cups on the table and echoing onwards. The frightened gaze of the wide-eyed lords turned suddenly to this overlooked apparition within their midst.

'Gentlemen,' announced Lord Tramford. 'Meet Lord Krarl our appointed Battlelord.'

Lord Byron was the first to rediscover his voice.

'Who...who is this...? Battlelord!? We have made no such

appointment, Tramford! What is the meaning of this?'

'Oh, you are correct, Lord Byron. This council has made no such appointment, but events have grown well beyond our parochial domain. Lord Krarl has been presented to us by his brother, Lord Morgan Ap Heston. Some of you will be familiar with this name, a name that has punched its way through our history.'

'This is madness!' spluttered Lord Breakspear. 'Have this man-thing removed from our presence at once!'

No one could recall seeing Krarl move but suddenly he was leaning over the obnoxious lord, an unseen but strongly felt force roiling out from him, bringing inexplicable fear to those in attendance; the weakest among them making involuntary sobbing noises.

'Weeth or weethout yuuu my bruudar weel make eez move. If you arrr nort ready orn this side, the fleeing Protectorate will flood into your lands seeking vengeance, wreaking havoc. You weel be divided arnd unprepared, your houses burnt, your larnd left in wrack arnd ruin. Your death inevitable. Choose arnd choose now. I leave art nightfarl, weeth or weethout you arnd your armies. CHOOSE!'

Straightening like smoke from a lamp, he flowed out of the stunned hall, leaving behind him a cavern of silence.

'And that, gentlemen, is that. Please, inform me of the outcome of your deliberations in ample time before nightfall,' said the Councillor and with a slight bow to his speechless lord, walked out in turn, followed by Sharleen, Horace, Luc and Scar.

As they emerged into the sunshine, Scar staggered and fell against the timber frame of the hall. Luc's hand snaked out and steadied his friend.

'Are you unwell, man?' he asked with a tinge of anxiety in his voice.

'Fuck!' said Scar. 'That man sends a bloody, cold spike of fear straight up my hot arse. He is very scary.'

'Yep, but I think his brother is even worse.'
'May the all-seeing goddess watch over us,' breathed Scar.

 Supporting each other, they wandered after their comrades in arms and in life.

CHAPTER XX

She swayed away from the slicing blade, her centre of gravity perfectly balanced on a point between her hips, then stepping swiftly in she flowed under the reversed slash, spinning smoothly aside and bringing her own sword into play. The clang of metal on metal and the numbing impact at her wrist was more than enough to tell her that her effort had been soundly blocked. Every morning was like this. Elisha was merciless, she did not use half measures but fought as if they were mortal enemies. Ahmya liked that. It forced her to improve. She missed Sharleen's lessons deeply though, as her technique was very different from Elisha's. It was calm and fluid, just like the big woman, whereas Elisha's was waspish and aggressive.

'You fight well, but you are too focused on hitting a target.'

The interrupting voice was honey deep and commanding.

'I have wasted many words on your teacher here, but she never listened. Now she is passing on her bad habits.'

She glanced at Elisha expecting to find the taciturn woman scowling fiercely but instead she was grinning from ear to ear like a happy teenager.

'Did you instruct Elisha in the use of the sword, Lord Morgan?' she asked the obvious.

'Well, to a fashion, but she had her own destiny to follow and was fixated on it. Flow is everything. Every attack has a counter, and every defence has a counter. Let go and find the flow. Now that you have a sound technique you must move on to the next level.'

'Care to demonstrate, old man?' invited Elisha, her grin becoming impish.

Morgan shook his head with pretend exasperation, drew his sword and stepped forward. He did not take a fighting stance but stood there with his sword held loosely in his hand, almost as if he had forgotten that it was there.

'Show me what you have learned then, my little blockhead,' he said casually to Elisha.

Ahmya had the feeling that they had transported themselves to a time long in the past and this was their familiar training ritual.

Elisha flew at him in a blur of movement.

Morgan seemed to simply step unhurriedly to one side and with a delicate swivel of his wrist appeared to wrap his blade around hers, then with a gentle flick, disarmed her, sending her sword spinning off into the air. Then with the point of his sword, tapped her twice on her neck.'

'Your speed has improved,' he said in a soft teacher's voice.

Ahmya expended a lot of effort to get her mouth to close. She had always been considered a very accomplished sword fighter, always included amongst the best. Then she had met Elisha and Sharleen and had realised she still had a lot to learn. She was just beginning to think that soon she would be able to hold her own against Elisha; now this! Her paragon example of sword expertise defeated in a second.

Elisha did not seem upset at all but quietly walked over to where her weapon lay in the dust, picked it up and began cleaning it.

'Would you like a second chance to overcome your sticking point, Elisha?' offered Morgan.

'I would like that very much, teacher,' was her very respectful reply.

'What about you Ahmya Yumi? Would you like to become my student?'

Ahmya brought herself up to her full height and bowed gracefully from the waist.

'I would be greatly honoured, Lord Morgan.'

'Excellent. I recommend that the two of you spend the rest of the day contemplating how to let go of everything you hold to be important. We will meet here at dawn tomorrow to start your training to the second level.'

As Morgan turned to leave, he saw the five youngsters from the Blue Mountains hovering uncertainly in the background. He knew what would be coming next and wondered how they would go about doing it. As he expected they came at him as one. He smiled inside, instinctively they had found their strongest point; they were pack, and as pack they hunted best.

'Lord Morgan, we were wondering if you would allow us to join in with the training?'

Morgan stopped and studied the young man. He wasn't the strongest but certainly the boldest, impulsive but fast in his decision making. A natural pack-leader in the making.

'Are you prepared to unlearn all that you have learnt; to start over from the beginning?'

'But…'

'Yes, Lord,' said the two young women in unison.

The three young men glanced at each other and nodded affirmation quickly.

Morgan could feel the loose-limbed one trying to communicate with his pack, but because they did not believe, they did not hear him. They all had potential, not half as much as their big sister, but enough to make them formidable as a group.

'Work on emptying yourself of everything you have been taught and meet me here at first light tomorrow,' he said enigmatically and continued on his way, sensing their confusion.

Bunched together they watched Morgan's broad back until he disappeared behind a tree.

'What does he mean by that, Kirk?' asked Vivian.

'How should I know. You and Steph were the ones who hastily agreed to his terms.

'Well, if he is teaching Big Sister, I thought we should be in on it,' defended Stephania.

'Too right,' added the muscular Reginal, 'but why did he look at you in such an odd way, Jake?'

The slender boy shrugged his shoulders in his trademark loose-jointed way and looked down at his feet.

The others frowned at him, looking puzzled. They felt that he was hiding something.

'Forget everything that we have learnt,' mused Kirk. 'We had better get started on that. We only have a day and a night to figure it out. Any ideas?'

'He said 'empty' not 'forget,' muttered Jacob.

No one else had anything further to add.

A grey light was just softening the black sky when Morgan arrived at the designated training ground the following morning only to find both Elisha and Ahmya already there. They were revolving smoothly around each other, their sword blades caressing with a gentle metallic sound as they performed a trance-like dance, engaging and disengaging in a sinuous and effortless flow. Morgan instantly recognised one of his training forms, the Feel of Feathered Blades. As the women stopped to acknowledge him with a bow, Morgan said.

'It's encouraging to see that you have not forgotten, Elisha, but disheartening to see that you were just plain ignoring what you were once taught. Please, continue.'

As the women continued their slow, graceful movements, Morgan sat down cross-legged on a moss-covered rock, closed his eyes and reached out tentatively towards them with his mind. Elisha's essence was struggling with itself. Pulsing erratically then smoothing out for a short time then pulsing again. Something had damaged her, but it was much more than that. Her nature always had an edge to it and either she did not know the cause or she did not want it revealed. Her essence was spiking much more than it had ever done when she was a young girl with a wild look in her eyes. Her struggle would be a long and hard one, and he wasn't even sure if she wanted to win. The other girl, in contrast, was a lake of golden light, very much like the young, lonely, plump boy who eventually grew up to become the secretive and feared Beggar Abbot. Her balance of mind and body was near perfect. It wasn't her abilities that were in question but her belief in those abilities. As soon as she opened herself to her gift, her training would truly start. Of all the people he had ever trained she was probably the most gifted. However, the possession of these questionable gifts was not an accurate indicator of how accomplished a student would become. His adopted son being the foremost example. His achievements were second to none yet he did not possess these so-called gifts. What he had was wondrously inexplicable, and that made him a very, very special person. He missed him.

As the entire awning of the heavens began to lighten with the silvered dullness of streaked metal, the Blue Mountains' youngsters straggled into the clearing, sleep still pulling on their full awareness. The forest birds were beginning their songs, and the mists still hung heavy within the gnarled branches of the trees but the air smelt clean and full of promise. Morgan felt more contented than he had for a very long time.

'Good morning, Lord Morgan. We are here to start our training,' said the outspoken one named Kirk.

'As you say, and what of your thoughts on my task for you?'

'Every attack should not be hampered by the one made before; every defence should not be hampered by the one before. Every move should be fresh, executed with clarity and full focus.'

'My compliments. Please, put your swords down and select a similar length of stick from the forest floor.'

As usual, the cub pack glanced at each other but went about their next task without a grumble. It didn't take them long to return to him armed with their sticks and an expectant look on their faces.

'Take ten paces away from each other. Bind your eyes with these strips of cloth and practice the forms your former masters taught you until you find each other.'

The youngsters did as they were told, stumbling around, disorientated, but doggedly practising what they had learnt in the Blue Mountains. Morgan watched them silently.

Soon the molten ball that was the morning sun peeped over the unending expanse of green foliage, transforming the world from grey to soft bronze and gold. A crowd of foresters had gathered at the edge of the clearing, now a training circle, making unhelpful comments and occasionally bursting into muted, mocking laughter, as one or the other of the striving youngsters fell over their own feet or stumbled over a protruding rock or interfering root.

Morgan's expression did not change, but he could feel the growing humiliation of the five students.

'Lord Morgan,' shouted an anonymous loudmouth. 'We are soon to be at war. Why waste time with these awkward children. Leave them to their game of sticks and train those of us who are true men and warriors.'

At first, Morgan pretended not to hear the spiteful comments and left the unkind spectators to have their fun. This emboldened them, and their poisoned verbal barbs flew with increasing thickness.

With the swift smoothness of an uncoiling snake, Morgan flowed to his feet and with a quiet voice and an imperious gesture he indicated two men, burly, strong-looking, rough and uncouth.

'You two! Come here!'

They hung back within the comfort of their brethren of mischief and did not come forward as commanded.

A hard voice cut loudly into the now still air.

'You heard the Green Warden. Step forward. Now!'

Greybeaver strode into the sunlight so that all could see him, his eyes fixed on the two miscreants, his mouth set in a grim line. With the five blindfolded students still working through their forms with slender sticks in the background, the two foresters straightened their arrogant spines and swaggered into the clearing and stood in front of Morgan. Not bothering to look at them he called softly across the open space.

'Jacob, would you come here, please.'

The loose-jointed young man, without removing his blindfold, walked unerringly over to Morgan. The men looked at him and frowned. They knew already that such a feat would not have been easy for them.

'Remove the cloth, Jacob,' continued Morgan in his soft voice. 'Here take my sword. I would like you to test the skill of these two fools.

Try not to hurt them too much.'

As the slender boy took his offered sword gingerly, Morgan stepped back out of the way.

Grinning confidently, the two ruffians drew their weapons and advanced on the frail looking lad with the attitude of well-practised bullies. The boy moved with the speed of a striking adder.

Where a split second before had stood a hesitant and unsure looking lad, there now materialised an unnervingly fast and competent swordsman. His borrowed sword slashed low, a searing horizontal stroke which had the nearest forester stumbling backwards in his haste to block it. Braced to receive a stunning blow on his blocking sword the brutish forester teetered off balance as Jacob, with the deft footwork of a born fighter, swivelled in a half-circle, allowing his sword to slide along the blade of his unprepared opponent without offering much resistance. Then as his body orientated itself half-way between the two foresters his arm came down in a blurring, two-handed, vertical slash which sliced a long line of blood along the shoulder and upper arm of the surprised forester, causing him to drop his sword. Adjusting his body from the hip, the boy ended his manoeuvre with a ripping upper slash which cleanly removed the first joints of the first two fingers on the sword hand of the second forester. He too dropped his weapon with a snarl of pain, and crouching over, clamped his bleeding hand between his thighs.

'Thank you, son,' said Morgan stepping back in and retrieving his sword. Please, return to your training.'

As Jacob bowed, fished out his blindfold, tied it back on and walked away, Morgan turned with a serious expression to the two furious and humiliated foresters and said to them in an even voice, still soft but edged with a tinge of power.

'You have just met your instructor in the use of the sword if you still wish to join these early morning sessions. The choice is yours to make.'

With that, he turned away to continue observing the progress of his students. There were no more interruptions from the watching spectators.

On hour later he instructed his two senior students to increase the speed of their martial dance, working them till they were pouring with sweat and they could hardly move their arms, making them switch their weapons from left to right hand, ensuring balance on all sides.

At mid-morning, under Morgan's leadership, the foresters broke camp and left the place of the Swearing Stones. As they moved through the unfolding greenery more and more warriors joined them and were organised into bands of fifty by Greybeaver and Francis Clearwater; each group was given a captain and a second in command. When they camped at the end of the day, it was no longer a gathering that was in attendance but a formidable army. Morgan called a meeting of commanders to put structure and function to this sprawling martial force. As was usual with a marching army, logistics would become the main concern. Despite his obvious faults, Stumpcutter the Pompous as he was now being called behind his back, was very good at number organisation and was placed in overall logistical command, reporting directly to Morgan. Greybeaver was to ensure that his calculations were transferred into reality and under him, bands of hunters and scavengers were sent out in waves ahead of the blossoming army to establish food cashes. Morgan's small training session was now a mass camp of striving warriors with the best swordsmen being made weapon masters in order to facilitate the growing numbers. Morgan directly took on the training of the best of the best, including the five youngsters.

Something had begun, something that was not entirely of Morgan's choosing, but it now had his focus. As always his plans moved with speed, boldness and surprise but this time, he also had his brother, a new, untried and powerful factor.

CHAPTER XXI

'Tell me again. Why did you stop the assault when your hand was almost cupping the rounded breast of success?'

The perspiring General paused, his mouth open, distracted by the vivid, sexual analogy to his decision. With an effort, he continued.

'Our scouts, Eminence, have reported the presence of a large army, disguised within the unnatural, creeping forests flanking our position. I thought it best that we prepare against an unexpected attack on our rear and to secure our lines of communication and supplies.'

'You did not think that this army was skulking behind trees for a reason? That perhaps they are but woodsmen who are timid of fighting like honest men in the open? That they were meant to achieve exactly as they have done? To divert you from your purpose?'

'But...'

'My goodness, darling! You are a general! Start thinking like one. Tactics, man, tactics! Someone is trying to buy time for our beleaguered rock squirrels. I do not recommend that we try to find out why at this juncture. Let's first crack their nut then we will have gained a fortified nest to better deal with the rest. Get back to your post at once, General, and stop wasting time.'

Her voice had not risen once, but he felt as if his ears were ringing with her admonishment. Embarrassed he glanced around to see who were the witnesses to his humiliation.

'Is there something else that you wish to tell me, General?'

'No, Eminence, I…'

'Then let me remind you, darling, that you have urgent matters to attend to. Matters that cannot be addressed whilst you grovel here on your knees.'

'Yes, Mistress…'

'Eminence, darling. My title is Eminence. Please try to remember that,' she said with a distracted air, already appearing to have forgotten the overly, armoured man at her feet and even why he was there in the first place.

'Yes, Eminence.'

Appearances were beside the point, distracted she certainly was not. Her mind was racing and time was trying to get ahead of it. It wouldn't be long before those cockroaches would find their way back to the Holy City and chitter into the smelly, waxy ears of the grasping First Citizen. He would undoubtedly make moves against her. Her family and estates lay vulnerable. She had not made the proper efforts to secure them, so swiftly had she executed her plans to advance to the frontier on a wild card. Still, one must accept collateral damage in every war, and this was war. Not just this little sordid battle that she was now caught up in, but her plans for her ultimate future. When she got to her goal, it would be time enough to salvage what she had lost on the way.

***

Krarl raced ahead of the small band of furiously galloping men. Their horses were lathered and blowing as their riders coaxed them onwards, grim and determined. Most of them were not surprised at the prodigious stamina and speed of the man they followed, but the newcomers to their party felt a deep unease, some might call it fear, of the unnatural display of raw energy expended in such a casual way. They, however, played it smart and kept their thoughts to themselves.

Long before nightfall, the lords had made their decision and had given the order to mobilize their armies, even the self-indulgent and peevish Lord Breakspear. In reality, their forces more resembled large bands of belligerent raiding parties rather than an army, but these raiders were accustomed to continuous, hard fighting where the risk of personal injury or death was an ever-present possibility. Numbers were not everything.

Krarl was leading a task force of elite fighting men and women. Their straightforward objective was to get to Stronghome Keep before it fell. They were all volunteers; Captain Horace, Luc, Scar, Pollock, thirty others chosen for their fighting skills, luck in battle and nastiness of attitude. All selected from a smattering of the other lords' fighting forces, and of course, Sharleen, who could exhibit all of the aforementioned qualities and who, under no circumstances, would be separated from Krarl. He from his brother's knowledge knew of a backdoor into the Keep; information that only three living persons now had. The plan was that he was to meet at the Keep with his twin, who would be leading a similar force. Would such a small party make a difference? The answer was a resounding, yes, as there were no other in this world as Morgan and Krarl, if they managed to rendezvous in time. Would it be enough to stop the Keep from falling? The answer here would be, no, as unfortunately, in the end, numbers did matter. But Morgan's planned objective was garnering on a different outcome, but only his twin knew what was on his mind.

'Leave orses ere,' commanded Krarl. 'Two to guard. The rrest, climb,' then he was off up the moon-lit mountainside, climbing into the hard, icy, cold. The others hastily scampered after him.

The route across the mountain's face was ice-crusted, bone-numbing and treacherously slippery, with both handholds and toeholds filled in with smooth, transparent ice. In addition, the wind scoured across the unforgiving rock canvass, chilling the traversing climbers down to their very core and tugging vengefully on their clothing as if resenting their effrontery. Two men, their fingers locked from the cold, were torn off and sent plummeting to their deaths, bouncing off of the diamond-hard rock-face, bones breaking and flesh bursting from the force of their spiralling fall. Their comrades acknowledged their fate helplessly and silently for there was nothing they could do about it. Everyman was an island onto himself, his personal destiny fused to his ability.

As the traumatised warriors inched their way down onto a broad, open ledge, their nerves and muscle fibres twitching uncontrollably from the strain and cold, they saw Krarl and another man, heads close together as if deep in conversation, the wind whipping around them, flapping and snapping their clothing. Huddled around them was another group of warriors, indistinguishable in the dark from the granite rocks of the mountain. The ledge appeared to be a dead-end, and Scar, the last off of the barely discernable cliff trail, wobbled over to Horace and Luc and sobbed out into the whistling wind.

'Did he bring us here to die!'

His words were whipped away and he had no idea, nor did he care, if his companions had heard him or not. He just wanted to feel warmth once again.

After a short interval, the stranger that Krarl had been conversing with, turned away and walked towards the cliff face. Krarl joined him and together they appeared to be straining at something, then with a shattering of ice like a rare collection of priceless, glass bottles, something heavy and ponderous, indicating a great, solid weight, grated and groaned, creating an open, dark maw in the rock face. The shorter of the two men turned and gestured, then disappeared with Krarl into the yawning hole. Men staggered to their feet and stumbled after them. As they entered the tomb-like space, the spiteful wind immediately died, but the cold, if that was possible, seemed to get even colder, a dead cold, and the darkness, so black that the imagination swept them away to a place of despair and loneliness with only their numbed sense of touch keeping them anchored in the world at the living end of the veil. They fumbled endlessly inside the bowels of a long dead giant and just when they were beginning to feel as though their skulls would shatter like the ice shards outside, a faint light could be discerned greying the endless, stygian blackness. Then their silence was invaded by the loud clamouring panic of warning bells, which made already jumpy and overstrained warriors snatch with frozen fingers at the even colder handles of their reluctant to draw weapons. Disjointed tongues of orange-yellow flames danced with agitation at the ends of their vision as hitherto unseen figures leapt surprised, to defend what was still theirs for the moment.

'Stand down, holders of Stronghome, we are allies rushed to stand by your side,' came a deep, commanding voice from their vanguard. 'We are not the enemy.'

'That's Morgan!' whispered Scar in Luc's ear.

'I don't care if he's the archangel, so long as he gets us out of this bloody cold!' shivered Luc.

'The arch who?' enquired Scar with chattering teeth.

'Never mind,' grumbled Luc.

'Whatever he is, he is not of this world and neither is his brother,' interjected a grim Horace. 'For their sake, I hope they stand down or they will all be dead before the enemy breaks their walls.'

'Stand down you stupid bastards!' shouted Luc at the menacing defenders. 'Can't you recognize friend from foe? For the goddesses sake, I want to feel warm again before I die! Do you have any ale left?'

At this some of the shielded warriors crouching behind the flickering torchlight began to grin, loosening their grips on their weapons and straightening their cramped spines.

'Who the bloody blazes are you!' came a booming voice from within their ranks.

'Morgan Ap Heston with volunteers from the Green and Lower Kingdoms come to your aid.'

'Morgan?' shouted a more youthful voice. 'Sheath your weapons, fools! The goddess has granted the dying wish of Housecarl

Stonerider.

'Shut it, you idiot,' grumbled an embarrassed Graham as he pushed his way through to the front.

With Captain Guy Bastonet by his side, the Stronghome warrior stood in front of Krarl and Morgan.

'Glad you decided to come back, Morgan,' said Guy with an open grin. 'Graham here has been dying to arm wrestle with you again.'

Graham frowned but spoke directly to Morgan, ignoring his friend's jibe.

'Welcome, Ap Heston. It is not the best time for a happy return visit but we are gladdened to see you all the same. You and your merry band of warriors.'

As his eyes roved quickly left and right they came to rest on Krarl, and his frown deepened.

'May I introduce my brother Karl. He is my equal in all things.'

Despite the less than perfect conditions, there was a pregnant pause as those in the know, more than two-thirds of the present company, digested this announcement.

'Welcome, Lord Karl,' said Graham smoothly. 'Please, I invite you to meet with our Lord. I guarantee that this time his arms will be more open than the last. If they are not, then I have a fool for a lord.'

Graham and Guy led the way out of the courtyard with Morgan and Krarl following and Sharleen in tow.

Horace looked down with a furrowed brow as Scar nudged him on the arm and indicated with his eyes and a gesture of his chin a small, separate gathering of warriors.

'Look it's that weird but gorgeous fighter with the pert backside and her mad, scary sword sister. The one's Sharleen was in the company of. And look aren't those the strange young'uns from the Blue Hills?'

'Blue Mountains, and yes, I see them.'

Immediately after the words left his mouth, Ahmya caught his gaze and wandered over to them with a fierce-eyed Elisha by her side and the Blue Mountain youngsters following.

'Well met, Captain Horace,' she said, grasping his forearm in a warrior's grip. 'I see you have also been invited to this little private party.'

Horace shrugged his thick shoulders.

'My companions and I always fight where the fighting is hardest. It's our duty in this life and will buy us a better one in the next.'

'Then why is that one staring at my sister with hunger lust in his eyes? Tell him to be careful, or he might just find himself in that better place short of one tiny appendage,' said Elisha in a loud and direct tone.

Scar immediately adopted a hurt and innocent attitude.

Ignoring them both, Ahmya nodded to Horace and said.

'Our roles are to protect the Lords Morgan and Krarl at all cost so my guess is that where they stand the fighting will be at its thickest. So there we will meet before this night is ended.'

Morgan and Krarl, led by Graham and Guy, found the Lord of Stronghome standing on the Keep's battlements, with four other Housecarls guarding his person. The moonlight shone coldly around them casting deep shadows in unexpected and unusual places. The broad walkway on which they stood was skewed and crooked, a testimony to the battering the walls had received and their near collapse. It was not a place to be loitering when the next assault took place.

'Lord Coulthain, Lord Morgan Ap Heston and his brother, Lord Krarl have come to us with reinforcements from the Green and Lower Kingdoms.'

'Ah, Lord Morgan,' said a noticeable aged Lord Coulthain, 'I apologise for misjudging your intentions on our first meeting, but unless you've brought an army with you, I'm afraid you may have come here to die with us.'

'May I present my brother, lord, and no, we did not come here to die but to fight. We entered your fortress by a long-hidden entrance at your rear. I suggest that you prepare to evacuate all noncombatants before it is too late. The longer we can delay the fall of your aerie the more time we have to sharpen the talons of the Lower and Green Kingdoms.'

'Ah, this is your plan then is it, Morgan Ap Heston? We are to be the damned goat tied to a bloody stake! And what of this back entrance that you spoke of? I suppose, Captain Bastonet, you also had knowledge of this? Another subterranean secret of my own home which you did not see fit to share.'

'It was not mine to share, lord.'

Sucking air over his teeth in irritation, Lord Coulthain turned his attention back to Morgan.

'This is still my fortress, Lord Morgan, and I will command here until I no longer have breath to breathe.'

'We are not here to wrestle away your grasp on what is yours, Lord, but your position is doomed. We have come to ensure that from this misfortune we may still throw a winning hand.'

'Graham,' said a disgruntled Lord Coulthain. 'Oversee the evacuation of the women, children and injured.'

'Be warned, lord, not all will be able to escape via this route. It is a treacherous way to be delivered from despair,' said Morgan in a level voice. 'We will have to rig ropes and pound spikes of iron into the very rock to hold them fast and prevent them from falling to their deaths.'

'Very well, Lord Morgan, get what you need and see to it. Graham will assist you in everything.'

'Thank you, Lord. May I have permission for my brother and I to lead the vanguard when your walls are breached?'

'No one here shall deny you further glory or death, Morgan Ap Heston. Feel free to forge your own destiny.'

'Thank you, Lord. My brother and I will start immediately on laying out the route of rescue. We are best suited for this task.'

The Lord of Stronghome had already returned to staring emptily at the icy, lunar landscape and did not bother to acknowledge him further, so Morgan turned to the quietly observing elder Housecarl, John the Grey-beard, and added.

'Please, would you send word as soon as the hostilities are rejoined?'

The wise, old fellow nodded gently but did not speak.

CHAPTER XXII

The smell came first. A mixture of wood smoke, putrefaction, blocked and open sewers and the assorted aroma from a broad selection of animals and their natural produce. Then as the spiralling road crested a bare hill denuded of all vegetation except for the occasional twisted and blackened brush, there on a flat plain by the sea, was that famous vista. Most would describe it as awe-inspiring and spectacular, a select few would name it a blight on the face of mother nature. All would think it significant; a statement of mankind and what he was capable of, there on the stage, to be played over and over again until he was exterminated. Energetic, restless, irrepressible and inventive. Like detritus from a massive wave dumped before a large, gleaming cliff that was a huge defensive outer wall, were buildings of every description, from ramshackle, hovels to well-ordered stone and wood houses protected within neat white-washed enclosures. Everything here was without planning, space used that was available or acquired by some means, legal or otherwise. Occasionally, a tree or small, green patches could be seen, but mostly, the entire earth before the wall was covered with the irregular dwellings of man, heat sizzling in the air and a great feeling of thirst prevailing. Then this tidal sweep of buildings seemed to break on the very wall itself, some sticking to its sides like barnacles on sea-polished rock. Entrance beyond this demarcation of authority was guarded by an impressive, bronze-clad gate, which at the moment, lay open, but its servants, iron garbed men, controlled and checked all who sought to enter, extolling from them payment in various guises, turning away those who could not pay the required toll. Beyond this wall was stamped order, rigorously designed and policed. It all had the appearance of sanctums within sanctums, with each check-point becoming more secluded and exclusive. In all, the way inwards was demarcated by three, circular, sentinel walls, each more impressive, one way or the other, from its outer sisters. At the centre of this remarkable fortified city, sat an immense, marble citadel, overlooking and towering above all like an indisputable god over its subjects. This was the Holy City, and the three tired and road weary emissaries did not stop to admire the marvel laid out before them with their red-rimmed, dust-clouded eyes. They had been witnesses to its gloriousness a myriad of times before, and their simple desire was to unburden themselves of their duty and sink into the sumptuous, luxuriating baths designed purely for the privileged. As they neared the outer city, their dulled, exhausted minds barely registered the roar of unwashed humanity going about its daily chore to find existence. They were not harassed or bothered as they trudged onwards for the badges they wore were well known and death awaited anyone stupid enough to delay the messengers of the god.

They passed through, from the Gate of the Believer to the Gate of the Promised, through the Gate of the Virtuous and into the Enclave of Heaven, a tranquil space filled with singing birds and running water, where they were escorted immediately into the presence of the First Citizen.

In the middle of an empty room made of cold stone, a fat man with a long, wispy beard and piercing, intelligent eyes, sat on a hard, undecorated, wooden chair. Everything about him seemed soft, except his gaze, which glittered like broken glass. At his feet, shackled to an iron ring fastened to the rough, uneven paving stones, was a man of middle years. He was exceptionally handsome, slim and elegant and although he tried to portray an image of serenity and calmness, the corner of his mouth twitched incessantly and uncontrollably. As the three emissaries were ushered into this barren reception, they fell to their knees, prostrating themselves before the fat man and pressed their foreheads into the bare floor. They pretended that they had not seen the chained man, but they knew him well. Their bellies tightened with nerves for they recognised that they were caught like mice in the squeezing trap of a power struggle and the news they were bringing would mire them even deeper.

'How did the bitch answer to her crime of ambition?' was the direct opening question; no false pleasantries, welcome or preliminaries pretended.

None of the emissaries moved, and the face of the shackled man twitched violently.

'Well? Are your ears clogged with dust and your tongues stuck with glue? I asked a question!'

Even the voice sounded fat, but this observation caused the three men to shake even more.

'She claims that all she does is carried out with the interest of the Holy City with its people in mind and since she is already there, then she is the one best suited to deliver this task.'

'Do you see, merchant, how your ungrateful niece conducts herself? She brings shame to your house. As its head what do you advise me to do?'

The fat man appeared to be addressing the man on the floor at his feet, but his attention was riveted on the emissaries. The chained man tightened his lips and did not respond.

'Emissaries, let me introduce you to my guest, the Merchant Lord of the House of Wuzetian. I am sure you are familiar with that august name. Even though they are foreigners and newcomers we have treated them more than fairly and allowed them to grow. Now they turn their backs on us for none other but selfish reasons. This saddens us deeply.'

Then his voice rose, rebounding around the chamber.

'Tell me, Lord! What am I to do? What am I to do with this niece of yours? This wanton woman who threatens us with our own armies? I await your advice. Tell me!'

The man questioned did not answer, but tiny beads of perspiration sprang out around his stylishly greying temples despite the coolness of the room.

'I did not hear you, Lord,' said the fat man, his voice low and conversational once again. 'Please, repeat what you said.'

The three emissaries very much wanted to leave, but their unknown parts in this play were not finished yet, and they had not been dismissed.

'No, no. I shall not risk a civil war by doing that. Men's loyalties must always be clear. Give me another option.'

Silence deafened the space.

'What!? That is indeed a hard measure. Do you think that it will make her come to her senses?'

The disturbing monologue continued.

'Emissaries, My adviser, Lord Wuzetian, has suggested that we send a hard message to our wayward Cardinal showing her that she is in danger of losing far more than she will gain if she continues on this present course. He advises sending her the head of her dear mother to debate rightful action.'

The elegant and stately man squeezed his eyes shut but could not stop the tears from escaping. The three emissaries stared at the flagstones at their feet. The First Citizen was indeed risking what he said he would not. The House of Wuzetian was powerful and influential. It was very much possible that this decision could force the hands, hitherto being sat upon, of the remainder of the Conclave. Driving them to either unite behind the First Citizen or polarize their positions. No one knew for sure how much Cardinal Wuzetian had seduced them to her hidden agenda. They thanked the god that it was not their duty to inform the First Citizen of this.

'Emissaries, I grant you the honour of delivering this message in person as a reward for your sterling service to our city. You will depart with the rising of the sun on the morrow.'

The three men turned pale, and if they had been allowed a meal beforehand, they would have emptied their stomachs there and then. They had just heard their death sentence, and there was no escaping their fate. With minds blank with incomprehension as to the road they had found themselves on, the emissaries bowed low to the man who had condemned them without good reason and set out to prepare for their last journey on this good earth.

The First Citizen hardly noticed their departure. He was a direct descendant from the holy line going right back to the saintly Cardinal Smithers, one of the very founding fathers. Who did this interloper think she was to dare to challenge him! He would send her entire family to her, piece by piece, until she returned to his city to receive his judgement. He had been made aware of her scheming, but he had not expected her to have made such a bold move. None of her family had martial skills, and none were connected to any of the generals. Yet there she was, in control of frontline veterans, men who had been fighting at the very edge of the Empire for years and may not even have seen the Holy City. The god knows where their loyalties may lie. First thing was first, however. His primary duty was to secure the Conclave. He had to find out who her supporters might be and outmanoeuvre them. He had the city guard, but even here he would have to start overturning some stones. He did not want any more nasty surprises hiding in dark places.

Heaving his bulk from his creaking chair, he walked absently from the stone chamber leaving the Lord of Merchants chained to the pavement. He had already forgotten of his existence.

***

'We have received word from our benefactor. She urges us to move swiftly.'

'Of course, but did she indicate in which direction? I don't remember her seeking our advice before embarking on this risky venture! She has exposed our hand and left us jumping at shadows.'

'She has always been impetuous, but now the First Citizen is awakened, and the god knows what his demented mind will conjure.

She pushes us to engage the Shadow Guild.'

'Those who put their hands in a basket of snakes will be most certainly bitten. I for one, will not go there, and there will be others of a similar mind.'

'But you are the Spy-master, Father! Can you not get our sympathisers in the Conclave to take action?'

'Action!? The only action they will take is to burrow deeper down. If we show them too much, they will throw us to the wolves to save their skins from the wrath of the First Citizen.'

'Then what do you suggest we do.'

'We eliminate all loose ends and find some scape-goats to offer up to the purges that are expected to come any minute now. It is time for us to survive and await the outcome.'

'What about Cardinal Wuzetian's family? Should we not help them.'

'We were not the ones to abandon them. She has killed her own. Do you not wonder what she would do to us? It is time to play smart, Father. It is the only way for us to survive this mess.'

***

The Lord of Merchants had risen to his once high position by using his knowledge and skill to gain the right patronage, by being patient, and by knowing how to keep secrets; lessons learnt from his ancestors. More than being the Lord of Merchants he was the Lord of Secrets. People would go to great lengths to accommodate you if you owned a part of something they did not want to be known and if you demonstrated to them that future mutual profit was an end play in the negotiation, then they would become your friends forever. Armed with his secrets, it didn't take long before he arrived at the poisonous gates of the Shadow Guild themselves. Used by the Empire for generations to track down and kill potential leaders in conquered lands, they had steadily acquired great wealth. The partnership between wealth and secrets was a great opportunity and an intelligent, educated, capable yet private man who stood well-respected in the light of the state was best placed to oversee this partnership. His position was known only to those whose roles made it essential to be informed. Not even his family knew. His promising niece, whom he hoped one day to become his heir, was unaware. The Conclave did not have a clue and only the god knew what knowledge the First Citizen had. The shining light around him camouflaged the dark. To them, he was just a self-made, trumped-up merchant king, but in reality, he was Guild Master to the Shadow Guild, the Guild of Assassins. Despite all of this he was powerless to save his sister and maybe even his family, but perhaps the time was right to assure the position of his niece; she had forced her graduation day upon him, like any gifted student, and it was up to him to move with it rather than fight it. He loved his family, but for every gain, one must accept a loss.

Chained to this floor was not such a bad thing. It would make people feel injustice towards his fate and soften them up for his eventual approach. It would put the First Citizen in a bad light; the light of a bully. Not that this would change much for the First Citizen was formidable, if a bit mad, but this madness made him unpredictable and twice as dangerous. Unless this madman decided on a whim to have him executed in this empty chamber, he would bide his time. Eventually, his solitary confinement would come to an end. When this happened, he would start the subtle manipulations of the musical strands that made up the orchestra of his domain.

CHAPTER XXIII

A deep horn, bass and urgent, reverberated through the Keep and echoed forlornly up the sides of the frigid mountain. Morgan and Krarl, working swiftly together, had run both a hand line and a foot line along the treacherous face of the icy mountain, pinning the ropes intermittently to iron, bolt anchors. Their movements were sure and coordinated, giving the impression of two beetles moving crablike across a wall. They were in the middle of helping a group of severely injured warriors across, a man each tied to their backs when the warning horn was sounded. They instantly increased their pace, scuttling at an alarming rate across the abyss. Then having delivered their packages, sprang onto unseen handholds and traversed back above the heads of the toiling and straining evacuees, who could only stop and stare at them in amazement and wonder as they raced along where it was impossible for any normal man to even inch his way across.

'Do you think that their father was a mountain goat?' shouted Graham into the ear of Guy who was staring open-mouthed at the unmatched pair of climbers.

Guy shook his head but did not comment as first Morgan then Krarl leapt down from fifteen feet above their heads onto the slippery rock on which they were standing. They did this effortlessly and did not even miss a stride as they headed for the tunnel entrance passing deftly the queue of noncombatants waiting to cross to safety. Before they entered, Krarl turned and gestured to the two astonished men; he appeared to be grinning but they were not sure.

'You may think he has been invited to a feast,' grumbled Graham as he edged his way after them.

The interior of the besieged fortress was a place of mayhem, noise and organised confusion. Commanders yelled until they were hoarse, at armed units of men who seemed to be tramping this way and that without a discernable pattern. Morgan paused for a short moment, took stock of what was happening, then began to give crisp, clear orders. Whenever men or groups of men hesitated, Krarl stepped in. The sixty manned unit brought in by the brothers demonstrated precisely what was required by their disciplined and efficient reactions to Morgan's commands. Contrary to prior assumptions, Morgan sealed off the huge cavernous hall where the Lord of Stronghome Keep had placed his forces earlier in the expectation of making his last stand. This selfsame lord fumed and raged impotently as a disturbingly, chilling and smiling Krarl supported by Sharleen, Horace, Luc, and Scar, blocked the barricaded, double-leafed, oaken door to their attempted entry.

'This is my House!' he yelled. 'And nowhere is barred to my person. Move out of my way immediately!'

It was Housecarl John who diffused the dangerous situation.

'Lord, there already lies a formed line behind us. Should we not join them instead of splitting our forces?'

Lord Coulthain glanced at the spot indicated by John to find Morgan standing quietly at the centre of a four ranked phalanx of shield warriors with Elisha on one side of him and Ahmya on the next. Behind them, on an elevated platform were three rows of bowmen. All eyes were focused on him, grim and anonymous behind helms of iron. So as not to appear a great fool, he came to his senses and strode towards Morgan, his shoulders thrown back and his chest pushed out.

'You are standing in the spot meant for the Lord of this Keep, sir. Stand aside!'

Morgan did not answer or bristle to the belligerent affront but stepped, relaxed and unconcerned to his right. Lord Coulthain advanced into the vacated space with his Housecarls. However, despite his action, the pinnacle of the defence immediately adjusted and re-centred around Morgan.

Before the newcomers could even settle themselves behind their shields, the fortress shook as if struck by the angered hand of a god. From beyond the inner walled partition where the huge common hall once lay, there came a thunderous, muffled sound, like an avalanche of rocks tumbling down a mountainside, followed by a loud cracking and breaking as the ceiling and roof gave way. The Lord of Stronghome felt the heat of embarrassment seize his face and neck with a red and ruddy glow. If he had been allowed his desire, he and his men would now be dead without even the chance to lift their swords. He resisted the urge to glare over at the man on his left who stood nonchalantly with his insufferable brother now by his side.

'Shields up,' drifted over a controlled command and the Lord felt himself obeying and gritted his teeth in annoyance. 'Archers ready!'

Shouts of triumph and bloodlust vibrated echoingly through the partitioned wall, then after a pause, the resounding boom of assault by battering rams made clear their intent. By the third set of blows cracks began to split the mortar, and by the fifth, stones began to fall out. At first, slowly, then with increasing speed, becoming a river of falling cut stones. Before the dust could clear, Morgan's steady voice broke through.

'Archers, Release!'

The buzz of a myriad of deadly darts tore through the dirtied air, followed closely by dull, wet, thwacks as iron barbs pierced armour and found living flesh.

'As one! Hold your line! Push on my command,' said Morgan, his authoritative voice forging unity amongst the warriors.

'Now! Push! Swords! Stab! Stab! Hold the line! Hold the line!' Together we stand! Separate and we die! Push!'

Warriors, born for single combat, itched to jump free of their comrades, swords swinging, but Morgan's iron voice kept them leashed to his will. They did not break as wave after wave of maddened and frustrated Protectorate soldiers flung themselves on their shields, tearing at them with bleeding fingers, oblivious to the iron that ripped out their bowels, fighting until death pulled them away from the living.

Even Morgan was taken aback by the ferocity of the enemy. He felt Krarl containing himself, fighting with technical skill, matching Morgan's every move, a weird grin on his face. Sharleen, ever by his side, mirrored him with a serene, detached calmness. On Morgan's other side was Ahmya, sinuous and fast, using shield and sword as both weapons of offence and defence, and next to her was Elisha, every move intending to kill. Her savagery was breathtaking, and a bit unnerving. Everyone who had chosen to follow Morgan and Krarl of their own violation was in the front line. Morgan felt a surge of pride as he once used to feel in the old days, when he was young of mind and fresh of vision, when he saw himself as one with humanity.

Morgan's plan was to delay and contain, not win. As long as this fortified, ice-encrusted rock stood, the people who lived on either side of it would not unite. He needed it to fall, but he also needed the seasoned warriors fighting to keep it from falling. He needed their skill and numbers to fight on another front but with the fire of brotherhood in their veins, not just for the exhortations and gold of an unworthy lord. Although the widest and most furious, this was not the only point under attack. Barricades of rough stone and mortar had been thrown up to block main corridors but as he and his chosen fought here, they were being torn down one by one, with crazed soldiers, long denied their goal and driven to please their mistress and Empire, flooding into them like wasps, hungry to kill the armoured ants within. Men had been given orders to retreat steadily before this flood and not allow themselves to become overwhelmed by it. Coordinating this ordered retreat and protecting its open lines were captain Bastonet and his giant friend, Housecarl Stonerider. They seemed to be everywhere, driven by an energy unmatched, pulling men back and sending them scrambling through the tunnel, joining the long line of escapees who were increasingly being caught in a bottleneck.

'Can't they move any faster?' asked Guy, with despair colouring his voice.

'No, my friend. I'm afraid some of us will have to die,' answered Graham sadly. 'Morgan Ap Heston knows this. The men and women he brought here are his sacrifice for us. This broken rock will be their tomb.'

'Do they know this?'

'Yes, they do. That is why they volunteered. They are the best of the best. Noble and courageous despite their low standing in our world.'

Of the chosen sixty, only half remained in the open halls of dust, blood and ruin. Among the dead, eyes open and sightless, was young Kirk, his body broken by a mace. They had been fighting as a unit within a unit; covering each other. Jake was the fastest, better than all of them with a weapon in his hand, his reflexes snake-like and loose-limbed. He kept them from splitting, but Kirk was the thinker, always sensing when they were about to step out of line or drop too far back. Regi was their rock, enabling them to stand firm, strong as an oak tree when all they wanted to do was to break and run. Stephi was second to Jake, weaving her shield and sword around Vivian, the weakest in the line, keeping her out of harm's way, snapping this way and that. Their breaths came in desperate gasps, and their arms felt like they were wrapped in lead, but they kept going, not wanting to disappoint, not wanting to fall short of the mark set by Big Sister. It was then that fate cut one of their strings. Jake slipped, on what, no one knew, but his shield arm dropped. A short, stocky Protectorate soldier, a master of weapons by his movement, in a blink of an eye, seized the moment. His muscled arm whipped down knocking Jake's shield wide, directly into Reginald's face, breaking his nose and bursting his lips in a shower of blood. Then in a blur, his arm heaved back, projecting the short, heavy mace gripped in his gauntleted hand with terrifying force and velocity. Kirk saw the danger and flung himself across his friend, intending to bring his shield to cover, but time was not on his side, so he used his own body. The thud of the mace and the crack of his spine had a finality to it. With a small cry, Jake twisted and spun low, lancing his sword up into the groin of his friend's killer. The agonised scream of the soldier was spitefully rewarding. It was in that moment of shared anguish that the Blue Mountain's youngsters truly bonded. Their minds linked with a pure vengeance and they became a thing to be feared.

Morgan, Krarl and Ahmya felt the explosion of their grief and the impact of what came next. This is what Morgan had wanted them to achieve through their training, but it wasn't to be. Only the grim reality of battle could unlock their potential. Deep down, Morgan knew that this was why he had allowed them to come and felt shame.

The defenders had retreated as far as they could go and as instructed by Morgan, the back rows began to melt away through the two doorways at their backs. First, the archers, then the fourth and third ranks of the shield warriors.

'Hold! Hold!' shouted Morgan above the hubbub. 'First rank, on my mark! Forward!'

With a mighty heave, back muscles and legs close to giving way, the exhausted front row dug deep, pulling on their last resources, pushing the colossal weight of the enemy backwards. The Lord of Stronghome was still with them along with the last of his Housecarls, old John. The others lay dead in the dust and dirt. On shaking legs he screamed and cursed, his shield shattered, but his sword cutting and pummeling in a demonic weave, all his pent-up frustration, anger and disappointment from life come raging to the fore. John, economical and efficient with his moves, tried to keep his Lord protected, but he surged beyond the sheltering wings of his shield line. They were soon beset on all sides by sweating men, howling in a beastlike manner, who were anxious for their blood. Even with the canny Housecarl by his side, the reckless behaviour of Lord Coulthain was counting heavily against him and his finely made mail shirt was rent and torn, bright blood oozing between the links giving it the colour of rust. As the devil possessed lord exchanged blistering blows with two soldiers on his right, three came at old John on his left. The Housecarl did not retreat but stepped forward boldly, smashing his chipped and dented shield in a metallic bang of boss on boss, into that of the oncoming antagonist, then with a deft movement of his feet and balance, turned his opponent enough to hinder the approach of the second soldier advancing behind. At the same time, his sword arm flew straight out with the point of his weapon slipping between the third soldier's shield guard, bursting the link of his mailed shirt and skewering his pumping heart. Then fate took a perverse hand to mock his martial skill. As the soldier crumpled towards death, his ribs locked the sword piercing him in place. Before the unexpectedly encumbered Housecarl could react and kick the body free of his weapon, a roaring Protectorate sergeant reared up as if from nowhere and brought a nasty looking battle-axe tearing through the air in a vicious sweep. The old campaigner tucked his chin and head down between his shoulders and relaxed his body, allowing his knees to collapse under him. He felt the breeze of death as the heavy blade whistled centimetres above his skull, and quickly sent a prayer of thanks to the goddess of mercy. But fate wanted to have her way despite her divine sister's intervention. The axe blade continued on its unwavering journey and cleaved with a solid thunk into the back of Lord Coulthain, shattering his chain mail asunder and sticking wetly between his ribs. With a roar of agony, he spun, sending a lightning reverse stroke clean through the jugular of his unintentional attacker. This deadly and instinctive response, however, left him open and of his two previous attackers, one sent his sword blade crashing down on the Lord's shoulder, snapping the clavicle in half, and the other stabbed his sword point directly into the throat of Coulthain as he turned back, spitting with rage. With a wet, gargled sound he pulled back and fell on the hard stone of his Keep, his eyes still burning with challenge and fire. Then an unleashed Krarl was there, flinging men away, stamping on their shocked bodies, breaking bones and sundering limbs. The enemy soldiers, even filled with battle lust as they were, fell back with dismay and fear, leaving a broad circle free around old John as he bent low to cradle the head of his dying Lord.

With Krarl's sudden and unexpected departure on his personal mission of rescue, fired by what reasoning no one maybe except Morgan could figure, the embattled front-line warriors now on their own, began to fray and break apart. Morgan, seeing this, removed the shackles from his restraint, and like his brother, released what he truly was. Hurling his shield from his arm, it became a deadly, spinning missile, which took the head of an enemy commander clean off of his shoulders. Then moving forward with graceful speed and sinuous action swept up a discarded sword with his now free left hand. Armed with twin swords he became a whirlwind of destruction, slipping and weaving through the enemy ranks, his arms too fast for the eye to follow, his body a picture of sublime movement, swirling like smoke, untouchable. Lost in his wake, it was here that Ahmya found her awakening. She felt rather than saw the presence of a supreme battlelord. All her training manifested itself in his flawless example, and she relaxed into it and found herself; her gift was released and blossomed within her, becoming holistic for the first time in her life. Energy pulsed deep in her abdomen and her mind entered the battle void. She became a killing machine, a man killer, second only to Morgan and Krarl.

The brothers drew abreast of each other and immediately joined in a mystic link of destruction. For the first time ever they had become one in battle. As if in a trance they swirled around each other, changing sides, flowing with unpredictability, killing in a fashion both beautiful and appalling. Men pulled away from them, both friend and foe, feeling awe, fear and sometimes revulsion. They were the brothers of death, and as death bringers, they were similarly admired and hated, for the taking of life should not have been so easy to do. Their every touch appeared to be mortal, and men died before they knew that they were dead, so swift was their passing.

As the enemy, unable to flee for the weight of their own numbers behind them, pushed back on themselves, creating a no man's land where all were afraid to tread. Guarding this stretch of emptiness stood a now still and dangerous looking Morgan and Krarl, Ahmya, Elisha, Horace, Luc, Scar, Old John, Sharleen, Pollock, Greybeaver and the Blue Mountain youngsters. The others had either perished or were withdrawing through the twin doors at the back.

In the silence of the broken, dust filled hall, there was a great oddness as the vanguard of an army of thousands stood rooted to where they stood and stared in trepidation at fifteen defenders, like buffalo before wolves.

The stalemate did not last long. A man wearing the ornate armour of a Protectorate general stood up from the top of the ruble where the outer wall once lay and shouted into the stillness.

'Don't just stand there you craven idiots! Kill them! Kill them all!'

This cold slap in the face as to their duty galvanised the soldiers back into action. But mostly, they felt guilt and anger that they, an all-conquering professional army had been hamstrung with fear by fifteen rock warriors. With a roaring challenge, more to give them courage than to overawe the enemy, they charged back into the hall.

They did not get very far.

Morgan and Krarl, still linked as one, took two steps ahead of their comrades and planted their feet in the face of the charging horde. Instinctively, they placed a hand on each other's shoulder, but it wasn't because they needed reassurance. They were taking the first tentative step in sharing, joining and focusing their power. Behind them, Ahmya, Sharleen and young Vivian appeared entranced as if transported to a place without their own volition; pulled into a semi-dream state. Only the three other youngsters noticed this strange behaviour. Everyone else was focused on the unusual twins who were their undisputed leaders. These two men seemed frozen in place as they stared into the heart of the onrushing enemy, like two marble, guardian statues.

Suddenly, the first line of running, howling soldiers faltered, and the second line crashed into them, bowling them off of their feet. Then they too faltered, their eyes rolling up into their heads, they bowels turning to ice, their minds filled with the frozen tendrils of fear, eating into their very being. Men pressed their hands to their stomachs and folded onto the cold, stone floor as if overcome by a potent dose of the flux. Others gripped their heads between shaking hands, teeth chattering uncontrollably and wondered about in dazed circles, whimpering and trembling. With a domino effect, the phenomenon spread back through the ranks and overtook even the general who fell to his knees mumbling incoherently.

Captain Horace turned to his amazed brethren and commanded in a hoarse, urgent voice.

'Go, Go, you fools! Time has been bought for us! Let's not waste it!' Dazed to a man they turned and ran, dragging the three seemingly incapacitated women with them, leaving the pitiable groans of a helpless army in their wake.

When they were gone, the brothers turned, as if leaving the stage of a theatre's play, and strode after them, calm and surreal.

In a widened corridor, leading to the small courtyard before the tunnel, now crammed with nervous and expectant warriors, Morgan and Krarl came upon the last of the Chosen forming a rear-guard with Housecarl Stonerider and Captain Bastonet. Before they could open their mouths, a bewildered looking Scar staggered to the front.

'Are they dead? What did you do? Did you kill them all?'

His voice was filled with both dread and awe as if he was speaking to the gods themselves.

Both of the brothers frowned down at him, but it was Morgan who answered to a fashion.

'This delay is only temporary. They will soon reorganise and come at us with vengeance in mind. You all know what must be done.'

Captain Horace, Luc, Elisha, Greybeaver and a dazed-looking Ahmya and Sharleen all nodded in solemn unison. Graham and Guy glanced at each other. John's face was unreadable.

Krarl addressed them all, but his eyes lingered on Sharleen.

'Be strorng. Will corm bark for you.'

Saying this, they passed them, turned and loped for the steep, winding stairs that led to the very summit of Stronghome.

'Where are they going?' whispered Guy. 'That way is a dead-end. There is no way out but through this overcrowded tunnel.'

'For you and me, my friend, but not for the likes of them,' replied old John.

'Are they abandoning us?' enquired Scar, a tinge of panic in his voice.

'We are the Sacrifice,' said Ahmya. 'Fate willing, we shall meet them again.'

'Hopefully in this world and not the next,' muttered Sharleen.

'Take your places,' commanded Captain Horace. 'There is work yet to be done.'

'I like you, big man,' said Elisha to Horace. 'All action and no fun at all.'

A brief look of concern crossed Horace's blunt face, and for the first time in years, he saw Sharleen smile. His anxiety increased.

'Sacrifice?' asked Scar, to no one in particular.

They all took their places in a shield wall, spanning the width of the corridor, two ranks thick, with the bigger and heavier ones in the fore, shield edges overlapping. Sharleen, Horace, John and Graham at centre, with Luc and Pollock on either side, flanked by Scar and Guy. The others formed up loosely behind them in the second rank. Ahmya armed herself with two short swords and hefted them for balance. Elisha spat on her palm and twirled her long-sword in a showy way, winking at Horace when she saw him look back at her. Greybeaver stroked a newly acquired bow, then spun it like a fighting staff, loosening his shoulders. The youngsters spread out slightly, giving their elders room to manoeuvre. Their plan was simple. The front line to stem the rush, the back line to kill them. No one made any speeches, they just waited quietly. They were the Chosen, and they had work to do.

Distant drumming drifted into their ears, like something being carried on a rushing wind. As it came closer it developed into the echoing sound of uncountable, iron-studded boots on stone and the rattling of loosely tied weapons; pounding forward with intent. There were no voices, no shouting or yelling, the usual hallmark of a charging army, just silent running, which seemed much more ominous and threatening.

'The gloves are off,' said old John. 'They are coming to kill us and grind us into dust.'

'That too, is our intention,' replied Greybeaver over his shoulder, as he strung his bow and tested the draw.

Ahmya placed her two swords neatly at her feet and with a smooth, practised movement, swivelled her short, recurved bow from her back and stepped up to join Greybeaver.

'Here come the bastards,' muttered Graham.

'Ready bows,' came Horace's gravelly voice.

He had not needed to give that order, the two behind him knew more than the majority what they were about.

Although they had been tracking them, the mass of soldiery bursting around the bend of the corridor almost caught them by surprise with its suddenness. Even so, two arrows flew out to greet them almost immediately, racing for warm flesh. Before the iron barbs could puncture their targets, three more were on their way, two from Ahmya, one from Greybeaver. Five men went crashing to the ground, tripping a fair portion of their comrades behind them. At this point, throats and passions were released, and a wall of belligerent sound smashed into the small rear-guard of defenders. More arrows lanced out to meet them, the force of their impacts, throwing men backwards into the arms of death. The distance was short, the time too little, they were on them. The two archers sprang back, dropped their bows and grabbed their weapons of iron.

The shock of the collision took their breaths away and stripped their minds of all useless thought. Big and strong as they were they were almost driven to their knees by the avalanche of aggressive weight and were sent skidding back a couple of spaces until they were braced by their comrades at their backs. Teeth gritted and neck muscles corded with the strain, they pushed back with everything that they had, keeping their centre of gravity low on their hips. Over their heads sharp-edged weapons lanced and cut at the enemy, preventing them from skewering the overburdened front line who were unable as yet, to bring their own weapons to bear. Ahmya, Elisha and Greybeaver were everywhere at once, cutting and slashing with vicious energy, merciless in defence of their own. Joining them was Jake, growing in confidence with the stalwart examples swirling around him. The others hung back, unsure as yet on where and how to contribute.

'Hold the line! Hold the line!' growled Horace. 'One! Two! Three! Now! Push! Push!'

Grunting, snarling, spitting, and cursing they heaved against the crushing force being applied on their backs and shoulders. Scar sobbed, but his effort was no less than the others. Graham bellowed loudly and pushed his shield forward, locked with Horace's and Sharleen's and slowly, slowly, inch by inch they began to exert pressure back on the Protectorate lackeys.

'Shut...it...you...bloody...ox!' sobbed Scar through gritted teeth, drool running in a slimy string from his open gasping mouth. 'Giving...me...a...bloody...headache.'

'Now!' yelled Horace with a hoarse roar.

The line stepped back neatly as one, causing the enraged soldiers of the Empire, with resistance suddenly withdrawn, to overbalance, and fall forward into the well of space created. With a snarl, the Chosen were on them like dogs on a stray cat, stabbing and chopping in a cold frenzy.

'Shields!' roared Horace once again, and with a snap of wood and metal, the fence of shields closed with a resounding crunch, and shoulders aching and bruised, pressed and crouched behind their wooden wall, pushing, panting, and heaving once again, the back line swinging swords of fury over their heads onto that of the cringing enemy.

Their very souls crying out from expended energy, sucking an empty hole of despair in their burning bodies, the Chosen fought with all their might for every toe-hold that they lost. Scar, the smallest on the front line, his body trembling and shivering, as his overused and abused muscles protested, barely moved his head out of the way of a plunging spear point that would have buried itself in his eye and brain. He knew it would come again but couldn't be bothered. He just wanted to end this endless torment. Suddenly, he was yanked backwards off of his feet and dumped on his backside in the space behind. He watched dully as stout legs marched past him and took his place in the line. Reginald, simmering with an inner conviction, smashed his shield driven by muscles born to apply force, square into the face and chest of an onrushing soldier, who had thought that a boon had been granted him and he could slip past these fighting demons and have at them from their undefended rear. He was wrong and knew this as he was flung back into the entangling arms his comrades, cheekbone broken.

'On your feet, lecher!' spat a black-haired, dancing harridan with a sword, weaving a magic of death over the heads of his brothers. 'There is still work here for you to do!'

'The gods help me!' Scar prayed, pushing himself to his feet and leaping at a small crack in the wall, plunging his sword into the screaming mouth of a berserker soldier who was clawing his way through. The scream cut off into a horrible gargle and the man fell back and disappeared.

'Take that, you bastard,' he yelled with hysterical glee, feeling an unknown source of energy surging through his limbs.

Behind him stood Vivian, her hand still resting on his shoulder from when she had helped him to his feet. Her eyes held the weird expression of an afterglow from a lighting strike, and she seemed a bit unsteady on her feet.

Jacob felt a oneness that he had never experienced before. He knew where every one of his childhood friends were in the heat of battle, he knew what they were feeling, he experienced the mist of conviction as it settled on Reggie's broad shoulders, he felt the strange bolstering coming from Vivian, he spun backwards with Stephi as she dodged a thrown spear, he could almost tell what they were thinking. He felt a great belonging, a part of something more than himself.

Still, the best of the Chosen, the last survivors of sixty, were being driven back and were on the point of being split, when the remnants of the fortress rocked as if the god of the underworld was fed up with their squabbling and was warning them to correct their antics. The two sides drew away from each other cautiously as mortar and chunks of stone fell around them. Before the dust could settle the overdressed general peeped up once again from many rows back. A lackey held a cone-shaped tube up to his superior's mouth and when he spoke his voice boomed across the distance.

'This is not the place to be when our mighty god is angry. If you wish to live and value your lives, I urge you to give yourself over into our hands.'

'Well, kick my ass! That man's got a big mouth. Tell, him to stuff his head in it, Captain,' offered Scar.

'They have collapsed the tunnel, Horace. It's time to follow Morgan's last command,' interjected Sharleen in her usual deadpan voice.

'What's she talking about, Captain? What command?' asked a confused looking Scar.

'Our leaders are dead!' shouted Horace to the peacock general. 'We were hired to fight, but there is no one left to pay us. We wish to discuss terms of surrender.'

'There are no terms to discuss, mercenary. Drop your weapons and let's end this farce.'

Horace looked around him at his companions. Most of them knew what was going on except, Scar, Luc, Graham, John and Guy. The rest nodded.

'Very well,' muttered Captain Horace, a troubled look in his eye. 'We surrender!' he shouted and dropped his battered shield and sword.

The others followed his example.

'Shit!' said Scar.

CHAPTER XXIV

'A delegation from the Merchant's Guild is asking to see you, Eminence, and has been coming to the Enclave every day for the past three days. They refuse to leave before you hear their petition.'

'And why are you bringing me this tale, Spymaster? Do you think I am unaware of what happens on my own doorstep? Are you perchance taking illegal employment elsewhere? Being a messenger of Guilds is not, if I recall correctly, part of the duties of a highly rewarded Spymaster. Have you become a messenger boy for rent then?'

'Not at all, Eminence. I was waylaid on route to you in order to answer your summons. Besides this, knowing what happens under your roof is why you have posted me in this honoured position. I'm paid to be your eyes and ears.'

'Bah! Then you are three days late. I know what they want. They want their precious Merchant King, but I'm not finished with him yet. You can run back and tell your bosom pals this when I've concluded my business with you, Spymaster.'

'I am your loyal servant, Eminence.'

'Of course you are. I want you to tell me who in your opinion, among my haloed peers have been stroking the velvet purse of Sybil Wuzetian and please don't try to feed me time-wasting crap.'

The Spymaster was well accustomed to the First Citizen's crudely turned phrases and avoided answering in kind.

'What I have to say will come as no surprise to you, Eminence. The positions occupied by most of the Conclave is due to and intricately linked, to their dealings in commerce. Being rich is almost a prerequisite and contrary to widely held opinions this is not a sin.'

'You are preaching to the converted, Father. I think I warned you not to waste my time.'

'Not at all, Eminence. What I was trying to suggest was that maybe we should put our questions to the Merchant King himself. I'm sure if we promise to spare his family further harm he might be grateful enough to drop some sweet gems in our ears.'

'I'm not sure that I am convinced by your analogy, but I get the essence of what you are proposing. Why not pay a visit to our guest in his prison cell.'

'Ah…he is not in the prisons, Eminence.'

'Is he not!? Where is he then?'

'You have left him chained to the reception floor, Eminence.'

'Have I? Oh yes. Hope the chap is still alive. Go fetch him then. Don't just stand there playing with yourself.'

'Yes, Eminence. At once.'

***

The Merchant King in question was far from dead. Someone had seen to it that he had received just enough water to keep him comfortable and a clay pot to empty himself in. It was no more inconvenient than his monthly fasts. He suspected the sly hand of the Spymaster behind it. It was very much in his interest that he did not perish in an absent but peevish purge by the First Citizen. Belief in the one god had long died, a thing of memory, and had been replaced by the pursuit of wealth which in turn bought influence and status irrespective of the qualities of the possessor. Men without wanted because they did not have, and men with, wanted just to have more than those who had. Power was forever sought after by those whose souls were empty, and these men were fertile ground for the growth of the Shadow Guild. The Spymaster was dangerous, for he understood these things and played them with the finesse of a magician but even so, he could rarely outplay the First Citizen for his mind operated somewhere outside the realms of this world and this made him unpredictable with every move and countermove; he was both in the game and outside of it, all at the same time. He could almost feel the strands vibrating as both men cast their webs about them. They would soon send for him, and as always he was ready, for he knew what these men desired above all else.

Lo and behold, as the third day was fading into the west, two court protectors arrived, unchained him and took him to the baths. Under guard, he was ordered to make himself presentable for an audience with the First Citizen. He was even offered a sumptuous meal from which he ate sparingly as a measure of personal discipline but also as a signal to the greedy that he was a man in control of his appetites. As lamps were being lit to drive out the darkness with tremulous fingers of wavering, yellow light he was brought before the august presence of the First Citizen, dressed in the full regalia of his office, the Spymaster and three priests robed in black, members from the Order of Questioners, no doubt, birthed by the suspicious and unhinged mind of the present First Citizen. They were a new addition to the pantheon but already feared by all. He would have been put to death for that thought on several counts had anyone been able to read him, but alas, he lived in a world of pretence, of smoke and shadows, so he could think what he liked with impunity.

'Ah, welcome Merchant Wuzetian. I trust that you are well and not to worse for wear due to the unfortunate turn of events instigated by your wayward niece?'

It was hard to tell whether the fat frog meant to be genuine in his regret or was just sticking the knife of sarcasm in a bit and giving it a little twist for perverse satisfaction. The Lord of the House of Wuzetian decided to answer in kind.

'I am as well as can be expected under the circumstances, Eminence, and I'm sure that my niece will learn wisdom and right course of action from the lips of my sister.'

The First Citizen stroked his wispy beard and stared at the Merchant Lord with flat eyes and a face devoid of movement or expression.

The Spymaster broke through the uncertain silence in between with a strategic clearing of his throat.

'This unfortunate thing with your niece, a revered Cardinal of the Empire, is yet to be decided, Lord Wuzetian, and remains at best uncertain. You of all people must acknowledge the uneasy pillow she has placed under our heads. However, we have called you before this tribunal not to harm you and yours but to inquire into who amongst us profit most from the dealings of your Guild. Think of it as a trading discussion.'

'I understand, Father. If you profit from my words, my family lives to gain more in this earthly life.'

'Crudely put, merchant, but dead on the head,' interjected the First Citizen.

The Spymaster hid the wince that involuntarily tried to seize his face and attempted to soften the situation.

'What you choose to say could be very much in both our interest, House Wuzetian.'

'If I allow you to weaken the base support of my niece would you guarantee her life, livelihood and position?'

The Spymaster glanced at the First Citizen but he remained immovable and unreadable.

'Yes, we are prepared to do this. Your niece, believe it or not, is very valuable to the Empire.'

'With all due respect, Spymaster, I would be more reassured if I were to hear this from your Lord and Master.'

'If I did not like or agree to the words of my servant you would certainly hear my voice, merchant. This is all the reassurance you will get. Now, do we have a deal or not?'

'Your word, as always, is your bond, First Citizen. Ask your questions, and I will answer to the best of my knowledge.'

In the end, he answered all of their questions to the letter without any guile or subterfuge. His skill lay in only giving exactly what was asked for and not volunteering anything other than the specific. The Spymaster saw what he was doing, and his questions were like the thin knife of a surgeon. Those of the Questioners were probing, spiteful and vindictive. The First Citizen was silent throughout and even the highly experienced and intelligent Merchant King felt some nervousness, for this man, mad as he was, had attained the office of First Citizen at a very young age and had held it secure in a fat grip of iron ever since. He could not be underestimated.

Whatever the outcome, he walked out of the enforced negotiations with his head still attached to an unbroken body and without imperial guards breathing all over his person. He had no faith whatsoever, in the word of the First Citizen, which in reality, was never given, but he had bought himself time and the assurance of an ally in the slippery form of the Spymaster. Their shared interests it seemed, were very much aligned. He knew that he only had a small window of time to prepare for a private visit from that self-same individual. His niece had inadvertently forced his hand. Sitting on the fence was no longer an option; it was time to take sides and throw the dice.

By the time the Head of House Wuzetian and the Spymaster had sat down together to work out a strategy for mutual survival, the First Citizen had already denounced three Cardinals within the ruling Supreme Council of Nine, as hypocrites to the faith and a moral threat to the Empire. He had stooges drawing their alleged lust for earthly things on the walls of marketplaces and priests of the people haranguing their flock on these Cardinals' hidden desires for rich food and the forbidden flesh of their daughters. Angered by what they all coveted but were not well-placed or connected enough to attain, the multitude rose up in protest and demanded accountability and right example from their leaders. At this, the First Citizen took the unprecedented step of appearing before them in person, elevated on a humble, portable platform made from unadorned wood, promising them that he would see to it that the misguided Cardinals led astray by the base desires of mankind, address their shortcomings and take the road of true humility before them. The truth of these charges was now neither here nor there. The people believed and had to be appeased, otherwise, riots and civil unrest would become the order of the day. The speed of these events caught all concerned on the back foot, ill-prepared to raise a defence and carried helplessly onwards on the tide of foment, stirred up by the unpredictable First Citizen. Unbeknown to the affronted populace, these very same Cardinals were the highest placed supporters of Cardinal Wuzetian, a person held in exalted regard by the people who were now clamouring for her political backers to be brought low.

'You have to give him his due. He does know how to go on the offensive. He has the makings of a great general,' said Lord Wuzetian in a neutral tone.

'Making chaos his faithful servant is certainly one of his hallmarks. You must know that your family's safety is still not assured,' replied the Spymaster in a matching voice.

'None of us are, Father. We can only continue to ride the storm until a port presents itself.'

'Wise words, Lord Merchant, but words are not enough in these troubled times.'

'What are you proposing?'

'I propose nothing, but if you have useful tools, think about sharpening them.'

Was the priest bluffing, or did he know more than he was supposed to know? He decided to play the game a little further.

'The exchange of goods for a financial return has limits as a cutting tool, Father. A merchant's reach can only go so far before he is at risk of losing his arm.'

The Spymaster studied his host with quiet eyes for just long enough for a possible message to be read.

'If you say so, my Lord. If you say so.'

'Do we know how far the First Citizen will go? Does he intend to limit my niece or destroy her? Can he be contained?' asked Lord Wuzetian, changing the direction of conversation slightly.

'Many questions, Lord Merchant, and all may be interpreted as treasonous. The answers to them all depend on how our Master wakes in the morning. I am not sure he has a plan any further than winning the day. Which leaves us all a bit helpless.'

'He has already seized my niece's estates but has not made any move against mine. A good reason for this may be that he still values his investments placed in my hands. It can only be assumed that he will also appropriate the wealth of the accused Cardinals when the time is right. So he is also refilling his treasure box. He must, contrary to your belief, have a plan, for the amassing of treasure has never been an aim in itself for him.'

'Yes, you see more clearly than I do in this, and of course, the generals support him. Unfortunately, the unorthodox move of your niece has inadvertently strengthened his hand. Her usurping of the Honey General's position has made them very nervous, and one must not forget that his family is a military one and well thought of.'

'So you see his hand at last, Spymaster. He is putting on a show; an elaborate show to expose any septic teeth being hidden behind closed mouths. To over-react will put our necks under the falling sword.'

'So much for being just a merchant, eh, Lord Wuzetian? Maybe you should have the role of Spymaster.'

'You flatter me, Father. I am poorly qualified for that compliment. I will stick to what I know best.'

'So we have come full circle and not advanced our cause one inch further. We await the pleasure of our First Citizen. God help us.'

'To god we pray, but in our wits we trust. Patience is a worthy ally in any game, Father. Those who are unlucky or unworthy will fall. We must ensure that we are not among them when the last piece is moved on the board.'

***

The First Citizen was satisfied. Both the Spymaster and Cardinal Wuzetian had played right into his hands in different ways, allowing him to take what he needed. They had given him an excuse to bring the people into the game. He could now take control of the generals or in any case, will soon be able to do so. They would willingly surrender their authority and expertise over into his palms as a balancing act against the ruthless ambition of Cardinal Wuzetian. She had allowed herself to be seen as outside the status quo of the Empire, something other, a threat. Generals did not like that. In their eyes, to avoid a civil war, they would have to form a powerful and unified front, and the only way to do so was to unite themselves under the most ancient office of the Empire, that of the First Citizen. Even the Merchant Guild, with their fingers stuck deep into every honeypot the Empire had to offer, would now toe the line or be seen to be taking the side of a rebel. Their Grandmaster, because of family ties, would have to appear ultra-loyal, which would neutralise any counter moves he might have been able to take to interfere with the First Citizen's plans. The only loose end was the dreaded Shadow Guild. Why had he allowed them to grow so strong? He knew nothing of them. Where they hid. Who they were connected to and who their leaders were. At one point he had suspected the Spymaster himself but had no evidence or leads in that direction. Besides this one blind spot, he now had enough finances and support to buy and equip his own army if need be. If he had to do so, he would sweep all opponents aside with fire and sword. He just needed a trustworthy general to elevate. His hopes had been pinned on the Honey General, but he seemed to have disappeared on the route home, and his whereabouts still remained unknown. Could the she-bitch have had him assassinated? He wouldn't put it past her. She was a worthy opponent, and he still harboured the secret wish to re-exert his control over her so that when his time came to cross the bridge, he could make her his successor. She would make an excellent First Citizen but not before he was ready to leave this world behind. In fact, he saw the title of First Citizen outdated. The Empire was prepared for an Emperor, and he was destined to take on that role. His first step, however, was to do away with the useless, near-sighted, bumbling idiots that made up the Ruling Council of Nine. This would be his legacy. He would be the first Emperor of the Protectorate Empire not just a first Citizen among a long line of First Citizens.

CHAPTER XXV

They took turns kicking him. He lay curled up on the icy ground, arms pulled up tightly around his head and neck, knees tucked against his stomach. He did not make a sound, except for an occasional grunt forced from his lungs from a particularly accurate blow. His battered companions looked on with visages blank and impassive. They were impotent to intervene, but inside they burned with a cold rage. As dry, light, wisps of snow swirled around the abusers they drew away laughing, taunting, nasty words spitting on the fallen man, whose hair and face was caked with frozen blood.

'Get up you pansy bastard! Not so tough now are you!?'

The captured warriors were corralled and penned into two separate groups among sundered walls and broken stones of a once great and proud fortress; five women on one side and eight men on the other. In the frigid space in between, they were dragged out one by one and beaten. The purpose was pure vindictive and cruel for no information was being asked for or being sought. At the moment, only the men were on the receiving end of this hospitality, but they all knew a worse fate awaited the women when their captors managed to work themselves up to it.

Horace and Luc watched the frightful mistreatment of their friend and felt the cold knot of revenge growing inside them. It was easy to forget how tough this small man was. His constant wise-cracking and griping disguised the hard warrior within. When the beating was finished, he had pushed himself almost to his feet when rough hands grabbed him, kicked his feet out from under him and dragged him over to the pen.

'Whose next, my pretty, little, babies?' asked a particularly unpleasant soldier, who, although he didn't yet know it, had the mark of death hanging over his greasy head.

As Scar was flung unceremoniously into the pen, old John was seized by the arms and head and roughly steered from his open-air prison. The elderly Housecarl, already bleeding and bruised from head to foot, was the picture of stoicism. His face remained impassive, and although he favoured his left side, he did not wince even once as the beatings and blows rained down on his tortured flesh.

Breathing heavily, the soldiers eventually stopped, disappointed that their victims were not fully cooperating with their torture.

'Bah! No fun in beating these old bastards. They are already dead. Shall we see what the little ladies have to offer?'

John moved. He moved with lethal efficiency, even though his arms were tied behind his back. His large, rock-like skull covered with tangled, dirty-grey hair, smashed down on the nose of the filthy mouthed soldier. The loud crunch followed by a spray of bright blood, and an agonised mewling sound, sent satisfaction into the hearts of the watching companions. Spinning, the tough Housecarl sent a low back kick into the knee of another soldier, snapping his leg and eliciting a high pitched scream which raised the hackles of all present. Continuing into the spin, he dropped his shoulder and bullied yet another off of his feet and stamped on his ankle before he could recover. They were on him, battering him viciously until he collapsed onto the hard, ice-encrusted ground unconscious. Then they dragged him back to the pen by his ankles and dumped him. They would have done more, but his comrades, as one, closed ranks around him with eyes and posture filled with belligerence. These soldiers had seen these warriors in action, and despite their taunts and cruelty, they feared them. Backing away they locked them back into their frigid cage. Filled now with the need to show that they were men and unafraid they turned their attention to the women captives, but when they looked into the eyes of Sharleen, Elisha, and Ahmya, despite the latter's stunning beauty, they saw death and quickly averted their gaze.

Mister Foul-mouth, nose bleeding and flattened messily across his face, spoke up in muffled vindictiveness and bravado.

'Leave the big cow for last, and that mad bitch next to her will bite our tongues out. Let her watch a bit first. That one with the devil's eyes will have to be softened and warmed up a bit. Don't want her making our cocks fall off with frostbite, do we boys!'

Rough, nasty laughter followed and the soldiers, drunk on cheap alcohol, victory and perversity crowded forward. With spears levelled at the three lethal women, they quickly grabbed the cowering form of Vivian and dragged her from the cage. Like all bullies, they zeroed in on the one they perceived to be the weakest. Realising her inevitable fate, the young girl came alive, kicking and struggling against the odds, against the tearing hands that sought to expose her. Suddenly, she went still, and the animals around her smelled the scent of victory, but they were wrong. Perched on the edge of losing all that she had, Vivian, felt the link of her Blue Mountains family, her pack. With a strength that she did not know that she had, she reached into the sick minds breathing foully on her and twisted. Five men, intent on unspeakable evil felt a pain in their heads like sharpened, shards of ice cutting through nerves, soft tissue and blood vessels. They screamed a scream so terrible and forlorn that the others with them froze in abject terror, unable to move, unable to comprehend, unable to speak, and watched blankly as five men fell dead at their feet. At the same moment, young Jacob, swayed on unsteady legs which folded under him, caught by the puzzled grips of his fellow captors.

As the male warriors glanced at each other in confusion, the women, Sharleen and Ahmya understood, but it was Ahmya only who had the ability to lend her spirit to her imperilled sister. With a cold, icy certainty, she sent her strength across the space to join with Vivian. The girl rose to her feet like a wraith, exuding deadly confidence and ability. The men around her staggered back, appalled by the sudden turn of events and the supernatural chill in the air. Many held their fingers and thumbs up in the warding sign and muttered hasty prayers to whatever entity they believed might protect them.

'What is going on here!'

The voice, colder than the already frigid atmosphere, cut away the last remaining vestiges of control in the now cowed and frightened soldiers.

'Attention!' barked a commanding, parade ground voice, obviously disturbed by what he was witnessing. 'Stand to attention for her Eminence, fools! Back! Back! Form your lines! Form your lines!'

The cold voice continued.

'General, take every fifth man in the vicinity of that girl and execute him immediately. Do you understand!'

'Yes, Eminence. At once, Eminence. I am sorry…'

'Not now, General. Do as I've commanded!'

A look of sheer terror crossed the faces of the men in question and they did their best to step away, but there was no escaping their fate. The sobs of those selected punctuated the enveloping silence as they were led away by their own to meet their maker.

Serene as a queen of ice in her gown of pure snow, Cardinal Sybil Wuzetian surveyed the gathering around her. She studied the battered, grim-faced but proudly standing, captive warriors in their cage, her expression unreadable. Then she turned to the even more impressive women warriors.

'Bring these women to my tent,' she said simply and glided away into the thickening snowfall.

As if awakened from a very satisfying nap for something annoying and trivial, the General stared with contempt at his soldiers and snapped.

'You heard, her Eminence! Lieutenant and you too, sergeant, select an escort that doesn't think with its balls and show our guests to her headquarters. If they are harmed in any way en route your lives are forfeit!'

The five women, dirty, grubby and smelling of stale perspiration combined with the stink of leather and blood, were ushered into the presence of the most unusual High Cardinal of the Protectorate Empire.

'When I first heard that there were women warriors opposing us, my primary thought was that such a thing was both perverse and demeaning. My imagination conjured up tall women, not unlike you, my dear,' she said, glancing at Sharleen, 'but with beefy shoulders and maybe sporting a beard or at least the shadow of a moustache. In other words, I expected to find men in all but name. I decided to put aside my prejudices and go see for myself. I must say, I'm pleasantly surprised and greatly impressed. You are a marvellous bunch. Heroines from the pages of an ancient saga.'

The five women stared at her.

'I'm sorry. I have embarrassed myself. Let me start again.'

She turned her back to them with a graceful, fluid motion and began pouring a rich, red wine into a collection of silver cups.

'Welcome to my tent. Its warmth is yours. My name is Sybil, my title I think you already know. I am deeply sorry, but unfortunately, not surprised in the least, at the treatment you have received by the hands of some of my men. I can assure you that they are not all like that. Be that as it may, there is no excuse for such behaviour. May I ask your names in turn?'

The Cardinal glanced at Sharleen, for she seemed the natural leader and was once again surprised when Ahmya answered.

'We thank you for your timely rescue, but do not mistake us, we are sworn enemies of the Protectorate, and our aim and duty is to drive you back to the walls of your city.'

'I do not doubt that, Lady, but can we not put our enmities aside even for a short moment and address each other as women, unusual ones for that matter, in this world of men?'

The genuine tone of the question wrong-footed Ahmya and she slowly centred herself before responding. She could feel the similar surprise in her sisters.

'You have a voice of honey, Cardinal Wuzetian. We have heard of your reputation, and it makes us over cautious.'

'Sybil, please, call me Sybil,' said the Cardinal smoothly as she glided towards them offering her tray of wine.

They each selected a cup for want of nothing else to do and for fear of appearing boorish, but none ventured a sip. As Vivian reached out and took her offered cup, Sybil Wuzetian caught her eye and frowned slightly. The others did not miss her reaction, fleeting as it was.

'Does this mean that you refuse to offer me your names?'

'Not at all, High Cardinal. My name is Ahmya Yumi. These are my sisters, Lady Sharleen Allbright, Elisha the Prophetess, Lady Vivian and Lady Stephania.'

'Prophetess,' whispered the Cardinal. 'Interesting! I am honoured to meet you all.'

Stepping towards Ahmya, she removed her cup from her fingers and replaced it with hers then took a sip. She did this all very casually as if it were the most normal thing to do. They all stared guiltily at their cups then following her example and took a hesitant sip themselves.

'You haven't got a hot bath behind those curtains, have you?' asked Sharleen out of the blue.

A soft, musical tinkling emanated from the Cardinals painted lips, and they all realised she was laughing with pure joy and amusement.

'I have indeed, Lady Sharleen. It was amiss of you not to offer in the first place, but I did not wish to sound presumptuous or condescending.'

'Condescend all you want. We need a bath.'

'As I said, and I do mean it, the hospitality of my tent is yours. I am curious though.'

'Oh-oh,' muttered Sharleen.

'My General has reported that before surrender, one of your number claimed that you were all mercenaries and that your leaders were dead. Forgive me, but you do not appear to be nameless warriors for pay.'

'Our ladies get together is beginning to take on the appearance of an interrogation,' said Elisha to no one in particular.

The Cardinal smiled and took another sip of her wine.

'There many oddities about you as a group and those caged wolves outside, Prophetess. You cannot expect a girl in my position not to be curious.'

As she said this, she glanced once again at Vivian.

No one took the time out to enlighten her.

'Oh, very well,' she said with another musical laugh. Your bath awaits. Feel free to guard each other's backs whilst disrobed, but you'll excuse me if I don't offer you your weapons. Sharp things make me nervous.'

She rang a small bell, and a stout, grumpy looking woman strode in.

'What do you want now, child?' she asked in a weary and disrespectful voice.

'This dragon before you in the guise of a woman is my nursemaid from childhood. She will see to your needs but please do not expect any courtesy from her.'

With another laugh, she glided from the tent.

Outside in their rude cage, shivering from the cold and mistreatment, Horace and the rest of the chosen, sat huddled, anxious but grim, around young Jacob, whose soft reassuring voice kept them calm despite their deep scepticism.

'How can you know for sure that they are alright?' asked Captain Horace.

'I just know. It is something that I can feel.'

Reginald nodded in affirmation.

'That's not a very comforting answer, young man. A feeling is just a feeling. I don't feel at my best right now, but that doesn't mean I'm going to die,' responded Luc.

'Such great logic has certainly got me lost,' muttered Scar, rolling his eyes.

Everybody ignored them.

'What that lass did with those would be rapist certainly makes me think that Morgan did not choose them purely for their good looks and youthfulness. I for one believe what the boy is saying,' said Greybeaver.

Old John, Graham, Pollock and Guy all nodded in support.

'Right, but where do we stand in all this?' asked Horace.

'Up the creek without a paddle but still alive at the moment,' replied Scar.

'I agree with Scar here,' said old John. 'The Hope in all this has just gone up a notch.'

'Did I say that?' enquired Scar.

'Shut it!' responded Luc.

Before any of them could say any more, a subtle stiffening of their guards alerted them that something unusual was happening or about to happen.

Stepping delicately across the frozen, uneven ground, surrounded by four of her personal bodyguards, glided the ghostly, angel-like figure of the Cardinal.

'Ah, we are truly blessed. Two visitations in less than an hour by the high and mighty. Wonder what she wants?' muttered Scar.

'She wants information,' said old John. 'She has heard of something inexplicable and is intrigued. She thinks we might have answers.'

'Right, the price is strong wine and warmth, you hear me, Captain! Nothing less!'

'Not selling yourself short then? Good to see that you can still strike a hard bargain,' responded Luc.

The Cardinal, a white, hooded, ermine cloak pulled closely around her, stood by their cage and studied them. They, in turn, remained squatting on the frozen rocks and regarded her without expression.

'Is there one among you who can speak for the others?'

The question rang clear through the chilled air.

'That will be you, Captain Horace. You've been doing a great job so far,' said Graham in a low voice.

The others nodded.

With a grunt, Horace pushed himself to his feet feeling the strain of the past few days weighing down on him. He wasn't sure exactly how old he was, but he had been in this game of violence for a long time, and it was taking a toll. He walked steadily over to the waiting Cardinal and stood in front of her with a calm, patient gaze, direct but without challenge.

'And you, dear man, how may I call you?'

'I am Captain Horace.'

'A captain. How sweet. Captain of what, may I ask?'

'A Captain of myself and the fate of my people here imprisoned.'

Her laughter rang like a pure bell.

'I like you, Captain. You are more than you appear. I shall be straightforward with you then. My men reported that you claim to be mercenaries and that your leaders have died before rewarding you for your services.'

'That is what I said.'

'My men also reported two men who stood at the fore of my army and stopped them dead in their tracks using dark magic. Were these men your leaders?'

'They are more than men, and their destiny is to lead us all.'

'I took you for a fighting man, Captain, but your words have the ring of an evangelist. Are these men dead?'

'They are not men who can be easily killed.'

'Where are they then, Captain? Did they escape with the others through the collapsed tunnel?'

'No, that way was blocked. They took another path,' said Horace in a low monotone and glanced at the looming, mist-shrouded mountain.

She hesitated, with a fleeting look of uncertainty passing across her eyes.

'Are you trying to say that they fled up the side of the mountain? That is not possible for any man.'

'They did not flee, and as I said, they are more than men.'

'Your answers are beginning to concern me, Captain. Are they wielders of dark magic as my soldiers claim?'

'I know nothing of dark magic, but they have a power which I am unable to explain.'

'I see. And is this power limited to them only or do others have it?'

'They chose their followers carefully. What you say may well be possible for I have witnessed too what has disturbed and intrigued you.'

'As I said, Captain. You are more than you appear to be and I can see why you were chosen, and chosen to lead a very unusual group, a dangerous group I might add. I am of two minds, Captain. One is to execute the bunch of you and put behind me all of this nonsense, but I realise even if I did so, this matter will not be ended. My second course is to offer you employment amongst my personal guard. You will be well rewarded for your services. What do you say to this?'

'I am truly sorry for you, Eminence,' said Horace with regret, for the first time using the proper title of the unusual woman standing before him. 'You are now trapped here in this place your ambition drove you to seize. You have one avenue left to follow. Take your army and march with full speed through the gap still left open to you and return to your city. Do so now before the gate is closed and you are annihilated. What happens to us, my brothers and my sisters, now caught in your hands, is not important. We are Sacrifice, and we did so willingly.'

'No Captain, on the contrary. It is I who am sorry for you. You have chosen to lead those in your care like sheep to slaughter before the altar. And for what? For a cause in which you will never see the outcome. You will find that it takes quite a lot to defeat me, Captain. May the god have mercy on your souls.'

She turned her back on him and walked away, the wind immediately blowing into the spot she had left vacant, filling it with shifting snow.

'Bloody hell!' he heard Scar saying. 'Warmth and wine, Captain! That wasn't much to ask for!'

'No, it wasn't,' he found himself thinking.

CHAPTER XXVI

The brothers had gone separate ways. Krarl to lead the attack from the Lower Kingdoms and Morgan to coordinate an assault from the Green Kingdoms, which were, in reality, weaker, due to their reliance on foresters who had lost their expertise in open warfare, having long since abandoned the sword and shield for the bow. Their countries were also occupied by the enemy so in many ways they had to watch what was behind them as they attempted to move on the aerie above them. This fearsome highpoint was no longer as unassailable as it once was, most of its claws now pulled by the long and terrible siege that it had struggled against and its resulting cataclysmic fall. Simply put, its defences had all been torn away leaving it an emptied shell of what it once was. The good of this was that the Protectorate no longer had a fortress from which to fight behind, only a high place to defend.

The survivors of Stronghome Keep, although small in number, were an essential force for Morgan. They had a fire burning in their stomachs, and they were hungry; hungry for revenge. They were also expert shield warriors, and Morgan had them placed in charge of reforming the fighting green bands that were so fierce and feared during the time of the Green Warden. He was gambling that their sudden reappearance on the battlefield of freedom would draw their countrymen to their ranks as they saw a national symbol of their independence reborn. Stumpcutter, believe it or not, had done a marvellous job, combined with the steady and expert advice provided by the ex-Protectorate General, and all fighting men were equipped and armoured for battle. Food stashes were adequate and safe places for the injured secured. To keep the attention of the occupying forces diverted, Morgan was leading lightning raids on depots in far-off directions other than the base at Stronghome, but he knew this tactic would not last long. The Protectorate was arrogant but not stupid.

They would soon learn that a large force was gathering to attack their frontline. It was whilst returning from one of these raids they came upon the dedicated but exhausted messengers of the Holy Conclave.

The three men were slogging along on their now almost blown express ponies, bred for speed and stamina, so totally secure in the belief that their forces ruled the world, that they took a long time to comprehend that they were now surrounded by and in the hands of an enemy. Even then they reacted with bluster and outrage, at the men who dared delay them in their sacred duty.

'Stand aside, fools! The penalty for interrupting a messenger of god is dismemberment by slow stages! Stand aside, at once!'

Morgan watched the dirt-stained foresters, some grinning openly, circling the three men like hyenas that had come upon the unexpected boon of an unprotected child. He saw the bravery of the messengers who now fully appraised of their dire situation were determined not to back down. He also saw the sad predatory nature of man no matter what side, good or bad, they proclaimed to fight under. He strode forward into the open.

'Stand down,' he said in a soft commanding voice.

He noted those who stepped back immediately, those who frowned in irritation before doing so and those who ignored his command. Yet another thing to deal with in the so little time available. The road ahead would be long and hard. He still wasn't sure that he wanted to travel along it, but his brother seemed committed.

'Stand back!' he repeated, his voice thinly laced with something else, something dangerous. 'I will not say again.'

This time they all hastened to obey, leaving a large circle around the three defiant messengers.

'Good evening, gentlemen. You journey far from the triple walls of your city.'

'Good evening to you, sir, but be wary, we will not be questioned by wayfarers. Our Empire knows no walls and our laws protect us from all upon pain of death.'

'A two-edged sword I was led to understand many years ago.'

'What you say is true. We are bound to speak only with the receiver or our tongues be cut out and our lungs punctured till we drown in our life's blood. Our service is an oath of blood. So you will know it is useless to try and coerce or force us from the path.'

'That sealed leather case you carry. I am familiar with it. In my day, it always contained a message that did not need words to explain further. Usually, it also meant death for the bringer of such a communique. You are brave men worthy of your position. May your god go with you and embolden others to show you mercy. Please continue on your path, we shall not delay you longer from fulfilling your fate.'

Eying Morgan suspiciously, the three urged their horses hesitantly forward. One of the two who had remained silent, halted his horse and looked directly at Morgan, his eyes showing a glint of canny intelligence.

'May I ask your name, sir? As a way of thanks.'

'My name is Morgan Ap Heston. May this knowledge spare you pain. Farewell messengers of your god.'

'We should have used this opportunity granted to us by good fortune to question them further, Lord Morgan,' said a rangy lad of about twenty summers.

Ever the patient teacher to those he led, Morgan explained.

'To what purpose, Anton? What they said is all true. Besides they have provided us already with a wealth of information.'

'I don't understand, Lord.'

'Have you seen men walking into a battle that they know will be their last? These men have that look. The leather case they carry is filled with a potent spirit, named by those who love black-humour as Dead man's Coffin. Can you guess why, Anton?'

'It contains someone's head preserved?'

'Exactly! Someone close to our Cardinal on yon hill. A Cardinal now more besieged than the castle she was once besieging. She is isolated in many ways and can expect no orders of aid from her city and her peers. She is almost ours, Anton. Let's hope the sacrifice will not be too high. Come, let's be on our way.'

***

Krarl was becoming more and more impatient. No one could tell this for he sat coiled on a chair as still and unmoving as a viper warming itself in the sun. Some had even forgotten that he was there so caught up in their bickering were they.

'I say we blockade our side and let the bastards rot up there in the cold!'

'What good is that! You don't win a fight by sitting on your arse.'

'You should know, that's how you've won yours in the past!'

Back and forth, to and fro, round and round, on and on since he had returned with news of urgency to move. He was giving them their chance but not for much longer. Many of the true warriors sitting and standing around the clearing were not speaking. They were looking to him, and he felt it. Here in the Lowlands violence was all they knew, all they respected; violence and excellence in combat. That is why Captain Horace was so respected, why Sharleen was so admired, and they had chosen to follow him. They had also heard rumours. So they, in turn, looked to him. The so-called Lords were something else altogether. They loved to talk, and argue, and drink. All except wise Tramford, who like Krarl, sat and listened.

A loud noise, like a crack of thunder in the heavens, broke in the clearing, throwing the gathering into stunned silence. The huge, oak table, some lord's prized possession, split and tumbled into the grass in two sections. Krarl straightened, uncurling his balled fists and flexing his hands absently. No one had seen him move from his chair, even those who had been watching him.

'Time to fight,' he said, to no one in particular. 'We attack art dawn. Tonight quick raid for fun.'

'A…attack…f…fun? You've already got my best men killed with your headstrong foolishness. We attack when we say so. We ar…'

Lord Breakspear's apoplectic voice choked off in mid-flow as Krarl's eyes like deep pools of darkness pinned him to the spot. With a mewling sound of horror, the Lord sank trembling into the green grass splattered with bright dandelions and pissed his britches in front of a war gathering. No one else could find anything else to say.

'Tramford taak charge orf centre. Kraxton, left flarnk. Byron right. Be ready. I weel starnd with centre. Now raid…volunteers?'

Several warriors leapt to their feet and came forward. The three named Lords walked away wordlessly to do their duty, leaving their peers behind with feelings of impotence and uselessness. To challenge this man was the same as asking for an early death.

***

The night was black beyond the capabilities of human vision to see light and so cold you could cut it with a knife. The remnants of the chosen lay huddled together in their cage, their skulls gnawed upon by the icy frigidness, their eyes unseeing, their mouths dry and lips cracked and bleeding, their limbs both stiff and yet trembling uncontrollably, their hearts beating dully in their chests and their thoughts forlorn. They all felt lost and abandoned with only the hope of death their comfort. Not even blankets had been given to them, and they all knew that they had been sentenced by the snow queen;

sentenced to death by freezing. Their time was not long in coming. No one complained, no one went down the vindictive path of laying blame. They were the Chosen, they were the Sacrifice. Their only consolation was that the girls, it seemed, had been spared their fate.

Sleep was not theirs to have, and they all lay awake listening to the mourning wind thinking absently of how much it echoed their feelings. Then the voice of death cut itself in between the emptily wailing element and mocked them, startling their fogged minds to a waking point.

'Nort dead yet then?'

'Did you hear that? Goddess have mercy! The bastard is here for us already,' whispered the croaking sound of Scar's terrified voice from their midst. They all thought him the closest to death and were trying to shelter him.

'Who's there!' challenged Horace, ready despite his inevitable fate, to spit in the eye of the grim reaper.

'Don't frighten him, Captain,' continued Scar's rasping whisper. 'Just kiss the bastard and draw him close. I've had enough.'

'We fight till we die!' grated Greybeaver. 'That's the way the Green Goddess formed us.'

'Don't see no plants growing here, Forester,' muttered Pollock.

Scar giggled.

A deep snuffling sound drifted to their ears, blown away quickly by the wind.

'That's a bloody bear, I tell you!' exclaimed Guy. 'They've put a bear in here with us for the black sport of it.'

'Much better way to die than freezing my arse off,' replied Graham. 'Come here to daddy, my furry friend,' he called out into the darkness.

'Always knew there was something wrong about you, big man,' whispered Scar. 'Too large, too hairy.'

'Would you all stop that useless gabbling so that I can listen!' commanded Horace with irritation and some nervousness in his voice.

They all fell silent.

'Marn so weak, so noisy. Dornt know even howr to die,' drifted in the deep voice again. Seemingly right in front of them.

Horace lashed out with all his strength but his blow cleaved through empty air.

A woofing, snuffling sound came to them again followed by a now curt, no-nonsense voice.

'Storp thart! Time to go.'

'Lord Krarl!' exclaimed a bewildered Horace. 'How...'

'Who else, stupid marn? Corm, time to go!'

Two rough hands grabbed his wrists, and with a short wrench, the frozen ropes that bound his hands were burst asunder. Pain lanced through him like thorn needles as the sluggish blood began to flow into his fingers again.

Like a breath, Krarl moved between the unbelieving men breaking the knots that tied them like sheep.

'Why wemane in big tent?'

'The snow lady took them away because she too is a woman and likes other women,' said a helpful Scar. He seemed very bright for someone who was just about to die.

'Cannort rescue them frrom there. Must go now. Too bard.'

His tone sounded regretful, but it was hard to tell with this man.

'But what about the guards?' whispered Luc.

'Whart about guards? They dead!' replied Krarl. 'Corm, we go now.'

Krarl swiftly guided the Chosen through the frozen, fog-shrouded camp, where the guards and the guarded hunkered down trying to preserve the little warmth left in their bodies. They had no idea that the prisoners marked for an icy death, were slipping like thawing water, through the cracks in their defensive ring. On the outskirts, they met up with the volunteers who were there as a backup to repel any pursuers if the escape had been discovered and to assist the exhausted men down the mountainside.

***

Inside the heavy material of the warm, command tent, Ahmya, Sharleen and Vivian sat up simultaneously, pulled from a deep sleep.

'Krarl!' moaned Sharleen aloud and shuddered.

'Shush, sister!' replied Ahmya quickly. 'Our brothers have been rescued. We must now see to our own uncertain fate.'

'The Cardinal will not be pleased,' whispered Vivian. 'Why did Lord Krarl not come for us as well?'

'Not without rousing the entire camp and throwing his efforts into the wind,' responded Ahmya. She felt Elisha's silent and watchful wakefulness as she listened to the unfolding of events that she was unable to sense herself. She also felt a faint thread of distress leaking from Sharleen and detecting something that was vulnerable about this woman made her feel inexplicably uncomfortable.

'Let's get as much rest as we can so we can face the outcome of these developments in the morning with a stronger heart and mind.'

She heard her own confident words but inside hidden from all was an emptiness, a foreboding even, and she secretly longed to see the reassuring face of Morgan once again.

She closed her eyes and lay back but, blissful sleep was a long time in coming.

CHAPTER XXVII

'The Shadow warriors feel that it is time to progress our agenda. To hesitate when an opponent is distracted is a wasted opportunity.'

'To move to the killing blow when your opponent is merely feinting is a sure way to die.'

'Yes, Master, but how do you know what is real and what is shadow?'

'We are dancing with an insane grandmaster. What is real to him he turns to shadow, and what is shadow he turns to reality. He pours oil on the dancefloor and capers about with a firebrand in his hand. We have to watch him, but also we must be wary for we are not the only ones waiting and looking.'

'I'm sorry, Master, but this strategy will lead us to nowhere.'

'At sunrise, on this very morn, three of the highest will be dragging themselves in their underclothes on hands and knees through dirty streets to be taunted and abused by rude and excited men and women; brought low by unsubstantiated rumours and false utterances. Our foe does not care for truth and does not recognize lies. He uses the masses to forward his cause and they see him as one of them. He is no such thing but as I said, truth does not matter in his unpredictable world. No, becomes yes, and yes, becomes no, in a blink of an eye and all without sound foundation. If we cut off the head of the snake, chaos will pour out unchecked from his rotten neck. What shall we do then, friend, when the people root us out of hiding, and the lurking vipers sink their fangs in us as we try to run?'

'We are helpless then?'

'I do not remember saying that. We are the ace card held against the chest. When we reveal it, events must be totally in our favour. The board must be swept clean in one stroke.'

'What of your niece, our once hope for the future? Will you not move to bolster her position?'

'I cannot. He wants me to do so in the guise that I bear as a merchant. He will be then able to observe the eddies of my actions and read my secrets. I fear our top card will be exposed prematurely. My niece in pursuing hasty ambition before consultation is the very thing he has been waiting for. He has easily isolated her in the field. She is not his target, Tasker, it is us, and by us, I mean all the influential guilds. He wants to turn our stones over so that he may peep underneath. We have to control the situation and learn from the sidelines.'

'It took a long time, a lot of coin and hard work to get her into her elevated position. It hurts me to watch it all go to waste.'

'My niece is very resourceful, Tasker. He sees this as just another test for her. We should view it in the same light. If she survives, her position will be even stronger.'

'There are a lot of unanswered questions here, Master. Will both her and you survive? Her memory is long. Will she still honour you when she looks back to this very day and remembers that your hand was not there when she most needed it? Will you be still useful to the Shadow when this episode is all but done?'

'We all have a purpose in life, Tasker, and none of us is irreplaceable. My instructions remain the same. Stay in the shadows and await my call.'

***

The First Citizen was in a buoyant mood. The fools could continue skulking behind doors and corridors. He would expose them to the people, their lies and their truths all in a mixed bag, and leave them to judge. Today will be a grand stage on which to perform. His audience was waiting, although they didn't know it yet. He could already hear the mob baying although the hour was yet early and the penitents were still being prepared. The poor souls had had to spend a night on their knees confessing their sins, real or imaginary, to the Black Crows; *'For God did not spare the angels when they sinned, but cast them into hell, delivering them in chains to be held in gloomy darkness until their judgement.'* The poor buggers. No doubt, they were innocent of the charges brought against them by the dubious claims pulled from the rotten soul that was the Merchant King, but all god's children had a purpose to serve, even vaunted Cardinals, and serve they must. The unfortunate idiots would be expected to divest themselves of all earthly signs of wealth, in this case, their clothing, and crawl through the filthy streets outside the walls on bared hands and knees. To help them on their way, they would be given the infamous three lashed whips of the Flagellants. He was always amazed at how the worst of the Old World managed to squirm out of its fall and continue to worm its way into the new. The sins of man will always be the sins of man. He intended to be in on the show from the outstart. He wasn't going to miss this splendid spectacle for anything.

His official entourage was nervously awaiting him outside of the closed door. Let them wait, the sycophantic bastards, whilst he enjoyed the view and his moment of reflection. He was set to be master of the world, and if he decided to be late, then everyone else will have to bloody well swallow it.

Finally satisfied with his self-glorifying and therefore, well-deserved reverie, he gathered up his voluminous purple robes and waddled towards the double-leafed doorway guarding his privacy -decorated with green intertwining plants sporting small, white, budding flowers- and pushed them open with flamboyant suddenness. He did not seem to notice when two of his officials were bowled over by this unexpected violence and ignoring the startlement and confusion stirred, bellowed enthusiastically at all and sundry.

'A marvelous, wonderful day, is it not gentlemen?'

He did not wait for an answer but swept through them and ploughed onwards, a man with the confident expectation that the world will follow him no matter what he did.

In stark contrast, the vociferous throng surging at the cordon of city guards keeping them from the throats of the cowed and frightened Cardinals, witnessed the coming of a solemn and dignified procession -swaying its way in sorrowful unison to a stately drumbeat- towards them. At its head was the unmistakable figure of their First Citizen, head bowed in regret. They fell silent in reverence as he and his entourage drew abreast of the thieving, greedy miscreants. Occasionally, a voice would break the silence and call out.

'Hang the bastards, your Honour sir!'

'Don't let them get away with this, Holiness!'

'They be dirty scum. Send em to hell!'

Three men ran forward and placed the small end of a large, extended cone before his mouth then slowly the First Citizen's head rose into the sunlight, his eyes glassy with unshed tears, and his hand, tremulous in the air, waved a joint blessing and a plea to be heard.

'You are my children. We are god's beloved children. We all, sometimes in the dark, sometimes in the light, do wrong. Only the god can see us at all times. Like the benign father that he is, in his wisdom, at times, gives us another chance. With your permission, with your agreement, I would like to grant these pitiful sinners grovelling at our feet, a second chance, but only on your say so. Still, they have to repent! They must bear the mark of repentance! On their backs! On their knees! On their souls!'

His powerful voice was beginning to rise and magnified by his instrument, boomed in the air over the now hushed crowd. Then his tone fell again.

'Sadly, the house of the god, built as a stepping stone between earth and heaven, built as a sanctuary to succour those who should represent you and your affairs to the all-seeing father, has become filled with narrow, short vision doubters! Listen to me! They take on many guises! Merchants! Priests even! Administrators! Some stand in the fullness of sunlight and lie into your face with a smile! They cheat you! Others hide in the shadows and threaten our peace with vile threats of death! I beseech you! Help me to root them out; every one of them, and put them to the test! God's test! Help me to bring them before you like these three misguided sinners! Help me to bring them to the test!'

His voice finished in a crescendo of emotion, echoing over the heads of the enraptured mob.

'Walk with me, my children. Walk with me. Help me to guide these wicked, weak sacks of flesh back onto the path of righteousness and honesty! Walk with me! Keep me upright in my sorrow, in my disappointment, so that I can carry the burden of this onerous task to the end! Walk with me! Be my staff! Do not let me falter! Walk with me and help me scourge the evil from these three willful children of mine!'

The crowd roared and gathered around their talisman dressed in robes of purple, screaming at the terrified Cardinals to get crawling on their way through the streets of purgatory. Dirty was their streets, but the true filth lay hidden in the pristine corridors of the Inner Enclave. The First Citizen had called on them. He would lead them on a Holy Crusade to cleanse the skulking, black souls; to drag them back into the light. These three were just the beginning. He would point the finger at the rest, and they would descend upon them with the wrath of god.

CHAPTER XXVIII

The Peacock General was feeling the enormous strain of his once much-coveted position. A face which in the not too distant past was considered youthful and handsome, now exhibited hard care-lines where vengeful, crow's feet dragged their talons deep in the corners of his ever squinting eyes. 'Be careful what you wish for,' he thought. 'It might just well come true.' His ambitious dream had become a nightmare. He walked along the rag-tag lines of the once mighty, front-line, assault troops, smelling their unwashed stink and noticing the haunted expressions in their vacant expressions. Not too long ago, they had marched under the rampant, fluttering banner of the Honey General, thoughts of conquest, fame and riches to the forefront of their minds. Now, all that occupied that space was the hopeful opportunity to be somewhere else, other than in this cold, inhospitable and barren place. He had potentially two fronts to face, two fronts to defend, low morale, fading food supplies and the tag of rebel placed over his head. His counterpart based in the Green Kingdoms had refused to come to his aid, citing revolts and disturbances within his domain. But the sad truth was that his City, the Empire, had turned their backs on them. Any person or persons offering them assistance would be given summary execution. On the same hand, anyone deserting their beleaguered ranks would suffer the same fate. This order, he was left to understand, had come directly from the First Citizen. The beautiful, once influential and clever Cardinal, a woman out of her own time, who had had the audacity to venture into the field of war and usurp the post of an active general, was now persona non grata, an exile, with her ravishing head under the shadow of an axe. He had betrayed his own commander by taking his command, so he deserved his fate. He was, for all intents and purposes, the Snow Queen's man, and he would stick with her to the bitter end. What other choice did he have!

'Sir, we have visitors approaching.'

He pulled himself back to the bleak situation in hand and strained his vision to peer through the blustery, snow-devils as they swept back and forth across the rocky, icy mountainscape, restless it seemed for something to happen. The ever-present whiteness made his head hurt, constantly.

'So we have,' he muttered in response. As none of his outriders had come galloping up the treacherous slope to bring him warning he assumed that the as yet unidentified visitors were known to them.

Gesturing for his horse, he mounted wearily and clicked at it to move it ploddingly a little to the front of his line. Immediately, the four horsemen veered towards him.

The lead rider, an army scout renegade, saluted him smartly and said.

'Found these three wandering like lost sheep in the foothills, Sir. They claim to bring a message from the First Citizen to our Snow Queen.

They all called her that. He looked at the three riders behind the scout, and any fool, except a Green Kingdom renegade, could clearly see that they were indeed messengers of the god. His glance fell on the leather casket on the shoulder of one of the horses and an involuntary groan escaped his lips.

'Who said things couldn't get any worse,' he thought.

Nodding to his second in command he said.

'Take over here. I'll escort them through myself. See to it that I'm informed of any changes to our situation. Emissaries, please follow me.'

Clicking to his horse once again, he turned it and led the way back to the imperial audience tent.

The four guards at the entrance recognised him at sight and the messengers by reputation and swiftly pulled back the huge, heavy flaps to allow them entry. He found the Snow Queen in the midst of a full audience with the members of her entire court. Arrayed in front of her were the female captives from now functionless Keep, where so many of his men had lost their lives. They were not in chains, but it was apparent that their free will had been taken away from them. Still, they sat there proud and self-contained. He did not like them. To him, they were haughty and arrogant. Why her Eminence tolerated them in such an elevated view, he had no idea but did not think it was right. Maybe, she saw them as pampered and exotic pets.

The Snow Queen had stopped whatever she had been saying and was looking towards them with an unreadable expression. The entire gathering had fallen into hushed expectation, and every eye was fixed on the newcomers.

'I see you've brought us familiar guests, General. Please, bring them forward,' she said suddenly, her unique voice carrying clearly across the warm space.

With an erect and martial stride he advanced through the central corridor formed by courtiers, and arriving before her dais, fell to his knees and bowed his forehead into the thick carpet. He could feel the messengers shifting uncomfortably behind him as only the First Citizen was greeted in such a fashion. His risky but spontaneous gesture was not lost on all of the informed audience. The room went even more silent if that were a thing possible, except for a soft, musical peal of laughter from his queen.

Pointedly ignoring the three standing messengers, Sybil Wuzitian spoke directly to him.

'Have we heard anything from our craven, double-crossing enemies as yet, dear General?'

Everyone knew that she was not referring to the warriors of the Green and Lower Kingdoms.

'No, Eminence,' he answered carefully. 'There have been no sightings as yet.'

'What a pity. The sooner we can get this overblown farce over with, the better for all of us, eh, Messengers of the God? I had not expected to have you back with us so soon. What ill breath have you wafted at us this time. You certainly are earning your wings.'

'We have been tasked, Eminence, in bringing you your final message.'

'I'm sure it will be even more delightful than the first. Please, proceed.'

Her composure was truly admirable. Whereas everyone present was staring with morbid fascination and anxiety at the leather casket, she did not glance at it once but studied the carrier with quiet, penetrating eyes.

Donning a shiny looking glove made from the stomach of a goat, the messenger under observation unsealed the container and gingerly withdrew its grisly contents and without so much as a grimace offered up the contents for the Cardinal to view.

Her face remained as soft and delicate as a freshly formed flower.

'I commend you, Emissary. Professionally done. My dear mother has never been so gently and respectfully handled except by those who loved her during her too short a life. The vile beast who ordered this has also deprived you and your family of this respect in the future that you have now given both my beloved mother and me. I am sorry.'

The Emissary did not flinch as his death sentence was given but bowed his head slightly in recognition of its inevitability. His comrade, however, was not so accepting.

'Eminence, hear me. We have something else to offer you!'

'If my memory serves me correctly, of the three, there is but one sanctioned speaker. Only if misfortune strikes is another mouth opened. This, sir, is an unprecedented break in protocol, is it not? You cannot be heard.'

'Tell her! This is not the time to be silent, fool! We have been abandoned to die! Tell her!'

The Speaker's eyes remained fastened to the carpet and refused to acknowledge the pleas of his fellow messenger.

'Take them away,' said the Snow Queen, her soft voice betraying a cold edge and a hint of the strain she was under.

'The leader of the rebels! I have it! His name is Morgan Ap Heston!' shouted the fellow desperately.

'Silence!' shouted the Queen. No one had ever heard her shout before. 'Take this man out, remove his tongue, and cut off his head.'

As her guards grabbed the three messengers, she said again, her voice once again soft.

'No, just that worm. Leave the other two.'

As the cowardly messenger was dragged kicking, pleading and sobbing from the tented chamber, the Snow Queen regarded his two waiting comrades quietly. They felt fear in their hearts, wondering why that given name had caused such a vengeful reaction.

'I am honoured to add bravery to your growing list of commendations. Your duty can be one of the hardest to fulfil in the name of our city.'

Neither man moved or tried to speak.

'I am still a High Cardinal of the Protectorate Empire and of the powers invested in me, I rescind your contract with us and command you into retirement. As a reward, you are instructed to take your place in the vanguard of our army and given the distinction of being the first to receive and repel our enemies on this very day. Your families shall be granted your life pensions. You may go. All of you! You may go!'

Caught by surprise by the turn of events and the abrupt ending, the courtiers numbly turned and filed after the two messengers being escorted to the exit.

***

Ahmya, Sharleen, Elisha and the two Blue Mountain youngsters, Stephania and Vivian were unsure exactly why they were being displayed in such a fashion. Cardinal Sybil Wuzetian against expectations had not seemed angry at all when she learnt of the escape of their brothers. In fact, she did not seem concerned in the least. She instead, had invited them to sit with her during an audience with her court. Why? Elisha thought that they were her trophies nailed on the wall. Sharleen said that she didn't care in the least, one way or another, as long as she did not kill them, fed them, and allowed them a bath now and again. Live and opportunities would present themselves, no matter how careful their captor, and captives they were, a small thing they must not forget. Ahmya thought it was much more complicated than that. In a way, this powerful, accomplished woman needed their approval as she perceived them to be also powerful, independent women in their own right. She, in addition, sensed that they possessed something that she did not have, and was intrigued. She wanted them to tell her what it was and whether or not she could make use of it. She also wanted to demonstrate that she could dominate and awe them with her dominance in a man's world. In a nutshell, the Cardinal had undefined and confused emotions and regard towards them. When things conflicted in the judgement of a woman such as she, the situation could change on the drop of a hat and become dangerous for them. Despite their apparent access to comforts, they were as much in a cage as their brothers had been. They too needed to escape, the sooner, the better, if they wanted to survive.

Sitting in silence through the extraordinary happenings during the morning, made Ahmya realise her worst fears. Beneath her calm, strangely sensuous exterior, the Cardinal was unpredictable, ruthless, determined, intelligent and now, she aspired to be a queen. She experienced a hollow feeling as the tent emptied on Sybil Wuzetian's emphatic orders.

The Snow Queen sat unmoving for a long count of ten, seemingly deep in thought. She appeared to be suppressing and rightly so, deep and private grief, which she refused the world to see. Then as if speaking to herself she started.

'I truly regret this. I was hoping that we would be able to keep each other's company on the long journey ahead. I need the company of sisters, sisters equal and worthy of me, but I'm afraid it is time for you to pick back up the stick your master threw down for you. How did you refer to yourselves? Ah yes, the Sacrifice. Believe me, I truly understand the sentiment behind this word. Well, darlings, now you must become my Sacrifice. Guards! Chain these women together!'

Ahmya caught the flame of anger as it leapt into Elisha's eyes and doused it with a barely perceptible, negative shake of her head. She glanced at Sharleen's calm face to confirm her own thoughts; wait, be patient, our time will come, then we strike. The two youngsters looked confused, unable to understand the quickly shifting nuances of their situation. They did not offer any struggle or show of resistance as neck rings were placed around their collars attached by links of blue metal; the chains of a slave. This was an outrage, a thing of shame even in the Empire of the Protectorate where from its founding, slavery was not permitted.

'Stake them in place ten yards in front of our vanguard. Let that undying bastard from the pages of our history and his annoying rebels pound their flesh into the rocks before they can get to us. Their shed blood shall be the first sign of his final destruction!'

The last of the Chosen captives hardly recognised her voice, barely remembered the charming, controlling Cardinal who had allowed herself to be transformed by a name into an entity of rage and unreason; the Snow Queen had become a queen of fire.

After the warmth and comforts of the past few days, the cold struck them in the face like a sudden and unexpected punch. They did not see any sympathy in the eyes of the soldiers leading them like leashed dogs. In fact, they sensed the satisfaction of long denied justice seeping out of them, especially from the over-decorated General marching in the lead.

Dragged through the ranks of a hate-filled army that had seen far better days, they were shoved roughly to their knees, and two burly, bearded and grim looking soldiers armed with sledgehammers on short handles proceeded to pound two iron stakes into the hard rock.

'Glad to see they're taking her literally,' uncharacteristically mumble Sharleen.

'Bah!' replied Elisha, spitting onto the frozen rocks. 'I'm not a lady overly fond of waiting. Should have strangled the bitch when I had her in front of me.'

It was her way of saying that her sisters had given her ill-advice.

'Quiet, scum! Your black curses will not help you now,' yelled the Peacock General at them, and stomped off with his men.

'Why do you think she did a flipsy when she heard Morgan's name?' asked Sharleen.

'Maybe she was a jilted lover back in his bad old days,' muttered Elisha. 'He can't have lived that long without deflowering a few fillies.'

'Goddess help me, your mouth is even dirtier than Scar's,' observed Sharleen.

Elisha grinned at her.

'Whatever he must have done, the cut is deep enough to have left a terrible unhealed wound inside her,' answered Ahmya to Sharleen's original question. 'But maybe the murder of her mother had something to do with it as well. Her mind was not entirely hers when Morgan's name was uttered.'

'Maybe so, but let's not forget what a cold bitch she is. However, that man seems to have messed up a lot of things in his long life,' commented Sharleen.

'All men do,' commented Elisha. 'Most of the time they only have one thing on their minds.'

No one noticed that Ahmya's cheeks had turned a bit flushed despite the leaching cold.

'Don't talk about Lord Morgan like that. He is the One!' said Stephania.

They all fell silent for a while, thinking their own thoughts. Then Sharleen's voice broke it, heavy with chagrin.

'Yeah, him and his bastard brother.'

CHAPTER XXIX

The barbarians had breached the gates and overrun the walls. The fighting now taking place in the narrow streets was pitiless and violent. The palace soldiers fought desperately, hand to hand, dodging flying and falling pieces of burning rubble and trying their best not to get tripped up or foiled by stampeding citizens, wild-eyed and panic struck, attempting to find safe refuge where there was none. Their sole function in the streets of the lowly townsfolk was to buy time for the royal family to escape with their treasures. They had ruled this port, growing rich on the taxation of ships and their cargoes of oil and wine that had needed to navigate this narrow strait on which fortune had allowed them to squat for millennia, to save time and avoid pirates and treacherous open seas. They had become a dynasty of despots, lording it over those they should have been serving and preying on everybody else. Leading the uncouth ruffians who called themselves citizens of the City State, was a warrior who had looked like any other man with nothing much to distinguish him from the rest of the multitude. He had come before them as a representative of the country folk beseeching the palace on their behalf, to lessen the burdensome yoke of taxation on their necks and allow time for the back payment of said debts. They had laughed at him and told him to mind his own business as a foreigner should, or he would find himself as their guest in the dungeons.

The goddess knows what he said to so incite the people to turn on their betters, but now here they were tearing down what they did not have the intelligence to build in the first place, destroying what they could not understand, greedy to take what was not theirs to have. And the man at their head? He was not a man, but a fiend in disguise. No one could touch him in battle, no one could equal his strength and cold ferocity. He planned our destruction and unleashed hell upon us. In one brief morning of fire and sword, we were thrown into despair and poverty, driven from our rightful home, our sanctified royal seat. Our memory is long, and with every passing year, our desire for revenge grows. We tracked the passage of this demon who had brought our house down into wrack and ruin, the Royal House of Wuzetian. We followed him from generation to generation, waiting for our time. We saw what others did not. We saw him for what he was, a devil, a timeless devil. His name we whispered to our children and our children's children. Do not forget! We soaked his name in our family's blood and made an immortal pack with the goddess of death. We will have our revenge! We will bring death to this Morgan Ap Heston no matter how long it takes! He is ours, and we shall have him! It is our primary duty above all else, so do we swear.

'What can you tell me about Cardinal Sybil Wuzetian?'

'She is a complicated woman from a complicated family, Lord Morgan. I may be able to provide a better insight if you make your questions more specific,' answered General Montford, aka the Honey General.

'Fair enough. Is she a capable military leader?'

'She is extremely intelligent and a fast learner, but to my knowledge, she has never studied military tactics.'

'Is she someone that people tend to follow?'

'That one is more difficult. She is very charismatic. Men are beguiled by her. She fascinates them and oozes sensuality combined with the ability to issue clear instructions that cut to the heart of things. She can also be ruthless and is driven by ambition.'

'If she is cornered would she negotiate or fight her way out?'

'Both, I'm afraid. Negotiations for her are just another battlefield.'

'Is she loyal to the Empire or to herself?'

'Family and ambition lie top-most for her on the scale of life, but which comes first I am unable to say. The survival and expansion of the Empire are essential for both these things to flourish.'

'How is she regarded by the Conclave?'

'As a newcomer, an outsider and an interloper. Most of the nine are afraid of her for the First Citizen has never moved or sided against her. Her uncle too is very influential and appears somewhat of an enigma.'

'Her uncle?'

'Yes, he is the Head of the House of Merchants, but he conducts business with confidence that hints of hidden support from as yet unknown corners.'

'Is he on good terms with the military?'

'Yes, of course. He, through his contacts, funds many of our enterprises. He tends to do these things through his niece, but his House and mine have had cordial relations for years.'

'And the House of Montford is a strictly military one.'

'Yes.'

'There was a royal household that once carried the name Wuzetian. It was of a different time and a different place. You have said that they are seen as newcomers. Could these people be survivors of this once Royal House?'

'Many think so. They, as far as I know, arrived in our city many generations ago. They were refugees but seemed to possess finely honed skills in trade negotiations, knowledge and logistics. They understood both land routes and sea routes, especially sea routes, and had extensive comprehension on all things to do with ships, sailing them, building them and equipping them. The Merchant Guild apparently found them very useful.'

'Thank you, General. You have been very helpful.'

'I'm happy to help in any way I can, Lord Morgan, my way back to my former life is a pass that is truly blocked. If it is not presumptuous of me, what will you do next, Lord? If we venture out from these woods, the Protectorate at our rear will have us and if we don't march forth the Cardinal keeps her unassailable perch.'

'You know her better than I do, General. Ask yourself these questions. What does this perch as you call it, this perch that she has given so much of her soldier's lives so to gain, now mean to her? How much longer can she sit up in that cold place whilst her army freezes and want for sustenance? What is happening to her position and allies in her city whilst she sits on a bare rock of indecision?'

'She will come for you.'

'Yes, General, she will come for us, and what position will we be in then?

'No matter what their orders are, the occupying force in this land will join her in a two-fronted attack. Now we are the meat between the crusts.'

'Yes, General. The game has started. Prepare yourself for battle.'

The Honey General leapt to his feet and hurried off to don his armour. With this man in their lead, things were bound to escalate very fast.

***

The Peacock General was troubled. The weather was deteriorating rapidly, and he was not comfortable in leaving a full army of hungry men standing at the ready in such an exposed position. The expected attack had not materialized, and his scouts' last report had clearly stated that the enemy still remained hiding in the shadow of their beloved trees. The first thing they should do when this land of skulkers was truly subdued is to cut every one of those useless plants down and turn them into functional and profitable timber! He strode back towards the audience tent with a firm mind to demand that his Queen allow the men to stand down. To his surprise he found an army of servants dismantling the huge canopy and packing it away. He found the Snow Queen serenely sitting in a much smaller affair warming her hands absently over a brazier. He stood to attention and cleared his throat.

'Yes, darling, what can I do for you?' she asked huskily.

As usual, in the presence of this woman, he began to lose his concentration.

'Our men are freezing to death in the open, Eminence. If they are not allowed to stand down, they will join the frigid rocks around them.'

'Has the enemy been sighted?'

'No, Eminence. They have not left the cover of their trees.'

'Then we shall go and force them out.'

'Eminence?'

'You heard me, General. Prepare the men to march. That should bring warmth to their limbs at least.'

'But...'

'I'm tired of sitting here on this barren rock of failed enterprise, General. Let us do what we do best. Let us seize back the initiative and force that undying bastard into the open. When we attack, our reluctant countrymen on flat ground will have no choice but to follow suit. We will have them, General! We will have them all!'

'But...'

'Stop stammering like an idiot and issue your orders, General. We descend in fighting order at once. Leave a rear guard behind us to protect against a nasty bite.'

'Yes, Eminence, at once Eminence.'

***

'Get moving! Slow mind'yu! Any funny business and we fill your guts with arrows. Walk!'

That was easier said than done. Crouching and kneeling on the hard frozen rock with a frigid fog leeching whatever was left of your warmth away did not provide the ideal conditions to spring to your feet and stroll down a mountainside. They all struggled to their feet, slapping their thighs and rubbing their leg muscles in an attempt to dispel the crippling 'pins and needles' that sent lancing stabs of agony through them. All, except Ahmya who stood smoothly and helped a staggering Elisha to steady herself. The woman looked at her and frowned but did not say anything. None of them spoke, conserving their energy and watching, waiting for that chance that still had not presented itself. They were glad to be moving for movement presented opportunity. Chains jingling in the cold, misty air, they set out down the slope at a measured pace, followed closely by the vanguard of the Snow Queen's army.

They descended between the broad, cleared space cut through the tree line and down to the flat cultivated plain, now left unattended, the fields strangled by weeds, as the hardy farmers thought it best to stay out of the way of men at war. Still, nothing happened and the army, tense with expectation, kept their heavy shields raised on trembling arms and their chins tucked down into their throats, helmets glinting in the dull sunlight.

Shouted orders reminded them to fan out into ordered ranks, their officers not taking the word of their scouts as to no sign of the enemy, too seriously. Everything before them seemed quiet and undisturbed, even the large, black crows picked and stabbed at any bit of grain they could find in a cocky and unconcerned manner, strutting about in arrogance, now and again breaking the silence with a croaky squawk.

'Oh, it's so nice to be warm again,' said Elisha. 'I'd forgotten I had hands and feet.'

'What's Morgan up to, I wonder?' mused Ahmya. 'I sense nothing but emptiness.'

She glanced behind them over the heads of the solid fence of the massed army and noticed the heavy baggage train followed by the bunched up courtiers inching their way noisily down the incline. In the middle of this, fluttered the Cardinal's personal banner.

'She's making sure this time that she is recognised by all, I see,' mumbled Sharleen.

'She is a forthright and shameless hussy,' muttered Elisha.

On a long line of stones, piled by the dirt farmers to clear their fields for easier tilling, a man appeared standing. No one could tell if he had been waiting there all this time and had not been noticed or if he had suddenly materialised out of thin air.

'Morgan!' exclaimed both Ahmya and Vivian at the same time.

'How can you tell?' asked Sharleen, sheltering her eyes with her hand. 'It could be anybody at this distance.'

'It's him,' said Ahmya with no doubt at all in her voice.

'How embarrassing for the One to see us like this,' commented Stephania in a small voice.

'We're alive, aren't we?' replied Elisha dryly.

The Peacock General, for all his faults, responded immediately. He leapt on his horse and thundered out towards the lone man, five mounted troopers from each flank, manned by cavalry, raising out to join him.

'Hope he kills the bastards!' muttered Stephania darkly', as they galloped by them.

Morgan watched them coming and felt the change in pressure as a wind began to pick up behind him. He glanced upwards and began to calculate, picturing the possible unfolding of events and the time it would take them to unfold.

The General pulled back savagely on his mount's reins causing the bit to saw harshly against its mouth. The tormented beast, nostrils flaring, skidded to a stop, rearing up in protest, blowing and stamping. His men continued in an encircling motion, surrounding the lone man who gazed at the General, unsettlingly unconcerned by their aggressive and intimidating antics.

'Who the blazes are you!' demanded the Peacock General, eying the unarmoured man whose only weapon appeared to be a short, streamlined, slightly curved, slashing sword, sheathed in a plain, leather scabbard and pushed as if by after-thought, through a broad belt cinched around a narrow, athletic waist.

'My name, General, is Morgan Ap Heston,' replied the man in a soft, deep voice.

The General and his men seemed startled into stillness. Then in an arrogant tone, the General continued.

'I'm afraid then, Morgan Ap Heston, you will have to come with us.'

The man who had just named himself as the hated leader of the forest rebels seemed to be now idly looking up at the mountain rising in front of him.

'You had best go back and do something about defending your rear, General, and while you're at it, would you kindly extend an invitation to your Cardinal to talks?'

'What in tar…,' the General followed the line of the lone man's eyes and froze in horror.

The wind, now gusting energetically around them, had cleared the mist and fog shrouding the mountain from which they had just descended. An extended ring of armed men, about six ranks thick and stationed in checkerboard squares stood just above the treeline, weapons and helms flashing in the now brilliant sunshine.

'Hurry along, General. We will not tarry much longer before testing the ability of your men to fight on both fronts. Deliver, please, my message to your High Cardinal. I will wait here for her answer.'

The astonished General whipped his head from looking at the army on the mountain threatening his weary troops and the calm, stern man standing on his pile of stones. Closing his slack-jawed mouth with a snap, he issued his orders.

'You five, stay here! The rest of you, follow me!'

With that, he spun his horse and raced back to his Queen.

CHAPTER XXX

In the nest of pit vipers that constituted the players within the walls of the Holy Conclave, Father Prior was probably the most loyal. He held his position purely by the luck of catching the eye of the First Citizen when he was still just a young, fresh-faced, soon to be ordained priest. A novice who had been fingered for duty within the Great Library due to his skill in making clear sense of small, seemingly unrelated, details. He suffered from chronic ill-health which had left him with weak lungs and the loss of all bodily hair and so, he had never harboured any hopes of rising very high within the church's hierarchy. Then one day, purely by accident, he had found a small, non-descript scroll written in the neat, scrawling hand-writing of the very first, First Citizen, the architect, designer and founder of the Holy City. In this scroll, written in code, he found the forming of the fledgeling ideas of the Holy Father, and this one, in particular, was directed to the members of the Holy Conclave itself. It took him over a year to break the code, and his findings poured cold water over the tradition that elevation to the Nine was a thing voted on and approved by a joint sitting. This, he was able to show, was not the intention of the Great Founder or his successor Cardinal Crispin. Ascension to the Nine was the sole prerogative of the First Citizen. He had strengthened the hand of the then sitting First Citizen in one fell swoop, in a way that could not have been imagined and the holy gaze had been focused on him ever since. He was now his servant, his fate tied to his like a ball to a chain. He served when he had suddenly found himself chief librarian of the secretive and holy archives, and he served now in his present role as Spymaster. At heart, he was still a young priest who believed in the god, in his church and in the supreme office of the First Citizen. Given a chance, he would take a sword in the stomach for the great man. Many, however, saw him as independent thinking, ruthless and a dangerous player who had amassed secret information on everything and everybody. His master had unleashed chaos, and the webbed strands of power-politics were thrumming with energy. His job was to listen to them, pick them up and follow them to the source. The most dangerous, he knew was that of the enigmatic Merchant King. With his niece neutralised, for now, he could bend all his formidable talents on him. There was something not quite right for a man who professed to be merely a merchant, be it a rich and influential one. He was a bit too confident, even bold in his contacts and contracts; too assured in his person. He had his suspicions, but he needed to find proof. It was too dangerous to try and remove him at this moment for his presence kept the scales balanced, but he needed to give his master a subtle means to control him. Yes, he was loyal, but he certainly was not a fool. His Master was unpredictable. That was a fact that required no detail to study. He also considered people only as so far as their usefulness to him. If they were no longer useful then that made them expendable; an object to be thrown away or traded in a deal. He was not entirely sure of where he stood in the First Citizen's books at the moment. Chaos reigned, and he had to find his way through it. His first step in this vibrating web of deceit and stealthy ambition was to look more closely at the dealings and relationships between the House of the Merchant King and certain powerful military families, in particular, the House of Montford. It was those who pretended to be the most faithful and obedient that the greatest surprises can spring forth and bite the unwary and unprepared.

***

'Has there been any further news on your brother?'

'No, Sir. He seems to have vanished on the route back. He left with old Turpin and one other. A member of his staff, I think.'

'From a General to an outcast! How could he allow such shame on the family?'

This last came from a long-nosed, straight-backed man with short-cropped, grey-streaked hair and wearing the frock of a priest.

'Do not be so harsh on your brother. We do not know for sure the details of his decommissioning,' replied the first speaker. An old man seated in a rocking chair with a tartan blanket draped over his knees but with a voice as hard as granite.

The second speaker, a tall man, lean, with long grey hair and a ram-rod posture who stood by an open window gazing at the rolling hills in the distance with bluish-grey eyes that calculated everything, spoke again.

'Our brother has the mind of a general but the appetite of a cook. He was always too complacent with those he deemed to be on his side.'

'Yes, and he allowed himself to be flanked by a bloody politician!'

The exasperation in the old man's tone was clear to his two sons.

'Do you think she had him murdered?' asked the eldest son casually, still looking out of the window.

'Be wary of treasonous words, brother. They are not tolerated by the church. Like it or not we are dealing with the actions and decisions of a High Cardinal.'

'Do not forget that your first duty is to your House. Blood is blood. The Montfords fight and die for their city, not for individual Cardinals. You are a Montford if my memory serves me correctly. Do not forget this.'

The old man's reprimand barked into the space, and the three let an interval of silence sooth the differences in opinion.

After a time, the eldest son spoke again.

'Uncertain times have found us again, Father. We must ensure that our dealings and actions are open and in keeping with the interest of our great city.'

The old man responded testily.

'We have always done so. I'm afraid this may not be enough to safeguard us entirely. There is no one out there who can threaten the Empire. War is in short supply, but unfortunately, there are many competent generals walking around with nothing better to do but fill their coffers with coin and make a mess of politics. Military Houses are no longer bastions; we've become expendable.'

'Then maybe it is time that we withdraw from those questionable enterprises that you've just mentioned, Father.'

'There is the thing, my strategist. It is easier said than done. Our feet are somewhat mired in the bog of profit and the light from an unpredictable burning fire may soon descend upon us.'

'God help us all,' said the priest. 'I should be the last to say this, but we need a war to survive.'

'Be careful what you wish for, brother,' muttered the eldest.

***

The First Citizen was pleased with himself. His torch in the form of a mob was already burning away the chaff from the corn. Many so-called loyal houses had already decamped and headed for their country estates. They were still within his reach, and could not escape and if necessary, his finger would soon start pointing, and the dogs of fire and righteousness would descend upon them, scorching the sins from their souls. He was not yet ready to do so for many had valuable properties and possessions which he could make good use of. Why destroy when you had the option to just take? Not for himself of course, but for the people, for the City. The Merchant guild was already sending him donations for this and that, but the wily Merchant King was making sure that these gifts were all widely known to the people before they were presented on his doorstep. No matter, he was having the last laugh, for with this coin he was funding free bread to the poor quarters. So in the long run, making the merchants cut a percentage, small though it may be, from their coffers by using their own presents to stop them from emptying the pockets of the poor. He was still the darling of the people whilst they were showing themselves in an increasingly bad light as grubby, mean, coin grabbers, giving gifts to those already wealthy at the expense of those who have nothing. Now, he wondered, what was his little digger in the dirt was up to? He had the knack of appearing at his elbow without warning, literally as well as figuratively. He must never overlook the inconspicuous, little bastard. He did not want to win the world only to have it snatched away by a concealed stiletto in the throat by the little cricket you thought to be a pet.

'Where are you boy!?' he bellowed. 'You can stop hiding. I have no interest in fondling you!'

A young, flustered, brown-robed novice appeared in the doorway, one of his many assistants.

'Go and find me the Spymaster. Tell him I have important matters to discuss, and he must come to me at once!'

'Yes, Eminence,' the boy stammered and fled down the dimly lit, wood-panelled corridor.

CHAPTER XXXI

Krarl led them out at dawn. The handful of Protectorate scouts nosing around in the darkness would never see the light of another day again as Krarl eliminated them one by one, tearing their lives away before they even knew that death was upon them. And so it was, that the rear-guard, left behind by the Peacock General to act as a screen against surprise, was a victim of their worst fears. Before a slate-grey, dawn sky could lighten the hard, rough landscape below, silent, figures of war broke in on their bleary-eyed vigilance, bent on their annihilation. They descended on them in a manner hard, fast and merciless, putting them to the sword in such a ruthless and grim fashion that none could escape to warn their comrades. Those who tried to break away and flee were brought down by the deadly impact of well-aimed, cold, iron barbs. Before the dead, lying lifeless on the icy rocks, could lose their last residual warmth, a memory of life, uncaring feet marched upwards over their corpses and took up their positions of dominance on the crown of the mountain. They had just deployed when a blustery wind split apart the cloying, cold fog shrouding them and the now mid-day sun, bathed them in its burning, brilliant light, turning their gear of war into reflecting, metallic mirrors. The armies of the Lower Kingdoms stood united in their first test against the might of the Protectorate Empire.

As they stood revealed by the sudden dispersal of the mists, the unease of the unwary army below them was a thing clear to see, like a ripple of a flock of geese on a lake preparing to take uncertain flight at the sight of soaring eagles in the heavens. The unnaturally far-seeing eyes of their leader, standing well ahead of the ordered field, could see necks with anxious faces attached, craning back at them and still, beyond, a horseman with five others tailing him, racing pall-mall back from another group stationed out on the plain around the figure of a lone, standing man.

'Harving fun, brodar?' chuckled Krarl.

***

The Snow Queen felt the palpable change in the atmosphere around her. The shift, like a displacement in the fabric of time, happened in the blink of an eye; a thing felt but not seen. She sensed the ripple of uncertainty like a pebble thrown into a pond, flowing through her forces, switching them from steely determination to ready flight. Following the panicked curve of their eyes to the point of terror, her heart skipped a beat. Sitting on her shoulders stood an unimagined army; something she, her general and her advisors, had thought possible but highly unlikely. But yet, here they were, fangs bared and ready to bite her rear.

Before her mind could think of a suitable response, she caught sight of her army's commander whipping his horse in a cloud of frantic dust towards her position.

'Bad news comes in threes,' she muttered. 'That's two so far.'

Skidding his horse to a sliding stop her General flung himself from his blowing mount and went down on one knee before her. Chest heaving from his exertions he said.

'Eminence, it is the leader of the Green rebels himself, Morgan Ap Heston, who stands like a cockerel alone on the open plain. He calls on you to join him in parley. Just say the word, my Queen, and I shall strike him down.'

'Oh, Queen is it,' she responded but did not sound displeased. 'No, General, my family knows of this fiend. Ten men of arms will not be enough to do the deed, and I would be sending you to your death if I gave you such a bold command. I am not yet ready to see you dead.'

The General glanced up at her a perplexed look plastered on his face.

'Never mind,' she continued, her voice still smooth and sensual. 'I take it you have seen his forces arrayed in a commanding post behind us. No doubt, he claims another stands waiting to appear at our front. I would like to hear what this devil has to say and even to see the form he takes. His name unhinges me with hate, but yet I am intrigued. Whenever he appears, members of my family die. Yet, my curiosity must be appeased. Tell him that I will agree to a meeting but only under certain conditions which I will specify by this eve. And General, do not provoke him.'

The now jealous man bowed low before his beloved Queen though still on bended knee and pounded a clenched fist over his heart. Then lurching to his feet, he leapt back onto his sweating horse to deliver her will.

The elevated General, now turned messenger, galloped back to his mark and announced his Queens reply with haughty arrogance.

Morgan did not move his gaze from idly examining the forces on the hill.

'General, inform your Queen that if she is not here before me within half an hour my forces shall move against her and no quarter shall be given. She can bring whomever she wants to the talks and will find me here waiting alone for I will need no other. Go, General, go now, before my mind is changed.'

All this was said in a quiet, absent voice, but the threat was there clear for all to hear.

With his Queen's warning hanging over his head, the faithful man turned angrily and carried out his duty.

When the Snow Queen received his ultimatum, she laughed, her voice a clear musical instrument, ringing pleasantly against the magnificent backdrop and in the tense air. She took her General, his five men of arms and three courtiers, and sauntered out in a slow, stately fashion, to meet the nemesis of her family and fate.

Morgan had not moved once during this time, not even to ease his stance. He seemed both carved from stone, like a temple guardian of old, yet at the same time, so relaxed and at ease that he portrayed a figure with lethal intent contained in a frightening way, within a thin layer of sun-bronzed, strangely reddish skin. Those who were left to keep him in sight and under control were afraid to breathe in his presence for fear of awakening that which they sensed but could not see. As the Snow Queen and her entourage drew up before him, he spoke without taking his gaze from the mountain.

'As a preliminary to our discussion and a show of good faith, I formally request that you free the brave warriors tied like dogs waiting to be put down. Their indignity does them nor us any good.'

The Queen studied the man perched on his pile of stones as if he bestrode a mountain and who seemed ordinary yet not, then with a gentle nod of her elegant head, spoke to her General.'

'Do as he asks, and invite them to join us here; all in good faith.'

No more words were exchanged during the interval it took for her General to carry out her command. Everyone except the two antagonists was unsettled and decidedly uncomfortable by the surreal mood infiltrating the short wait.

The General and his men soon returned, their horses plodding at the flanks of the five captive women corralling them as if they were cattle being led to slaughter. Their neck chains were still in place linking them together, yet they strode forward with the pride of queens, unbowed, unbroken, making their escort appear to be petty bullies rather than conquerors.

Although his expression did not change, Morgan's thoughtful, brown eyes began to dance with flecks of gold, and inexplicable energy began to buzz in the air around him. Those who thought themselves his guards were startled by this unnatural and unexpected phenomenon and their horses shied away, tossing their necks and rolling their eyes in consternation. The Snow Queen, her poise momentarily broken, strived to control her agitated mount, a perplexing frown marring her beautiful, smooth features. Tightening her facial muscles and that of her hold on the unruly animal she sat astride, she turned her annoyed attention to her general with the thought to chastise him, but it was too late. A snap of power blew through the air, seizing the disgruntled man and pounded him into the hard earth, driving his breath and his resentful thoughts out of him. The Snow Queen felt the coldness of dread coursing through her as she became transfixed by the eyes of her nemesis, now a maelstrom of swirling gold, unearthly and inhuman. Energy danced and darted through the air like sparks from a fire, unseen but felt, lifting the small hairs on arms and necks, and tingling the skin uncomfortably. Ahmya and Vivian, chained as one, fell into a simultaneous trance and without conscious thought, drew on the wild energy unleashed by Morgan, syphoning it up and pouring it into their bonds of iron. The mettle began to scream with the energy channelling through it and reaching a crescendo, burst asunder, with broken links flying in all directions, piercing the soft flesh of their hapless warders.

'Good faith is all I asked!' Morgan's deep, bass voice thundered through the confusion.

Bringing down her rearing horse the Snow Queen yelled a hasty reply.

'Stay your hand, Morgan Ap Heston! This misunderstanding is the unfortunate action of the overzealous! Let us not rip the cloth before it is made!'

The Snow Queen spun her horse on her soldiers who were beginning to draw their swords.

'Stand down, you fools!' she commanded. 'Enough mischief has been made for one day. Let's not compound it!'

Their hands froze over their pommels as shame and fear took hold.

'As for you!' she said to the General as he rose shakily from the dirt. 'You will answer to me later.'

The five once captives ignored her and her disgraced men and walked forward, stood before Morgan and bowed respectfully.

They were all surprised when he smiled at them, returned their bow and said.

'Welcome back, best of the Chosen. I have missed your presence.'

'We did not lose faith in you, Lord Morgan,' replied Ahmya. 'You are the One.'

The Snow Queen observed this interplay and realised that she had had something in her hands far greater and precious than she had appreciated. She did not intend to be on the losing side of another opportunity again.

'Lord Morgan,' she said in her most sensual voice. 'I hope that we may still have our talk. I am most willing.'

Immediately, the green, piercing eyes of the exotic beauty with a fearsome power residing in her, flashed her a warning.

'Oh, how wonderful!' she thought with delight and hid the smile that rose within her. 'Best not to aggravate this one too much but still, I could never resist a challenge.'

Morgan answered, his voice deep and even, unflustered and unheated by the recent events.

'I believe our discussions are already well underway. Will you continue them as an independent Queen or as an instrument of the Empire?'

The amusement in her died quickly. This one, it seemed, had a way of presenting things in a stark and transparent fashion.

'An interesting observation, Lord Morgan. With you, I think, I shall start writing the pages of a new book.'

'Be certain before you put ink to paper, Queen. There will be no way back after this day.'

'My brother is not a patient man, Majesty, time is short. Will you fight with us under our command or face annihilation after these proceedings are complete?'

'You are asking me to join with you against my own city and family? Why would you even think that I would entertain such a thought much less such an action? You speak of an army but my scouts tell me that you lead woodsmen with little knowledge of field warfare.'

'There is no middle ground here, Queen of a borrowed army. Your First Citizen has you isolated through your own actions. You have been neutralised and unable to influence anything political in your former power base. Your army is tired, with food supplies and weapons running low. Many of them will simply want to return to their homes from which they are a long way. You did not know of an army behind you of such a force. Would you like to gamble on what lies hidden in front of you? Shall I continue, Majesty? I offer you a life-line. Take it or die.'

'You will find that I am not so easy to kill, Morgan Ap Heston!'

'I do not doubt that at all, Sybil Wuzetian, but the outcome will be the same nevertheless. Even if your countrymen disregard they holding orders and seize the bull by its horns and rush in at our rear when engaged, they will not be able to save you. Your hopes are futile.'

'Your argument as to our destruction is eloquent and persuasive, Lord Morgan. We would like time to withdraw and consider its merits and repercussions.'

'I'm afraid not, Majesty. You are now a Queen and no longer a member of the ruling nine. A consensus is not necessary. Decide and decide now or may your god have mercy on your soul and those under your command.'

'You are giving us very little chance, war master.'

Morgan did not bother to reply but regarded the Queen evenly. She knew that the negotiations were over or in reality, the terms of her surrender.

'My Queen, we cannot join with this devil of dark magic against our Holy City,' whispered the Peacock General in her ear.

'What do you suggest, General, that we throw our lives away in one last glorious flash of righteous flame?'

Before he could say any more, she turned back to Morgan dismissing the commander of her troops from her mind.

'Very well, Lord Morgan, but we join with you towards what end?'

'To drive the Empire back to the territory it started from when your very first First Citizen betrayed the brotherhood he once led.'

The Snow Queen stared at Morgan for a long moment then without looking at her henchman said.

'General, tell the army to stand down. They will not be any fighting on this day.'

CHAPTER XXXII

'She has done what!?'

His chin wobbled like that of an over-fattened turkey, and he used his full bulk and height to dominate the messenger, whose forehead was now flattened onto the hard stone paving. His oddly, small feet in their soft slippers of velvet and golden thread were but inches from the man's prostrated head.

'She has joined with the forces she was once assaulting, Supreme Eminence,' mumbled the petrified man.

'Speak up! Speak up! Didn't your mother never tell you not to mumble!? Speak so that we may all hear this outrage!'

The messenger sat back on his haunches and repeated the words he had been instructed to deliver, his face white with strain, to repeat the words that had caused such an outburst from the First Citizen.

'Did you hear this, ladies and gentlemen? Our beloved Cardinal has been forced to give herself over into the hands of a dirty barbarian to save her army! She has been forced to belittle herself whilst this, this man's general, sat on his hands and did not raise his finger, not even the little one, to assist her in her beleaguered state!'

'But, but Eminence, our orders were...'

'Silence! You were not given leave to speak further! Orders, you say? Your general's orders were to stand back and do not hinder the war efforts of our dear Cardinal Wuzetian. How shall I take this news to her doting uncle? A stalwart child of our Holy City. How? Someone, please tell me how? How will I break these disastrous events and circumstance to our citizens who love this lady above all else? That foolish general appointed without my consent has interpreted my words to suit his own spiteful spirit; he has changed do not interfere, with do not help, to forward his own and his hidden masters' nefarious interests. What should we do with such a man!?'

'Bring him down!' shouted the gathering of courtiers and generals. 'Bring him down! Bring him down!'

Many listened to this and were appalled. Since when did the Audience Chamber of the Empire become a place of rabble-rousing?

'First and foremost, let us bring him back! Bring him back before the people! Let him answer to them! Let him explain why he acted as their enemy. An enemy of the people! We shall bring him back!'

Amid a roaring chorus of 'Bring him back,' the First Citizen waddled arrogantly from the chamber.

When the heavy doors were shut firmly against the noise, he turned to his secretary priest and asked.

'Where is Father Prior? Those fools will soon realise that what I've just fed them does not make sense.'

'He awaits you in the old chamber of the Founder, Eminence.'

Without a thank you, the First Citizen swept away, his flesh wobbling obscenely.

As he entered a small room decorated in faded green and gold, he spied the Spymaster sitting demurely and patiently on an ancient, ornate chair.

'I need answers, Father,' he said without preamble. 'What is she up to?'

'She had very few options open to her, Eminence, and she is very good at surviving. I would assume she did it to buy herself space and time.'

The First Citizen grunted and farted loudly.

'That's better, he mumbled, then addressed his Spymaster once again. 'Does her uncle know of these new developments?'

'There is very little he does not know, Eminence. I've recently discovered a shared information network between him and some of our military houses.'

'The merchants are working with the military?'

'Not as far as that, Eminence. Just a sharing of certain channels.'

'Sly bastards! Give me names, Father. Time to do some finger pointing and let the good people indulge in a bit of gardening.'

'I would urge caution, Eminence. We may be in need of expert military guidance in the months to come.'

'How so?'

'The leader of the rebels is no ordinary man.'

'What is that supposed to mean, for the love of god! Out with it man! Stop being a coy girl.'

'His name is Morgan Ap Heston, Eminence, and that name goes back to the very early days of our city.'

'Some sort of a family vendetta?'

'Much more than that, Eminence.'

'I've already warned you about being coy, Spymaster!'

'Yes, Eminence. My studies seem to be indicating that this same man is responsible for the murder of our Founder.'

'What! Are you saying that this rebel bugger is over three-hundred years old!? You are not spouting this ancient magical crap again, are you? Stop believing everything you read, Father. It's time you get out of dark rooms and pull your nose out of dusty scrolls and live a little in the real world.'

'As you say, Eminence.'

'All right. All right. You win. What is your evidence for this foolish theory, to use one of your borrowed words?'

'Did you know that our Holy Founder was once a leader of a secret sect of brothers?'

'No, that's new to me. So, what's so important about that? We all have to start from somewhere.'

'This brotherhood spent many generations actively searching for knowledge from the Fallen World. It is through their interference that many things from that ancient, lost world are now back with us today.'

'Spilt milk is spilt milk, Spymaster. What are you trying to tell me? Get to the point.'

'They recruited to their number only people who had special gifts. People whose very being had been perverted and tampered with by the cataclysm that ended an almost godlike civilisation. The unspeakable methods used by the ancients to kill each other, altered the very fabric of some of those few who survived, giving them a legacy that is hardly comprehensible to those of us who have not been tainted.'

'And so?'

'And so, the Founder was one of these tainted, god forgive me. His sect intended to do the work of the almighty using stolen knowledge, and create for themselves a master being; someone to rule over a broken and violent world, bringing peace to all.'

'And did they succeed? I'm a little afraid of what you're going to tell me next.'

'In part, yes, Eminence. This Morgan Ap Heston is their creation. He is not altogether human.'

The First Citizen eyed his servant for a long pause with an inscrutable expression. Then, all of a sudden, he burst out laughing.

'Oh, oh, that's a good one, Spymaster. What a lot of rubbish! You are in danger of getting yourself arrested for heresy. Bloody hell! Now, use your time more wisely and find out more about the cooperation between the Merchant Guild and the military houses. And bring me names! You hear me! I want names!'

Chuckling to himself once again the First Citizen waddled out of the cluttered and cosy little room.

With a weary sigh, the Spymaster settled back into his chair. He was exhausted, and his eyes burned so much that they ran with water. He had dug deep into the secret records of the Founder, a treasure trove. Even more interesting, were the scrolls written by the Holy Cardinal Smithers. A man like himself, who believed in rediscovering secrets. A man who was obsessed with the 'why' of things. He stared at the steady flame burning within the shelter of its glass frame as it sat on a far table, and with a thought, extinguished it.

***

'Welcome, House Montford. Thank you for agreeing to meet with me in these uncertain times.'

'Thank you, Lord Wuzetian, but my father still rules.'

'I meant no disrespect to the great general, but you are his eldest and acknowledged heir. He would be proud to hear you so addressed. His legacy is assured.'

'You make me smile, Lord. You truly are deserving of the title

Merchant King. Your tongue is pure honey.'

'The truth is always sweeter to the ears, General Montford, than the sick treacle of lies that are flooding our city at present. The more the people lap it up, the closer they come to reveal the hidden contents of their stomachs.'

'A disturbing analogy, Lord, and a dangerous one to speak out loud.'

'Which leads us to the reason behind this meeting, General. What danger does this Morgan Ap Heston pose to our Empire?'

'He sits on our borders with a growing army, fed by the people of two Kingdoms flocking to his black wolf banner. Swimming in this growing cauldron of potential turmoil is your niece and her annexed legions. If unchecked he may well form a substantial threat to our outlying districts.'

'That's only half of it, I'm afraid,' said the Merchant King gravely. 'Have you heard of this Morgan Ap Heston before?'

'Can't say that I have. My still missing brother is the one who seemed to have made a point of knowing something about every military leader he could find.'

'Maybe he had it right. A man by that very name has been listed on our account ledgers more than once.'

'Surely that's not unusual seeing that your guild is one of merchants. Your trade must be wide and varied.'

'Yes, it is. The unusual lies in the passage of time. The first entry was made over two hundred years ago.'

The eldest son of House Montford stared at his host for a long period.

'A family name perhaps?'

'Yes, perhaps. The alternative is unthinkable. However, the footnote next to his name always repeats the same; leader of men, untouchable in battle, the Defiler. Why would a merchant say such a thing?'

The General froze, his eyes suddenly becoming focused. Then he shrugged and did not venture an answer, but his eyes were troubled.

'Has our First Citizen been alerted?' he asked.

'And put ourselves in the position of explaining how we became acquainted with a new enemy's name so quickly? Something maybe we should avoid just now. However, his fox disguised as a hound has already been sniffing. I am sure he knows.'

'Our Holy Father seems more concerned with consolidating power in his hands than the defence of the Empire.'

'Perhaps the two are the same, dear General. One dependent upon the other. One must not underestimate our Supreme leader.'

'No, we must not. Another point on which our houses agree.'

Having gauged each other, the two longtime associates relaxed in informal conversation, sipping wine and toasting the health of their respective families, despite the ill fortune both houses and recently undergone, one the death of a sister and the other a brother missing in action.

As he watched the erect back of his departing guest, Lord Wuzetian wondered why he had not mentioned the connection between the rebel leader and his family. Maybe for the same reason, the General did not acknowledge recognising one of the names from the ledgers of merchants past. At first, he had intended to. This strangely, long-lived man had been their effigy of hate since their royal demise, and alas, here he was again, but this time during his watch. It was enough for now that he had sowed the seed of doubt rather than reveal too much of his family's vulnerabilities, he supposed. 'Let's hope House Montford has taken the bait,' he whispered to himself. 'Our future survival will depend on it.'

CHAPTER XXXIII

It felt like old times for the Honey General. Morgan had ordered the now combined army to march quickly into the narrowest point of the mostly ploughed land dividing two stretches of dense forest. Stakes were swiftly pounded into the soft, tilled soil, effectively plugging the bottleneck against a surprise cavalry charge by the belated but fast assembling Protectorate army. The foresters, trained bowmen from birth, held the two wings. One commanded by the Honey General and the other under the command of Greybeaver. The Snow Queen's army was effectively split up by Morgan and mixed in with the Lowland Kingdom's solid infantry. Amongst these were inserted bands of supporting archers. This section, making up the centre, was under the direct command of Morgan and Krarl. The reserve horse held back for advantageous opportunity or to stymie disaster, was made up of the surviving cavalry from the Queen's army. They had been placed under the firm and experienced control of Captain Horace. All in all, they appeared a formidable army, but they were not cohesive as the different elements were highly suspicious of each other. As always, Morgan's strategy carried a high degree of risk. The Honey General realised that Morgan could usually get away with this due to his incredible martial prowess, a thing that was admired by warriors universally and more than likely, forged unity amongst disparate groups. Now with his brother joining in next to him, things could become interesting.

The Honey General was familiar with the rival General although he had never met him personally, he knew of his family. His House was relatively new, only two generations deep. His Father had been a middle-of-the-road officer, who had never done active front-line service but who had landed a plump position, through high-level patronage of some sort, advising and explaining to the sitting cardinals the actions and decisions of Generals fighting on the borders. The son, however, was cut from a different cloth. He had been hungry to prove himself and had been continually lobbying to obtain a front-line commission. He had even competed for the Honey General's former post, but the revered reputation of his House had allowed him to win the day. He laughed at the irony of it.

'Are you well, sir?' asked old Turpin, who was attempting to sketch the layout of the potential battlefield while perched incongruously on a spirited war-horse.

'Couldn't be better, old friend,' he replied with a fond smile. 'Was it wise for you to pick a warhorse for our gentle reconnoitre?'

'I didn't choose him. The young, stable hand had mischief in him this morning and was looking for sport. He said that this horse was old and his frolics were only a memory of better times. I didn't have the energy or inclination to dissuade him from his nonsense.'

'I see,' said the Honey General, returning his eyes to studying the land. 'I now understand why Morgan moved us forward so quickly. Where we're standing is the narrowest and highest point and the land slopes gently downwards afterwards. Galloping a heavily armoured horse up to this position will be tiring for the beast as it will also have to contend with loose soil and ploughed ridges. The Protectorate has been caught doodling.'

'Do you not find it strange the way we now see ourselves?'

'Yes, Turpin, but these two brothers will turn our world upside down. Many shall be changed by them.'

'It's so quiet and peaceful here. You wouldn't think that the Empire's destiny hangs over this rural setting.'

'No, it's all very unreal. Come, we had better report back to Lord Morgan.'

After stabling their horses, they picked their way through the sprawling encampment towards the modest, field tent where Morgan had set up his command post. They found him and his brother sitting in conversation with the group who were now known to all as The Chosen.

'But why, Lord Morgan? Our duty is now to fight by your side and Lord Krarl's, to protect you from the unforeseen and unexpected. You will now be the sole target for the malcontent and shadowed assassin. Why send us away now?'

This plea came from a short, muscular, blond girl who sat before the brothers like a coiled spring.

Krarl chuckled quietly in a deep, throaty voice, sounding more like the low growl of a wolf than anything humorous and benign.

His brother glanced at him then replied to the girl.

'Stephania, we are not kings. A royal bodyguard is not required. You are the Chosen. We will ask you to do things that none other are qualified to do. You are the very extension of us.'

'What exactly do you want us to do, Lord Morgan?' asked Ahmya.

Morgan paused. Once again he was taken aback by the strength of the gift in this warrior. He had felt it when she and Vivian had broken their chains by harnessing the residual elements of his unleashed power, and he felt it now in her simple, straightforward question. It was more than words. She had communicated her feelings and commitment directly inside him.

As before he glanced at his twin who shrugged.

'I want you to move behind the enemy lines and capture or kill their General. Ahmya, you will lead. Elisha, Scar, Stephania, Luc, Pollock, Reginald and Jacob, will be your team. Jacob, you are second in command. Vivian, you will remain by my side and you Sharleen is seconded to my brother. Lord Graham and Lord John take personal control of the Queen's infantry divisions stationed amongst us. Make sure that they follow the orders of my brother and I. Captain

Bastonet I would like you to join and support Captain Horace with the reserve horse. The rest of you already know your duties.'

'When do we leave?' enquired Ahmya.

'Within the hour. Ah, welcome back, General Montford. Please, share with us your observations of the field.'

'It is as you said, Lord Morgan. We have stolen a march on the enemy General and have bagged the choke point. Their cavalry will have a hard time getting to us and will not be able to find room to outflank us. It is either punch through our forces or surrender the field.'

'What if they refuse us battle and just withdraw for a more favourable location?' asked Ahmya.

Sharleen snapped her mouth shut as her sister warrior had just beaten her to the observation.

The Honey General looked at the striking, young woman and smiled in approval but it was Morgan who answered.

'That is why your mission is so important. I wish to goad them into hot action. Also, I'm counting on the General not to want to lose face in the eyes of his superiors but to seek glory in stopping us where one of their vaulted Cardinals have failed.'

'Quite a gamble, Lord Morgan,' said the Honey General. 'To the uninitiated, it seems just a bit more than a hope and a prayer but I for one, am convinced to your way of thinking. Speaking of dice throwing, why isn't the Queen's General not invited among our gathering?'

'There is a simple answer to that one, General. The queen has stripped him of command.'

Krarl chuckled.

'Would that not leave a festering wound in our ranks?' continued the Honey General.

'Yes, it will,' Morgan answered but did not give any further qualifications.

'Well, if there aren't any further questions, let's get to work, ladies and gentlemen. We have a lot to do in a short time,' said Morgan, wrapping up the meeting.

When they had all departed Krarl said.

'Snow Queen dangerous. Nort to be trusted.'

'I know, brother, she too gambles, eh?. She has set up her disgruntled General to turn traitor. Her hope is that he leaks our plans to his City in spiteful pique. This way she remains untarnished but flexible.'

'Clevar womarn; dangerous. Why put young cub second to Ahmya? Elisha bettar.'

'Yes, very. Her joining with us is purely a gambit to survive and buy time. We will use her all the same. As for young Jacob, he needs experience and responsibility to grow. He has great potential. Elisha is too much of a hot head. Like you, brother.'

'Haaaa!' laughed Krarl. 'See, murch bettar to lead!'

Morgan smiled, his face losing all its cares and taking on a youthful look. Joined in a common purpose, the brothers felt as they once did as boys. They were One.

Two days after, Morgan stood with Vivian in the shadow of the trees watching the growing army of the Protectorate. New troops were arriving hour by hour, and their sheer size was frightening to the untried girl. She imagined that when they deployed they would become a juggernaut, a thing unstoppable. Morgan seemed unconcerned, but this did not reassure her.

'Can you feel his presence?' his voice was soft but resonant.

After a moment of seeking, the third time in an hour, she replied.

'No, nothing.'

'Nothing is your starting point, girl,' said Morgan. 'Stop trying. Just let it happen. Find that place where there is emptiness; find the void or rather let it find you.'

Once again going through the steps that he had been gently teaching her she opened herself and relaxed. For a long time nothing happened, then suddenly, she felt a trace of anxiety creeping into her mind; the only thing was, it wasn't of her making. In her excitement, she lost control, and the feeling was banished.

'There! You have it! Now, stop reacting and welcome it in. You have touched your spirit brother. Let him in.'

'It feels wrong, Lord Morgan,' she said a bit breathlessly.

'He is the true leader of your spirit circle. The two of you will determine the strength of your wolf pack. It will only be wrong if you make it so. Open yourself, girl. Let him in.'

Slowly she became lost in a trance-like world where her concept of self began to fade. What she had first thought of a feeling of anxiety revealed itself to be that of unease, caution even, a sense of treading in the unknown. Yet, at the same time, a determination not to disappoint; a belief in someone familiar but untouchable and mysterious. Expectation began to grow, and a surge of adrenaline spiralled her away.

'They are close!' she panted, her eyes unfocused and slightly confused as she separated self from other.

'Well done, Vivian. You have accomplished what only a few of the best can do. Come, we must return to the camp.'

As they trotted along a barely discernable game trail, Morgan reached for his brother. He experienced a wave of unbridled power as his psyche touched his twin, a seemingly inexhaustible supply of energy barely contained. Krarl was overseeing the constant drilling of the disparate troops, trying to get them to work as one under their commanders within the time scope available. It was a task he enjoyed. 'Be ready, brother. It is time.' He felt an acknowledgement swimming back at him, almost in an offhand way.

Krarl was there to greet them as they jogged across the open fields towards the encampment. Behind him the army was reforming into their allotted units, their commanders shouting, swearing, cajoling, pushing and bullying them into position.

'Could be worse,' he said to his brother, who he found gazing in amusement at a spot behind Morgan.

Turning, Morgan saw Young Vivian, bent over, hands on knees gasping uncontrollably and retching into the weeds.

'This worn even weaker tharn you, brodar,' observed Krarl.

'She'll do fine,' replied Morgan with a smile. 'She made contact with her pack, and they are running close to their prey. We must be ready when the distraction comes.'

***

The infiltration team, as they preferred to see themselves, rather than the skulking assassins that they were, had decided to split into pairs; Ahmya and Jacob, Elisha and Stephania, Luc and Scar, Pollock and Reginald. The first four, which were mostly women, would attempt to infiltrate by night and the male teams by day as it would be easier for them to pose as soldiers. The Protectorate army did not believe in the equality of the sexes. For them, women had a role in life and men another. War was the exclusive domain of men. There was no longer room for a society of warriors, merely the functional process of conscripted soldiers and career officers. The teams were to operate independently, gathering information but mostly seeking an opportunity to carry out their deadly work. They had agreed on a rendezvous point where the teams would revolve and gathered intelligence exchanged.

The first day and night had been frustrating. Pollock and Reginald had managed to slip in amongst the baggage train which was manned by mostly conscripted locals under the command of Protectorate officers. Their muscular frames allowed them to fit in quite well, but all they got out of their efforts was a day of hard, back-breaking work. Luc and Scar, being a bit more belligerent in their approach had managed to bushwhack two sentries who had wandered into the trees to relieve themselves. As they trudged back towards the turmoil of motion and confusion that was the enemy's military camp, Scar commented.

'Bloody bastard pissed all down the front of his trews! How am I to be inconspicuous with my front soaked?'

'It's not the wet, mate. It's your smell that will make you fit in like a seam in my old gran's bedsheet,' replied his friend with satisfaction in his voice as to Scar's predicament.

'Don't recall your grandmother ever owning a bed,' grumbled Scar.

However, despite or maybe, in spite of their borrowed uniforms they didn't get very far. An officer, seeing them seemingly abandoning their duty, ordered them back out to patrol the perimeter. They, too, arrived at the rendezvous point that evening truculent and foot-sore.

The night shift didn't fare any better. They had a chilly time hiding in shadows and dodging camp guards. Twice they had to run for it, scampering blindly through the snoring camp, tripping over guy ropes. They too returned dirty and disheartened without even gaining sight of the General's pavilion.

The men were just preparing to set off again to try their luck with the rising of the morning sun when an opportunity appeared to be brewing. Under a large, rampant Protectorate banner, the General had decided to tour his troops. They watched him as he moved from one section to the next but unfortunately, always in the thick of his men. Somewhere around mid-morning on that second day, fortune smiled.

The man must have been overcome with the greatness of his god for seemingly on the spur of the moment, he swung his field-staff wide and took them on a climb up to the top of a low promontory hill. Here they stood discussing what lay before them and to them, did the waiting wolves split and start their hunting run, knifing towards his position from several points, their minds and weapons sharp and ready.

Crouched low and moving swiftly behind his big sister, Jacob was hit by a wave of sudden dizziness and missed his footing. Instantly and instinctively, Ahmya twisted in her tracks and with her hand darting as fast as a striking snake, steadied him. The disability lasted only a fleeting moment, but they both knew what it was and looked into each other's eyes for confirmation, then resumed the hunt. Scar, following next in line, wondered what slip in the wheel of fate had him following after madmen and women. He shook his head and continued the hunt behind said lunatics.

The General and his senior staff were preoccupied in viewing the splendid vista of their immense and war-like camp. Dominated by cavalry units, the plain below the sloping neck running between the two stretches of forests left unviolated to help bolster the defence of what was once the unassailable Stronghome Keep, was covered with large herds of unsaddled horses, waiting for their riders. They nor their assigned bodyguards were not expecting their own Protectorate tactics to be turned against them. Standing on a hillock in the midst of a vast field, once a cultivated breadbasket for the Kingdoms, they felt secure in their power. They did not see the two prongs of four manned teams running in on their viewing platform; not even when their would be assailants hit open ground. Ahmya led one group, Elisha the other, and speed was their ally. As they flew up the embankment almost simultaneously, a guard, idly glancing around, caught sight of the band headed by an implacable, grim-faced Elisha. With a start, he whipped his head around and opened his mouth to shout a warning but never got the chance. Ahmya's knife, thrown with force and accuracy from an apparently impossible position, struck him between his perfect teeth and with a strangled, gurgling sound, he was hurled off of the back of his now bolting horse. Then all hell broke loose in a flurry of commotion and lethal confusion as the wolves were on them, silent and with deadly intent. Two of his field officers and three bodyguards were down and bleeding their lives away in the dirt before the General truly comprehended what had befallen his team and the predicament he was in. In a surge of desperate, self-preserving panic, he kicked and spurred his protesting war-horse down the steep and precarious embankment on his side with the only thought in his head being to put distance between him and certain death swirling behind him. Ahmya and Jacob, now free of all insecurity, leapt and dodged through flying hooves and wildly slashing swords, cutting a bloody path to where the General had disappeared over the edge. Scar and Luc tried to follow but were soon left frantically trying to defend themselves from the determined counter-attack by the guards and officers of the Protectorate, now fully awake to the danger and grimly prepared to see off this audacious assault.

Elisha and her band of new reivers in the form of Stephania, Pollock and Reginald, were pressing the beset guards backwards. Elisha and Stephania were like ravening hell-cats, twisting and cutting, fast, ferocious and furious. Pollock and Reginald were like a brick wall, immovable.

Ahmya was the first to get to the drop-off, just in time to see the forelegs of the General's colossal warhorse buckle as a mud-rock split and broke under its crushing weight. He was catapulted over the top of its head, and the two of them rolled down the embankment in a tangle of legs, spraying dirt and dust in every direction. She did not have time to witness the outcome as she saw a phalanx of madly dashing horseflesh thundering towards her. Left no choice, she turned and leapt into thin air, hearing the terrified screeching of horses as they careened off the lip of the drop behind her. She had no idea where Jacob was.

Jacob watched Big Sister jump into the air like a shining angel of death and felt a surge of pride in his chest. Then he glimpsed the avalanche that had caused her to so leap and spun away like a dust-devil, his spinning sword slicing through the flesh of the nearest madly racing horse. The sound of its agonised winey was heart-wrenching and in reaction to its pain, swerved into the path of its fellows just as they neared the edge, causing them to somersault down in cataclysmic disarray of rolling and screaming horse and man flesh.

The General crawled groggily from under his horse's neck which was clearly broken and rose shakily to his feet, amazed that he was still in one piece. He looked up the steep hillock to see how his men were faring and immediately regretted it. A lithe and deadly figure was coming at him at a breathtaking speed, bounding from rock to rock in an amazing and inhuman fashion. How in heaven's name it kept its feet and balance at such a pace was incomprehensible. Behind this vision of mythology, rolled and slipped a mass of broken men and horses in a cloud of dirt and dust. So horrified was this commander of men, that his feet grew roots and he was unable to move. The last thing he saw on that day was a slashing sliver of light as the shining figure raced by him, then he was covered in crushing darkness as the living avalanche knocked him down and rolled over him.

CHAPTER XXXIV

'He is down! They've got him!'

Her black eyes were shining with uncontrollable excitement, and her breath was coming in short gasps as if she had been running from certain death.

'Calm, child,' said Morgan gently. 'Explain it to us.'

Vivian looked at Morgan's reassuring, almost fatherly face then took a quick glance at the unreadable but fearsome visage of his brother.

She quickly returned her gaze to Morgan.

'They have killed the General…I think. Big sister's strike should have taken his head off!'

'Should arve?' enquired the grating voice of Krarl.

'She barely escaped the falling horses and men behind her. They buried the General before she could confirm the kill. Now they are scattered and running for their lives. We must go and help them, Lord Morgan.'

'Give orders to pull the stakes and sound the attack. We move now.'

'But Lord?'

'They are on their own, child. They knew this from the beginning.'

She blinked the warm tears from her eyes, and the two men were gone.

***

'His helmet protected him somehow but even so, he has several broken bones, and of his organs, I cannot tell.'

'We need the men to see him! You have to do something!'

'I'm open to suggestions. I've done all I can. If he wakes, stick this paste under his tongue. It's opium and may dull his pain.'

'You will do it yourself! Your place is by his side.'

'But I will be needed elsewhere! Can't you hear what's happening outside, man?'

'You will do as I command, otherwise, you will have need of that disgusting paste yourself! Am I clear, medic?!'

'Yes, quite clear,' came the defeated and disgruntled voice.

He tried to open his eyes, but his whole body felt dull, broken and unresponsive. Something heavy lay over his mind, and he imagined he could hear a roaring sound and what seemed like the clash of arms. He attempted to open his mouth to ask a question, but the message did not get to where he wanted it to go.

***

'Who gave those fools the order to charge, god help us!' screamed the man on whose shoulders had fallen the responsibility of the injured and incapacitated General.

'We aren't sure, Sir. As we deployed, the rebels appeared on yonder ridge much faster than anticipated. The light cavalry deployed on their own volition on both wings and sallied out to meet them as our infantry centre was not yet in position.'

'That still does not tell me who gave the order!' the man's voice ended in a shrill note which did not calm the growing unease among the surviving field commanders.

'What are your orders now, Sir?'

'Now you ask!? Now you ask when a third of my horse now lie feathered with black arrows in a peasant's cornfield!? The bastards have the high ground, and they have archers aplenty. We hold this position and tempt them to come to us. Order those fools to pull our horse back in reserve. They will be the hammer when the time is right. When I give the order! Do you understand? When I give the order!'

'Yes, sir,' replied the colonel, sending a messenger scampering off to convey the command of the Brigadier now in overall command after the decimation of the field officers on the knoll of assassins. 'But what of our footmen, sir? They are still not ready and look, sir. They are not waiting to be tempted! The whoresons are coming at us without pause!'

'Bloody stinking, god-less savages! Why in the name of the almighty are our shield fences not raised yet!? What are the fools waiting for!?'

'They think the General dead, Sir. They need to see him still in command.'

'Then see to it, Colonel! Superstitious fools! Give them what they want! Get the General on a horse! Get him to where the idiots can see him. Do it now, Colonel! What are you waiting for!?'

'Yes, sir,' replied the man doubtfully and galloped his fretful mount towards the dust-shrouded command tent in the distance.

***

Morgan and Krarl, standing a clear two lengths ahead of the ordered field, watched the swirling mass of enemy light cavalry storm around the milling centre of foot and charge up the slope towards them. They resembled the two curved horns of a bull, aggressive and dominating.

'Looks impressive,' muttered Morgan.

'Looks foolish,' countered Krarl. 'Marn stupid. Horse tired soon.'

'Passion counts over reasoning when distracted. This is what we counted on. Are our wings ready?'

'Yarp.'

The horns had now joined at the centre forming a formidable front of thundering, armoured horseflesh. The vast dust cloud thrown up by their iron-shod hooves gave the intimidating impression of a pyroclastic flow spewing forth from an angry volcano bent on destruction, but to the keen eyes of the brothers, it was evident that the juggernaut was beginning to show signs of labouring under the task set before it.

Despite his twin's assurances, Morgan glanced to his left then to his right. General Montford sat easily on his mount to the side and fore of his silent bowmen, ranked in their straight, implacable lines behind their newly implanted stakes, sharp and slanted. Greybeaver stood within his similarly dressed foresters, one with them but clearly in command. The two commanders' style of leadership was starkly different, but Morgan was pleased to see that they both chose to lead from the front. The centre stood firmly behind their shields with the second row holding long spears with nasty hooks sprouting from the sides, at the vertical, sharp, polished tips of iron, pointing skyward and glinting in the sunlight. The Housecarls Graham and John had arrayed their archers in front of them in two long ranks. The first on bended knee and the second standing behind, all with arrows aplenty, resting to the ready at their sides. Morgan and Krarl walked back to these men of the bow and stood at their rear. The four commanders in charge of the opening engagement, knew their business, so the brothers did not interfere.

The first line of cavalry came rolling up towards them like a threatening thunderhead, dark, rumbling and ominous. It was a sight to strike awe in the hearts of men, but the rebels stood firm as the earth shook beneath their feet, reverberating up into their skulls, jarring their clenched teeth. At about 250 yards out, they couched their lances and levelled their points. Morgan's voice cut through the thundering sound of clobbering hooves and jingling bridles.

'Mark!'

Immediately, and in unison, each commander shouted out sharp orders to the bowmen in his charge.

'Nock arrows, to the ready! Draw! Loose!'

From the wings and the front, a rain of iron-tipped arrows flew into the mass of oncoming horsemen, thudding and slicing into them at less than 200 yards, spilling men and animals into the ground with screams, shouts of alarm, breaking bones and rupturing organs. A split second after this first volley, Morgan's hidden card was revealed in an effective and deadly fashion. Stationed beneath the shadowed thickets and trees of the forest fringes were lines of camouflaged bowmen. These rose, as one, and released a storm of lethal arrows into the flanks of the enemy horse as they galloped by, bringing down their wings in crumbling chaos of surprised and wounded soldiers and their panicked mounts. The riders desperately pulled their horses inwards in an attempt to avoid the barrage of death pelting them from the sides, resulting in a crush of men in the dead centre. This allowed for such a concentrated charge that although they impeded each other, they also threatened Morgan's foot warriors. At a sharp bark of command from Morgan, the bowmen melted back through the ranks whereupon, the front line raised their shields and the second line presented their long spears to the almost horizontal, thick shafts resting on the shoulders of their brethren, showing the charging horsemen the semblance of the back of a hedgehog. The horses, seeing this barbed obstacle, shied away, causing the weight of those coming after to bowl them over, collapsing the front line of the charge, rolling and kicking into the loose earth. The archers, now sheltered, altered the angle of their bows and sent a black rain of death over the heads of their brothers in arms and onto the oncoming enemy lines, stymieing their onrush and sowing further confusion amongst the massed forces. At the same time, the archers on the flanks, arrows exhausted, stormed out of the trees armed with whatever weapons lay at hand, swords, hatchets, even the mallets used to pound defensive stakes into the earth. If none of these was available, they drew their knives or swept up whatever weapons they could find on the battlefield, sometimes torn from the dead hands of fallen enemy riders. So armed, they swarmed over the compacted enemy, dragging them from their blowing horses in a frenzy of violence and sent their souls flying onto the bridge of light. The surviving enemy horsemen, frightened and appalled by this savage onslaught assailing them from three fronts, turned and fled back down the slope, losing even more men to deadly barbs as they presented their backs. Their ill-timed and poorly thought out attempt to destroy the rebels in one fell swoop, thrown into the gutter of defeat.

Behind them, the victorious rebels did not waste time in celebration. The bowmen, who had been responsible for carrying the fight to the enemy, were now exhausted from their efforts and looking down the open field, it was clear that the Protectorate had only committed a small fraction of their forces. Both the Honey General and Greybeaver had their hands full in recentring their concentration and redressing their lines. Many of the men appeared to be begging to be allowed to sit in the dust and put their heads into their trembling hands. Had the enemy chosen at this point to make a second assault the rebels would have been defeated. Morgan, Krarl and all the experienced commanders knew this, and they spent an anxious moment watching the Protectorate camp whilst they wings raggedly reformed.

Morgan knew that he could not allow the enemy to sit tight and fortify. They were blocking the entrance to the Green Kingdoms like a cork in a bottle, and he had to prize it open or retreat back up the mountain. If he did that, men would soon begin to abscond, especially the Queen's men, and this entire enterprise would be finished before it even got started. Signalling to his small, tightly controlled reserve horse commanded by the highly experienced Captain Horace, a brute of a man bred for conflict, he sent them racing in a circular probing run to hit and provoke the still milling infantry centre of the Protectorate and to harass the remnants of their fleeing horsemen. Krarl, chomping at the bit, ran with them, not to command but merely for the sheer thrill of it.

***

As the Colonel galloped off towards the command tent, the Brigadier watched with his eyes popping from his skull sockets in frustration, the highly disciplined and compact mounted rebels punch a hole into the sides of his unready shield wall, scattering them left, right and centre. Many turned and fled under this swift and unexpected attack. However, it wasn't just this audacious charge that had caught his horrified attention but a man on foot, silver hauberk flashing dully in the sun and a mallet in his hand, tearing into his men like a berserker from the burning cauldrons of Hades, smashing them from their feet and stomping them into the ground in an unearthly display of unbridled violence and carnage.

'What in tarnation is that!' he exclaimed in apoplectic rage. 'Bring it down, you fools! Bring in down! And where are my bloody men of horse!? Why are they not countering this outrage!? Where in the name of the god, are my bloody horse!?'

'You've ordered them to withdraw, sir,' came a laconic reply.

'What!? Then rescind that order, you fool! Send those cowardly idiots into the fray!'

'Yes, sir,' responded the same laid-back voice, and another of the dwindling supply of junior field officers galloped off towards the rear of the army with his new set of conflicting orders.

'You!' shouted the Brigadier once again. 'Haul your arse over there and tell those incompetent fools that command my men-at-arms that if they don't pull their fingers out and get their charges in line, they will be relieved of their rank and flogged publicly in front of the army before nightfall! Did you hear me! Go tell them this!'

'Yes, sir.'

They were now only four nervous looking officers, all on clerical detachment, left fidgeting with their bridles around the distressed Brigadier.

A flurry of movement by the command tent distracted the man from his fuming, and he turned his horse to have a better look, raising his eye-piece to his red-streaked eyeball. The General's high stepping, reserve black charger was being led to the entrance where its master stood slumped in the arms of two attendants. Even in his incapacitated state, the great man was not being allowed to lay down the onerous duties of his position. Tied to the back of the elevated, leather covered, wooden saddle, was a cross like frame to which the General, after being heaved astride the dancing animal, was firmly lashed. The indignity of this exercise was not lost on the man who had so commanded that it should be done. The colonel, the person whom fate had fingered to do this dirty work, grabbed the hanging reins of the baulking steed and led it towards a high ground overlooking the field, followed reluctantly by the General's aids and his medic. As the comatose Protectorate General was brought to a halt, his snarling, dragon banner was unfurled over his head, and all eyes were turned in his direction. A roar of relief and welcome broke raw from the throats of thousands of soldiers and a ripple, visible to the naked eye, ran through their unformed lines. Their plighted attitude began to transform into a firmer stance, one determined to throw these low-based barbarians back up the hill from whence they came. Soldiers stopped looking for opportunities to take to winged heels and began heeding the calls of their unit leaders. This change was felt by both friend and foe. It was felt by the Protectorate rank and file, it was felt by the mounted warriors under Captain Horace as having disengaged, were now winding their way back to their waiting comrades in arms. It was felt by Krarl, who snapped his jaws together in annoyance and it was felt by a keenly observing Morgan, who realised that the real battle had still not yet begun.

'They are rallying to a man who already has one foot in the other world, Lord Morgan,' said the Honey General.

'That may be true, but they are rallying, nevertheless,' replied Morgan in a matter-of-fact voice. 'We will soon have our hands full.'

'What are your orders, Lord Morgan?'

'We must not allow them to settle. We will carry the fight. Bring as much of the light siege machines from your former troops to the fore, General. Keep your archers in their ranks behind them to cover. On my signal let hell loose. Let's move with speed, General.'

As he gave these orders, Krarl came trotting over.

'Brother, how fare our shock troops? Are they in position to make another foray?'

'Tharr arrr ready. Horace a good marn.'

'Excellent, brother. Lead them out again. Harass and distract their right wing. Tempt their cavalry out. Do not engage, brother. Run before them. Bring them to me.'

'Good furn. We go nowr. Be ready, brodar.'

As his brother loped away, Morgan sensed the presence of Ahmya like a pleasant aromatic smell in his mind. He found it strange that his awareness would embrace her in such a manner but did not have the time to examine this niggling thought.

'My spirit brother is close, Lord Morgan,' said the soft voice of Vivian, who had attached herself like a shadow to him; constantly but silently, at his elbow.

He nodded but did not speak, finding it interesting that he had detected Ahmya before she, Vivian, had been alerted to the proximity of Jacob.

Three events unfolded at the same time. Captain Horace with Krarl in attendance, began their second hunting run, lancing down the gently sloping incline in a tight, fast-moving formation, an arrow pointing at the heart of the Protectorates' right flank. The Honey General was swiftly erecting the remaining ballistae with men once under his command who now seemed extra keen to make up for their perceived former shortfall in his eyes. Lastly, he could now hear the approach of the Chosen as they hurried to where he was standing, their elation on a mission accomplished palpable to his senses.

***

Pain brought him back. Lost in a swimming, fogged world of cloying opium, pain reached him and dragged him to the surface. He opened eyes, glued together and encrusted with dried infection, and blinked away confusion by summoning a considerable chunk of will, a will driven by the perseverance of a life-long held ambition, an ambition to lead armies. He understood that he was on horseback although he could not remember how he had gotten there. He also could not comprehend why he was unable to move. This inconvenience, however, did not overly concern him for in a moment of clear vision, he saw the mess that was his army. He saw the commotion as his core, front-line infantry troops milled around like apprenticed boys on a practice field. He saw his highly trained, mounted shock troops, seemingly attempting to attack and retreat at the same time, disrupting the concentration of their fellows and stymieing any possible cohesion of purpose. He saw terrible leadership in a shocking display of incompetence, but most frightening of all, he saw that they were under immediate attack.

A tight, compact threat in the form of a lightly armoured unit of horsemen, suspiciously familiar, was tearing down the incline, lances couched and destruction evident in their purpose.

'Close shields! Close shields!' he mumbled incoherently. 'Close shields and present pikes!'

'The General is awake!' someone shouted annoyingly in his muffled ears. 'The General is awake!'

'Calm yourselves, sirs. He is trying to tell us something!'

'Finally, someone with common sense!' thought the General.

'Pull back the cavalry. They attempt to draw us out! Raise shields and present pikes. The centre is our counter. Issue my orders! Do it now before all is lost!'

'You heard the General! Do as he says! Signal the infantry and recall the cavalry!'

'Yes, Colonel!'

Two General's taking control of an army simultaneously was not a good thing. Such an occurrence when under assault by a well-versed enemy, was a recipe for disaster. Still, the infantry had rediscovered their self-belief and was now a force to be reckoned with. Their General was back with them and under his watchful eye, or so they believed, they closed up ranks and threw up a formidable shield wall, shields clacking together with the sharp cracking sound of wood and metal. In quick time, they erected a wall which any mounted opponent foolhardy enough to come at, would find their deaths on their pikes, skewered like pigs at a banquet. The cavalry, however, had no such clarity of thought.

Given conflicting orders and faced with a situation in which they were unsure of who was in command, the vaunted Protectorate shock troops did not know whether they were coming or going. Their section leaders were divided and were either too hasty to react or spent too much time arguing with each other the right course of action. Now they had jointly decided that doing something was better than lingering at the back of the field twiddling their thumbs, despite the signal to the contrary coming from the Dragon banner on the hill. In essence, they disobeyed a direct order from their General.

'What's that fool Colonel think he is doing!?' screamed the Brigadier. 'His simple job was to show the General to the troops, not issue orders in his name! Take some men and go up there and arrest him immediately! The idiot is sowing confusion faster than a pox in port!'

The five clerical officers around him glanced at each other uncertainly.

'Why are you still standing there looking like star-struck idiots!? Are you deaf or shall I have you arrested as well!?'

Not knowing what else to do, two unskilled and untried officers trotted off on their horses to do a task they had no idea of how to even start.

The Colonel, a seasoned battle commander, saw them detach from the Brigadiers dwindling group, a now forlorn pocket of impotence shrouded in dust and the potential heart of a possible embarrassing defeat and knew what they were about. He saw, however, something even worse. The light cavalry had disregarded the General's signals and was storming out to intercept the enemy horse.

'Sir, the cavalry did not heed your command. What are your orders?' he asked in a level voice.

The General was no longer there. The opium and his severe injuries had taken him away once again. His reality was one of delirious dreams and gnawing pain.

'Fuck!' was the Colonel's understated response.

'The Brigadier has sent us to place you under arrest, sir,' came a timid and respectful voice.

The Colonel ignored this intrusion and watched the scene, for which he already feared the outcome, unfold on the field beneath him. The enemy horse turned suddenly with the discipline of highly trained troops and raced across at right angles to the infantry's front, increasing their speed with each stride. Amazingly, a man on foot ran easily by their side but wide, taunting the shield wall with his daring presence. This seemed to inflame the passions of the pursuing cavalry even more, and they spurred their mounts recklessly in hot pursuit, cheered on by the raucous and belligerent shouts of the encouraging shield wall.

'Do you recognise the enemy horse, gentlemen?' asked the Colonel in a conversational voice to the two waiting junior officers, who seemed to have momentarily forgotten their duty and had joined in with the watching. 'That's the Honey General's troopers. Impressive aren't they? Never thought the day would come when I'd be fighting our own.'

A huge cloud of obscuring dust was being thrown up into the air from the many angry, pounding of hooves, covering everything and everybody in a dirty grey mass. It soon became impossible to tell foe from friend except by guessed at proximity cued from the thundering sound. The Colonel and his party, the anxious Brigadier and his, and the animated front line, all watched in anticipation as the two forces, hidden from sight, chased across their eye-line. Then as they roared past and the dust began to lift and fade, the horror of the enemy's planning leapt into their consciousness. There on the sloping plain, appearing like a mirage carrying the harbinger of destruction, sat a row of primed and ready ballistae flanked by rows of archers.

'Fuck!' muttered the Colonel, the second profanity in less than twenty minutes, a thing forbidden by his religion. 'The bastard! Used a dust cloud, half of our own making, to steal a march to our door front.'

Before the last words had left his mouth, the ballistae bucked back on their cradles like maddened donkeys and released a volley of their terrible, thick bolts, which with a loud crack, tore through the surprised shield wall, ripping through hide and wooden defences and impaling men standing ready in disciplined ranks, flinging them bodily from their feet and dead into the dust like ragged dolls before they really knew what had befallen them.

'Fuck!' the third curse and his god had noticed. The bell as the priests were so fond of saying, had tolled thrice.

Up on the roughly ploughed incline, with dust still billowing up into the air like black smoke pumping out from the damp hovels of a village that had been put to the torch, the men-of-horse, led by Captain Horace, wheeled about in a superb military manoeuvre and like a vengeful lightning bolt from the hand of an angry god, crashed headlong into the chasing vanguard of the Protectorate cavalry. So swiftly and smoothly was the turn executed, that the angry pack bent on exacting retribution, only became aware of the danger they were in when an inhuman force of nature wielding a mallet like a crazed god from the myths of the old days, smashed into them, tearing men from their saddles and knocking spooked and terrified horses off their legs. They did not have much time to contemplate this sudden apparition of death, for close on its heels, came an unforgiving horde of highly schooled horsemen with their fates written on the tips of their lances, levelled and aimed at their hearts. Horses reared up on their hind legs and toppled backwards, falling on and crushing their hapless riders, from the sudden impact bowling into them from higher ground with no quarter given in mind. Many on the flanks reeled away in an attempt to escape the crush and gain space, but a disciplined group of longbowmen raced to a position opposite and on the parade ground commands of their captain, a tall man with heavy grey in his beard, formed swiftly into a long line and released volley after volley, point blank into their baulked formations. So decimated were they, that the survivors forgetting that they were there to fight, turned and fled pall-mall, back the way they had come for the second time that day.

The Brigadier may not have been a good general, but he was a brave man. Witnessing the fate of the first and second row of his indomitable shield wall, he raced his mount down to stand by their side, to stand with them in their hour of need. As he galloped up to them shouting orders for them to reform and make preparations to storm the enemy's artillery position at double pace, he was just in time to be greeted by a second blistering volley. A stray bolt pierced his chest and flung him from his horse, stone dead before his body rolled to rest in the earth. The fruitlessness to his short rise to power was starkly shown in the fact that the hard-pressed men-of-arms, to whose side he had so recklessly hurried, hardly noticed his passing from this world nor wished him fortune in his journey to the next. And thus, Colonel Jethro, next in the chain, found himself in sole command of a fully formed and active Protectorate field army.

Being a phlegmatic man accustomed to the whims of fate, he did not miss a stride. He signalled for all surviving field staff officers to rendezvous with him under the now dead General's Dragon Banner. He then beckoned for the infantry to withdraw out of artillery range and plant defensive stakes. At the same time, he dispatched his light skirmishers to harass the enemy and slow them from advancing any further. Finally, he sent a runner out to instruct his reserve of horse which consisted of heavy cavalry, to form up on the now abandoned right wing. He then waited patiently for his orders to fall into place. Seeing all ranking, field staff, united under the regiment's banner, the army settled down to business. In many ways, the skirmish on the high ground between his cavalry and the enemy horse served his purposes for it tied down the enemy's mobility. Yes, this Morgan Ap Heston was clever and familiar with war, but his resources were limited both in men and equipment. He just had to hold him till he wore himself out, like waves pounding on a granite cliff during a brief storm.

'Find the commander of the Crossbow division and ask him to move his men in squares of eight and three, alternately placed, between our blocks of infantry. Inform him that he has ten minutes to deploy,' said the Colonel quietly.

'Yes, sir. At once, sir,' replied smartly one of the officers who had earlier been sent to arrest him.

The General, newly elevated by default, was satisfied. All was ready to face the demon from the hidden annals of his City's history. God help them all.

CHAPTER XXXV

'In my opinion, he has lost his chance, my Queen. He cannot hope to win against a fully fielded army of the Empire. We should make contact before it is too late.'

'Are you counselling that we should sneak away like thieves in the night or even worse, like beaten dogs with our tails between our legs, dear man?'

The Snow Queen, her demoted Peacock General, and a few of her more hardy courtiers sat their horses on an advantageous plateau overlooking the two armies facing each other on the dusty plain below.

'You would be welcomed back with open arms, my Queen. The City loves you, and you won't return alone. Many of our men would heed your call and turn on this rebel cur, disrupting his forces from within.'

'Oh, you think that, do you, dear man? Have you also failed to notice that their beloved Honey General stands with them again? Having once failed him they seem to me embarrassingly over keen to make up for lost failures. I must admit, I've underestimated his survival abilities. Good on him.'

'I have placed men loyal to you only next to him, my Queen. You only have to give the nod, and he shall be removed.'

'So, now you advise assassination. No. Stop this whispering on my shoulder. I have made my bed with this Ap Heston. Maybe I shall entice him to lie in it with me. What do you think, dear man? I feel myself growing heated at the very thought.'

The ex-general, but still adorned like a peacock, turned red of face and squirmed with discomfort on his saddle. Summoning a great effort, he replied.

'This man, it is rumoured, is not altogether human, my Queen. I beg you to be wary.'

She gave a soft, silvery laugh and turned her back on her once general, giving her full attention to the moves and counter moves of the two opposing commanders. Despite the straightforwardness of what she had said, she had been paying close attention to everything. Information had been surreptitiously garnered and all options considered. Nothing had been ruled out.

'Can anyone give me the name of our newly acquired commander down there in the opposing field?' she asked. Although, the answer she already knew.

After a heavy, uncertain pause, a young courtier, with long, thinning blond hair, plucked up the courage and responded hesitantly.

'His name is Colonel Jethro, ah…Majesty. His House was once great, but for two generations, has fallen into near obscurity. His patron is thought to be our Spymaster himself, but the evidence for this is difficult to confirm.'

Although she did not show it, Cardinal Sybil had been caught by surprise. This young, knowledgeable fish had it seems, been swimming beneath her notice. She did not even know his name, much less who he was. He also seemed to be in possession of knowledge that she had not known. The connection between the dangerous Spymaster and this Colonel Jethro was utterly new to her. There was always so much work to do. She pretended as if she had not heard his offering and keeping her back to her courtiers, continued to observe the battlefront. The outcome was difficult to discern at this point. She would continue to hold her hand close to her bosom. For now.

***

Most generals faced with such a situation would have chosen to hold their forces, even pulled back, in order to appraise this new stalwart and expert deployment of a much larger, highly trained army with an unknown but obviously competent commander at its head. Not so Morgan. It was easy to forget that under his outwardly sober persona, there lay the kin in spirit to his savage brother, Krarl, wild and dominant. Morgan was a risk taker. He was super confident in his approach to life and like his twin, knew no fear. He did the unexpected. He attacked.

The rebels, despite their recent successes and the high ground that they held, were not in a very secure position. The longbowmen, drawn in the majority from the foresters who had put on such a lethal display of firepower, were now exhausted, their supply of arrows mostly used up. The light cavalry, hitherto used in two very effective skirmishes, sat on blown horses and were certainly not in a position to launch a third. The artillery which had knocked back an overconfident enemy infantry onto their heels had been swiftly withdrawn to save it from the darting attentions of the highly mobile, enemy skirmishers. All in all, the only part of Morgan's newly assembled army which was combat ready, was his strong infantry centre; the men of the Lowland Kingdoms, hardened to war by constant internal conflict. They were to be the heart of Morgan's audacious and highly risky countermeasure. Summoning his section commanders to his side, he quickly outlined his plan.

'We have to be moving before our foe's heavy horse is in place, gentlemen. Speed is of the essence. Let's go. There is work to be done,' he advised them after he had outlined his intentions and the parts he needed them to play in it.

They all nodded curtly and sprinted away.

In short order, barked commands could be heard echoing up in the air from all along the lines of the battlefront. With a bit of jostling, the tight squares of infantry began to unfurl, forming a uniformed and extended front of interlocking shields, blocking the enemy's view as effectively as a fence and at the same time, presenting a defensive wall which had the feel of something offensive in its reality. Behind this curtain, a burst of energetic activity was taking place. Under the command of the Honey General and Greybeaver, the artillery machinery was manhandled over to the left flank, where the archers who still had in their possession arrows, also assembled. The remnants, under shouted orders of Housecarls Graham and John, armed themselves with whatever fallen weapons they could find and joined the shielded frontline. Some of them laboured hurriedly at bundling and lashing rolls of thick brush together, forming huge round bales, as were found in farmers' fields at harvest, to which they attached hemp and leather ropes. Of these, some were constructed light and others heavy, with boulders secreted within. Behind all this, stood the now dismounted horse warriors, resting, grooming and watering their tired mounts. They were the reserve and had to be prepared to serve once again in a short time; ready or not.

Morgan, with his brother by his shoulder, watched these proceedings with steely eyes and a deathly calm. As the fruit of his instructions came to a conclusion, each section commander gave him the signal of readiness.

The Snow Queen, perched on her plateau was also keenly watching. She heard and ignored the outburst from her once general.

'What in the god's name does he think he is doing? Is he mad? Why isn't he retreating to safe ground to consolidate defence!?'

She was finding this Ap Heston more and more intriguing. Underneath that calm skin, he was a man born of the wildness of nature. Water and fire. He was a man of water and fire whereas his savage brother was all air and fire; dangerous and unpredictable. Not suitable as a consort to rule the world with, but this Ap Heston…maybe.

Morgan and his twin turned and strode to the very front line of the shield wall, then in a deep, bass voice that cracked and reverberated throughout his tense foot warriors, he barked.

'Warriors, are you ready!'

'Ready, General!' rolled back the thunderous reply.

'On my mark, break right. Ignore their centre. Now! Break! Break!'

Morgan and Krarl surged forward, like the point of a thrown spear, followed by Ahmya, Sharleen and the remainder of the Chosen who had not been allotted a specific command or vital post. They were the Brothers of Destiny's self-appointed bodyguards, and they would stand or fall at their side as fate decreed. The entire shield wall pealed right after them, breaking into a double trot but yet, amazingly, keeping formation. As they did this, they dragged the light brush bales behind them, throwing up a storm cloud of dust into the air and at the same time, lit torches to the heavier ones and sent them hurtling -a myriad of disturbingly, bouncing and pitching, fiery balls and roiling black smoke- towards the enemy lines.

***

'They're on the move, General! The bastard is moving! But I can't make out... Fireballs, General, fireballs!'

'I have eyes, major. Be calm. Send a quick signal for the ranks to open and allow them passage through.'

'Yes, Sir,' replied the excitable major, frantically signalling the veteran front-line sergeants, who already knew what had to be done and were already shouting appropriate orders.

Keeping discipline, the Protectorate infantry parted smartly to the commands of their troop sergeants, but the slope, roughly furrowed by countless years of overuse by farming implements, made the tumble of the burning projectiles unpredictable, and although many bounced harmlessly through, a fair few crashed with destructive force amongst the massed men, scattering them in panic and injuring many. Even so, the damage was contained and had minimal effect. However, choking smoke blew through and obscured the field with its swirling blackness.

'He is trying to hide his intent beneath dust and smoke, but I see you, bastard,' muttered General Jethro under his breath.

In a louder voice, he continued.

'He is aiming to punch a hole through my left wing. Send out the heavy cavalry to counter, ready or not. Let's tear out his side and spill his guts, once and for all. These godless peasants will thank us for making their barren fields fertile again. Eh, major? Prepare to sound a general advance on my signal.'

The heavy cavalry was more than ready. The armoured riders were so eager to get started on their run that their rampaging emotions were spilling into their restless mounts, making them stamp, prance and chomp at the bit. In fact, they were so quick of the mark, that the General suspected that they had anticipated his signal. He smiled in appreciation of their martial prowess.

They swept out onto the field in impressive style, forming a flying wedge and driving with implacable speed and force directly at the heart of traversing Lower Kingdom infantry. Nothing it seemed, could stop them from achieving their objective. The General and his army held their breaths at the sight of their thundering magnificence. Then, a devastating broadside ripped out from the throat-clogging dust cloud and cleaved into their middle. Heavily armoured horses and their proud riders were hurled inwards as if the hand of god had swept them aside. Their terrified cries as they hit the ground rolling, spinning and sliding tore into the shocked hearts and minds of their watching comrades, jarring their souls and suspending their self-belief. Even so, with their centre gutted, the juggernaut, stuttered, stumbled and picked back up the pace, absorbing this unexpected barrage like a giant shrugging off a blow to its head. Still, with unstoppable forward momentum, they ploughed in turn, into the heart of the shielded Lower Kingdom warriors, collapsing their running fence, imploding it as if it were but a mere tinder wood obstacle, sending men flying in every direction and crushing others under the merciless weight of iron-shod hooves.

'The bastard is clever,' muttered General Jethro. 'But now I have him. Sound the advance, major.'

As a cacophony of horns burst out across the field, Morgan and Krarl crashed into the enemy's shield wall with the spear-point of the surviving infantry packed tightly behind them. Krarl struck first, his mallet, swung with full force, shattered the shield of a burly soldier as if it was stiffened paper and cleaved through his armoured chest, breaking nearly all the bones in his rib-cage and flinging his lifeless body into two of his comrades, hurling them off of their feet and into unconsciousness. Morgan, armed with battle-axe and sword slipped into the space created by his brother like a dark, avenging spirit of death. As Krarl reversed his stroke with the fury of a berserker, sending yet another three soldiers catapulting into their startled brethren on the other side, the chosen stormed in behind him, carving a larger breach into the gap. Morgan was a wraith of speed and power. Whereas his brother smashed all before him with unmatchable force and destruction, his fighting technique was like water and iron. As the enemy swung and stabbed their weapons at him in increasing desperation, he melted and swayed under and around their attempts like a living creature without bones, smooth and elegant, evading iron points that no man with mortal eyes could possibly have seen, anticipating all. Then he would counter. The power in these counters was awesome and matched that of his unleashed twin. Men lost their helmeted heads in his forehand stroke and were hurled backwards and into the air by his backstroke. The brothers were the living embodiment of something out of the war myths from ancient mankind; terrifying incarnations of death-givers, demi-gods of battle and destruction. Ahmya, a step behind Morgan on his left -and strangely linked to him- mirrored his style, flowing and darting in his shadow. Sharleen, fought in Krarl's lea, silent and deadly, and behind her, Elisha battled, a ball of dark fury, killing all that her sister missed. Bolstering their ruthless spearhead, were the three other children of the Blue Mountains —minus Vivian, who had been posted with Captain Horace- with Jacob in their lead, fighting as a unit within a unit, grim and effective. The warriors of the Lower Kingdoms, poured into the space left open by their wake, their martial spirits uplifted by the paragon examples of carnage that led them. They were hungry to follow.

All, however, was not going the rebels way. As the spearhead led by Morgan and Krarl delved deep into the Protectorate infantry's left wing, breaking their cohesion and shattering their will, the Protectorate heavy cavalry was wreaking havoc where the rebel counter-strike marched the thickest, denying them the manpower and weight they would need to break and roll-back the enemy. As Morgan twisted and turned, slashing and cutting, pounding the Protector soldiers side by side with his indomitable brother, he saw the danger. It was the point of all or nothing. The point at which fate herself, driven by the three sisters, would turn. He seized the moment.

General Jethro had watched appalled as he witnessed the gutting of the most prized mounted assault force that his army possessed by the unseen and unexpected blizzard of hell driven bolts, launched from the storm clouds of dust and smoke that shrouded the battlefield. He watched with pride in his chest as the vanguard of his decimated horse, picked itself up, shrugged off the abuse that had hammered through its centre, and tear into the sides of the enemy as planned, like an arrow into the rotten core of an apple.

'You tricky devil! Take that, you bastard!'

As he muttered his curse, his eyes were drawn to his left wing where the enemy foot had formed a wedge and were sprinting in a bellicose and frightening manner towards his shielded wall. He watched in grim trepidation as the point burst into his armoured men, lancing through it like a hot needle through an overripe boil, spewing the guts and blood of his stalwart foot into the air.

'May the god protect us!' he muttered again, trying not to show his alarm. 'What manner of warriors are those!?'

'It's the bastard General himself, sir!' answered the worried looking major. 'Local gossip has it that he has been fashioned from the cauldrons of dark magic! Both he and his inhuman brother.'

'Brother!? I knew not of any brother?'

'He is not generally spoken of, General. He is the bogeyman lurking under every child's bed. To mention him is to invite ill luck.'

'Bah! Superstitious, godless peasants! We need to kill that spearhead before it sparks a rout. Already it is causing our advance march to swing inwards. The bastard will soon have us flanked on the right by his reserve horse. Signal our reserve foot to march left to bolster. What of my light horse? Have the survivors reformed yet? Ready or not, signal them to shadow our right wing.'

'Yes, General.'

As old generals like to say, it is the man who makes the first mistake that loses the battle. In his fast flurry of orders, his nervous major erred in his signals, sending both foot and horse reserves to the right instead of foot to the left and horse to the right. This gave Morgan a chink of light in the window of fortune.

Stepping back into the small island of calm behind his raging brother, Morgan managed to catch the eye of Jacob who was wielding sword and shield in a tight, efficient and deadly manner. With a brief hand signal, he conveyed his intent to the young man who immediately dropped back behind the cover of his two Blue Mountain wolf pack companions. Here he closed his eyes, and a look of concentration suffused his youthful features.

Without waiting for any visible show of results, Morgan sent a quick mental impression to his twin and leapt back into the fray. Anyone, with the luxury of space and time to observe him thoroughly, would have seen him suddenly transformed as if a dampening blanket had suddenly been ripped away from his head and shoulders. His spirit appeared to instantly burst into flame, and his thoughtful, brown eyes ignited with swirling gold, becoming luminous and unearthly; a thing to freeze men's hearts and freeze them he did.

'To me, brothers of the sword. To me, win or lose, give me all you have!'

His deep bass, shouted words were clearly heard by friend and foe above the heated din, and both sides drew up their heads in readiness. Then the enemy was struck by a devastating double surge, the likes of which they had never experienced before in battle or anywhere else for that matter.

It began with those close to the extraordinary brothers. At first, they experienced a cold numbness in the brain, like drinking icy, melt-water on a baking hot day after strenuous exercise. With this feeling came an overpowering and unreasonable sense of fear, as if all courage had left them and something unseen and horrible in the darkest corner of the night was visiting them, seeking to drain them of their very lives, something unnamed and evil beyond bounds. Many turned to run, finding themselves trapped in place by the press of their comrades behind them which only increased the overwhelming terror in their hearts and minds. Caught in this place of purgatory and suffering, they were struck down, sent crumbling with trembling spasms into the churned earth as the return of a glacial driven cold burst the blood vessels in their brains, their spirits fleeing, bemused and bewildered onto the bridge of light. As these horrid and inexplicable sensations spread outwards, ravaging the petrified soldiers, Morgan, Krarl, the Chosen and their Kingdom followers, fell on them like ravening wolves. Like a tide, reversing out to sea, they broke and fled before this unnatural onslaught. There were no reserves in place to stand in their stead and stem the flood.

'Major, why are my reserves of foot heading for the wrong flank? Recall them, man! And hurry! Send them to where they are sorely needed!' exclaimed General Jethro his voice held low but brimming with urgency. 'You sergeant! Get down there and tell the advance to hold in place before we spiral into oblivion, god be our protector.'

The General swept an experienced eye over the rest of the field. All was not lost despite the dire circumstances on his left flank. The heavy cavalry was still rooting the enemy infantry into the earth like hogs would do to turnips. Good on them. Serve the bastards right! Let them feel their loss and weep like women. His centre-right was still in place, untouched if twisted at an odd angle, but then he saw what he feared might happen. The enemy light horse, the same disciplined troopers that had had two successful charges at the expense of his forces, were storming back down the hill towards the slight gap on the right flank of his centre-right. A black arrow of thundering horsemen, lances couched and ready.

Captain Horace had been standing by his mount watching the give and take being played out on the field, his face as readable as a rock. Besides him was the slender figure of Vivian, left in post by Morgan to aid communication. Suddenly, she held out a hand to steady herself against his muscled bulk and closed her eyes as if fighting dizziness. He switched his gaze to her, his eyes and thoughts undiscernible.

'We have to ride. Now!' she said in a hollow voice.

The Captain frowned and rediverted his attention back to studying the field. Then with a grunt, he mounted his horse heavily, pulling its head up and around.

'I'm sorry, Captain. That's all I have,' continued Vivian, looking up at him with apologetic eyes.

'You did well, girl,' he replied. 'I'll take it from here. I know what must be done. You stay here.'

With that, he turned his horse and signalled for his men to follow. They scampered hurriedly to fall into line and within a heartbeat of five were thundering down the slope heading for the enemy's right flank.

The Protectorate General was not the only one who had seen the danger. The veteran battle-sergeants with coarsely bawled orders managed to halt the advancing soldiers on the right, even before they received instructions from their General to do so, but getting their charges to shuffle backwards and adjust their lines was a lost cause. In their minds, they were moving on the enemy, and this was not the time for a back step. They could see the success of the heavy horse, and they wanted some of that for themselves. They had not seen the danger on the left wing nor did the majority see the threat coming at them from the hill. Even so, let them come, thought those who were aware. A light cavalry charging heavy infantry only had one way to go; straight down to hell. As an armoured block, they had no sense that they were drifting off line, pinned to the whims of the overall battle as they were. They did not see their vulnerability as their general and battle-sergeants saw it. They would sweat and bleed for that lack of oversight.

As Captain Horace and his troop tore around the hastily adjusting enemy lines, hugging the forest fringes and drinking in the sudden fear of the heavy foot, they became alerted to the hugeness of their task. Speed was everything. The Protectorate ranks were six thick with the second and third ranks armed with long pikes, bristling with iron menace. If they managed to address their lines, he and his horsemen would all be spitted like pigs at a spring fayre. Clenching his jaws and thighs, he urged his gelding to greater speed.

Back up on the slope, the commander of the heavy cavalry, cantering his horse through blood and gore mixed with dark earth, wheeled his men in a disciplined circle. Now to deal with the rest of these upstarts who were causing such a ruckus on the left. He would send them along the same path as their now barely recognisable brethren. As they turned their backs for a downhill charge, rain in the form of black-tipped arrows fell on them. They had forgotten the Honey General and his archers.

General Montford had long realised the high risk in Morgan's strategy. As the senior officer left in charge, he had taken it on himself to provide as much cover and distraction as he could. As Morgan had said, he needed smoke, smoke and mirrors to win the day. As soon as his artillery volley had flown their cradles, he had sped his archers over to the round of the hill, not even bothering to observe the results. He had also left orders for the artillery division with Greybeaver now in charge, to manhandle their machinery over to his new position as best they could. They had not yet arrived, but his few remaining longbowmen were ready. As he looked down on the bloody carnage below him and the mounted juggernaut that had caused it, he felt the urge of retribution as he gave the signal to unleash their volley of arrows. Their efforts took the horsemen by surprise, and many fell from their horses injured, but even so, their armour, the paucity of missiles, and the distance, limited their effectiveness to distraction rather than decimation. The horse commander seemed to toy with the idea of coming at them to punish them for their audacity, but when he saw the artillery machines and their handlers pelting up to take position, he galloped off with his men.

'Well, I hope we've bought Lord Morgan a little more time to prepare,' he said to a panting Greybeaver.

Grey beaver nodded, but he seemed distracted. His attention was focused on the bloody field of broken bodies below them.

'One of our own may have survived. There is movement down there.'

As the Honey General followed his gaze, he saw a dirt-covered apparition heave itself out of the ground. Looking about in a dazed and unsteady fashion, it suddenly lurched off, staggering towards an untidy pile of bodies where it began methodically digging.

'I think he has lost his mind, poor fellow,' muttered the Honey General. 'Let's go to him.'

***

The last thing old John remembered was a crushing blow which sent him hurtling into oblivion. The first thing he became aware of was being buried alive, a thing he feared most of all, a nightmare that visited him most nights in the darkest of hours, a terror that always brought him gasping to the surface drenched in sweat and thankful, in the end, that he was still alive.

'Bastards didn't even have the decency to check my pulse. Buried me without a bloody prayer,' was his second thought, filled with belligerence and clean air. He had pushed himself clear of battlefield detritus that had been covering him.

Wiping the dirt from eyes, he surveyed the carnage around him clinically and impartially. He had been in this situation before, and each time he prayed that it would never happen again, but his curse was to keep living whilst all around him died. This time he hoped, something might be different for he spotted a familiar stripe of colour lying under an unrecognisable pile of bodies. Taking another deep breath of sweet air, he staggered over for a closer look, not allowing any emotion to mar his investigation. Pulling splintered limbs and crushed torsos aside as respectfully as he could, he focused on that splash of colour. Finally, his fingers closed over it, and he heaved backwards with all the strength remaining in his body. A loud groan emanated from the large man he had in his grasp, followed by a generous wad of spit mixed with dirt and blood.

'Fuck! Am I dead? Bloody well doesn't feel like the Hall of Plenty!'

'You're still here with me on this pissing earth, big fellow. Pain isn't finished with us yet.'

Housecarl Graham Stonerider collapsed on his bottom on the trampled thigh of a dead warrior.

'Sorry, mate,' he muttered. 'I'm all done in. What the fuck happened, John?'

'The sky fell on us, I think,' replied Housecarl John, swaying precariously on his feet.

Before Graham could answer, Greybeaver and two other foresters ran up to them.

'Glad you made it back to us, lads. We've still got more fighting to do so don't die on us yet.'

'Charming!' grumbled the huge Housecarl.

***

Morgan felt drained, and a glance at his brother confirmed that he was no better off. They had never used this destructive aspect of their gifts on such a large scale before and certainly not in the middle of a battle. It had been successful, however, as the Protectorate men-of-arms were falling over themselves to get away from them. They may soon rally, but the objective had been achieved for now. He heard Karl snarl and looked up to see the enemy heavy horse beginning to make their run towards them. His plans did not cover this, although he knew it would have been a real possibility. It was time to improvise or die.

***

The Protectorate field army was in imminent disarray, and its General knew it. His light cavalry which should have been guarding his right flank was all but destroyed. His massed infantry, his centre, his powerhouse, was wheeling out of formation, out of effectiveness. The cross-bow division, hidden amongst them, neutralised. His centre-right was desperately trying to correct its inward swing to avoid being flanked by a rapacious enemy horse, and his left had been routed with the remnants bending under an extreme assault. The only unit that could now offer him deliverance and ultimately victory was his heavy cavalry, which should have been guarding his left flank but had had to be switched to bolster his right. He cringed inwardly as the past mistakes paraded through his mind; ineptitude after ineptitude. The enemy general had played them all for fools. He watched his heavy horse turn from its small victory and begin its ponderous advance on the bastards who had put his left wing to rout –why had they run in such a wild manner anyway- and balanced it against the daring charge of the enemy light horse as they raced around the hedgehog points of his pikemen. He found that he was unable to draw breath; unable to breathe. God be his protector.

***

Captain Horace and his men, for they were his now, whipped around the hurriedly back stamping mass of pointed pikes. Most of them made it, but an unlucky few were hooked and skewered, screaming from their saddles, to be trampled into the dust by the drumming hooves of their own fellows' wide-eyed mounts. He could clearly see the panic in the eyes of his foe as those on the edge tried to heave around their heavy pikes, breaking their hard-pressed formation even more. Into this boiling mess of piss and sweat, his horse plunged -stumbling as men were crushed underneath- its huge muscles bunching as its iron hooves broke flesh underneath, adding blood to the fetid mixture. He felt a sharp pain as a pike point ripped open a gash on his thigh and instinctively swatted it away with his sword, then in a reverse stroke, tore open the throat of a howling soldier as he madly lunged at him. Fancy swordplay was not needed in this hot melee, only speed and ruthlessness. This was where the Captain was at his best when the fighting was at its most brutish. This was where he had earned his fighting reputation and why warriors followed him into the horrid field of battle. A place where companionship and belonging threw the gut-twisting, cold hand of fear out of the window; where warriors bonded into a fellowship of iron.

The first few moments went well for them as they tore into the unprotected belly of the terror struck footmen. Their rapid momentum took them deep, but then the densely packed bodies of the soldiers brought their bucking horses to a standstill as effectively as if they had been stuck in sucking mud. The Captain tried to spin his horse in tight circles, giving it free rein to lash out with its iron-shod hooves, cutting left and right about him with a cold fury, cleaving skulls and splitting armour. Even so, he felt grasping, vengeful hands trying to pull him from his saddle. He knew they were in a bind and could not hold out much longer. He prepared himself for death and strove with a maddened energy to take as many of the bastards with him before his time came to meet the maker and spit in his eye.

***

Morgan's prediction had been proven correct. Under the bellowed commands of their battle-sergeants, most of the foot soldiers had stopped running. Even the Protectorate General had ridden over in an attempt to stem the flood, and his Dragon banner could be clearly seen fluttering urgently in the rising breeze.

'Two squares, brother, facing all fronts before horse and foot descends on us!' he shouted to Krarl. 'You take one. I will lead the other. We two shall face the horse. Leave an avenue between.'

Krarl leapt into action, racing through the massed Kingdom troops, splitting them, pushing men left then right, dividing them from their centre. At the same time, Morgan's deep voice thrummed over them.

'Break, break! Form two squares! Move or die! Be ready on all fronts! Move!'

The Chosen surged into the milling men, joining the brothers in shoving the shuffling warriors into position.

'Be Ready! Be ready or die!' Morgan reminded them.

Morgan glanced around him to assess the field. The heavy Cavalry was now in full gallop, their lances lowered with deadly intent. The earth trembled with their coming. The enemy foot too were beginning their advance if a little bit uncertainly and with a ragged line. The horse would be the first on them. A classic hammer and anvil technique.

'Shields! Shields! Raise shields, you bastards! Show me a wall! Show me a wall!' bellowed Morgan.

'Starnn Firrm!' roared Krarl. 'Starrnd firm, you weaklings!'

'Close up tight, warriors of the Lower Kingdoms! Show these bastards how we fight!' shouted Sharleen. She had taken up position in Krarl's battle square, tucked in on his left. Her popular presence, a figure known and respected, centred the men.

'Widen the gap!' commanded Morgan. 'Leave the whoresons room to funnel! All with javelins, be ready to throw! Be ready! Here they come!'

He noticed the silent figure of Ahmya by his side, her green eyes flashing with anticipation and determination. He felt her power.

'Ready! Men of the Lower Kingdoms! Are you ready?! Are you ready for war?! Are you ready to kill?!' he roared with thunderous might.

'Ready! Ready! Ready! Was the booming response from a thousand throats.

'Then follow me to victory! Let no man falter! On my mark! March! Left! Left!'

'Shields up!' yelled the simultaneous voices of Ahmya, Sharleen and Elisha from their respective squares. 'Tight! Tight!'

'Tight as a virgin's arse,' bellowed Pollock.

A roar rose from the mass ranks of the stomping warriors, and they all took up the cry.

'Tight! Tight! Tight!'

They marched belligerently towards the oncoming horsemen. They marched for two reasons; to gain cohesive courage and to put a little distance between them and the reformed Protectorate infantry.

'Halt!' roared Morgan. 'Shields up! Swords out! Javelins at the ready. Stand firm and do not move! Brace! Brace!'

His call was echoed throughout the ranks, and the warriors hunkered down, shoulders against shields, overlapped and braced. A solid wall of wood, leather and iron; facing outwards on all four fronts with a broad avenue in between.

'Stand firm or you die where you stand!' reminded Morgan in his battle voice. 'Kingdom men. Why are we here?!'

'Tuurr fiiite!' bawled out the savage voice of his brother in a defiant answer.

Another roar lifted from the battle-ready warriors as they took up the call as one.

'To fight! Fight! Fight! Fight!'

The oncoming heavy cavalry, now in full gallop, crashed through the wall of sound that rolled towards them, and broke through, shredding it with their own bellicose war cries; bolstering their wildly beating hearts with bands of vengeance and valour.

Krarl unexpectedly gripped the muscled shoulder of Sharleen. At first, startled by his physical contact, she settled, as she felt a joining, something primitive, mind to mind. Then a thing unknown opened inside her, and she felt Krarl pulling it gently from her. She watched in fascination with a sort of inner eye as this psychic union filled her. She had never felt such a thrilling thing before, and her mind expanded with energy. Krarl guided this energy, fused it with his, funnelled it, and sent it blasting outwards.

As they bore down on the two solid and immovable squares of determined warriors, hoping to intimidate and scare them into breaking formation, a roiling energy of fear and despair boiled around them, cloying to the spaces created before they knew themselves as men, an area that generally lay dormant in the inner recesses of their minds. Hardened horsemen were thrown back hard into their saddles in dismay and near despair from this onset of inexplicable anxiety urging them to abandon this unnecessary foray towards certain death. Even so, with the desire to turn their steeds and flee compelling them, the elite Protectorate men of horse, kept their seats and their objective.

With the earth literally jumping under their hooves from their battering, the fully stretched avalanche of horseflesh, seeing before them what they thought to be an unbreakable and unscalable fence, baulked at the last moment. Those riders, still glassy-eyed and unfocused from Krarl's attack, sailed over their horses' lowered heads to land inside the armoured squares, only to find their deaths waiting there. The others clung on grimly as their mounts turned right angles at full gallop and tore along the shielded front, many sent crashing to the hard earth as thrown javelins sunk into both man and horseflesh. Finally, finding an opening to escape this abuse, the now terrified animals, overcome by the roaring noise of unseen men and the smell of their own blood, fled along its course, seeking escape. The thundering noise now on both flanks drove them to even greater speed where they spilt out into the open field between friend and foe. Here their recovered masters tried to turn them to continue the elusive contact. As they fought the bit, spinning and milling about, churning the earth, they acted as a barricade, hampering the rallied ranks of their own foot soldiers advance. With their fronts facing in all directions, it was easy for the two fighting squares to join as one, and reverse with an implacable intent on the now ineffective heavy cavalry, pushing them onto their own infantry's shield wall, disrupting their formation and fighting effectiveness. Under these impossible conditions, both men and horse began to abandon the battleground, seeking safety in the far distant line of forests. Morgan, Krarl and the rebels had won the day.

***

Down on his knees but still gutting men with his broken knife in a frenzy of killing, his breath whistling through his cracked front teeth, captain Horace refused to go down. The crush bearing down on him was almost unbearable and giving in began to seem a rosy option. He hated flowers anyway. Suddenly, the horn of the goddess started to call for him, and he steeled himself to make a good impression. Strangely, the sun began to shine on his face, and a cooling breeze eased the suffocating heat from his body. He smiled. She had come in person to take him across the bridge.

'We live, Captain! We live!

He opened his eyes to see the battered but grinning face of young Captain Bastonet. Never in his life had he seen such an ugly and unwelcoming sight. Where was his adored, shining goddess?

***

General Jethro knew that all was lost as soon as he saw the fighting squares being formed. Underneath his anger, he admired the sheer audacity of this Morgan Ap Heston and his warriors. He had learned a lot from them. He signalled for the general recall to be sounded and watched his battle-sergeants organise the disengagement and begin to carry out an ordered retreat. There were many here who he intended to give a field promotion on this very day. He despised his City's policy of only giving officer command to the pampered sons of military houses. As long as the rank of General rested on his shoulders, he would make the changes that will matter in the days, weeks, months and maybe even years to come.

'Surely we cannot run before this rabble, General!' protested his serving major.

'We are doing what is sensible and prudent, Major. This is only the first of many engagements. Our world has begun to change. We must learn and be ready. Come, Major. It's time to go.'

With these words, he turned his horse and with his Dragon banner still fluttering proudly in the breeze, vacated the field of battle.

CHAPTER XXXVI

'You should not be going to her! You are flying the wrong colours, Lord Morgan. To all eyes, you are giving the impression of surrendering the high ground to the White Bitch!'

'Well said, Elisha. There is a General in you yet,' replied Morgan, with a bare hint of a smile. 'Every manoeuvre, however, has an inherent risk.'

He felt Ahmya's silent agreement with Elisha's voiced sentiment and his brother smelled of amusement.

The Snow Queen, as soon as she saw victory assured, had set up a lavish camp on a high, flat point of the sloping plain. A considerable pavilion had been erected, and her courtiers and service staff had been working double time to put on a sumptuous celebration. She immediately issued invitations for the victorious generals and their commanders, knowing fully well that it would have been boorish for Morgan to refuse. As always, she viewed everything with a political eye. She even sent an emissary to the City to offer opening talks of peace and compromise, making it appear as if this triumph was won under her guiding hand. The Honey General advised Morgan to cut her short before she fomented trouble for all of them. Housecarls Graham and John agreed with him, and Elisha advocated stripping her naked and sending her packing back to her Gomorrah. Sharleen nodded keenly to this and Krarl laughed at them all. Ahmya kept her council, but her green eyes glittered like cold, stone emeralds from time to time. Morgan listened to them all with a calm, unreadable expression, then accepted the invitation.

As Morgan, Krarl and their entourage strode onto the array of plush carpets and rugs spread within the large, tented arena, the Chosen spread out before him, deflecting the approach of the Queen's courtiers. Morgan was their target as no one in their right mind would dare approach Krarl directly.

The Queen sat on what was in all intents and purposes, a raised throne. She was once again, attired in a flawless, glowing, white gown, cut low and revealing. Her elegant neck was adorned with a simple silver chain on which was attached a perfect diamond nestled precisely within the hollow of her throat. She rose immediately as the brothers entered and descended her throne gracefully with a long, perfectly formed leg emerging from her dress with each step and an apparently genuine smile pulling the corners of her full, painted lips.

Elisha made a deep sound of disgust.

'Welcome, victorious Generals. Before our very eyes, you have accomplished the impossible and done what has never been achieved before. You have defeated a Protectorate army in the field of glory. We stand before you awed in your light.'

'Can't say that I noticed,' commented Sharleen to no one in particular.

If the Queen heard her, she gave no sign.

'Lord Krarl, I watched you in the field from on high,' she said, bowing before him. 'You were magnificent. There is no one in this world, who can rival you in battle.'

Krarl did not answer but watched her as a mongoose would a snake. She quickly turned to Morgan, and her smile widened revealing perfect teeth that matched her gown in whiteness.

'Lord Morgan,' she continued, her throaty voice growing more husky and sensual. 'Your presence here fills me with gratitude and joy. You are a genius of war and its tactics; a paragon of martial prowess. The world and this queen awaits your pleasure, and we are humbled.'

With these words of honey dripping from her red lips, she glided towards him, her face uplifted and her eyes shining, intending to kiss him as an equal on both cheeks.

'You will stand back from our Lord Morgan!'

The words of power cracked and rolled through the space like a dark, ominous cloud of lightning and thunder. Ahmya, her beautiful face transformed into a goddess of wrath, seemed to double before all eyes in size and stature, dominating the assembled group, her shadow encompassing all and especially the queen, with threat and fury. As the power in her words lashed and echoed around the pavilion, the Queen stepped back hurriedly, her visage turning the colour of her gown, drained of all blood. She reached trembling fingers up to the diamond at her neck as if to draw strength and stability from it and her eyes turned nervous and uncertain.

The entire room was struck dumb with shock and trepidation, and the thought of dark magic raced its course through the superstitious minds of most. All except Morgan and Krarl. Morgan glanced calmly at Ahmya and Krarl made a low, deep chuckle. The only sound in the hushed pavilion.

'The Chosen are very protective of our safety, Eminence. Maybe, it is wise that we listen to them and follow their suggestions,' said Morgan amiably.

The Queen, a superb and balanced political in-fighter, recovered quickly. She did not lack personal courage, but nothing in her world had prepared her for such an encounter even with those earlier anomalies that had awakened her intellectual curiosity and the observation of the impossible done by the brothers in battle.

'Yes, you are right, my lords. I forgot myself and your positions.'

She turned slightly towards Ahmya, her eyes now guarded, and gave her a hint of a bow as a ring fighter would to his opponent who had struck him with the first skilful blow. A battle of sorts it seemed, was joined.

'No harm done,' replied Morgan.

This time he stepped forward and gently cupped the Queen's elbow and indicating his brother who had already wandered over to the feasting tables, guided her after him.

'Shall we all enjoy this wonderful victory banquet you've laid on for our warriors, my Queen? They wait outside for your permission to join us.'

'Of course, Lord Morgan,' she answered quickly. 'This celebration is for the honour of all.'

As a wave of noisy and ravenous looking warriors invaded the pavilion behind them with their uncaring, dirty boots, Morgan leaned in on the Queen and said.

'Time is short for us and them, my Queen. We march tomorrow.'

'March, Lord Morgan? But surely we have already won our victory! You have recovered for the Green Kingdoms their provinces.'

'Yes, my Queen, but my brother assures me that this is just the beginning. I encourage you to spend the night contemplating my words and the role you wish to play in the future. Why, what manner of meat is this, my Queen? It is delicious!'

'I'm not sure,' replied the Queen absently. 'My culinary skills are not very developed.'

'Never mind. My compliments to your chef. My thanks and my apology, my Queen, but it is time for me to leave. There are a lot of ingredients for me to prepare for tomorrow's march. My brother shall remain in my stead. He is not what he appears to be. Take some time out and talk with him. I guarantee that you will be somewhat surprised by what he has to say.'

With this ambiguous statement, Morgan turned and departed, followed by most of the Chosen.

The Queen did try to talk with Lord Krarl but found their conversation both frustrating and disconcerting. Half of the time she did not understand his words and suspected that he was deliberately making it so. With the other half, he was so direct that she was not sure whether or not he was being serious or was just having fun on her behalf. She decided it was best not to linger to find out. The hulking woman who was always at his shoulder did not make things any easier either and the occasions that she had caught her leering down at her bosom made her skin crawl. The evening had not turned out in the manner that she had anticipated, but she was not angry. She now realised that Morgan was not the straightforward military man that she had expected. He knew how to play at politics and acknowledged that he and his staged actors had outmanoeuvred her at her own game. With a toss of her beautiful, coiffured head she departed the pavilion for her private tent, leaving behind her the rude transformation of her carefully constructed royal banquet into the semblance of a soldiers' mess hall.

'The courtier who provided me with information on General Jethro. Do you recall him? What is his name?' she enquired of her Peacock en route.

'I'm not sure, my Queen.'

'I see. Find him and bring him to me.'

'But…'

'Now, please, and hurry.'

'Yes, at once, my Queen.'

Impatience was beginning to crawl into her mind, animating her finger into tapping on the arm of the chair on which she sat when the Peacock finally arrived in a blustering flurry. In his wake walked the gawky, young courtier with his long, thin, blond hair whipping about his face in the stiff breeze. He seemed uncomfortable and clearly did not want to be dragged into the centre of affairs where eyes could focus on him. He stood there like a sage fowl considering flight from an imaginary fox; nervous of the world.

'You may leave us,' said the Queen.

The Peacock seemed unable to register that she meant him and he looked confused. She regarded him quietly for a long silent pause before the coin dropped.

'Oh!' he said hurriedly and bowed jerkily, spinning on his heels and stomping away.

'You have been discovered, and still, you remain standing in the shadows. Incredible! I find it disconcerting that you have found your way into my court, under my very nose, and I did not even know of your existence. Tonight you shall tell me your story, dear man.'

He remained silent and she was starting to feel that he might try to defy her but then clearing his throat, he responded.

'My story is not worth the telling, my Queen, for I descend from an unremarkable side-line and I have no House to belong to.'

'Your line runs parallel to the House of Saint Smithers himself, and that makes you a blood relative of a sort to our First Citizen. That, I think, is hardly unremarkable but certainly dangerous.'

He hid his surprise well and covered his discomfort with a small cough.

'My line goes back to a half-sister of the saint, my Queen. She never served in office, and neither did any of her children's children down through the generations.'

'Do not play games with me, young Flavius. You stand well placed among the strands of influence that camouflages your activities. Is the First Citizen even aware of your presence? I wonder? What would this information be worth to him? Your death or my demise? Tell me, what do you hope to gain by remaining in the dark, Shadow dancer?'

'Reward usually comes to those who are patient, my Queen.'

'My, my. You are a bold one. I think I like you, but even so, why do you think, I should not have you killed?'

'The arm of the assassins is very long, my Queen. We are instrumental as an ally, and you will be surprised at how many secrets we hold that lead back right to your very doorstep.'

'I am happy to see, dear man, that you do not disappoint. You are as sinister as the organisation to which you belong. Pray tell, what secrets are these?'

'Every secret has a price, my Queen. And trust me, you are not yet ready to meet the value of what is hidden beneath your nose.'

'I revise my earlier comment. You are not bold. You are merely insolent. Remember, for all your dark connections, you stand alone in my household. At the moment your life hangs by a thread between the scissors of my indecision. Go, I do not wish to speak with you any further on this night. You leave me in need of a bath. Get out of my sight.'

'My Queen,' said the assassin, bowing low and padding silently off into the darkness beyond the reaches of her candlelight.

CHAPTER XXXVII

News of the defeat had flown to the city on the heated wings of rumour. On its way, it took on several forms, each manifestation flying into the eager ears of those most receptive, based on their nature and their intent. The good citizens, grown fat on victory after victory, were enraged by this affront and took to the streets in raging mobs. They demanded swift retribution. They called on the Ruling Nine to send out the legions to destroy these unwashed upstarts; to capture their leaders and drag them back to the Holy City in chains to be judged and punished before the god. Whilst sending this message, the good people attacked all known foreigners in their city and burnt their belongings and hard-earned properties to ashes, beating those caught to within an inch of their lives. The authorities did not see fit to intervene. In a closed sitting, the First Citizen insisted that his children had the right to express their righteous passions and those parasites who had been feeding on the City's largess for countless years were now justly being offered up as altar lambs before the god. Strangely enough, his private words soon found their way to the people's ears within the hour, shouted from unruly street corners by impassioned priests, rousing the populace to even greater levels of mass worship and purification. The Ruling Nine, swayed by the people's just desires, issued orders that the war legions be raised and sent to the borderlands and there to crush the heathens and rescue their beloved Cardinal Wuzetian from their vile clutches. Her claims that the victory was hers were dismissed as coerced propaganda. Their proclamation was echoed through the tree-lined avenues and dirty back streets alike, lancing the general unrest like a hot boil and bringing a tense peace to the City of the god.

There were others who felt, if not fear, then the first tendrils of concern. Among these were the Spymaster, the Merchant King and many of the military houses, primarily the House of Montford. This latter had now received word of the fate of their House's missing son. They were not sure what to make of it. Had he turned traitor to his kind as the First Citizen had loudly claimed? Or had he made a conscious decision for self-preservation, bearing in mind the manner in which his command had been stripped from him. Only time and opportunity, they hoped, would tell. Both the Spymaster and the Head of House Wuzetian, knew of this Morgan Ap Heston. Many of his exploits were documented in the City's secret histories, and most of them had been to the detriment of the Protectorate regime. Some even stated that he was in some way, responsible for the death of their mysterious and powerful, First Citizen. His ventures were not to be taken lightly, and many in the high echelons of power knew that he had defeated not just one as was commonly believed, but two field armies, in a matter of a couple of years. He was a real danger, and they full heartedly and publicly supported the mobilisation of the war legions with the Spymaster pushing for the man he was the secret patron of, to be put in overall command. Lord Wuzetian also knew, that his niece's position was much more precarious than advocated. He had been keeping track of her through the Shadowy Guild, but recently, all information had dried up. His subordinates inside the Guild claimed that all their operatives had been eliminated by Ap Heston and his crew, but he had his suspicions, and they were not altogether reassuring. An even more real danger was, of course, the First Citizen. No one really knew the full extent of his knowledge of the facts and of the situation. No one really knew what he believed and most scary of all, no one knew what his intentions were. He stirred the people pot at every opportunity and continued his erratic and merciless campaign to eliminate rivals and perceived rivals. He claimed that the truth was false and that false things were true until no one really knew what to believe or even worse, stopped caring. He had become the First Citizen of chaos. Now it was feared, that in this dry cauldron of confusion, Ap Heston was intending to march with a firebrand in one hand and a sword in the other. God help them all!

The First Citizen couldn't care less about receiving help from his god. He watched them all, scurrying this way and that. He would get them so scared that like a dog they would fart and by their stink, he would find them out. This Ap Heston was the Sandman of their childhood nightmares, and he would use him; use him to fish out their eyeballs and deliver them to him so that he may see the light of their desires fade from them.

***

Morgan sat his horse as the early morning sun turned the world to soft gold and watched his army file pass beneath him in marching formation, tight and disciplined. He was pleased with their sterling performance but knew that they would be tested again and again in the days and weeks to come. From this forging in fire, he intended to emerge an army of iron with the deferent elements fused together to make an unbreakable sword; a sword pointed at the heart of the Empire. Standing with him were his commanders and the Chosen. His brother stood alone on a jutting outcrop ahead and separate from them, his expression unreadable, but Morgan smelt an eagerness coming from him, something more than just the usual battle eagerness. He wasn't sure what to make of that. At the rear of the army with a large gap dividing them in an attempt to avoid the worst of the dust, came the Snow Queen and her travelling court. They were like a palace on wheels.

'They are part of a web of intrigue, Lord Morgan. They are versed in using deceit and betrayal as political tools. For them, nothing is personal, only business as usual. They know when and where to bite. Where to inject crippling poison. Where to wound a man to bring him low and where it hurts most; for they are the children of vipers and know no better,' drifted the matter-of-fact voice of the Honey General, bringing him back from his musings.

'You sound a bit bitter this morning, General. Did you not sleep well?'

'Very well, thank you, Lord Morgan. Please heed my words, my Lord. Medicine has a taste of bitterness but so does poison. My former homeland was built on political poison. We were weaned on it from our mother's milk. Do not trust this White Queen, Lord Morgan. She may love you, but that will not stop her from betraying and killing you. It is who she is.'

'I understand all this, General. I keep her close for a purpose. All strategy has inherent risk. You of all people should appreciate this.'

'Yes, Lord Morgan. I understand, and that is why I am fearful and sad. If we learn from our enemy, think like them, act like them, so as to defeat them. Do we not become our enemy and in the long run, defeated?'

Morgan glanced at the silent Lord Tramford who was trying his best to appear as if he was not listening. He had kept a low profile, not seeing himself as a military man, until Morgan had sought him out and brought him back into the fore of events.

'That is also the reason why I keep you and these good others by my side. To keep reminding me of who I am and why we have begun this fight.'

'You are wise, Lord Morgan.'

'I am old and wary, General. Wary of myself more than any other.'

EPILOGUE

In a dusty, open courtyard surrounded on three sides by an angular, pillared and flagstone patio and by tall, elegant trees on the other, three figures battled furiously. The leafy cover from the trees cast a cooling shadow over half of the courtyard, but the shade was the last thing on the minds of the combatants. A tall, blond, athletic-looking man, shirtless and with a fighting stick held in each calloused hand, swirled in constant motion. His face was serene despite the intense pressure he was being put under. His opponents, both women, were pressing him hard, merciless and deadly. The shorter of the two, slender, with piercing green eyes and flaming red hair, wielded a long, hardwood staff with fast, economic efficiency. She did not twirl it or flourish it with showy and useless energy but jabbed its ends at his face, throat, groin and joints with vicious purpose. When these were swiftly deflected or evaded she would step away fluidly, spin her weapon, and slash down with a crushing sweeping force at her adversary's skull, legs or any body part that seemed exposed and vulnerable. In contrast, the other woman was well beyond the average in height, and her limbs and back were sheathed in long, hard muscles. Framing her dark, granite face, were tightly plaited locks with bells, shiny trinkets and colourful feathers, knotted into them. These whipped about like writhing musical snakes as she moved with blinding speed and ferocity against the blond man in the centre; attacking in tandem and with smoothly executed coordination with the redhead. In each hand, she held a long knife; real ones with sharpened edges, not training toys. With these she darted in on the tall man, cutting and stabbing. He covered everything, never missing a beat as a rhythmic and primitive drum beat echoed into the fighting space, beaten out by a group of wild-looking women who sat cross-legged on the sidelines between the cylindrical stone pillars.

'That's it, sister,' shouted encouragingly the older and larger of the women. 'We have him cornered. See! He is unable to attack. Only defend. He is a man. All muscle and bluster. No stamina.'

As if to belie her mocking words the blond man executed a blinding counter, trapping the downward stroke of the redhead's staff between his sticks and stripped it from her grasp, sending it clattering to the flagstones.

'Shit!' she yelled with venom.

The man laughed and immediately had to leap backwards in haste to avoid a wicked knife slash to his stomach. His recovery was exquisite for as the follow-up slash to his throat came flying towards him, he swayed like smoke under it, then in a hardened counter, riposted with two rapid whacks, separated by a quick gasp of breath, across the stomach of his second opponent. She grunted audibly and stepped back.

'Lucky shot,' she said in a flat voice.

The young man laughed again, his handsome face bursting into a ray of sunshine, infectious and full of humour.

'Gabrielle, I thought you said he was tired and we had him cornered?' panted the beautiful redhead, wiping a bead of perspiration from her brow.

Before the dark warrior could answer, they were interrupted by a spindly limbed, white-haired, court official, who despite his advanced age moved with pompous alacrity towards them. He frowned with disapproval at the seated women then turned his disapproval on the trio in the open courtyard.

'The Queen commands that you stop wasting time in tomfoolery and present yourself to her within the hour,' he announced in a loud, sour voice.

As Nat and Elaine bowed to him in an irreverent manner, he uttered a loud 'hurrumph' and switched his beady gaze to Gabrielle.

'You too…erh…erh…Miss,' he continued, summoning up as much disdain as he could muster in his posture.

Gabrielle glared at him and muttered darkly, 'Silly man.'

Nat sniggered, and Elaine struggled hard not to laugh, giving out an involuntary snort.

Lifting his robes in disgust, the old courtier stalked off.

'Ladies should behave like ladies,' they heard him muttering.

'Old Crow is in top form today,' laughed Nat.

'Leave him alone, you ruffian,' said Elaine, also laughing.

Not a hint of a smile touched Gabrielle's lips.

'I wonder what the royal sister wants with me? I hope she doesn't start with this silly nonsense about frilly dresses again,' she said ominously.

The laughter immediately dried up for both the young lovers and they regarded the wild, steppe warrior silently. The thought of this woman in a frilly dress was very disconcerting.

Shaking himself all over as if emerging from an icy shower, Nat said.

'We had better make ourselves presentable and go find the Queen before she sends Crow for us again.'

Elaine nodded, and they moved off hand in hand followed by a glowering Gabrielle and her band of warriors.

***

Having scrubbed and changed clothing, Nat and Elaine found the strange and enigmatic, steppe chieftain waiting as motionless as a rock in the corridor outside. Accustomed to the oddness of their friend, they nodded to her as she fell in beside them, without a word. It was hard to tell if she had bothered to wash. Certainly she was wearing the same outfit from before, and the usual smell of horse and fresh air drifted from her. It wasn't unpleasant, it was not just a scent one expected to find in a palace.

After many enquiries, they were directed to a small rose garden which ran around the throne room. Here they found both the Queen and her consort busily pruning the fragrant, red flowers. With them, incongruously, was a short, broad-shouldered man who seemed to be constructed from bricks. The King saw them first and grinned at them, but continued his chore without rising to greet them. The Queen, on the other hand, quickly tucked her secateurs into the pocket of an apron she was wearing, wiped her hands on it and walked forward to meet them, followed closely by the short man whose face could only be described as dour.

'Glad you could make it,' said the Queen simply.

'How do, lads and lass,' he said, glancing with a small frown at Gabrielle.

The warrior shook her head in a small show of exasperation. It was a game that they had been playing for over a year now.

'Hello, Duncan,' said Nat. Gripping the man's huge forearm in a warrior's grip.

Elaine reached over and kissed him on the cheek. She was taller than him.

The Queen cleared her throat gently, and they all gave her the fullness of their attention.

'The gods of war have turned on their own.'

'My Queen?' asked Nat, his brow creased in puzzlement.

'The whereabouts of your father and mentor have been located.'

Sensing more, Nat kept his face still and placid, suppressing the surge of joy in his heart. He saw and felt the glow of emotion coming from Elaine, however.

'He has gathered an army around him like new clothes and has defeated yet another Protectorate army in the field. This time he intends to march to the gates of their City, come hell or high water. He will not be able to do this without the help of friends and allies. We wish to lend support to our King of old.'

The Queen's voice as ever, was as dry as a parched desert and none present dared to interrupt her flow.

'I suspect that he plans to supplant the Protectorate and make himself Emperor though, he may not be aware of this yet. We need to be by his side to ensure that he doesn't become worse than they are.'

Nat stared at her, not quite believing what she was saying.

'We need you to go to him. You will head our contingent, yes, to fight for him, but mostly to calm his demons. And believe me, these demons swim closer to the surface than you might think. Will you accept this duty in our name, Nathaniel Woodsmoke, Guardian of Kings?'

Nat fell to his knees before his Queen.

'Without all my heart and soul I accept.'

'Very well. I hereby anoint you, in the presence of my faithful consort, subject and ally, to be our royal emissary and representative in all things. May the goddess of light guide your young heart to do the right thing and see through what must be done to its bitter end.'

'I will also go. Morgan is close to my heart and me to his. Besides, my place is with Nat, now and forever.'

The Queen's eyes softened for a brief moment, but then the dry, hard desert returned.

'I'm sorry, child, but I need you here by my side. The fate of your former Kingdom balances on a knife's edge. Only your father keeps it from the tipping point. Having you nearby and safe fortifies and arms him to deal with a precarious and tormented King. If civil war rears its ugly head my army will have no choice but to march. Your place will be at its head.'

The steel inside Elaine that many in the past failed to see before it was too late rushed to the surface and confronted the Queen.

'In that case, my man will not be going anywhere until we are wedded.'

At this, the Queen's face broke into a wide smile and her eyes danced with merriment.

'Then by royal decree, you shall be wed in three days' hence and the nation shall pay homage to your bonding with feasts and dancing.'

'My warriors and I shall ride with Nat for he is foolish and needs protecting from himself. Especially now that he is to be given in life service to our warrior sister,' said Gabrielle in a voice that brooked no contradiction.

Nat glanced at her with consternation but did not object. The Queen nodded her consent but knew that in reality, she had no power to direct the wild women warriors. It was, however, an outcome that she had hoped for.

'Duncan and his men will also accompany you along with most of the Watchers who have followed you previously. They all volunteered to a man. You are a natural leader of men, young guardian, and men think highly of you.'

To save Nat further embarrassment from the Queen's open and unusual praise, Elaine said.

'Morgan promised us that he would come to our wedding. He was to stand by Nat's right hand. What of my father? Will I be allowed to invite him?'

'Of course, dear. You may invite whomever you wish, but you know of course, that your father will not be at liberty to come. Life and politics have a way of making the most simple and pleasurable things difficult if not impossible. If he sets foot outside the borders of his Kingdom, he will never be allowed to return and that, as you also know, will mean war. We are all trying our hardest to avoid such a thing.'

Nat and Elaine walked away from the rose garden with a mixture of heady emotions swirling through their minds. Along with these emotions was the niggling feeling of bitter-sweet loss. The world they were looking at would soon change. For better or worse they could not tell, but the outcome rested in the alien hands of Morgan Ap Heston; father, guardian, builder, king, destroyer, and soon to be Emperor, all rolled into one.

The End

ABOUT THE AUTHOR

Over many close years, the author shared a love for movies and fantasy books with his son. As his son grew into manhood and blessed retirement presented itself, the author gained long lost spare time and freedom to reacquaint himself with his imagination. What a better way to present his son with a personally signed gift of thanks than to write a novel for him. From this wish The Brothers of Destiny series was born, with The Turning (Fate's Seal) Part I, being the third. His plans for Part II remain as yet, undecided.

You can follow the author on: https://www.amazon.com/author/jcpereira